THE ONE
PAUL REED

Crescent

First published in 2003 by Crescent Books,
an imprint of Mercat Press Ltd
10 Coates Crescent, Edinburgh EH3 7AL
www.crescentfiction.com

© Paul Reed 2003

ISBN 1 84183 0550

The publisher acknowledges subsidy from the Scottish Arts Council
towards the publication of this volume.

Set in Minion at Mercat Press
Printed and bound in Great Britain by
Bell & Bain Ltd., Glasgow

*Dedicated to the loving memory of
my mother Christine Reed*

Thanks to
Sylvia Cunningham M.B.E., Alison Cunningham, Ronnie Hill, John Reed, Dr Peter
Lefevre, Dr Brian Venters, Irvine Welsh, Anne Reynolds C.P.N., Lindsay Reed, Mark
Reed, David Taylor, Davy Flucker, Karen McFarlane, Dr Neil Murray and all the staff
at Ward 6, Royal Edinburgh Hospital.

Special thanks to Quintin Jardine.

The rapping on the front door brought Jools to an unexpected semi-consciousness and he rolled over and threw up. The hammering grew louder and his head throbbed in time with it.

'JAY, IT'S ME, MAN!'

BANG! BANG! BANG!

'JAY, C'MON MAN!' the voice shouted.

'I'm still alive! The big man upstairs says it's no ma time,' he said to himself and staggered to his feet. He felt dizzy, throwing a hand out to steady himself.

'JAY! JAY! IT'S ME, MAN! OPEN THE DOOR!' the voice echoed up the hall.

A sudden flash of white light behind his eyes sent a sickening pain through his head.

This was a day Jools never expected to see. The pills hadn't worked.

It should have been enough to kill him, the amount of tablets he'd taken. Around eighty in all. He looked at the alarm clock on the dressing table. Five-thirty. He couldn't judge how long he'd been out but it felt like ages. He remembered he'd fed the cat, putting extra food out, enough for two days, then gone to his bed and taken an overdose. A confused fear spun his head and he felt a knot in his stomach. He gagged and threw up again.

BANG! BANG! BANG!...

'JAY!'

....BANG! BANG!....

'IT'S ME!'

….BANG! BANG! BANG!….

Jools staggered downstairs and opened the front door. It was Kev, his pal.

'Ah've been trying to get hold ay you for ages, man. Where the fuck have you been?' he asked.

Jools waved him into the sitting room. His head felt like jelly inside and he had drained to a deathly white.

'You awright bigman? You look terrible,' Kev said.

'Ah feel terrible,' he croaked. Then he told Kev about his OD.

⊙

Jools awoke from a feverish sleep. Someone was there in the room with him.

He could sense another's proximity in the pitch darkness of the bedroom. His heart pounded and he froze, hardly daring to breathe. The other took on a human form although it seemed to lack substance, as if made of shadows. It moved towards Jools who was trembling like a child, then it started to enter his body. He let out a scream as the head of the dark shape squeezed into his. He could feel the shape inside his body, breathing. The taste of its breath in his dry mouth made him want to vomit. Jools tried to scream again as he felt the other enter his mind. He was no longer alone in his own head. It lay motionless inside him watching. Jools was frozen stiff. The hair on his neck stood on end and his eyes were wide with terror. He leapt up, flicking the bedroom light on, and his eyes darted round the room but he could see nothing. The shadow continued to watch then gradually began to fade and fade.

Jools slept on the couch that night and left the light on.

⊙

Next day Jools awoke around 1pm. He sat up and rolled a joint, burning his fingers on the hash, and made himself a cup of tea. He pondered on last night's events.

'What the fuck was that last night?' he wondered. He was totally positive he had been fully awake. Had it been some kind of ghost? It really happened, he was sure of that. He shuddered as he went over it again in his head.

'This fuckin hoose gies me the creeps,' he said to himself as he tried to shrug off the thought. He turned on the TV as a distraction and flicked through the TV guide. The film, *Who Framed Roger Rabbit*, was on. It reminded him of the time he'd attended a psychic fair in a hotel a few years before. He'd always had an interest in such things and had taken part in a psychic reading. He'd lost his mother suddenly a few years back and wondered if a reading would hold any messages for him.

A china plate was passed round the audience. On it people placed small personal items, a ring, a brooches. Jools had taken off a small enamel badge with the Japanese character 'NIN' on it and placed it on the plate. It was handed to an assistant who took it to the front of the small function suite. The psychic, a thin man in his forties, then picked up each item in turn and gave his message to the anonymous owner. His message for Jools had been not to worry, he would have children one day, he should relax more, he would probably in future study old ways and religions and did Roger Rabbit mean anything to him? The last one had him flummoxed.

Since then he'd often wondered what that had meant.

Today by chance the film was on so he decided to watch it to see if anything became apparent.

He rolled another joint and ran a bath, then sat down in front of the TV. His mind flashed back over the events of the night before and his OD attempt and he found it impossible to concentrate on the screen. All he could fathom from the film was that the rabbit was a nervous wreck. He thought hard. Did the psychic sense the nervousness in him? He'd certainly been a bag of nerves since he and his brother had found his mother's body that morning and he'd spent a lot of time since in counselling. A sudden wave of fear sent him reeling. He felt as if he was being watched again and the feeling terrified him. The shadow was back inside his mind, this time in the broad daylight. He could feel its gaze in his head as it observed his most private thoughts. It sat in his skull not moving but seeing all in Jools's mind, terrorising him. Jools dropped to the floor on his hands and knees. The blood ran cold through his veins. He tried to stand but the thing in his head had immobilised him and he found his legs had turned to jelly, making movement impossible.

'What's happening tae me?!' he screamed out. Suddenly his ears where deafened with the sound of brass band music and his body shook violently like he was being electrocuted. His mind's eye lit up like a picture screen. He could see clear as day the marching jackbooted army and they were coming for him. A loud rumble began to get louder as huge tanks thundered into view. The panic hit him again. A large flaming swastika burned into his brain as he recoiled in terror and he found himself praying to God.

'HELP ME!', he screamed. 'AH DINNAE KNOW WHAT TAE DAE!' he howled hysterically. With an almighty effort he wrenched his body off the floor. His whole being trembled.

'What's happening tae me?' he asked.

The visions in his mind subsided. The marching band started to fade. He wiped the tears from his face and he found himself crying like a child.

'WORK!!! YA WEE FUCKIN JEW!!!' the loud voice screamed in his head.

'Wh… who are you? What dae you want?' Jools asked.

'WORK, YA WEE JEWWWWWW!!!' the voice replied.

'Get oot ay ma heid! Leave ays alone!' Jools blurted out between sobs.

The presence inside him faded and he felt alone again.

Jools was scared. He'd barricaded his front door, jamming a steel weightlifting bar between the latch and the bottom step. He took down the samurai sword from its wall rack. Unsheathing it he checked the keenness of its edge. 'Sharp enough,' he thought, before returning it to its scabbard. The phone rang and Jools jumped. He walked over to it and his heart pounded. He found himself unable to pick it up. He was shaking badly. He got together everything he might need and decided to lock himself away in his bedroom. No one would even know he was in the house. What had they done to him? Why were they coming for him? Who were they? All he knew for certain was that they had been inside his mind and they had been watching him. They could see his every move from the inside and this terrified Jools. The visions had looked like video tape being played through his mind, crystal clear. He was totally confused. He'd never seen anything like this before and was at a total loss what to do. It started to get dark. He opened the bedroom curtains to allow the street lamps to illuminate the room. He'd been too scared to risk putting the light on. They would see it and know he was in. He sat in silence. His cat scratched at the room door.

'The cat's at the door,' the voice said.

Jools froze. The voice was gone again.

He sat for a while thinking it over and finally decided he would get out of the house. Trouble was, he'd nowhere to go. Muirhouse had changed. The old community had all but died out, it seemed. The area had seen a massive regeneration in the last few years. Almost half the scheme had been knocked down and rebuilt with many faces coming and going. Jools had felt the change like an earthquake. It had shaken his world, crumbling what little stability he had left in his life.

'Ah'll take a walk,' he thought.

His ground-floor flat opened right onto the street and he immediately noticed the large black car parked across the road. It seemed to be some Eastern

European make and there were two occupants. He sensed something threatening about them. The feeling was strong and hit him in the guts. He went back inside and closed the door, running upstairs to his bedroom cupboard where he kept his old martial arts weapons. When he was a teenager he'd trained in ninpo, a martial art of feudal Japan, and had kept up his training ever since. He kept his collection of weapons in a large black holdall in the cupboard. He unzipped the bag and picked up a jutte, a 12-inch iron truncheon with a forked prong sticking from the handle, and stuck it down his belt. He left the house again feeling a little safer now he was tooled up. The black car was still parked across the street and Jools walked towards it. He could make out the driver. He was male with a thin weasel-like face and a goatee beard. He wore a black leather jacket and smoked a cigarette. The passenger was female with bleached blonde hair. Both of them watched Jools as he passed the car and his hand tightened on the jutte.

'The cat's at the door,' they had said. Was this her? They were watching him alright. Jools walked round the block. They were up to something, that's for sure. Why the fuck were they watching him? he wondered, as he passed the Gunner, the pub on Pennywell Road. He took a left and headed down towards the roundabout at the bottom of the road. The streets were quiet and it began to spit with rain. He turned back in towards the estate. A mangy-looking fox ran along the grass verge in front of him and he stopped to watch it. It sniffed around for a couple of minutes then crossed the dual carriageway and disappeared into a garden. He circled back round to the flat and when he got there the black car was still there. He let himself in and barred up the door behind him.

'The cat's at the door,' the voice came again, louder than before. The voice sounded like it was coming through a mobile phone but he heard it in both ears.

'What dae ye want!? What does she want?' he asked.

'She wants you!' came the reply.

'Why? What does she want wi me?'

'Coz you'll no work! COZ YE'RE A JEWWWWW!!!'

'Who's a Jew? Ah'm no Jewish,' Jools protested. 'Ah'm fuckin Church ay Scotland!'

'YE'RE A WEEEE JEWWWWW!!!' the voice screamed. 'WORK!!! YA WEEEEEE JEWWWWWWWWWWW!!!! YA WEEEEE JEWWWWWWW!!!!!!!'

Jools grabbed his head. 'AAAHHH!!! Fuck off!!! Leave me alone!'

'YOU'VE HAD ENOUGH TIME, CUNT!!! D'you think you can live your life the way you've been going? WORK!!! Well, you're fucked now. We're gonnie make sure ye pay yer way in life, ya fuckin dirty Jew cunt!'

'Ah canny work! Ah'm fuckin ill! The doctor signed me off,' Jools answered, trembling.

'WORK!!! You've never done a day's work in your life. Dae ye think this country will support shite like you for ever? YA WEEEEE JEEEWWWWWW!!!!!' The presence retreated.

'Who are you? How can ye talk in ma heid?' Jools asked.

There was no reply.

Jools got his head down early that night but didn't sleep too well.

⊙

He slept late into the next afternoon. He got out of bed and decided he should go shopping. He'd not really eaten for a couple of days and the hunger made him feel weak. He planned to do his shopping in Davidson's Mains, about two miles up the road. This would give him the chance to see if he was being followed. He stuffed the iron truncheon down his trousers again and pulled his jacket over the top to conceal its braided handle. He left the flat. There was no sign of the black car, much to his relief. He walked along Muirhouse Gardens to the shops at the foot of Martello Court, Edinburgh's highest multi-storey flats. Jools had lived there as a child. 'Terror Tower', the press had dubbed it in the 1970s. It had been reduced to slums, and crime of every kind flourished in its vertical 230-foot high walls. The council had since sold it off as private flats and it had become a desirable place to live again with its views out over the River Forth.

Jools bought 10 cigarettes at Jas's corner shop then started his walk, going through the primary school. He cut through the school at the back where 15-foot high steel gates separated the scheme from its more affluent neighbour, Silverknowes. These gates had always pissed Jools off. They locked them every day at 5pm and if you got there too late you had to double back and take a long detour. It was as if the gates were there to keep the Muirhouse punters out of their precious little area and it made him feel like scum.

The spring sunshine warmed him as he walked up through Silverknowes' whitewashed avenues. He reached the bridge at the top of the road and started along the disused railway towards Davidson's Mains. A girl in a school uniform walked towards him. He eyed her up as she got closer, then ducked into Safegates and did his shopping. There didn't seem to be anyone following him and he felt at ease being away from the house. He'd bought enough groceries to last him a week and thought he could maybe hole up till next payday. He walked along the main street carrying his heavy bags.

'BIGMOOTH!' someone shouted at him from a passing car.

'FUCK OFF!' he bawled back.

He passed Ferranti's factory on Ferry Road, made his way down Muirhouse Green and was soon back home again.

He got in, unloaded his shopping and sat down with something to eat. After a while he sat back in his chair and dozed. He drifted on the edge of sleep. He could hear his neighbour playing around with the kids through the thin wall. A plane passed overhead, a dog barked and an ice-cream van sounded its chimes some distance away. His breathing had become slow and heavy as he relaxed and the early evening sunlight shone through the window. It was the most he'd relaxed in weeks. The phone rang. He picked it up.

'Hello.'

It was his aunt.

'I'm just phoning to find out what you want to do for your birthday,' she said.

'Ah've no really thought about it.'

'You feeling OK? You sound like you're in for the cold or something.'

'Ah'm awright,' he lied.

'Well, if you think of anything give me a phone and let me know.'

'Ah will do. See ye later.'

'Bye.'

Jools sat listening to the radio till late that night. He kept the volume turned down low so he could hear anything going on outside. He sat in the dark smoking and pondering over his predicament. He peeked out the window. There was now a red van where the black car had been.

'Is this the new watch?' he wondered. He couldn't see if there was anyone in it from this angle. He decided to move back upstairs to the bedroom.

⊙

Jools awoke in the early hours. It was just before dawn and the sky was a deep blue. He felt it right away. It was watching him from inside again.

'Aye, Ah'm here. Watching youuuuuu,' it said.

'Get the fuck oot ay me!' Jools screamed.

'WORK! We will get you, by the way. We've been watching you for ages. D'you know Mr Love?'

'Who?'

'Jimmy Love.'

'Ah've nivir fuckin heard ay um.'

'Well, he sure knows you,' the voice sniggered.

'What do you mean?'

'Jimmy Love's been watching you for quite a while. He's gotten to know your... habits, as it were.'

'What's he watching me for?'

'It's what he does,' the voice said. 'He's been watching you, taping your... antics for a while. Yes, we have you in some rather... compromising positions.'

Jools's face flushed. He felt violated.

'Our Mr Love has been watching you with an infra-red camera. It can easily make you out in some of your less... graceful moments,' the voice went on.

'What—an x-ray camera?' Jools asked.

'Got it in one, old chap. Latest technology, shipped from Eastern Europe. Thermal imaging. Used to use this gear in Bosnia, apparently.'

'But why the fuck are you watching me?'

'We're here to teach you a lesson. Jimmy Love has you over a barrel. We can do what we want with you. You're in no position to do anything about it, with what we have on you. We think you're a sick puppy, mister. Funny the things a man will get up to when he thinks he's alone, hmm?'

Jools was embarrassed. He tried to hide his inner thoughts.

'What have Ah done tae youse?' Jools asked.

'YOU HAVE BEEN A SICK WEE BASTARD FOR TOO LONG!'

'But what have Ah done to you, personally?' he pleaded.

'We are sick and tired of... shit like you in our society. Well, we've decided to do something about it. We're taking a stand. We're disposing of all our waste just now. Your uncle's next.'

Jools shuddered at the thought of them harming his uncle. 'The black car. Was that your people?'

'It was.'

'Who are you?'

'We go by many names. Have you heard of the masons?'

'What's the masons efter me for? This doesnae make sense!'

'You see, you were told to work. Get a job, they all said, but no. You'd rather lie around sucking the life out of this country like a giant leech. There is no one can help you now.'

'What dae ye want me tae dae?' Jools asked.

'Oh, we'll be in contact.'

The watcher retreated and Jools was left alone.

Jools wondered why they'd singled him out for this. He'd hardly left his house since he'd given up the drink after a spell on the purple tinnie, the extra-strong super lager. Those had been his darkest days, and he'd tried to pull his socks up since. He just wanted to live in peace now he had put those days behind him.

⊙

Next afternoon Jools was sitting quietly thinking to himself when the front door went. He crept up to the door and peered through the spyhole. It was Kev.

'Awright, mucker?' he nodded.

Jools waved him in. 'C'mon in.'

Kev sat down, pulled out his cigarette papers and started to build a joint. They got down to a good smoking session and soon they were both pretty stoned. Jools forgot his troubles for a while. He enjoyed smoking with Kev. They could discuss the deepest subjects when they'd had a few joints and they were definitely on the same wavelength. They had been talking about the philosophy of the martial arts this afternoon and Jools was on a roll.

'In our art we're taught that you must have both philosophy on one hand and martial arts on the other. This creates a balance. Like yin and yang. *In Yo* in Japanese.'

Kev sat and listened, puffing on the joint.

'Like your left hand and right hand,' he went on. 'If you train only the body the mind gets weak. It creates an imbalance. You must train mentally and physically.'

'That's pretty interesting shit that,' Kev said.

They sat and talked for a while and Kev built a few more joints. 'Was there any birds in your martial arts class?' Kev asked.

'Aye, a couple,' Jools replied.

'Ye should huv seen the fanny up the toon the day. Tidy as fuck, man.'

'Aye?'

'Aye man. Saw doon this birds tits on the bus. She got on at the college. Nae bra on. She looked a right dirty cow. Hud a fuckin ragin stonker aw the way up the West End, man,' he laughed. 'How come ye always get a hard on on a bus? Usually just before your stop, tae.'

'True,' Jools nodded.

They had a cup of tea then Kev went home for his dinner. Jools felt a little better after their talk. The smoke had relaxed him. He microwaved a vegetable casserole, and sat down to eat in front of the TV. He had a bad case of the munchies and scoffed down his food. He fed his cat, had a bath and soon it began to get dark. Jools was beginning to dread the darkness. He still didn't dare put the lights on.

⊙

'We have some messages for you,' the voice said in his mind.

Top of the Pops had just started on TV.

'Keep watching. Jimmy Love's been busy,' the voice laughed.

Jools watched the screen nervously.

The band REM came onto the screen. Jools watched as the singer sang

> That sugar cane, that tasted good…
> C'mon, c'mon, no one can see you cry…

The lead singer danced around the stage then stopped dead, stared Jools in the eye and licked his lips. He could see Jools through the screen.

'FUCK OFF!' Jools shouted. He felt a flush of adrenalin speed through his veins. They were slagging him off on TV. He began to panic. 'Why are ye daein this tae me?'

'YE'RE A POOF! YE'RE A JEW! SHUT YOUR MOOTH!' the voice shouted.

Jools began to cry. They were humiliating him on TV. 'AH'M NO A FUCKIN POOF OR A JEW,' he blubbed.

The voice just laughed. 'SHUT YER MOOTH!'

REM finished their performance. The studio crowd cheered and the cameras panned to a different stage.

'And now a lady who's reputed to have over 400 pairs of sunglasses in her collection,' the DJ said. The cameras turned to Anastacia who was standing in the gantry being interviewed.

'What are ye daein this for?' Jools asked in his mind.

'Just shut up and watch,' the voice replied.

Jools turned back to the screen just in time to catch Anastacia say: 'I don't know what's going on', then she went to the stage and started her number.

'That was about you but you missed it,' the voice said.

'What, was she slagging me tae?'

'She might have been but you missed what she said. We told her about you.'

'What, me? Anastacia?'

'Don't tell me you're not that bothered. We have your escapades on video tape the last time Anastacia was on TV. Thought no one could see you? PEEK A BOO!' the voice laughed.

Jools's face went scarlet and his eyes welled up with tears.

'Yes you always had a little… weakness for Anastacia, didn't you? Well, she knows aaaaaaall about you now,' it sniggered.

Jools got up and turned the TV off. He was totally mortified.'Ah'm no fuckin watchin any mair ay this,' he said.' Fuckin slaggin me off on telly. What are you doing this to me for?'

'You are a threat to national security.'

'If Ah was a threat the polis would lift me or shoot me or somethin. Dinnae talk shite.'

The voice retreated and he was alone again.

He decided to get out of the house. It was dark outside. He walked along Muirhouse Parkway, the golf course stretching down one side of the road, multi-storied flats on the other. The rain had stopped and a cool breeze blew. He headed along the pavement, hands in pockets, head down, looking around every so often to check he wasn't being followed. He'd reached Lauriston Farm when a car passed him.

'BIGMOOTH!' he heard in his head.

Jools turned to see a black car with tinted windows speed past. Another car approached.

'BIGMOOTH!' he heard again.

Four cars in a row passed.

'BIGMOOTH!'

'BIGMOOTH!'

'BIGMOOTH!'

'BIGMOOTH!'

Jools reached Davidson's Mains and headed up to Queensferry Road. The four-lane traffic was busy even at this time of night. A large lorry passed him.

'BIGMOOTH!'

As he faced the oncoming traffic he began to notice there were more cars coming towards him than from the opposite direction. Every second car someone would call out 'BIGMOOTH!' Jools started to cry. He sat at a bus stop and broke down in hysterics. Had everyone seen them slagging him off earlier? Would they know that they had been referring to him? Who were these fuckers calling him bigmooth? He felt as if he could never face anyone again. He started to think out loud.

'How the fuck am Ah a threat to national security? If Ah was Ah'd get lifted or the jail or shot or something. They wouldnae let me walk aroond, surely.'

'It's your type that's the threat to national security,' the voice interrupted.

'But how could Ah harm anyone?'

'I told you before, you're a piece of shit. We're here to make sure you get what's coming to you.'

Jools started to walk. 'You dinnae have tae dae this tae me though. How come you didnae just send someone tae break my legs or shoot me or something?'

'We are not animals. You are the threat to society. We are simply here to remove it. You do realise you'll have to go?'

'What d'you mean? Move hoose?'

'Eventually.'

Jools was terrified. He'd lived in Muirhouse all his life. The scheme was as much part of him as he was of it. Now they were going to force him out. He continued walking. 'But why dae Ah have tae leave?'

'You talked.'

'Talked aboot what?'

'Other people's business.'

'So you're going tae ruin my life by publicly shaming me and chasing me out. Is that it?'

'Don't look for any help. You've had your chances in life. There is no one can help you now.'

'How far away dae Ah have to go?'

'Oh, there are masons everywhere. Pretty far, I should imagine.'

Jools shuddered at the thought. He felt physically sick. 'What about ma family? Will Ah be able see them?'

'You should have thought about that before. They'll be alright as long as you don't tell them too much.'

Jools broke down again. He couldn't take it in.

'BIGMOOTH!'

He reached the Barnton roundabout and turned into Cramond. The roads were quieter.

'Do you hear that plane?' the voice asked

They were in hearing distance of the airport.

'Aye,' he replied, wiping his eyes.

'We're tracking you from that plane. It's tuned into your brain frequency. They can hear everything you think up there. Another little gem from our Eastern European friends.'

Jools looked up at the landing lights circling above. He turned up Gamekeeper's Road and could see the lights of the scheme above the golf course.

'BIGMOOTH!' A jeep passed.

'Hurry up. Get home quick,' the voice ordered. 'It's not safe for you to be out. Anyone could be listening to the signal. It works on radio.'

Jools picked up his pace. He was scared at the fact that others could hear inside his head and decided to get home double quick.

'BIGMOOTH!' Another car passed.

⊙

Jools sat in the darkness of his room and listened to his radio. He lay on his futon mattress looking at the badly aertexed ceiling. A dog barked in the distance. His clock radio read 3am.

'It's the silicon age,' a gruff voice said. It was a different voice from before.

'Who are you?' Jools asked.

'Don't worry. You're not on your own. We're here to help.'

'What, you the polis or something?'

'H. M. Special Forces.'

'What, SAS, likes?'

'Stay calm.'

'Thank fuck you're here!' Jools said.

'Try not to get too scared. We need you cool if we're going to get through this. We picked up your signal and we're trying to track whoever did this to you. How do you feel?'

'Scared,' Jools said. He let out a sigh of relief.

'Listen, I can't be here all the time and we've got to keep our communications a secret. We can only talk late at night. The rest of the time you must keep as strong as possible. This thing is a bit bigger than you might realise.'

'Ah canny believe this is really real! They said it was a guy called Jimmy Love had been taping me through an x-ray camera.'

'That's who we want. He lives in the next block to this one. He's the old guy lives in the bottom flat over there.'

Jools knew who he meant.

'You're not the only one he's done this to. Mr Love has done this to many people. Some very important people have been through hell because of Mr Love. He's a dangerous man.'

'How can you talk tae me in my heid?'

'It's just a radio mic. They've tuned in to your brain frequency. Trouble is we can't find the digitiser to switch you off. It could be anywhere in the country.'

That's why we're staking you out. Hopefully you'll lead us right to them. They can't hear what I'm saying to you but they can hear you answering. You've got to keep your voice down. Specially at night.'

'How did he do that thing wi the swastika? I saw it clear as day in my heid. It was as clear as watchin a telly. Ah felt it like a shock going through me.'

'That's classified. Like I said, it's the silicone age. That gadget is top secret. You could get twenty years for just talking about that.'

'What? He zapped me with somethin? Like a stun gun?'

'It's a small gadget about the size of a cigarette packet. It's an official secret. He probably had someone drive him past in a car.'

'Well, do me a favour, will you? When you get this bastard, make sure you zap him. That fuckin thing had me terrified.'

'You better shut up about that. I have to go now. Remember, don't try and contact me during the day. We'll be listening in so don't worry so much. Keep the radio tuned to Virgin. If we need to contact you we'll put the message on air.'

'But wait! Ah need to ask ye something,' Jools said, but the SAS guy was gone. He fell asleep shortly after.

⊙

Jools woke early next morning. He was hungry and he thought he would risk going for a paper as there would be no one around. He dressed and walked to the corner shop in the shopping centre.

'Good morning,' Asif greeted him. He picked up some rolls and a few packets of crisps then went to the papers and couldn't decide which one to buy.

'Get a *Daily Mail*,' Asif had suggested, winking at him.

Jools put the goods on the counter. 'Ah'll take this lot and twenty Mayfair.'

'Twendy Mayfairr,' Asif repeated in his Pakistani accent. He rang up the till. 'Five twendy, pleese. Tank you.'

Jools bagged up the items.

'Do you smell gas?' Asif asked, sniffing the air.

'Aye,' Jools said. 'It's quite strong over at the freezer.'

'I'll need to call someone out.'

Jools walked home quickly as the sun rose in the east, casting a golden light over the buildings. Seagulls swooped and dive-bombed overhead, their squawking sounding amplified in the quiet of morning. He let himself into the flat, dumped the bag down and ran a hand over his crew-cut hair. He felt drained.

'You all right?' the voice said. It was the SAS guy. 'I thought I'd check on you, see if you're OK.'

'Ah'm fine,' Jools replied. 'Ah'm just shattered. Hey, what dae Ah call you?'

'Just call me Bulldog. I wanted to talk to you about a few things while it's still quiet.'

'Sure, fire away.'

'Have you ever heard of a man named John Mackenzie?'

'What, the millionaire? Him wi all the car businesses?'

'Multi-millionaire. Yes, that John Mackenzie. Well, we believe that he has been employing the services of our Mr Love. Have you noticed that his sponsorship on ITV has disappeared? That his businesses have been changing name? That's down to us. He's the one responsible for having this done to you.'

'But what have Ah done tae him?' Jools asked.

'He's dying and he's turned bad. We have evidence on him for murder. He's also involved in blackmail and he's stolen state secrets. We believe he's in Northern Ireland under protection of the UVF. He was heavily involved in the masonic lodge. He was a grandmaster. The guy's a bit of an Aleister Crowley freak. Into witchcraft bigtime. He poisons people with menstrual blood. He uses it in his magic rites. Have you been feeling ill lately?'

'A bit. D'you think he got me, likes?'

'Maybe. I'm more worried about the way he's had you done up with Jimmy Love. Anyway, we've got something on tonight. If Mackenzie likes using the TV companies, so can we. We've had the TV people run us up a little programme of our own. The beauty of it is everybody will think they're watching a piece of fiction when we in the know will see Mackenzie's crimes exposed on primetime. He's not got a long time to live and he's trying to clean up society before he goes. He's dying of AIDS. He caught it and now he's trying to wipe out druggies, alcoholics, immigrants, the mentally ill, anyone he deems unfit to live in society. It's his revenge. He blames them for spreading it. Thinks it's the wrath of God or something. Do you remember the black car that was watching you?'

'Aye,' Jools said.

'Those were his lot. The cat and her brother. They're Bosnians. A real evil pair. They're Satanists. Our intelligence says they are suspected of war crimes including cannibalism and human sacrifice. It was probably them that zapped you. They caught wind of us and they've left the country.'

'What do we do now?' Jools asked.

'Easy, we sit back and watch Jimmy Love. He might lead us to the digitisers and we can switch you off.'

'And the TV programme?'

'That should get Mackenzie shitting himself. I have Downing Street's say-so on this one.'

'Tony Blair? He's heard aboot this?'

'They had a meeting last night. Quite a few important people are in the know. You have a lot of well-wishers.'

'That guy told me Anastacia knew about me.'

'She does. She said she thought you were cute and she was praying for you. She'd like to meet you one day, you lucky sod, so you'd better come through this.'

Jools grinned from ear to ear. He was elated. 'She's fuckin tidy, man! Ah'm really gonnae meet her? She makes me go weak at the knees, man! Ah'm like totally intae her, bigtime likes! Even just her voice gives me goosebumps!'

'That's what she says,' Bulldog said. 'Speaking of well-wishers, we have someone here who wants a word.'

'Hello Jools,' a gruff voice said.

He recognised it right away. It was Rob. His martial arts *sensei*. He was the head of the Scottish branch of the Ninpo Federation.

'Rob sensei. Good tae hear your voice,' Jools smiled.

'How are you, son?' Rob asked.

'Ah'm OK. How are you?'

'You keep strong, son, and we'll soon have this mess straightened out. I'm here for you. I've set up a flat over the road so I can keep watch on your house. I'll be in the neighbourhood as long as you need me. They've given me a radio mic so we can talk.'

'It's good tae know you're aroond, Rob,' Jools said. He felt safe. 'Which hoose are you in?'

'The one over from you, with the Scotland flags for curtains.'

Jools got up and went to the front door. He peered through the spyhole. Across the street he could make out the window hung with saltires on the first floor.

'Don't keep looking over,' Rob said. 'Our friend might still be watching you with his camera.'

'Right,' Jools said, and sat back down in the living room. He lay back in his chair and relaxed.

'That's it. You take it easy. Try and get a little sleep,' Rob told him.

Jools drifted off with Anastacia on his mind.

⊙

He slept soundly for a few hours and woke up mid-afternoon. The sun shone through the drawn vertical blinds and the sound of a council lawnmower cutting the grass filled the air. He went to the bathroom and picked up his mail on the way back down. There was a large envelope which he tore open. It was a census form. He put it aside and picked up the newspaper. He skimmed the first pages. There was an article on someone who had died mysteriously. He scanned the next page, another suspicious death. A factory in West Lothian was to close, laying off its entire workforce.

'You'll not find anything in the paper about this,' the voice said. It was Bulldog. He was whispering. 'It's alright, Jimmy Love's out. He went out this morning so we should be safe to talk. Another couple of deaths in the paper, eh?'

'Aye, Ah've noticed there's been a lot of people dying mysteriously recently.'

'That's right. But you'll not find anything about this situation in there. It's all been kept hush-hush. They just report it as natural deaths.'

'What, you mean Mackenzie's something to do with this?'

'You can bet your life. You'll find out tonight when we air the programme. That letter, by the way. It wasn't the postman who delivered it. We were watching.'

'Oh, that's just a census letter.'

'It's one of his tricks. He's trying to get to you any way he can. He's trying to set you up. That letter, he can collect your DNA from the envelope. He can plant it somewhere to incriminate you.'

'Ah better get shot of it then, eh?' Jools thought.

'Don't throw it out,' Bulldog said. 'We can use it. Just fill it in and send it. We know you're here so if your DNA turns up far away we'll know we're on to him.'

'Where's Rob?'

'He went into Leith earlier. He's following Jimmy Love. He was along at the shops this morning. He's got access to the CCTV footage from the concierge. We're running through it now. He had a word with Asif in the shop. He's been tipped the wink and he's in for us, so just be guided. A couple of your friends are helping us try to track the radio signal. Big Steve across the road's there for us. He's been up all night with Rob in the car, tracking.'

'Big Steve's a barry guy,' Jools said. He'd been a community youth worker when Jools was young and had helped to run the local youth club. Jools probably trusted him more than anyone in Muirhouse.

'Listen, Jimmy Love's on his way back from Leith so I better maintain radio silence for a while. We can talk more later on. Oh, before I go, we've been on to the papers. Read the horoscopes in the *Mail*. We'll leave your messages under your own birthsign, Taurus.'

'OK,' Jools said. 'Ah'll catch ye later on.'

Bulldog disappeared.

The front door tapped. It was Kev. Jools glanced over at Rob's window as he let Kev in. He was finding it hard to keep all this to himself but decided he shouldn't tell Kev what was going on. Not yet.

'Ah've just droaped in tae borray yer hammer,' Kev said. 'Ah'm helpin ma brother dae up his new flat.'

'Aye, nae problem. D'you want a cuppa?'

'Aye, go on then. Ah'll get a quick one before Ah nash, likes.'

Kev pulled out his Rizlas and started to build a joint.

'None ay that for me,' Jools said. He needed to keep a clear head.

'Did ye hear Mikey McNab goat stabbed the other night?' Kev asked.

'Aye? What happened likes?'

'Three guys jumped oot a car ootside the Main Street Bar. Set aboot him wi baseball bats. They stabbed um four times tae.'

'Is ay awright?'

'Ay's in intensive care, Ah heard. Wee Donna Randal telt ays at the shops earlier.'

'She's a right wee gossip her, eh? Kens fuckin everything aboot everycunt.'

'She says it wis cunts fae Royston. The Trotters. They're meant tae have geid him it tight likes.'

'Fuckin mental, eh?' Jools said. 'This place gets worse.'

They talked for a while and drank tea. After a while Kev got up to leave. His mobile phone started to bleep.

'Fuck sake, man!' he sighed. 'My fuckin mobile's been switched on aw that time.' He held the phone to his ear. 'Fuckin thing's rang my hoose phone and got my answer machine. Run up the bill healthy.' He switched it off and put it back in his pocket. 'Huv ye goat that hammer?' he asked.

Jools gave him the hammer and he left.

Jools put the radio on to listen for messages. He tuned into Virgin UK and sat back and listened to the music. The new song 'Sing' by Travis came on and he whistled along.

'SHUT THE FUCK UP YA FUCKIN POOFY JEW BASTARD! STOP THAT FUCKIN WHISTLIN! YA FUCKIN BIGMOOTH CUNT!'

Jools jumped. It was the mason.

'What the fuck are you so happy about? We'll soon have that seen to, don't you worry. Stay away from red-fronted shops! We know about your little friend in the shop. Do you think we're stupid? You fucking filthy scum fuck. We're on to your little game. Don't worry, that bastard will get what's coming to him, just you wait and see. We nearly had you the other day. Nearly took out a Jew and a Paki in one go! Do you remember smelling gas in the shop?' he laughed. 'Yes, we had a couple of… gremlins loosen the gas mains.'

'But Asif's nowt tae dae wi it,' Jools tried to cover up.

'WE FUCKING KNOW HE'S BEEN TRYING TO HELP YOU! Don't lie to us you fucking worm. We see everything! Jimmy Love has contacts everywhere. Your friend also works for Jimmy Love. Yes, Kevin. Amazing what a few pounds will get you around here. He's been bugging you for us. Do you remember all those sick little conversations you've been having lately? We have you on tape discussing other people's business. You've insulted a few of the local hard men. You think you can get away with talk like that? Your tongue is evil. But it's all been behind people's backs. Never to their faces. You disgusting little bastard, you make me sick. Well, don't worry. Jimmy Love knows these people and he's been having a word here and there. George Grant's going to kill you and I'd stay away from the pub if I were you. Yes, we'll make sure you move alright. You'd better start making plans. You're not going to be around that long, I promise you that.'

Jools was terrified. George Grant was a psychopath. He'd done time for killing someone in the 70s and was thought to be one of the hardest men in Muirhouse.

'Do you honestly think we've been regenerating the area for shite like you to waste your days in? We've set the hard men of the area to work for us. People who get things done. They're the sheepdogs, you and your like are the sheep. We're moving all you dregs out of the area. Do you think we'll tolerate the likes of you in our society forever? Junkies, alcoholics, gays, wasters—you make us want to vomit. Not such a tough guy now, are you? You maggot. We have a job for you to do. Call it community service, if you will. We want you to walk for us. We want you to go into Leith. You must walk where we tell you to walk. We want you to do some sponsor work for us. We'll take some pictures of you for our client's businesses. We'll have you pose for us. Naturally we'll be watching you all the way. We've issued our people with ear pieces so they can hear what's going on as you walk. Jimmy Love's nephew wants a look at you. You'd better not fuck this up. Jimmy Love's nephew's laid out a lot of money on this one. He expects his return. Have you any idea how much it cost him to fix up all those cars with radio equipment?'

'Ah'm no goin anywhere,' Jools said. 'Fuck walking into Leith. You can stick it up yer arse! You're driving me oot ay Scotland, gettin me leathered, taking over ma thoughtwaves, invading ma fuckin heid and you expect me tae work for you? Fuck that. You can fuck off. Ah'm goin naewhere.'

'Oh, you'll go alright. We'll make sure of it,' the mason said.

'Well Ah'm no goin today, that's for sure.'

'As you wish. But you will before long. I'll be in touch.'

The mason disappeared.

⊙

Jools heard the DJ on the radio talking about what he'd watched on TV the night before. It reminded him about the Mackenzie programme. He turned on the TV as the news finished.

'And now on BBC1, drama in *The Bad Marine*.'

The programme showed the story of a wealthy man who'd served in the Royal Marines for twenty-five years. He'd lost his wife a few years ago and had a daughter who was a doctor. He was an obsessively neat and tidy man but had a darker side. He had a lust for young men and liked to pick up rent boys. One night he'd been out looking for business and had found a young man. They agreed on a price and they'd walked to a quiet spot under the eaves of a basement flat. The rent boy had asked for his money in advance and they started to argue. The rent boy pulled out a knife and demanded the marine's wallet but he'd refused and the rent boy lunged at him with the knife. The marine had been trained in unarmed combat and easily sidestepped the blade, turning the knife back on the attacker. The rent boy slid to the ground, his eyes rolling in their sockets. The marine wiped the blood from his hands and ran. A few weeks later he'd been contacted by a man. He claimed to be a friend of the dead rent boy and had seen the marine leaving with him the night he was killed. He wanted £50,000 or he would go to the police. The marine had refused to pay and the man had sent a letter to his daughter telling her all about the rent boy and his death. She'd decided to stand by her father and had set up a meeting with the man at her home where she poisoned him. The programme ended with father and daughter hugging each other and crying over the body.

mind. You're not that bad a guy, really. A bit misguided maybe but there's worse than you out there.'

'You can actually see my thoughtwaves? How's that done?'

'We just tuned your brain frequency into our computer. We can see what you're picturing on the monitor. Simple, really.'

'Fucksake, man.' Jools tried desperately not to think of anything dirty. 'Have you seen in many people's minds?'

'A few. Your mind's not that bad. You should see some of them I've worked with. Anyway, you get your head down. I'll speak to you later.'

'G'night man.'

'Be guided.' The SAS man retreated. Jools fell asleep quickly.

⊙

Jools put on a Happy Mondays tape. 'Step On' came on. He listened to the words.

> Hey rainmaker,
> Come away from that man,
> You know he's gonna take away
> Your promised land.

'This sounds familiar,' Jools thought. The words fitted his predicament.

> You talk so hip,
> You're twisting my melon, man

the song went on.

The words fitted too closely to his situation to be coincidence. He wondered if Shaun Ryder had been through this himself.

'IMBALANCE!!!' the voice shrieked in his head. 'IMBALANCE!!! MOVE!!! RUN!!!'

Jools jumped up, his heart pounding.

'IMBALANCE!!! HURRY!!! TROUBLE!!! GO, RUN, MOVE!!!'

Jools left the flat, running.

'THIS WAY! HURRY!' the voice bawled.

Jools ran past the Gunner. A crowd of youths hung around outside. He crossed Pennywell Road into Pilton.

'FUCKIN RUN!!! MOVE!!! THIS WAY!!! RUN!'

Jools headed into Pilton Circus.

'C'MON, FUCKIN MOVE! IMBALANCE!!!' the voice urged him on.

A siren wailed in the distance. Jools cut through into the West Granton estate. The black clouds overhead opened and it began to rain. He passed a stationary green mini-bus. Its windscreen had been smashed in and an alarm sounded.

'IMBALANCE!!! YOU'VE GOT TO BALANCE THE SIDES!' the voice screamed.

'I dinnae know what you mean,' Jools said, confused and out of breath.

'RUN!!!' the voice screamed.

Jools kept running. He got to the top of the road and could see that the rain clouds came to an end over the Forth. Fife was sunny. The black clouds seemed to be concentrated overhead, directly above him.

'Mackenzie's cutting the clouds,' the voice said. 'He's controlling the rain. It's mason's magic. You have to balance the scales!'

'How dae Ah dae that?' Jools asked. 'Ah dinnae know what you mean.'

'You have to run! Look for the signs.'

Jools ran to the new access road that joined Granton with Crewe Toll. The street lights lit up in sequence up one side of the road as if lighting the way for him. Jools followed them. A police car sped past, its blue light flashing. Jools got to the concrete bridge and took a breather. 'Now where dae Ah go?' he asked, bending over, trying to catch his breath.

'It's too late.' The voice sounded crushed. 'He's just had his face smashed in. They've just taken him away in an ambulance. It's your fault, you broke the balance. I hope you're proud of yourself. They've stabbed him with your knife.'

'What dae you mean with my knife?' Jools asked.

'They've been in your house while you've been out. They've taken a knife out of your house and stabbed him with it.'

'Who's been in my hoose?' Jools asked.

'Us!'

'Who the fuck are you?'

'Gypsies!' The voice retreated, laughing.

Jools turned and headed for home. He was exhausted from his running and wanted to get home quickly to check for signs of entry. The drizzling rain had soaked through his jacket and the sun began to break through, turning the air humid.

Jools reached home. He let himself in and barred the door behind him. He went into the living room and scanned the room. Seeing no sign of disturbance he ran upstairs. He shoved the bedroom door open, standing slightly back in case anyone was there. He entered the small room, checking around. He went to the cupboard and searched for his knife, a Japanese tanto. It was gone. Looking round his room he spotted a huge wasp on the bed. He looked closer.

It was dead. But the window was shut. 'How did it get in?' he wondered. 'They must have put it there. Left it as a calling card.'

He picked up the dead insect by the wing and dropped it in the ashtray.

'Fuckin gyppo cunts,' he said to himself. He wished Lenny McLean, the bare-knuckle boxer, was still alive. Uncle Len knew how to treat them pykies. How the fuck did they get in? There were no signs of forced entry. He went to the window. It was hard to tell if Jimmy Love was in. It was still light and there were no lights on in the house.

'Bulldog… Bulldog… Are you there, Bulldog?' he whispered. There was no reply. Jools thought about the man they had hurt. They had stabbed him with his knife. He couldn't have this on his conscience. The police would trace the blade back to him. His prints were all over it. He didn't want to hurt anyone. He had to get rid of his weapons. He took out the holdall. It was full of swords, knives, throwing stars and other martial arts weapons he'd collected over the years. He unrolled a black bin liner and dumped the holdall and contents into it. He went downstairs, opened the front door and checked around. No one. He crept along to the bin room in the stair and dumped the bag in the large metal bucket. He climbed up on the bin and reached down, covering up the bag with rubbish. He jumped down and brushed himself off. Returning to the flat he had a last look around to see if anyone was watching. The light in Rob's flat was on. Jools went in and went to his room. 'Rob… Rob… Are you there?'

'I'm here,' Rob answered.

'Rob, they've broken intae ma hoose. Taken a knife and stabbed somebody. Mackenzie made it rain. They said he was cloud-cutting.'

'I know. I saw the sky. Mackenzie's still powerful. It's not your fault the guy got hurt. You weren't to know. The police don't expect him to live.'

Jools felt terrible.

'We've got to get Mackenzie's troops. There could be hundreds of them. He's still a big influence on the masons. He has plenty of support in the lodge. The lodges are all interconnected. He has people all over Britain. It was Jimmy Love's soldiers that broke in.'

Jools was nervous. They could come back and let themselves in anytime.

'Don't worry. We'll be watching your door 24-7 from now on,' Rob said.

Jools felt done in. He ran a bath. 'I tried calling Bulldog earlier. He didnae answer me.'

'Bulldog's out tracking with Big Steve. They had a fix on that gypsy guy's signal. Somewhere in Niddrie this time.'

'They've moved it again?' Jools asked.

'Yes. It can be moved quicker than we can track it.'

Jools got into the bath and lay back. The hot water melted away the cold dampness from his bones. He wished he had a joint. A smoke would hit the spot around now.

'You ought to stop the drugs, Jools,' Rob said. 'They're not doing you any favours. You have to keep a pure mind. Sensei Tanaka's coming over from Japan soon. He won't be happy if he finds you on drugs. Damien, your old instructor, is coming over with him.'

'Sensei's really coming over?'

'Yes. He's been hearing about you. Thinks you'd make a promising student. He wants to help out with your predicament. It's not every day a Ninpo grandmaster comes to see you. His skills are on a par with Mackenzie's except he's devoted his life to dispelling evil instead of creating it. Tanaka sensei can cut clouds too. He's a powerful man.'

'Ah feel honoured,' Jools said.

'Drugs are your old life. Bad ways. Damien will have a few words to say about that too, I should imagine. He spent a lot of time training you. You're still saveable. It's not too late. Remember, "Taiyo, say no to drugs". The campaign we did a few years back.'

'It's only a smoke, Rob. Ah'm no into anything heavy.'

'I know, but you have to think of the example you're setting to the younger ones. They might not show your restraint. I'd brush up on your Japanese manners too if I were you. Sensei's a stickler for manners. Believe me, you wouldn't want to offend him. Practise the ninja *seishin*.'*

Jools went downstairs wrapped in just a towel. He dripped all over the carpet. He peeked through the blinds. Jimmy Love's light was on. 'He's in.'

'I'd better go,' Rob said. 'I'll teach you some special techniques tomorrow. Remember what Bulldog said about keeping a quiet mind during the day. It would be a great help to us. And another thing. Don't picture my face. They've got you wired up to a computer monitor too and I don't want them seeing my face. I don't need them ID-ing me.'

Jools's mind almost made a picture of his sensei's face and he fought it hard. 'OK Rob. Ah'll talk to you later. *Arigato gozaimas sensei*.'

Rob retreated and Jools was alone. He switched the TV on. A documentary on Belsen concentration camp on one channel. On Channel 4 an animated film showing a dog humping a rolled up blanket as he used to do when he was a child, pretending it was Purdy from the *New Avengers*. He recoiled in embarrassment. Channel 4 were slagging him off now. 'Bastards,' he thought.

---

*A traditional Ninja verse, used to guide the Ninja's heart.

These cunts had influence over all the TV companies. He turned the set off in disgust. He'd be a laughing stock if anyone was watching that. He went to bed and cried. He couldn't take being humiliated like this. He felt totally miserable. Still, at least Tanaka sensei was coming. He felt some hope. Tanaka sensei was as powerful as Mackenzie. He would even the odds. Jools was weary. He rolled over and cried himself to sleep.

⊙

Next morning Jools was looking through the freezer for something to eat. There was no food left in the house and he decided to go out for some supplies. He heard Big Steve's car start up over the street.

'He must be away out tracking,' he thought, and he felt grateful for the amount of time Steve was putting in. It made him feel wanted, cared about.

'Can you look at the wall for us?' Bulldog asked. 'Just stare at the wall, concentrate on one spot. Don't picture anything in your mind. Try not to drift away into a daydream. Just blank out your thoughts.'

Jools complied. He stared at a small mark on the wall. 'Now what?' he asked.

'Just stay like that.'

Jools's mind quickly drifted. He began to slouch and daydream.

'Don't think,' Bulldog said impatiently.

Jools sat up and cleared his head. He widened his eyes and tried again. Soon his eyes began to water and boredom set in. He wandered off track again.

'CONCENTRATE!' Bulldog hollered.

'Ah'm tryin!' Jools answered back, a little miffed at being shouted at. He wriggled into a more comfortable position and tried again. 'Ah'm hungry,' he moaned. 'Ah've had nowt tae eat aw day.'

'Just a while longer,' Bulldog said.

'Can Ah no just go for a scran?'

'In a while. Concentrate.'

Jools began to feel weak with hunger and this staring was giving him a headache. His stomach gave a loud rumble and he fidgeted. His mind began to drift onto Anastacia and he grinned to himself.

'FOR FUCK'S SAKE!' Bulldog shouted. 'JUST GO AND GET SOMETHING TO EAT! YOU'RE REALLY FUCKING ANNOYING ME TODAY!'

'Awright, fuck. There's nae fuckin need tae be like that, eh? Ah'm jist fuckin starvin man, awright?' Jools got up and dressed quickly.

'I'm sorry,' Bulldog said. 'I'm just really tired. I feel like we've been chasing these guys for ages. I've been up all night tracking. Now I have to organise a watch so you can go to the shops. If you see any of our cars don't stare at them for fuck's sake. They'll be tailing you all the way, so just be guided.'

⊙

Jools headed to the shopping centre. He was turning the corner outside the library when he heard a loud bang which startled him. A tall well-built man walked towards him and he glared at Jools. Jools sussed him straight away as another SAS man under cover. The man put his hand up to his ear and pinched his earlobe. Jools took this to mean he was wearing an earpiece. The man seemed to usher him out of the precinct.

'KEEP THE FUCK AWAY FROM THOSE SHOPS, I TOLD YOU!!!' Bulldog shouted. 'Go to the other ones.'

Jools scuttled back the way he came. He was pissed off at being moaned at. It seemed that everyone was getting on at him. He walked along Muirhouse Gardens. A bus passed him. A small boy of about seven or eight was standing with a golf club on the grass verge. He swung at the ball which clattered through the double-glazed window of an empty house.

'Hey! What are you daein, wee man?' he asked the boy. 'Ye'll get in tae trouble for that.'

'Smell yer ma!' the boy answered back, offering him a middle finger.

'Cheeky wee bastard,' Jools laughed.

He carried on past Martello Court. He went into the corner shop and bought a few tins, some bread, cat food, crisps, a paper and cigarettes. The Asian woman put everything in a blue carrier bag and he left. He got home and ate right away. Soon his blood sugar was back to normal and he relaxed. It had been a shitty day so far. The sun shone through the drawn blinds. He heard his next-door neighbour in his back yard with his kids and wished everything was back to normal, before the world had changed.

'It will be,' Rob said. 'Soon. Don't worry, son.'

'Ah'm glad you're here, Rob,' Jools said.

He went upstairs and lay on the bed. He felt safer in his little bedroom. The bright red carpet glowed in the sunshine and he was warm, protected.

'I've got something to tell you, son. You're not going to like it much but understand that I'm there for you no matter what.'

'What is it, Rob?' Jools asked.

'I'm a mason.'

'Rob. NAW! Surely no. Ye canny be,' Jools said, sunk.

'I'm a Billy Boy. I know it's a shock. Don't worry. I'm on the right side. I want to help you. I'm disgraced as far as the masons go. I can't go back to the lodge. They're after me too, son. I have to watch my family too. They could be targets. Anyway, being a mason I know their tricks. I can help. I want you to go out tonight. I have something I want to teach you. Will you walk for me?'

Jools sighed. 'Ah still trust you, Rob,' he said. 'Ah'll walk for you.'

'Thanks son,' Rob said warmly. 'I knew I could count on you.'

⊙

'YA WEEEEEEEEE JEEEEEEEEEEWWW!!!' the voice goaded him. 'YA WEEEEEEEE JEEEEEEWWWWW!!!'

'Fuck off!' Jools bawled, grabbing his head in both hands.

'YA WEEEEEE JEEEEEWWWWWW!!! WEEEEE JEEEEEEWWWW!!!! YA WWWWEEEEEEEE JEEEWWWW!!!!

'GET THE FUCK OOT AY MA HEID!' Jools screamed. 'We'll fuckin catch you. Ah guarantee it.'

'Shut it, Jew. Ye'll no catch me. Ah'm in Aberdeen. Aye, Ah'm a mason, and you're a wee Jeeeewwww.'

Jools pictured an old man with white hair talking into a mic.

'That's fuck all like me,' the old man said. 'YA WEEEEE JEEEEEWWWWWWWW!!!!'

'AHM NO A FUCKIN JEW!' Jools shouted at the top of his lungs. 'Ah telt ye, Ah'm fuckin Church ay Scotland.'

'YE'RE A WEEEEE JEEEEWWW!!!!'

'Fuck off, ya fuckin spastic cunt.' Jools was getting annoyed. 'Get the fuck oot ma heid. Leave me alone, ya fuckin radge.'

'Ah'll be back, Jew. HA'PENNY CHEEEEWWWWWWWW!!!!' The presence faded.

Jools's brain was fried. He was mentally drained and his head buzzed inside. He went downstairs and made a brew. The cat curled round his ankles, meowing, and he picked it up. It sniffed at his face as if it sensed that something was wrong. 'We'll be awright, puss,' he said, stroking its head. The cat purred contentedly.

⊙

Jools picked up the newspaper. ROBBIE DEATH THREAT the headline read. Robbie Williams had received death threats while on tour in the US. He was under protection of several bodyguards and was currently in LA.

'The cunts have got to Robbie,' Jools said. He wondered if it was because Robbie had come out in support for him.

'Mackenzie's US followers,' Rob said. 'They're gunning for anyone who supports you lot. After this is all over they want you to go to the US. You'll meet Anastacia, Robbie. Shaun Ryder will be there. Anastacia especially wants to meet you. She really didn't know what she was reading out that night on TV. She asks about you a lot, apparently. She's really there for you.'

'Anastacia really cares aboot me?' Jools beamed from ear to ear and his heart pounded.

'They're going to have a big party for you when this is over. Put you up in a big hotel. They want to talk to you about all you've been through. Probably end up on Oprah. None of this will get in the papers, not until it's all over.'

'It's amazing what doesnae get in the papers, eh?' Jools thought.

'Do you feel ready for our lesson?'

'Cool. Let's go.'

'Go for a walk. I'll guide you.'

Jools left the flat, looking around, checking the surroundings. A blue car passed by. Jools looked away in case he was breaking their cover.

'Don't worry,' Rob said. 'Bulldog has you covered.'

The sun was out and a light wind blew.

'This way.' Rob led Jools along Muirhouse Gardens.

He reached the roundabout at the foot of Martello Court. A large black Daimler sat outside. Jools stared at the occupants. A young guy in his thirties wearing a baseball cap. Jools stared at his unshaven face. The passenger, a black girl with short spiky hair, clung to his neck.

'Those are my people,' Rob said. 'This way.'

Rob led Jools through the school and into the leafy avenues of Silverknowes. He walked along the kerbside, the sun shining in his eyes making him squint.

'This way, up here,' Rob navigated.

Jools headed to the top of road and crossed over. 'Take a left.'

He walked along past the supermarket into Davidson's Mains. A red car passed him and Jools looked the other way in case it was his tail.

'Along here.'

Jools walked along the disused railway. He got to the bridge and stopped on top of it.

'I'm going to show you some secrets of the masons,' Rob said. 'You must promise to never, ever tell. Never.'

Jools descended the steps down the railway embankment.

'Look at the sky,' Rob said.

A cloud covered the sun and it went cold.

'That was me. I did that. It's mason's magic. That took years to learn. We've not got much time.'

The sun came back out.

'To be a mason you must walk with nature. Don't go against the grain. Just like in nature. In business the same principle. Don't go against the grain. Always walk with nature. Never against it. Walk on the right side.'

Jools nodded. 'Do Ah walk on the grass?'

A light wind got up from nowhere.

'Be guided,' Rob said.

The wind pushed Jools from behind.

'Be guided.'

The wind blew stronger. It started to blow Jools along.

'Walk with nature,' Rob said. 'Don't go against the grain.'

Jools went with the wind. He kept it on his back as it blew him along.

'That's it, good.'

Jools picked up his pace as the wind blew stronger. It blew him to the end of the road and changed direction.

'Be guided.'

It took him along past the playing fields at Craigroyston, his old high school. He reached Drylaw police station and the wind changed direction again, blowing him down Pennywell Road. He passed the pub.

'You best keep away from there for a while,' Rob said, and Jools remembered George Grant was out to get him. He took a long detour home.

'We'll guide you like this from now on,' Rob said. 'You can go and rest now if you want.'

Jools got in and wolfed down his food. He ran a bath, got undressed and sank into the hot water.

'You did well tonight,' Rob told him. 'Her Majesty would be proud of you. So would Tanaka sensei. Wait till Anastacia finds out what you've been doing.'

'Do you think she'll hear about this?'

'Yes. I told you, she asks about you all the time.'

'Well, tell her Ah says she's beautiful!'

'She knows you like her, I know that much.'

Jools was weary. His feet ached and he felt heavy. He dried himself off and went downstairs. It was just getting dark and Jimmy Love's light was on.

'Do you think we'll ever get anything on Jimmy Love?' he asked.

'Soon, I'm sure we will,' Rob said. 'Jimmy Love has another nephew. He's an MSP. He's with the left. He's been keeping his uncle out of trouble. I'm sure he's involved with transport. Runs the buses and trains.'

'Do you think he'd be any help?'

'Maybe if we could get to him, Jimmy Love would be easier to catch. We've not got much concrete evidence against him so far.'

'Ah'm tired,' Jools said. He sat in his chair and relaxed. He put the radio on and turned it down low.

'I'd better go,' Rob said. 'Jimmy Love will be watching. You know people round about have heard what's happening to you. They've started to leave a light on for you. If you look around you'll see how many people are there for you.'

Jools peeked through the spy hole on the front door. There were lots of lights on in the opposite block including Rob's. He looked out the living room window. Again there were lights on in all the blocks around him. 'They're all for me?' Jools gasped.

'All for you. They're leaving lights on all over Scotland for you. I'll be back to talk soon, OK?'

'Ah'll catch ye later, Rob.'

Rob retreated. Jools felt comfort at the fact so many people cared for him. He went to bed early and thought some more about Anastacia.

⊙

Jools got up early next morning. It was a dull grey morning and all was quiet except for the cooing and flapping of the pigeons that roosted on nearby buildings. He stretched his muscles and held a few yogic postures. He stood in front of the mirror and checked his eyes up close in the reflection. He took a step back and threw a punch, stopping an inch from the mirror. He practiced some kicks, ten with the left leg, ten with the right leg. He practised *muto* techniques, side-stepping the sword and disarming his imaginary attacker. Next he moved onto wrist locks and takedowns. He finished off with striking pressure points.

He had a quick wash and decided to go to the shops before the morning rush started. As he walked to the shops there were still a few lights on. He bought a paper and cigarettes. On his way out the shop door a woman smiled at him. He thought she must know about him. Maybe she'd left her light on for him. Returning home he noticed that Rob's light was still on.

'I'm up when you're up,' Rob said. He sounded tired. 'I've not had much sleep. I was watching you when you were out.'

'Where's Bulldog?' Jools asked.

'He's still out with Big Steve.'

'Ah was just thinking,' Jools said. 'About Kev. Do you think Ah should trust him? They said he'd been bugging my hoose for Jimmy Love.'

'I don't trust him. He's been trying to sell his story to the papers. They turned him down, most of them, but you can bet some of them bought it. They'll be sitting on it till they get the OK to print from Downing Street. You best get rid of him. He's only there for the money.'

'But Ah've known him for twenty years. How could he dae this tae me?'

'He thinks he'll come out of it looking like a hero. Trouble is, he's not doing any of the work to deserve it. If he is working for Jimmy Love he's a real danger to you. He knows too much about you. And you better get back that hammer he borrowed from you too. I think they're trying to set you up.'

'What? D'you think he'll use the hammer on somebody? It's got my prints all over it,' Jools said.

'Remember the guy you and his brother were fighting with in Cramond? I'll bet they'll use it on him. The police will find your DNA at the scene. But they don't know that we're watching you too. We'll have it all on tape. They won't have a leg to stand on. Then all we have to do is get Kev to stand up against Jimmy Love. You'd better get rid of him. Don't let him in.'

Jools sighed. He felt totally betrayed but scared at what Kev could tell them about him.

'Don't get too down, son,' Rob said. 'We'll balance these bastards alright when we get them.'

Rob retreated and left Jools to his thoughts.

⊙

Later on that day Jools turned the TV on. The band Starsailor were doing their number 'Good Souls'. Jools listened to the words. This song was all about him.

> You've been messing with a good heart
> You've got to pay what's JEW!

The singer glared at Jools through the screen.

Jools turned off. They were still slagging him off. When would it stop? Why were they still letting Mackenzie use the networks for his jibes and blackmails?

Surely someone at the BBC would stop this. He wondered if he should phone them. He decided not to put the TV back on. It was getting too painful to watch. He went to look out the window. Jimmy Love's back door was open. A cat sat on the step outside.

'Ma cat would fuckin leather it,' he thought.

'PRICK!' the voice said.

'Fuck off!' Jools answered back.

'Ah heard that. Aboot my cat. We'll see when ma nephew gets a hud ay ye.'

'Who the fuck are you, likes?'

'The word is Love. Jimmy Love. Ah heard you dinnae like ma people. Aye, gypsies Ah'm talkin aboot.'

'Nae fuckin wonder,' Jools said. 'Check what you're daein tae me.'

'Ma nephew's spent a wad ay money on his sponsorship deals. You better dae his walk for him. If ye dinnae, he'll have every face fae Muirhoose tae Leith efter ye.'

'Ah'm no daein it. Fuck off. Ye're a dirty bastard.'

'We'll see.'

Jimmy Love disappeared, leaving Jools feeling uneasy. He wondered if he'd made the right decision. He didn't need any more hassle than he'd already had. A helicopter buzzed around outside. He went to the window.

'It's the TV people,' Bulldog said. 'They're trying to get some footage of your house.'

Jools held back the net curtain and waved to the helicopter. He put two blue china liondogs on the window sill to represent balance. The helicopter buzzed overhead then disappeared. Jools lay on his bed and tried to relax.

'Can you look at the wall for us, Jools?' Bulldog asked.

'Awright, Ah'll gie it a bash.' Jools sat up. He stuck a thumb tack in the wall and settled down, concentrating on its shiny head.

'Don't picture anything. See how long you can hold it for. That's it, stay like that. Just be.'

Jools held it a few minutes. He started to think of Anastacia.

'Don't picture anything,' Bulldog checked him.

Jools cleared his mind. He widened his eyes and started to breathe rhythmically. He counted breaths: five… six… seven… eight counts in. Six… seven… eight counts out.

'Don't count,' Bulldog said. 'Just be.'

Jools quietened down again. Another few minutes passed. He thought of Jimmy Love's nephew.

'Quiet!'

'Sorry, man.' Jools got back on it. His eyes started to water. He tried to ignore it but they began to sting. He wiped his face on his sleeve and settled back down. He wondered what time it was.

'You're doing it again, Jools.'

'Sorry likes, but this isnae easy.' He took a deep breath and dropped the tension in his shoulders. He stared at the tack. His vision began to double. A few minutes more passed. His head began to hurt. 'How long do you want me to do this for?' he asked.

'As long as you can.'

Jools was getting bored. He straightened his back. His mother popped into his mind.

'Concentrate.'

Jools sighed. He emptied his head and refocused on the tack. His eyes began to play tricks on him. The tack began to move down the wall. He shook it off. Another few minutes. Jools started to drift. He began to wonder how long he could hold this. Another few minutes and he couldn't do any more. 'Ah'll have tae call it a day,' he said.

'You did OK,' Bulldog said. 'We'll leave it at that for today. If you could try and do this for a while every afternoon it would be a big help to us.'

'Ah'll try.'

Jools went downstairs for something to eat. His head throbbed and he was hungry. The low blood sugar made him feel weak. Big Steve's car started up across the road and Jools heard him drive off.

'Is that them away tracking?' he asked.

'Yes. Rob's not going tonight. He's staying in watching your door.'

It had started to get dark outside. Jools sat in the gloom and ate. The cat started to call loudly in the hall.

'It's them!' Bulldog said. 'They're trying to scare you. They're making the cat howl. Another one of their tricks. They can affect animals. Make them do things.'

'Dirty bastards,' Jools said. 'Using ma cat. They're making sure Ah dinnae get any peace.'

'It's the animal people.'

'How do they do it?'

'It's mostly done electronically. Some of them can do it using the power of their minds. The cat won't suffer any. It's safe. Poor thing probably wonders why it's acting like this. It must be strange.'

Jools lit a candle and flicked through the newspaper by its dim light. A Japanese ambassador, Mr Koji, was to visit Edinburgh.

'That's Tanaka san,' Bulldog said. 'He's travelling in disguise. He doesn't want to be seen before he's had the chance to help.'

Jools felt a lot safer knowing his grandmaster was in the country. 'We'll really see some fireworks now that he's here,' he said gleefully. 'When do we meet up?'

'After this is all over, we'll have a party. We can all have a good drink together.'

'Ah'll look forward tae that.'

Jools started to think that maybe everything would work out. Tanaka sensei would even the odds. Damien, his instructor, was there too. He thought of them out there somewhere watching over him and felt as if no one could hurt him.

'I'll have to go,' the SAS man said. Bulldog retreated.

Jools peeked out the window. Lights were on everywhere.

He went to bed and slept soundly.

⊙

Jools woke early. A copy of the *North Edinburgh News*, the community newspaper, had been posted through the letterbox. He'd done some work for the paper when he was younger and used to get his name in the credits. He flicked through it and noticed an article on Sinclair McKelvie's new book.

'It's about you and your mates,' Rob said. 'It's about you and Kev growing up. I've had a chat with him on the phone. He's asking for you.'

Jools felt honoured. 'He's really gave us a mention? In his book, likes?'

'Really.'

Jools read on. Sinclair McKelvie was to visit the *NEN* offices in a couple of weeks.

'He wants to meet you,' Rob said. 'Should be a laugh.'

'I'll need tae go tae that.'

Jools turned the TV on. The breakfast programme was on ITV. The female presenter was interviewing a Buddhist. The man spoke in a Scots accent. The presenter kept glancing at her monitor as if waiting for a cue. Jools got the uneasy feeling they could see him. They seemed to be waiting for him to switch on. The presenter asked the Buddhist about his faith. The man said that Buddhism could be studied along with any other religion. Buddha was not a god.

'SHITE!' Jools said. He switched off. 'They're no fuckin watching me. Fuck off.' Maybe the Buddhist had been from the centre at Portobello. That would put him nearer Prestonpans and the gyppos. They could easily have got the Buddhists on the payroll.

'Fuckin sneaky bastards.' Jools decided not to watch the TV again while this was going on. Every time he did they were at him, slagging him off. And now they could see him in the studio but only when his TV was on. He got ready to go out.

'We'll leave signs for you,' Bulldog said. 'Our guys will guide you with signs. Look out for them. I want you to do something for us. It's your chance to help us. Walk for us. The TV people will be filming you all the way. Our guys will be everywhere watching you. You'll be quite safe. It's your chance to show your side of the story.'

'Awright,' Jools agreed. 'Cool, likes.'

Jools left the flat. The wind caught him at the end of the path. It blew him along the road, gusting gently at his back.

'Be guided,' Rob said. The wind changed direction and he followed it down Gypsy Brae to the West Shore Road. A woman walked along leading a horse by the reins. Suddenly a man ran past and Jools thought he saw the man do something with his fingers.

The horse took fright, rearing up on its hind legs and the woman tried to steady it. The horse eventually calmed down.

'Excuse me!' she called to him in a posh accent. The woman asked Jools if he would hold the reins while she got on the horse's back. Jools took hold of the strap but the horse pulled away, spooked. He wondered if it could sense the presence within him.

'It was that man jogging,' the woman said. 'He scared the horse when he ran by.'

'One of Jimmy Love's men,' Jools thought. 'He doesnae trust me,' he said, and handed back the reins.

A gust of wind blew at his back and he moved on. The sun came out and it began to feel warm. A silver car passed.

'Shut your mouwf!!!' Jools heard the voice, a camp whisper.

'Shut your mouwf.' Another car passed. The wind blew him to Granton Square. He passed the Claverhouse on the right-hand side and Granton harbour. He remembered how he'd seen his dad off on a trip when he was a boy. His dad and uncle had been trawlermen and had sailed from Granton in the seventies until the boats were tied up and work moved away to Aberdeen.

The wind took him along by the sea front. The breeze blew him across to the opposite side of the road.

'Shut your mouwf!' The whisper came from a red Escort in the busy traffic. Jools passed the Old Chain Pier, the pub on the seafront with its colourful flowers and hanging baskets outside. He looked across the Forth to Fife. It was clear and he could see an oil tanker making its way upriver. The wind picked up again and he started to walk. It blew him back across the road and on to Harry Ramsden's restaurant in Newhaven harbour. He started to feel hungry and went in.

'Don't worry. We're with you,' Bulldog encouraged him.

Jools stood in the queue and wondered who his cover was. The place was busy. It could be anyone. He noticed a collection box for the lifeboat charity and dropped in a two pound coin. He always hoped that his dad would never need them. He ordered some chips and a cup of tea to go. He paid and went outside to sit in the sunshine at the quayside.

'Ah wonder if they're still filming me,' he thought to himself. Jools felt relaxed away from the busy traffic. He sat and took in the scene. A small picturesque harbour with its little fishing boats. A pile of lobster pots piled up on the other pier. It had a lighthouse on the end of the quay. He could see Granton pier in the distance. He tucked into the box of chips and stirred a packet of sugar into his tea. Seagulls swooped overhead.

'Watch this,' Rob said.

A seagull landed on a little red fishing boat. It stood and squawked loudly. Another one joined it.

'Balance,' Rob said.

Jools laughed. 'How do you do that with animals?'

'It's just a trick the sensei taught me.'

'Could Ah dae it?'

'Maybe. But it takes a while to learn. Animal magnetism. Seagulls are easy to affect. They're very easy subjects.'

'Are they still filming me?'

'Yes. They'll have got that on tape.'

Jools wondered if his dad had seen them slagging him on the telly. He looked around for the cameras and licked his lips like he'd seen the REM singer do.

'Who's the poof now, eh?' he smirked as he stared at where he thought the cameras were. 'What am Ah doin this walk for, Rob?'

'We're trying to flush out Mackenzie's people. As soon as they hear you're out in the open they'll all be out for a look. That's our chance to spot them.'

'Did you get many today?'

'Quite a few have shown themselves today. We've done alright.'

Jools finished his chips and knocked back his tea. 'Time to get moving,' he said.

'Don't go any further, Jools,' Rob said. 'Don't go past the mill. You don't want to go any nearer Leith. Jimmy Love's nephew's from Leith.'

'I'll just go home then.'

'OK.'

Jools crossed the road and stood at a bus stop. He'd done some walking and felt worn. A small child waved a plastic sword at him from behind her father's legs and he pulled a face at her. The little girl stuck her tongue out at Jools and he smiled. The number 32 bus came and he got on it, going upstairs to the back seat. Someone had written CHERYLS HOLE SMELLS OF FISH on the back of the seat and he laughed to himself as he wondered what little degenerate had tested that theory out. He sat back and closed his eyes. The bus was warm and the vibration rocked him gently. He thought of the seagulls on the boat. That was a great trick. His mind drifted and he thought of his ex-girlfriend, Natty. She'd never believe what was going on. He nearly drifted off and woke with a start just before his stop. He got home feeling weary. Rob's light was still on even though it was daylight. Jools went upstairs and lay on his bed. The sun shone in the west and beamed in through the net curtain. His neighbour was in the backyard with her granddaughter. An ice-cream van sounded its chime in the distance. A plane streaked across the sky leaving a white vapour trail. Some kids bounced a football, playing 'kerby' in the car park. Someone began playing loud music out of their window.

'This song was written for you Jools,' Rob said. 'It's just about to be released. The proceeds will go to help us.'

'They wrote it for me?' Jools asked.

'Yes. They believe in your cause. They're a new band. American. You'll meet them in LA at the party.'

Jools listened to the song, a slow R'n'B track. He couldn't make out the words but he liked the music.

'NIGGERS!!!' the loud voice screamed in his head. It sent a shooting pain through Jools's right eye.

'Ahrrggh!!!!!' he bawled.

'FUCKIN NIGGERS!!!'

'That wisnae me, Rob!' Jools pleaded his innocence. 'Ah nivir said that.'

'I know,' Rob whispered. 'We've got one of them playing silly buggers.

Probably just jealous. Decided to spoil it for everyone. We're tracking him now.'

'FUCKIN NIGGERS!!!' the voice screamed. 'Yer goin tae America. Yer gonnae stay wi Biggie Smalls!'

Jools held his head in his hands. 'GET TAE FUCK YA FUCKIN RADGED BASTARD!!!' he shouted at the voice. 'Biggie Smalls is deid!'

The presence disappeared.

'What the fuck happened there, Rob?' Jools asked.

'He's gone,' Rob said. 'We've lost him. These people are dangerous. They're trying to cause trouble.'

'Fuckin oot ay order, likes.'

'They must have boosted their signal. They had us locked out for a minute there.'

'Fuck's sake, Rob. Dinnae let them dae that.'

'Don't worry. We will catch these people.'

Jools's eye throbbed. 'Can Ah no outrun the signal? If Ah got far enough away Ah'd be oot ay range.'

'They're very clever people. The signal is tuned to your brain frequency. You can't outrun it.'

'Ah've no heard that voice before. He was a new one.'

'They're passing the digitiser around. They're having a shot of the radio mic. We can try boosting our signal. Maybe drown them out. For a while at least,' Rob said.

Jools went to the bedroom window. The sun started to set. The sky turned pink and orange. The yellow streetlights flickered on one by one. Big Steve's car was gone. Jimmy Love's light was on.

'He's been in Leith all day with his nephew,' Rob said. 'Do you feel like helping out tonight?'

'What dae ye want me tae dae?' Jools asked.

'Help us catch some spiders.'

'Spiders?'

'Mackenzie's people.'

'Show me how.'

'Be guided.'

⊙

Jools walked over the school playing fields. The mud squelched underfoot as he crossed the sodden grass, and he climbed the iron railings at the top. The wind blew him on across the road past the Doocot pub in Drylaw. It pushed him gently up Groathill Road and along towards the back of the hospital on Telford Road.

A dark coloured car passed.

'Shut your mouwf!!!'

'Got one,' Rob said. 'Tailing him.'

Another car sped past close behind.

The wind blew him along the kerbside. He stopped again.

'Shut your mouwf!!!' The camp whisper came from a milk lorry.

'On him. We got a bogey.'

Jools watched as another car raced after the lorry. The wind pushed Jools harder. He started to run.

'Shut your mouwf!!!' Another car sped past.

'Contact!' Another tail.

The road went quiet. The wind blew him across to the MacDonald's drive-in. He stood and waited a few minutes. A motor bike and a van approached and passed.

'Steady,' Rob said.

Some cars came all at once.

'Shut your mouwf!!!'

'Got him.'

Jools moved up the street. The breeze blew him back across the road and he moved along the road a few hundred yards to the red-brick bridge. An articulated lorry passed, followed by a breakdown truck. Jools walked to the bus shelter. He sat on the fold-down plastic seat.

'Shut your mouwf!!!' A small black hatchback passed.

'On it,' Rob said.

Another few minutes passed. Jools lit a cigarette. Some cars approached.

'Shut your mouwf!!!' The whisper came.

'Safe,' Rob said.

Jools stood for another hour catching spiders, then went home. He was totally worn down and went straight to bed.

Jools lay in the darkness.

'You did well tonight,' Rob said. 'We got a few of them. That's a few less to worry about.'

'Ah'm knackered, Rob,' Jools said.

'I know, son. But we're getting there. Anastacia would be proud of you.'

Jools smiled, then turned over and went to sleep.

⊙

Jools filled in the census form. He wondered about the possibility of them getting his DNA from the envelope and decided to wet the flap with tap water instead of his tongue.

'Fuckin analyse that!' he laughed.

He left the house. Rob's light was on. The sun was high in the sky. There was no breeze. Jools made his way through the scheme. He walked across the field past Martello Court avoiding the CCTV cameras round the high flats. The postbox had been vandalised and covered in gloss paint but he posted his form anyway. He went across the road to the corner shop and bought a paper and some cigarettes. A tall man dressed in dark clothes entered the shop and looked at him. He put his hand to his ear. 'He's got an earpiece in,' Jools thought. 'Must be one of Bulldog's guys.'

He left the shop and walked back along Muirhouse Gardens. A metallic blue estate car sped along the road stopping next to the post box. A man got out and went to the pillar box then got back in the car and sped off.

'You didn't just post that census form, did you?' Bulldog asked anxiously.

'Aye. Ah did. Why?'

'Shit! We'll have to get the keys for the postbox. They'll get your DNA.'

'Dinnae worry, man. Ah stuck the flap doon with tap water.'

'Thank God for that.' Bulldog sounded relieved.

'Aye, fuck them. They'll no get me in a hurry,' Jools laughed. He crossed the field back into Pennywell. Big Steve's window had a vase of flowers at each side.

'Balance,' Jools thought.

He crossed the car park and saw a neighbour along the block standing at his window.

Jools waved to him. He caught sight of Jools and gave what Jools thought was a Nazi salute. Jools was stunned. He'd known the man for ten years or more and now he was being like this. 'Fuck him,' he thought. Jimmy Love must have got to him.

He got in and sat down in the living room. This was getting to him. Even neighbours were turning against him. He thought about Kev and worried about the hammer he'd lent him. He decided to distract himself and do some training. He knelt down on his knees in *seiza* position and began to recite the ninja seishin.

Ninja seishin towa. Shin shin shikio shinobu...

He finished the verse and knitted his fingers in a kuji sign.

'SHIKIN HARA MITSU DAIKOMYO!!!'*

He clapped his hands twice and bowed. He clapped once more and bowed again.

Onigai shimasu!

He stood up and picked up his samurai sword. He bowed to the weapon, holding it at arm's length and stuck it in his belt. He stood in front of the large mirror. Drawing the sword in one hand, it cut through the imaginary opponent in one swift move. He resheathed the blade and relaxed his mind. He drew and cut again, this time faster, cutting diagonally left to right. He resheathed the sword again and put it down. He stood in the posture *ichi monji no kamae* and threw an upper block followed by a finger jab to the eyes. He repeated the move faster, then changed arms. A lower block, followed by a chop to the throat, then a stomping kick to the sternum with the sole of the foot. He stood in *jumonji no kamae*, a fire posture, fists crossed in front of the chest. He blocked underarm with his left and delivered an elbow smash with his right. He practiced the same move again with his other hand. He knelt down again and cleared his mind.

The front door tapped. It was Kev.

'Awright, man,' he said chirpily.

'Aye? What dae you want?' Jools responded bluntly.

Kev looked at him, waiting for the joke. 'What's up, man?'

'Ah dinnae really want any company the day. Ah'm no wantin you tae come roond,' Jools said, annoyed that he had the gall to come back. 'And can Ah get ma hammer back? Ah need it for something.'

'But Jay, man. It's me. What's up wi' ye?'

'Ah know all about it, Kev. There's nae use in trying to cover up.'

'But Jay, man, what are ye talkin aboot?'

'Get ma hammer,' Jools said, closing the door. He came back in annoyed. 'Ah hope he enjoys the money while he can,' he thought. 'Ah hope he got his money's worth.'

Jools went upstairs to his bedroom. He was pissed off. The sun streamed through the window and the room was warm. Someone played Eminem out their window.

'Don't worry,' Rob said. 'He's the one that'll miss out in the end.'

Jools thought about it. 'He could've come wi' me to LA. If only he hadnae been so greedy.'

*'Divine light guide us in your wisdom!'

'Never mind. Wait till you meet Anastacia. You'll not look back.'

Jools smiled at the thought. He read the paper. An article slagging off East Lothian council caught his eye. The article was about a no-smoking sign that had been posted up in their offices. It had been signed 'East Lothian Toon Council'.

'Us big city folk dinnae talk like that,' the reporter had joked.

'The Prestonpans mob will go mental aboot that one,' Jools sniggered.

'We're starting up a new political party,' Rob interrupted. 'It's all a sting so we can drain Mackenzie's bank accounts. We're going to be the Tory Liberals. We can bring together everyone opposed to Mackenzie so they can vote no matter what party they're from. Wear something yellow and something blue. They're our colours.'

Jools pinned a yellow badge to his blue shirt. 'Ah'm no too sure aboot the Tory bit, likes. Ah hate the fuckers.'

'There will be a general election in a few months and it's vital that this all stays quiet till then. We don't want that Labour lot getting in or we'll never get rid of Mackenzie.'

'Ah just hate the Tories,' Jools said.

'We've got some work for you to do,' Rob said. 'We want you to walk again. Sensei's been watching you, and him and Damien think you're ready for it. They want you to walk for them.'

'Aye, OK. Ah'll dae it.'

'Tonight.'

'Sound, likes.'

'Be guided.'

⊙

The wind pushed Jools along the road fast. He stopped when it stopped. It blew him along past the gasworks at Granton, the two giant blue gas-holders that could be seen from anywhere in Edinburgh. The yellow streetlights were reflected on the wet road. He crossed the new bridge and continued following the breeze. He climbed down the embankment to the disused railway under the bridge. It was pitch dark except for the stars and the glare of the streetlights above. He walked along the railway into the darkness, the wind urging him on. He stopped and turned around. There was a helicopter in the distance.

'Don't worry. We're watching you. We're just hanging back so we'll not draw attention,' Bulldog said.

The wind picked up and Jools was carried along further into the darkness. He felt reassured knowing Bulldog was watching. A fox trotted along and Jools froze so as not to scare it. The fox stopped and sniffed at a patch of long grass, then moved on, oblivious to his presence.

'Turn back little fox!' he heard. It was Damien, his ninpo instructor.

The wind blew him on and Jools was confused whether to follow the wind or turn back. He continued on and soon came to the road at the track's end. The wind took him across the road and into the harbour. He stopped at a hole in the gate, the wind dropped and he climbed through. He walked to the edge of the pier and looked over the side into the cold, dark water. Farther along the pier there was a slipway leading into the water. The breeze urged him along. He got to the bottom of the slipway and stood looking under the pier. The wind picked up, blowing him towards the water. He hesitated.

'Do Ah go in?' he asked, but there was no answer.

He rolled up his jeans and waded in. The ice-cold sea water filled his trainers and he shivered. The wind urged him on. He walked further in. Up past his knees. He almost lost his balance and steadied himself. He rolled his jeans up to his thighs and waded deeper. He reached out for the wooden pier but it was a few feet too far. He stood in the water shivering uncontrollably. He reached out with his feet and found a large brick under the water. A typical ninjutsu trick, he thought. The wind blew him on. He stepped onto the submerged brick and found he could reach the pier. He climbed onto a rafter and sat rolling his jeans down. He waited for a minute and let his eyes adjust to the dark. The pier creaked and groaned above him. The breeze picked up and he climbed along to the next spar. Then the next. He came to a small jetty sticking out into the harbour. A large black water rat perched on the edge of the jetty. It slipped silently into the water on his approach. He climbed down from the beam and the wind blew him along to the end of the jetty. The breeze died down and he stopped at two rubber dinghies tied to the pier. He put a boat in the water and climbed in, sitting on his knees. The wind urged him on and he began to row the boat with a paddle he'd picked up. He rowed out into the harbour trying to stick to the shadows. The wind direction changed slightly and began to blow him towards the quayside. He paddled towards the pier, the wind pushing him on. He stopped under the pier and pulled the boat along under the rafters. He had to duck in parts as he passed under a beam. He reached a wall and a ladder and tied the boat up. He climbed up to the quayside and found himself behind an old warehouse with barred windows. Looking up, he could see an open window halfway up the side of the building. A metal pipe stuck out from the brickwork just below the window frame. The wind blew him on until he stood directly under the window. He looked up and saw a small ledge. Using it as a handhold he lifted himself up the wall. He saw another handhold and swung his body over to it. He was now about twenty feet above the concrete ledge with the water below that. He reached the steel pipe, just touching it with his fingertips. He could hear the water below the pier in the darkness. He jumped for the pipe and caught hold of it, his heart pounding.

'When climbing, always keep three points of contact with the wall,' his teacher had once said.

He pulled himself up to the window sill, panting for breath. He sat there till his breathing had calmed.

It was quiet up here. Only the wind made a sound. He turned to go through the window. Suddenly he flinched and ducked as a dark mass fluttered towards his face, making him reach out to stop himself falling backwards. A bird flapped frantically out of the building and into the darkness, scaring the life out of him. His heart pounded. He took a deep breath and the wind blew him on into the warehouse. He stood in the darkness. The building was derelict. He walked across the floor and came to a large pole stuck through a hole in the floor. A piece of rope hung from the rafters above. He stood at the edge of the hole and looked down into another room. He slid down the pole. Two large loading doors were open and Jools could look down on the Ports Authority building lit up on the end of the pier. He sat for a few minutes and observed. He didn't want to be spotted and stuck to the shadows. He climbed down from the loading doors, dropping the last few feet to the quayside below. The breeze picked up again, pushing him on towards the end of the pier. He moved from shadow to shadow in quick bursts. The wind led him to a large hole in the wooden pier then it dropped. He climbed down onto the beams. The water lapped at the piles below in the darkness. He climbed onto a concrete ledge just wide enough for him to sit on and looked out over the Forth. Fife was lit up in the dark and the lighthouse on an island shone through the night. Jools looked up at a passing plane, its landing lights tracing a path across the surface of the water.

'They're looking for you,' Rob said. 'From the plane.'

'Ah better hide then,' Jools said, ducking in under the beams.

'They're tracking your body heat with thermal cameras. Stay hidden till it passes.'

Jools waited till the plane passed. He climbed back onto the ledge. He looked up at the black sky. It was clear and studded with stars. They seemed so much brighter here in the dark. He looked up at a constellation above him. He thought it might be Cygnus, the swan. It looked like a cross with one spar out of alignment.

'That's the Queen's personal constellation you're looking at,' Rob said. 'It's a secret of the masons. The three prongs that face one way represent Scotland, England and Wales. The fourth one represents Ireland out on its own. As long as the three remain strong together all the power will stay with the throne. It is written in the stars. You must never, ever tell, Jools, promise me.'

'Scout's honour.'

'Tanaka sensei thinks you deserve an honorary rank for this, you know. He thinks you're ready for third dan.'

'Nice one. That's sound, Rob.' Jools was over the moon.

'We've got some of the SAS boys filming this from a boat. Wait till sensei sees the film of this. He'll be impressed.'

'What am Ah here for Rob?' Jools asked.

'Look for clues. There should be a bit of a coat in there somewhere. Like a workman's rain jacket. It's evidence. It's from a murder scene. We believe it was dumped under here.'

Jools looked everywhere but could find nothing. A gentle breeze got up, pushing him along to the end of the pier. He hung over the edge, looking down at the water.

'If Ah fell in,' he thought, 'Ah'd have no chance.'

He climbed down onto a lower beam nearer the water. There was no sign of anything.

'Are you sure it's doon here, Rob?' Jools asked.

'Somewhere,' Rob replied. Another plane made its way across the water. Jools was confident he couldn't be spotted where he was. The plane quickly passed and Jools crawled round a corner along the concrete shelf. He could see across the bay to East Lothian. He sat looking at the lights on the coast. The red lights blinked on and off four times, then stopped for a minute or so.

'They're warning you to stay out of East Lothian. The flashing red lights are a warning,' Rob said.

The wind picked up again and Jools searched the ledge. There was definitely nothing to be found. He'd searched the area twice.

'There's nowt here, Rob,' Jools said. 'D'you want to call it a night?'

'Be guided.'

Jools climbed out and headed back along the quayside. The charred wooden frame of a chair lay in a corner of a fenced compound.

'That's what we were afraid of, Jools,' Rob said. 'They tied the victim to that chair, dowsed him in petrol and burned him to death. That's why we need the piece of the coat. It may be all that's left.'

'Ah'll come back in the light,' Jools said, heading up the road. There were many lights on all the way home.

⊙

Jools lay in bed unable to sleep. A party raged on in a nearby block. Their music was turned up so loud it was distorted. A woman sang along to a Tina Turner record.

> You're simply the best,
> Better than all the rest!

Jools heard a car door slam and an engine start up. 'Big Steve,' he thought. He went to the window. Jimmy Love's light was off.

Jools thought of Rob.

'Don't picture my face,' Rob said. 'They can see that on their monitors. I don't want them to see my face.'

'Sorry, Rob.' Jools cleared his mind.

'We'll have more work for you tomorrow. Will you walk again? We need you to help us catch more of Mackenzie's mob.'

'Awright,' Jools said. 'How did they tune me in, Rob? Wi' the radio an' that?'

'These people have been out there for a long time, Jools, in position, watching, waiting. They had the dentist put something in your tooth when you got that filling. It's a small tracking device and a mic. That's how they knew all your business. They could hear you. That's how they could pinpoint you to tune in the radio gear.'

Jools contemplated pulling the tooth with pliers.

'It'd do no good,' Rob said. 'It's too late. Once you're tuned in the only way to stop it is to find and destroy the digitisers.'

Jools heard the neighbours bang on the ceiling again.

'They're doing a good job. That'll be them changing tapes again,' Rob said. 'You better get some sleep. You don't want to keep them up all night taping you. They can't sleep till you do.'

Jools lay down and tried to sleep. The party across the street simmered down and the sky turned to dark blue. Jools was restless. He kicked at the duvet and rolled over. The birds started to sing and he found it annoying.

'Ah canny sleep,' he said.

The neighbour upstairs banged around again.

'This is fuckin hopeless,' he huffed.

'Shut up, Jools,' he heard from upstairs.

'Is that you, Greg?'

'Jools, go to sleep. We've been up all night,' his neighbour said.

'Thank fuck Ah can talk to someone, Greg. Can you hear me OK?'

'Aye. They gave us a shot of a mic. Dinnae worry aboot this, Jools. It'll be awright. We've had a barry laugh with Rob, by the way. He's mental.'

'Rob's sound, man,' Jools said. 'Thanks for helping oot with this, Greg. Tell the wife Ah said thanks tae, will you? This is a freaky set up, eh?'

'Aw what?! It's brutal, Jools. But we've got to get some sleep. We've got to get up early. We're recording in your sleep. That's when they try to sneak in and play with your heid. We can track them better when you're asleep.'

'Ah'll try again,' Jools said, and turned over. He lay awake for some hours and the neighbour banged on.

⊙

The wind pushed Jools through Inverleith Park. He walked along the avenue with its mature elm trees on either side. The breeze carried him along to the road at the end. He crossed and entered the west gate of the Botanic Gardens. The wind changed direction blowing him along by the holly hedge that ran down one side. The breeze pushed him along a small path that was hidden from view of the rest of the garden behind the seven-foot hedge. It stopped him just in front of a gap in the foliage. He peered through at the house across the road.

'Blackmail,' Rob said.

SLAM! a car door clunked shut. Jools took it to symbolise them being locked up and grinned to himself.

The wind picked up and Jools continued. A few metres along the breeze died down. Jools peered through the hedge at another grander house across the street. He heard some women cheering from inside the house and felt proud that his efforts weren't going unnoticed.

The breeze blew him along past another few houses and stopped again. Jools stood staring at the huge house in front of him. He took a step back and climbed up on the small retaining wall to a grassy hill above. The sun blazed overhead. Jools sat under a tree looking at the house.

A sparrow sat in the tree singing.

'Jools, you must learn how we get into messes like this.' It was Damien, his instructor. 'Blackmail causes misery. They manipulate the five weaknesses to get you to bend to their will. One little bird tells another little bird and it grows. Spreading out everywhere. Soon we'll catch these people.'

A loud bang disturbed the scene and the sparrow flew away from the tree.

'The one o'clock gun,' Jools laughed.

'They're going to jail,' Rob said. 'We've got enough on them to put them away for a long time. They didn't want a visit from you, that's for sure. You've freed the other ones from their blackmailing.'

Jools laughed. He felt like the grim reaper to them. They didn't expect him to come around with his accusing stare. The loud bang provided a final touch, marking their capture.

'The beauty of it is, Jools, you don't say anything. You just mark out who did what to who, we film it and as soon as you leave they get banged up. It's foolproof. You're exposing them one by one.' Rob sounded as if he was enjoying himself.

Jools walked along the tree-lined path, the breeze blowing at his back. A squirrel chased another one along the grass in front of him. The wind pushed him to a crossroads in the path and died down. Ahead of him there was a waterfall. Two crows hopped along the grass beside it.

'In your mother's memory,' Rob said respectfully. 'She was a remarkable woman. It's a fitting tribute. Her Majesty wanted to reward you on the quiet.'

Jools felt a lump in his throat and a tear in his eye.

'This is really for ma Ma?'

The breeze blew, turning him around 180 degrees. A little house stood in front of him. The door was open. A plaque read 'Prince of Wales Trust.'

'The door's always open for you here, Jools. They want you to work for them after this is over. Just come up anytime. The job's yours,' Rob said.

Jools turned and gave a quick bow to the four directions.

'Thanks, Rob. Ah always wanted to work here.'

'I know. We had a quick peek one night when you were sleeping,' Rob laughed. 'You're a good gardener.'

'You're really helping me sort oot my life. Ah fell intae a rut a few years ago and Ah've been strugglin a bit ever since. Ah appreciate it Rob. Really.'

The wind picked up and Jools followed. It blew him to the Irish bog garden with its pond and little house with a thatched roof. A solitary duck paddled in the water. The wind pushed him along the wooden decking across the little bridge. He turned to his left and walked on. A young man sat on a bench. His dark curly hair reached down to his shoulders. Jools couldn't see where his eyes were looking as the man had sunglasses on.

'Watch him,' Rob said. 'He's here to check you out for the Irish. The IRA are interested in you. They want Mackenzie out of Ireland. He's giving too much money to the UVF.'

Jools looked at the man. He dropped something on the ground in front of him. The wind blew Jools around to face the pond. The duck quacked. Jools counted ten times.

'That's not funny,' Rob said. 'They're using animals again. The duck. It's taking the piss. It just quacked at you ten times, right? What's ten in Japanese?'

'Ju,' Jools said, laughing.

'Small things amuse small minds. They must have someone nearby.'

Jools turned round again. The man was gone, leaving an empty bench. Jools walked over to the bench and looked around to see what the man had dropped. There were some peanut shells on the ground.

'He's calling you a monkey nut,' Rob laughed. 'Believe it or not, Jools, the IRA want you to do well. They're actually there for you. If we get Mackenzie out of the way the UVF's funding will be drastically reduced.'

Jools felt a bit anxious. 'Ah'm no really sure Ah want tae get into this, Rob. It's a bit heavy.'

The breeze turned Jools around again. An older man in a flat tweed cap walked over the bridge, stopping in the middle and leaning on the guard rail. He looked over at Jools and stood contemplating the scene.

'He's the boss,' Rob said. 'The other one was just here to check it was safe.'

The old man walked across the bridge and pointed to a sign nailed to the handrail as he passed.

The man disappeared into the crowds. Jools walked over to the sign. It was a life preserver. It read 'IN CASE OF EMERGENCY'.

'That's what they're saying,' Rob said. 'You can contact them, but only in an emergency.'

Jools felt wary. 'Ah'm no really wantin much to do with them, Rob. It's a bit too heavy for me. Ah appreciate the offer, likes.'

'Her Majesty will be thankful for that. She really has high hopes for you.'

'Still, it's good tae ken that there's so much support for us, eh Rob? Who'd ay thought a wee diddy fae Muirhoose could go that far?'

The wind pushed at his back and he moved on.

An old man talked to his granddaughter as Jools passed. 'He has a yellow forehead,' the man said, looking at Jools. Jools wondered if the man was talking about him or the duck. His forehead was throbbing inside, just behind his eyes. The wind pushed him onto the rockery, a tall hill in the corner of the gardens. A group of Japanese tourists passed him smiling. They sat down on the grass at the top in a circle and talked. Jools could hear some of them laughing. Maybe they recognised him from the TV. The breeze guided him down the hill and past the palm houses. He left by the east gate into the busy traffic and was directed up to Canonmills. He crossed the road and followed the breeze up Broughton Road into McDonald Road and past the fire station. He was beginning to feel worn down with all the walking and stopped at a shop in Leith Walk for a can of Coke. He left the shop and a small Asian boy ran past him giving a Nazi salute.

'Cheeky wee bastard,' Jools muttered under his breath. 'If Ah had done that tae him Ah could get done for it. One fuckin rule for them...'

The wind picked up and pushed him further up Leith Walk, then changed direction taking him along London Road with its parkland on one side and Georgian townhouses on the other. He crossed Easter Road and continued along past the traffic lights. He looked across the road. He noticed a painting in an art shop window and a burst of adrenalin hit him in the stomach. The painting was of Jools. It was a portrait of him but this version of him wore a depressed scowl like a cruel caricature. Jools felt unsafe. It looked like they didn't like him in this part of town. He broke into a jog and ducked into a shop. He bought another can of Coke and some cigarettes and the woman scowled at him when she handed back his change.

'Rob? Rob, are you there?' Jools asked. There was no reply. A little further down he passed a shop with Nazi memorabilia and a dummy in full SS uniform in the window. He started to feel nervous. He decided to get off the main road. He ducked down a side street. The wind tried to blow him back the other way but he kept on.

'Ye were right. They dinnae like Jews in this part ay toon. You'll do our walk for us,' the voice said. 'We're watching every move you make.'

'Who are you ?' Jools asked.

'Ah'm wi' Jimmy Love's nephew and you will do our walk, by the way.'

Jools headed into Holyrood Park. He looked up at Arthur's Seat and Salisbury Crags, the extinct volcano rising hundreds of feet into the Edinburgh skyline. He started to hurry through the park, breaking into a jog again. He found some steps and ran up onto Regent Terrace. The wind pushed against him as he ran along the road. He passed some buses parked at the roadside. In Waterloo Place he ran out of breath. He stopped at the foot of some steps leading up Calton Hill. He raced up the steps, still out of breath, to the quiet of the hill above the city. He sat down on a wall and called for Rob or Bulldog. There was no reply. Jools sat and tried to calm himself. A young woman dressed in gothic clothes passed him. Jools was confused about what to do. They must be following him. Had he given them the slip? The sound of machinery from a nearby building site broke through the silence. Jools decided to go home. He walked along to the set of steps. Two women sat at the bottom of the steep stairway. Jools wondered if they were watching him. He walked down the steps watching them. One of them bent over as Jools passed. He thought she was calling him a bender and whispered 'fuck off' in her ear as he passed. He walked around to the front of the St James Centre and waited for a bus. A police van drove past.

'Too late now,' he thought. 'They're never aroond when you need them.'

⊙

Jools sat in the dark smoking a cigarette. He'd lit a candle and read the newspaper by its flickering light. Sean Connery was in Edinburgh.

'He's here for you,' Bulldog said. 'He's an SNP man at heart but he's casting them aside for the Tory Liberals. That'll get us the SNP vote.'

'Will Ah get to meet him?' Jools asked.

'When it's over. He'll be at the party.'

Greg upstairs stomped on the floor.

'Ah wish he'd shut up,' Jools said. 'He's always fuckin banging aroond. It does ma fuckin nut in.'

'You're just tired. Greg's OK. He's been there for us. Don't be so grumpy,' Bulldog said.

He read the horoscope for Taurus.

'You've been very destructive in your past. Now is the time to repay your debt and learn in the process,' it said.

'What d'ye think they mean by that?' Jools pondered.

'It's to do with you,' Bulldog said. 'You've been a little shit since you were born. Think of all the damage you caused when you were a kid. I've had a look through your memories and you really have been destructive. I blame your peers and your surroundings. Remember when you burned that house down? You were only about seven or eight. You flooded all those houses that time in Martello Court. Remember burgling the camp site? You'd skipped school and gone thieving with your pal. You were only at primary school at the time. You went through about four tents. You hid all the stuff in the woods, remember? All the vandalism. You were a wild kid. Well, now's your chance to do some good for the community. They don't need Mackenzie's mob telling them what to do. The money's good just now but I don't think the people will put up with being shoved around. They'll rebel eventually.'

Jools put the paper down and went to the window. Jimmy Love's light was off.

'He's out,' Bulldog said. 'He's with his nephew.'

'One of his fuckwit wee Nazis was talking to me earlier. Told me Ah better dae their walk.'

'I heard. You did the right thing not going any further today. They were trying to photograph you all day. We caught a couple of them. They don't like you down that way. The Mackenzie support's quite strong down there.'

'That painting. That's fuckin oot ay order. Did you see it? It was meant to be me.'

'I know,' Bulldog said. 'We made them take it down after you left. They got a visit from the police.'

'Ah'm getting pissed off with this whole thing,' Jools said. 'Ah just want normality back. Ah'll pull my socks up. Ah'll get a job. Ah'll mend my ways but this has got to stop. Ah canny go on like this. It's all getting to me. Ah just want peace, left alone.'

'Take it easy, Jools. We can't stop this until we get the digitisers. There's nothing anyone can do. I'm sorry.'

Jools felt like crying. His head hurt and the lack of privacy at having people see his thoughts was getting to him. The thought of more of this was making him more miserable than he'd ever felt in his life. He wept as he thought about his mother. He missed her badly. He wished for his old life back.

'Take it easy, Jools,' Bulldog said quietly. 'C'mon now, don't get upset.'

Jools cried himself into an uneasy sleep.

⊙

Jools decided to go for a walk to clear his head. It was a windless rainy day and he walked down the top of the golf course at Silverknowes. The drizzle soaked through the bottoms of his jeans. He crossed the grass and headed through the woods at the bottom of the hill.

'They're fighting!' the female voice said, exhilarated. 'The laddie Wood and Jimmy Love's nephew.' She sounded excited.

'Who are you?' Jools asked.

'They're fighting! The laddie Wood's getting leathered!'

'It's fuck all to do wi' me,' Jools said.

'You canny go back to your hoose until they're gone. It's no safe.'

'Why dae Ah have to stay away fae the hoose?'

'They'll be watching. Stay away where it's safe,' the girl said.

Jools continued walking. He cut down the path next to the hotel and headed towards the beach.

'PEEK-A-BOOOO!!!' the voice laughed.

Jools got the feeling he was being followed and checked around. He wasn't sure if he saw someone duck behind a tree.

'We're the peek-a-boo people,' the girl said. 'We're the ones that watch you. We're gypsies.'

'Are you wi' Jimmy Love?' Jools asked.

'Me and ma people.'

Jools ducked into the woods. He heard a twig snap behind him and spun round, fists clenched. There was no one there.

'PEEK-A-BOOOO!!!'

His blood ran cold. He ran through the trees heading up towards the road.

'PEEK-A-BOOOO!!!... We saw you!'

A white car passed. Jools hoped it was his cover. He ran along the road next to the campsite.

'PEEK-A-BOOOO!!!'

Jools got to the bottom of the cattle track that led back to the scheme. He turned round and scanned the surroundings. He could see no one and he knew they couldn't follow him up the track without being spotted. It was a straight track about a quarter of a mile long.

'PEEK-A-BOOOO!!!'

The presence retreated. Jools walked home. He was soaked through.

Jools was hungry. He hadn't eaten all day and decided to go to the shops.

'Can you cover me, Bulldog? Ah need tae go oot.'

'We need you to look at the wall for us, Jools,' Bulldog said.

'Awright then. Just for a while.'

'We're tracking now. Got a signal. If you'd like to assume the position.'

Jools sat on the bedroom floor and focused on the tack stuck in the wall.

'Don't picture anything,' Bulldog said.

Jools wriggled from side to side and straightened his back. Images began to flick through his mind and he caught himself going with them. He refocused on his mark.

'Just be,' Bulldog said.

Jools's stomach growled loudly, causing him discomfort. He stared blankly for a few seconds and his mind wandered.

'Don't picture anything. Try not to have any thoughtwaves.'

Jools's eyes began to sting. Tears ran down his cheek and he wiped his face. His head began to throb behind the eyes. He settled back down and stared for what seemed like a long time. He began to slouch and started to daydream. His breathing deepened and his eyelids began to feel heavy. His eyes began to close.

'Concentrate!'

Jools sat upright, straightened his back and widened his eyes. He cleared his mind and took a deep breath. He was beginning to feel lightheaded. Hunger ate at his stomach. A few minutes passed. His head throbbed. Again he began to slouch. Thoughts began to flicker through his mind and he started to drift.

'Jools! You're dreaming,' Bulldog checked him.

Jools sat up and sighed. 'This is brutal, man. Ah canny dae this. Ah'm starvin and ma heid hurts.'

'Try harder. You can eat later.'

Jools's back started to go stiff and he had pins and needles in his legs. He stared hard at the tack and his eyes burned. He was restless with boredom and fidgeted as he tried to keep looking ahead. He let out a sigh as he caught himself drifting again. More long minutes passed. Jools could stand no more and stood up.

'That's aboot aw Ah'm daein the day, man.'

'A while longer,' Bulldog said.

'No danger. Ah'm fucked. Ah'm starvin. Ah'm no up for any more ay this.'

He got ready and headed to the shops. He went to the corner shop and bought a few tins, a paper and some cigarettes, then hurried home. He got in and wolfed down his food while he read the paper. Larry Wiseman, the American chatshow host, had done a full-page interview.

'He's over here to support us, Jools,' Bulldog said. 'He really is a Jew. He's also got connections with the Chicago mob. He's good to have on-side. He's popular and reaches a wide audience.'

Jools laughed. 'Larry's got mafia contacts?'

'Yes. The mob invest a lot of money in business. They have interests all over the world. D'you remember the mobile phone factory that closed down in West Lothian the other week? It's a Chicago-based company. It was mob funded. They lost a lot of money on that one. They said the money had come from drug dealing—cocaine, mainly. Mackenzie's soldiers tried blackmail but the mob just decided to cut their losses and leave. They pulled their money out and the factory closed. The government and MI5 are fully aware of it all but it would damage the economy too much to stop it. Wiseman's here to see if he can smooth things over. He wants to know how you're doing.'

'Fuck's sake, man. Larry Wiseman. The mob. This is mental, man. Ah'm just a wee bam fae Muirhoose.'

'It is pretty strange, I know,' Bulldog said. 'But the more support we get the better.'

Greg upstairs stomped on the floor. It sounded as if a child was running around.

A car started up over the street. Big Steve, he supposed.

⊙

Jools felt the presence enter his mind. It sat back for a few seconds then sniggered quietly.

'Who's there?' Jools asked.

'Peek-a-boo!'

'What dae you want?'

'Ah want you to shut up.'

'Ah'm no saying anything.'

'Shut up, Jools,' the female voice laughed.

'Ah telt you, Ah'm no sayin nowt.'

'But we want you to shut right up.'

'Fuck off. You're no makin sense.'

'Jools, ye've tae SHUT UP! Literally, just shut up.'

Jools began to get annoyed. 'FUCK OFF, YA FUCKIN LOOBY CUNT!' he bawled.

The woman laughed as the presence faded.

Jools went downstairs and turned the TV on. He flicked through the channels. Alan Titchmarsh, the TV gardener, was on. He was potting up plants in a greenhouse. He looked through the screen at Jools and put his finger up to his lips.

'SSSHHHHH!' he said.

Jools turned the set over.

'Fuck that,' he thought. 'Ah canny turn it on without something getting said. They must be watching for me switching on. Why me?'

On BBC2 Vanessa Mae was just coming to the end of a violin number. She looked into the camera and answered him.

'Destiny!' she whispered.

Jools wolf whistled at her. Someone in the audience whistled back.

'They must be able to hear me!' he thought. He started to panic and turned the set off. Someone in that audience had an earpiece in.

⊙

The wind blew at Jools's back taking him past the great mansions in Barnton. He passed the tennis club and walked to the bottom of the road. He felt scruffy and out of place around these streets. He imagined he could be arrested for just walking round such an exclusive neighbourhood. He wondered if the people in the houses even knew their neighbours. It was a long walk next door. Some community! The breeze took him down to the front gates of a grand house. The gate posts had huge stone lions on the top. He stood and looked at the house. A car door slammed in the distance and the wind picked up, blowing him back up the road.

'They're the Scots Tories,' Bulldog said.

The wind stopped him at another house further up.

'Blackmail. This lot have been trying to blackmail the Tories. He's a Tory MSP.'

Jools heard a door slam and the wind picked up again. He followed it further into Barnton, past even bigger houses. He came to a set of railings and the breeze pushed him on over them onto the fairway of a golf course. Two men with golf trolleys stared at him as he passed. The wind picked up speed and he began to jog over the cropped grass. He leaped over a sand trap and jarred his knee.

'Hurry up!' Bulldog said. 'They always get away before you get there. We need you there quick so we can nick them.'

Jools crossed the fairway and climbed the fence. It led onto a dirt track. The wind blew him over the fence and onto another golf course. A gust caught him and he changed direction. He broke into a run and soon he reached the clubhouse. The wind dropped a little and he slowed down. He walked through the car park of the hotel clubhouse. A man in a blue anorak walked to his car just ahead of him. Jools got closer and saw a familiar face. It was Jimmy Saville. It was definitely him. He stood for a second realising that Jools had recognised him and smiled.

'Now do you believe the stars are there for you?' Bulldog asked.

Jimmy Saville got into the car and the engine started. The wind picked up and Jools walked on. Now he was convinced. He walked further on along the busy road. The wind changed, blowing him across the road into Cammo. He walked up to the gates of the Cammo estate. The breeze took him up the path through the trees. The leaves rustled in the wind. He reached the ruined house at the top and sat on the wall lighting a cigarette.

'Gie me five Bulldog,' he said. He sat trying to catch his breath. The wind picked up and blew against him as if trying to rush him. He stayed put.

'Just gie me five minutes,' he said.

He smoked his cigarette and flicked the stub away. He started to walk. The wind took him to a long rectangular pond covered in duckweed. The breeze picked up, trying to push him into the water.

'There's no danger Ah'm going in there,' Jools said.

He walked around it and headed in through the long grass. The wind took him over a drystone wall and further into the bushes. The breeze dropped and Jools stopped under a tree behind a wall. He let out a titter like a schoolboy as he sensed something dirty had gone on here.

'Rosy-cheeked caperings?' he giggled.

'Don't you dare laugh!' Bulldog sounded serious. 'Do you know what happened here? It was a young boy. He was molested by those creeps here. He's not a laughing matter. How can you laugh at something like that?'

'Well Ah didnae ken, eh?' Jools said, embarrassed.

'These people are sick, Jools. You don't know how sick.'

The wind blew him further on into the trees.

'Peek-a-boo!' a bird whistled. 'Ya weeee Jeeewww!'

Jools spun around, terrified. The birds were talking to him. Paranoia ripped through him.

'Ah kin see you!' the bird whistled.

The breeze blew Jools into a swampy area. He crossed it, leaving deep footprints in the mud. He carried on until he reached a high wall and he climbed up it. He sat on the top and looked over. It was another golf course.

'Ah'm gonnie get you raped!' a bird twittered. 'Ya weeeee Jewwwww!'

Jools dropped down onto the grass and climbed the hill. Two men putted on a green and he wondered if they'd heard the birds.

'Peek-a-boo!'

He started to run scared as the bird continued to call.

'Ah'm gonnie get you raped!'

'That's them,' Bulldog said.

Jools ran across the golf course. The wind gusted more strongly at his back, urging him on. He came onto a narrow road and found himself behind the airport. An airliner was just about to take off and taxied down the runway, picking up speed. He started to get a bad feeling in his gut.

'Ah dinnae think Ah should go any further,' Jools said. 'Ah dinnae want to go near the airport. Something bad might happen. That's bad shit, man. Heavy, likes.'

'Safe,' Bulldog said.

A red car passed him. The driver looked at Jools, then looked in the direction of home.

'That's good enough for me,' he said, and started back. The sun was beginning to set in the west and it turned cooler as if it might rain.

⊙

Jools was hungry. He ate his food like an animal. This was the first thing he'd eaten today. The street light filtered through his drawn blinds. There was a loud click and his fire went off.

'The bastards have cut your electric off,' Rob said.

'Shit!' Jools said. 'What do Ah do now?'

'They must have someone nearby.'

Jools was cold and tired. He went to the window. Jimmy Love's light was on. He went upstairs and brought his duvet down. He wrapped himself in the duvet and sat in the dark, smoking. He heard Big Steve's car start up and drive away.

'This is the pits,' he thought, and lay back on the couch. His next-door neighbour's TV was turned up loud and Jools could hear the news starting. An ice cream van chimed in a nearby street.

'We want you to walk tonight,' Rob said.

'Ah'm knackered Rob. Ah've been oot aw day.'

'We need you to walk.'

'NAW! Ah'm no going oot the night. This is bullshit. Ah've been thinking, Rob. Maybe Ah kin outrun the signal. If Ah could escape, get oot ay Edinburgh. Maybe they'd leave me alone. The signal wouldnae reach me.'

'It's doubtful. I think they'd track you wherever you go.'

'Maybe Ah could go stay wi' family doon south.'

'Jools, there's no way you can walk away from this. It won't go away no matter where you go. Not until we get Mackenzie's people and find the digitisers.'

'Ah just want ma heid back. Ah want ma old life back.'

'Will you walk for us?' Rob asked. 'It's the only way to catch these people.'

Jools sighed. 'Ah'm no going far, Rob. Ah'm fucked. Ma feet hurt. Ah'm run doon. Ah need tae rest.'

⊙

The wind took Jools past Crewe Toll. He passed Telford College and the breeze stopped him at a bus stop. He stood and lit a cigarette. He spotted a poster that had been fly posted on the shelter. THIS MAN IS A CAPITALIST! it read. He studied the picture. A man stood wearing a beige jacket. The face! It was his face on the poster. Someone had scratched the eyes out. Jools was startled. He began to get the feeling not everybody was there for him. The wind gusted at his back and he moved on. He passed a man on the other side of the road walking the opposite way and wondered if he was walking with the wind too.

'Keep to the right. Always walk on the right,' Rob said.

Jools reached the hospital and the wind changed direction. He walked down Carrington Road past Fettes School. Tony Blair had once been a pupil there. The wind took him past the police headquarters. He cut through into Stockbridge and walked along Raeburn Place. The wind blew him along the pavement. His foot started to hurt and he started to limp. A shopkeeper at the Eight till Late stood on the pavement taking in a sign. He bent over as Jools passed and Jools avoided him deftly.

'They're trying to photograph you,' the female voice said in his head.

'Who are you?' Jools asked.

'They want you to pose with the man bending over. It's publicity for the gay chat line we're running. It was advertised on telly. You have to play the poof.'

'Fuck you!' Jools said. 'There's no danger Ah'm playin a poof. Ye can fuck right off.'

'Jimmy Love's set it up. It's sponsored. You better do it. You better play the poof.'

'Away and shite.'

'We'll get you if you dinnae. You'll get fuckin leathered,' the girl said.

Jools walked further on and the wind took him down a side street. He got to a bridge at the end of the road and the wind dropped, leaving him standing.

'Just come along here a bit. Stand under the bridge. We'll get a couple of photographs,' the girl laughed.

'Fuck off. Ah'm no a poof!' Jools was beginning to get annoyed.

'Ah know you're no really gay but Jimmy Love's got you promoted as the next big gay thing. He wants pictures of you to publicise his chat line. He's got a gay mag interested in pictures of you. You just have to act a bit gay, that's all. Just pose for a few snaps.'

'FUCK OFF!' Jools shouted. 'Ah'm no bothered what you say. Ah'm no playin the poof for nae cunt.'

'You've no really got any choice. He's publicising you as gay whether you like it or not. And you better do his nephew's walk for him. Ye'll get fuckin leathered if you dinnae.'

'Come ahead then ya fuckin bunch ay weirdos. That's it wi' you fuckers, eh? Ye'll sneak aroond fuckin wi' ma heid but ye'll no show yerselves, eh?'

'Ye're a poof! Ye're a Jew! Shut yer mooth!' the voice retreated, laughing.

Jools climbed the steps and arrived in Danube Street. The street had once been famous for its brothel. It was now a posh secluded side-street with Georgian townhouses along either side. Jools headed up the street and into Stockbridge. He walked for some time. The wind blew, pushing him back along Raeburn Place. He reached the bottom of Orchard Brae and started to climb the hill. His foot throbbed and he stopped halfway up the hill to adjust his laces. He lit a cigarette and continued up the hill. He was out of breath when he reached the top and sat down on a wall. Suddenly there were three bright flashes of light in his right eye.

'We've equalised,' Rob said triumphantly. 'The wasp is dead!'

'Who's deid?' Jools asked.

'Mackenzie. Our boys neutralised him in Belfast. He's dead.'

'So Ah dinnae have to worry any more?'

'We still have a long way to go, Jools. His followers are many. Now they'll want revenge. We've still got a lot of them to put behind bars but the boss is dead. Now we need to find the digitisers. You're not out of the woods yet. Be guided.'

Jools followed the breeze along to the Dean Bridge. He reached the end of the bridge and saw two identical red cars sitting at the traffic lights. The lights turned to green and both cars drove off. One car split left, the other split right in formation. Jools stopped and wondered if he should turn back. He decided to carry on straight ahead. He crossed the road and started to walk towards the West End. A tall man in dark clothing walked towards Jools. He staggered as he approached Jools and he thought the man was acting drunk. Maybe he was SAS trying to tell him to turn back. He felt confused about what to do next. He decided to turn back. He walked back down to the Dean Bridge and continued on to Orchard Brae. The wind picked up and took him to the steps of Bristo Baptist church. He sat on the steps and rested, lighting a cigarette. JESUS IS LORD a sign read. A taxi passed.

'The taxis are there for us, Jools,' Rob said. 'They're on the lookout for us. They'll watch out for you.'

Jools sat and smoked. The roads were quiet at this time of night. A car sped past. Jools thought he saw a camera flash as it passed.

'Fuck you!' he shouted after it. 'Cheeky bastards!'

The wind took him back across the road. A black hatchback sat outside an office block. Jools stood by the car as another car passed. He wondered if they were photographing him, although he saw no flash this time. The breeze picked up and took him along the road. His foot felt as if it was bleeding and he was dead on his feet.

'Ah'll need to call it a night, Rob,' he said.

'Safe,' Rob replied.

Jools looked for a shortcut. He vaulted a wall and found himself on the disused railway which was now a track for bicycles and pedestrians. It led to Drylaw which was only up the road from Muirhouse. He walked through the semi-darkness. The path was lit in places and he made it down to Craigleith when he stopped dead. Two fox cubs sat on the track playing in front of him. He crouched down slowly and watched them fighting, oblivious to his presence. He sat for a good few minutes watching them, then they both stopped and pricked their ears up. They got up and darted into the bushes, leaving Jools crouching there. Jools walked on, thrilled to bits at what he'd just seen.

'It was the animal people,' Rob said.

'They were sound. Did you see them Rob? Barry wee foxes.' Jools smiled warmly.

'I'll see them later. I'll watch your memories of them when you're sleeping, if that's OK?'

'Sound, man.'

Jools limped his way home. He checked the lights in the houses on the way. There were still a few on, even at this time.

He got home and ate cold beans out of a tin with a spoon. He finished the last of the bread and wrapped himself in the duvet. He went to the window. Jimmy Love's light was off. He lit a candle. The clock read 3. 20am. He lay back on the couch and soon began to drift off.

⊙

He woke with a start. Greg upstairs was banging around again. 'Fuck's sake, man!' The cunt was two floors up!

'They've been waiting up for you, Jools,' Rob said.

Jools could hardly keep his eyes open. He took his boots off. His foot was badly blistered and had been bleeding where the skin had rubbed off. He staggered through to the kitchen and fed the cat. He downed a glass of water and took his duvet up to the bedroom. He lay on the bed and listened to the night. Sleep took him quickly.

⊙

He woke after noon and went downstairs with his duvet. His foot stung and he cleaned it with cold water and toilet tissue. His eyelids were heavy and his legs and lower back ached. He peered through the spyhole on the front door. Rob's light was still on. He got dressed and limped along to the corner shop. He bought a few tins, bread and cigarettes and returned home. Eating cold food out of a tin wasn't very appetising but he tucked in. He read the paper. Another odd death. Jools flicked through the death column.

ANDERSON. Suddenly at home on the 8th of May. Edward, beloved son of Betty and Rab, died peacefully aged 34. Funeral to take place at Warriston Crematorium, 10.30 Tuesday 15th May 2001. Family flowers only please.

Jools wondered if it was the same Eddie Anderson he knew. The smack dealer from Granton. There had been rumours that he had the virus. He'd been done for spitting in a policeman's face and telling him he had Hepatitis B. Jools didn't know him well, only by reputation.

'It's time for you to assume the position, Jools,' Bulldog said.

Jools sighed loudly. 'Ah fuckin hate this, man, it's boring,' he said as he went to the bedroom and sat facing the wall. He zeroed in on the tack head and cleared his mind. He started to slouch and felt sleepy. His eyelids grew heavier and heavier. He straightened up his back and settled in. Images began to flit across his mind's eye. He struggled to clear them.

'Don't picture anything,' Bulldog said.

He sat a few minutes, managing to keep his mind blank.

'That's it. Just be.'

Jools began to breathe deeply. His breathing began to settle into a rhythm. He widened his eyes and refocused. Another few minutes passed. He began to slouch again. He started to daydream.

'Concentrate.'

He snapped out of it. He stretched his back and continued staring. His eyes began to sting. Tears rolled down his cheek. He wiped his face. Another few minutes. He began to think about meeting Anastacia.

'Don't picture anything,' Bulldog checked him. 'Concentrate, now.'

Jools glanced at the clock. He concentrated on the clock's ticking. He began to dream and snapped himself out of it quickly. His eyes began to close slowly. He began to bow his head. He began to picture things.

'Just be. Concentrate. Look, all I'm asking you to do is just be. Don't think!'

His head began to hurt. He zoomed in on the tack head and sat another few minutes.

'Keep oot ay Leith!' a bird whistled outside. 'Cheep cheep cheep. Ye've tae keep oot ay Leith!'

Jools sat bolt upright. 'Bastards!' he said.

'Ya weeee Jeeeeewwwwww!!!' the bird twittered.

'We'll leave it there for today,' Bulldog said. 'Looks like they're having fun with the birds again. They're trying to put you off.'

'Ah'm gonnie get you raped!!!' the bird whistled from a nearby rooftop.

'That'll be Jimmy Love doing that with the birds. Don't be scared. Like I said, it's the silicone age. He's doing it electronically.'

'Keep oot ay Leith!'

◉

Jools followed the breeze along the cycleway. The sun was shining and birds sang in the trees. The peace was disturbed by the ring tone of a mobile phone. A woman stopped a few meters ahead and started to talk.

'I'm just taking the dog for a walk,' he heard her say.

Jools approached a bridge over the walkway. A huge mural had been spray-painted across one side of the bridge. 'WE MUST WALK IN THE DARKNESS TO FIND THE LIGHT' it read underneath.

'That's one of ours,' Rob said. 'The mural was done by one of our young supporters. It refers to a civilian police force we're trying to establish. We hope to get it up and running soon.'

'Civilian police force? Like the Guardian Angels?'

'Sort of, but more low key. Less American. We're keeping it a secret until we get given the go-ahead. Don't mention this to a soul.'

'Dinnae tell me any mair secrets, Rob. Ah don't know what they're taking oot ay my heid when Ah'm asleep.'

'Safe,' Rob said.

Jools left the cycleway, emerging into the busy traffic. The wind took him along to Haymarket. A giant billboard showed a poster of Bruce Lee, Brandon Lee, Jackie Chan and Jean Claude Van Damme. He crossed the road at the clock. The breeze took him along the street and through a tunnel. There was no pavement in the tunnel and Jools walked along the kerbstones. As he was leaving the tunnel a black man walked towards him.

'NIGGER!!!' a loud voice screamed as they passed.

Jools was sure the man heard it and went scarlet. How could he deny it was him? There was no one else here.

The man kept walking and didn't turn back.

'That's fuckin oot ay order,' Jools said. His face was flushed and his heart pounded.

'He was a fuckin NIGGER!' the man's voice replied. The presence sniggered and disappeared.

Jools followed the breeze further along the road. The wind dropped as he stood next to an office block. It picked up again, taking him around the back of the offices. He was blown into a car park. He walked to a covered area and stood next to an air conditioner outlet. The breeze blew him further into the corner. He noticed a pile of cigarette butts on the floor. Someone had been standing here for a while, judging by the amount of butts.

'Blackmail,' Rob said. 'He's been watching the offices from here. He's also involved in industrial espionage.'

Jools stood and looked out over the car park. A man came out of a door at the bottom of the concrete steps. He looked at Jools and made an 'up your arse' gesture with some rolled-up papers he was carrying.

'He'll be banged up in Saughton by tonight,' Rob said. 'He's just been exposed by his bosses and he's trying to run. The police will pick him up later.'

The breeze picked up and Jools followed it back to the main street. He walked back down to Haymarket, crossing another car park. The breeze dropped and he stopped to light a cigarette. A man in paint-splattered dungarees walked along by an office block. He dragged a paint-soaked roller along the wall, leaving a long blue streak the entire length. Jools followed the wind up Morrison Street. It blew him up a side street and stopped him at the door of a tenement flat. He stood there wondering what this guy had done. A car door slammed up the street and the wind picked up. He followed the breeze through more back streets and thought he was lost. He emerged at the Meadows and stopped to sit on the grass. His foot was bleeding badly and his sock felt wet and sticky. He looked around the park. A group of young men played football. There were people sitting around on the grass talking in groups, students by the look of them. A man walked his dog up the avenue of trees. Jools sat for a while enjoying the sunshine. He stood up and felt light-headed.

His stomach growled and his legs had stiffened up. He walked back to the pathway and continued to limp along with the wind. His heart skipped a beat as a guy on a mountain bike skidded to avoid him.

'Walk on the right!' Rob said.

'Ah nearly fuckin shat maself, man. The guy on the bike.'

'One of ours,' Rob told him. 'They'll keep you on the right if it kills them.'

The breeze took him further along and changed direction, taking him past the old Royal Infirmary. Jools was beginning to feel weak with hunger. The walking had taken its toll on him and his blood sugar had crashed.

'Ah'm gonnie have to call it a day,' he said. He felt he couldn't go any further. The wind increased but Jools refused.

'Ah canny. No the day, Rob. Ma foot's pishin wi' blood and Ah'm fucked. Ah need tae eat.'

'A bit further,' Rob argued, but it was no use. Jools headed for the bus stop.

⊙

Jools got off the bus and followed the wind across the road into Pilton. He recalled how Muirhouse and Pilton had fought each other when they were kids. The tradition had carried on and still flared up from time to time as each generation had its go. The breeze took him along the deserted streets and it began to spit with rain. The wind dropped suddenly, stopping him outside a house. He turned and looked at the window accusingly. He heard a click from inside the stairwell and a gust whipped up, taking him further on.

'A paedophile ring was operating here,' Rob said. 'We've got to get these bastards. The house is full of videos.'

The street lights cast their yellow light across the empty road. The wind stopped him outside another house. He stood by the hedge, staring at the ground-floor flat. A man walked from the stair and slammed the lid down on a dustbin. The wind picked up and he limped on.

'This one had been storing photographs for them,' Rob informed him.

'Fuckin beasts,' Jools spat.

The breeze took him through Pilton, stopping him twice more. He limped to the bridge at Crewe Toll and the wind changed, taking him down the new road that ran to Granton. His foot started to hurt really badly and he stopped to rest.

'Ma foot's knackered, Rob,' he said.

'Don't stop now. We don't want to get there too late.'

'Ah'm no bein lazy Rob, honestly. Ah'm done in. Ah've been walkin for weeks.

Ah need tae rest. Ah wouldnae mention it if Ah wasnae desperate,' Jools pleaded. The wind gusted strongly at his back.

'NAW!' he shouted. 'Ah'm goin hame.'

⊙

Jools got home. Rob's light was still on. He flopped onto the couch and took his boots off. The blood had soaked through his sock and his foot stuck to it. The clock read 2.35am. There was no food in the cupboard so he sat in the dark smoking.

'You did well tonight, Jools. I'm proud of the way things are going with you,' Rob said. 'You've pushed yourself past your limits for us.'

'Ah'm no sure Ah kin keep this up, Rob,' Jools said. 'Ah'm run right doon.' Jools thought of the possibility of outrunning the signal. He wondered if he could escape without them following him. He could stay away for a while until all this blew over. His legs and back ached and his foot nipped badly. The raw patch stung where the skin had rubbed away and large blisters covered his heel. This was all taking its toll on his mind too. The lack of privacy had been hardest to handle. His every thought was there to be seen by anyone at the other end. His head hurt with trying to stifle his thoughts. He started to shiver and wrapped himself in the duvet. His cat jumped on his knee and started to purr loudly.

'Rob, how much longer dae ye think this will go on?' Jools asked.

'Hard to say. Until we get Mackenzie's troops. Until Jimmy Love's safely behind bars and we find the digitisers, I suppose.'

'Ah'm no sure Ah kin go on Rob. Ah've pushed maself too far,' Jools thought grimly.

'You'll be OK.'

⊙

Jools woke up late next afternoon. He felt sore all over and hungry and decided to go to the shops. He dressed and left the house. It was a grey, overcast day and the wind tried to take him as soon as he walked down the path. He ignored it and it seemed to blow stronger as he walked.

'Rob, Ah'm no walkin the day,' Jools said wearily. 'Ah need a rest.'

There was no answer but the wind increased, trying to blow him back the other way.

'No!' Jools put his foot down. 'Ah really canny walk the day.'

He hobbled through the scheme, avoiding the CCTV cameras at the bottom of the high-rises and made his way to the shops at the foot of Martello Court.

He bought a few tins, some bread and cigarettes at the corner shop and limped his way back home. Rob's light was still on even though it was daylight.

He got in and ate cold soup from a can.

'Keep oot ay Leith!' a bird chirped from a rooftop.

He could hear his neighbours on both sides talking and playing with the children. A crowd of kids played football in the car park. His headache had got worse. He went to the window for some fresh air. Big Steve's car was gone and there was no sign of life at Jimmy Love's.

'It's time for you to assume the position,' Bulldog said.

Jools went upstairs and sat down cross-legged. He stretched his back and started to concentrate on the tack head in the wall.

⊙

'Quick! Now's your chance! Jimmy Love's out. Go now!' the woman's voice shouted.

Jools was startled. 'What dae ye mean?'

'Jimmy Love's away for a while! You can get away if you go now! Hurry! Just go!'

Jools put his boots on double-quick. He grabbed his jacket and left the house. It was dark and there was little breeze.

'This way!' the woman shouted. 'Along here! Run!'

Jools tried to ignore the pain in his foot as he broke into a run. He headed down to Granton, past the gas works.

'Hurry! Before they realise you're gone!' the voice urged him.

Jools started to get out of breath as he reached the bridge. He stopped, panting heavily. His foot bled in his boot and throbbed badly.

'Which way now?' he asked.

'Down this way! Hide!'

Jools went down an embankment behind the shops. He hid in a building site a few meters from the road and tried to get his breath back.

'Just wait here,' the woman said. 'Ma people will be along to pick you up. Just wait here out of sight. They'll be here in a minute.'

'Where are we goin?' Jools asked.

'You're going to stay with some of ma people. They're coming for you now. They'll take you somewhere safe.'

Jools watched the road. A car slowed down as it passed and Jools thought it was going to stop for him but it speeded up and carried on again.

'That was them,' the woman said. 'They're too scared to stop here. Come down this way.'

Jools walked further into the darkness. He walked down the unlit path and could make out some lights in the distance.

'They've left a light on for you, Jools,' she said. 'They're ma people.'

'Who are you?' Jools asked.

'Ah just wanted to see you get away,' she started to laugh.

Jools approached the lights. They were shining from the porch of a large old mansion house behind the gasworks.

'Ah wouldnae like to live doon here,' Jools thought. It was too isolated stuck down here in the dark.

'They've left the door open for you,' she said. 'Just go right in.'

Jools went in the gate and started to walk across the gravel-chipped driveway. The crunching underfoot became noisy and Jools started to employ a stealth technique he'd learned in ninpo training. He crossed the gravel as silently as a shadow. He thought he saw someone duck behind a large yew tree.

'That's one ay ma people,' she whispered. 'He's been watching for you.'

Jools walked up to a side door. He pushed it but it was locked.

'Should Ah knock?' he asked.

'Just go in!' the female said. She started to snigger.

He tried the door again. 'Ah thought ye said they were your people.'

There was no answer.

'Who are you?'

'Ah just wanted to get you out,' the woman laughed. 'You canny go home now. They've got shotguns.'

'Who?'

'Ma people. We wanted you to stay with us for a while so Ah thought Ah'd get you out the house.'

'Who are you?'

'Awright. Ah'm a gypsy!' she started to laugh. 'And you're gettin fuckin shot if you go back to your hoose! Ah'm wi' Jimmy Love!'

Jools didn't know what to do. He started to run. He left the grounds of the house and ran down the path. It took him into the industrial estate on the Shore Road.

'You're gettin fuckin leathered!' the woman cackled. 'Ma people are oot everywhere lookin for you!'

Jools crossed the road and headed along a track by the sea. The waves lapped loudly as Jools broke into a jog. He held his breath as he passed the chemical works and headed along the beach in the darkness. He caught sight of a dark shape lying on the grass ahead of him. As he passed he tried to get a look at whatever it was. It appeared to be someone lying down. He avoided the shape and kept running.

'That was one ay ma people you just passed,' the woman said. 'Ma people are everywhere! You're gettin fuckin wasted if you go hame.'

Jools was scared. He ran up the set of wooden steps and stopped at the top to catch his breath. His hair was soaked with sweat. He started to hobble up the cattle-track to the lights of the scheme. He looked back now and then to check no one was following and soon reached the dual carriageway. He crossed into Pennywell and circled the block a few times to make sure no one was around then decided to risk going home. Rob's light was on. He was watching the door so he'd be OK. Jools got in and barred up the front door. He limped up to his bedroom and flopped down on the bed in the dark. He took his boot and blood-stained sock off. His foot bled badly and his legs and back nagged him. He felt badly run down and thought he'd end up in hospital if this went on. He tried to stand but his leg muscles had seized up. He lay in the dark listening to the night. Greg upstairs started to bang around.

⊙

Jools awoke in agony.

'AAAARRGH!' he screamed out as a violent cramp set into his calf muscle. It felt like the muscle was being ripped with a red hot knife. He sat up, grabbing his leg and trying to relax it. The spasm lasted a few minutes and started to wear off. He got up and walked stiffly downstairs. Picking his mail off the floor was an effort. He dressed and left the flat. The wind caught him the minute he stepped outdoors, taking him along the road into Pilton. The rain started. Jools passed an ice cream van parked by the roadside.

'They're in on it too,' Bulldog said. 'The ice cream wars in Glasgow were nothing compared to what'll happen here if we don't stop Mackenzie's people. Jimmy Love is just his man in Muirhouse. Think how many there are around the country.'

'Ah'm no sure Ah'm gonnie make it, Bulldog,' Jools said grimly. 'Ah'm really no too well.' He felt weak and his stomach growled. 'Ah'm no going far today'

He crossed into West Granton limping painfully. He decided to get some food. The breeze took him further into Granton. He began to shiver as the drizzle soaked through his clothes. He saw a sign saying Johnny's General Store and went in. He walked around the aisles and picked up a packet of chocolate muffins, a loaf and a tin of cat food. A radio played in the background.

'Steal something.'

'Steal something,' the song said.

Jools wondered if it was tuned to his station. Was this a message for him?

'Just steal something and get caught,' Bulldog said. 'The police will come and arrest you and when they find out who you are they'll put you somewhere safe.'

'Steal-some-thing, steal-some-thing,' the song went on.

Jools thought about it. He could do with getting away. He picked up a creme egg and pocketed it in full view of the shopkeeper. He walked to the counter and paid for the other items. The shopkeeper, a man with dark hair and a gold bracelet, hadn't noticed the theft. Jools bought some cigarettes and left the shop. The wind picked up at his back but Jools couldn't go on. He turned and started to limp home. The wind drove the rain into his face all the way back.

⊙

Jools got in and ate. He got out of his wet clothes and went upstairs to bed wrapping himself in the duvet.

'Assume the position,' Bulldog said.

'No,' Jools replied. 'Ah just canny the day.'

'Jools, the only way to catch these people is to do this; now assume the position.'

Jools sighed loudly. He sat cross-legged and focused on the tack head. The rain rattled off the window pane and the wind howled.

⊙

Jools sat in the darkness and smoked a cigarette. His body ached all over and his head hurt. A car started up across the road and drove off. He lay back and closed his eyes. Suddenly his mind lit up red inside like a TV screen. A cartoon picture of a face appeared on the screen.

'Jools, it's us,' the voice said. 'It's me.'

The voice sounded familiar but Jools couldn't place it.

'It's me, Mel,' the voice said. 'Ah'm just havin a rummage aroond.'

Mel was an old friend of Jools's. He was a boxing instructor and Jools had known him for years.

'Mel, is that you?' Jools asked.

'It's me and Johnny, from Johnny's shop earlier. We're over the road and we hacked into this system. We couldnae believe what they've done to you.'

'It's pretty brutal, eh?'

'We were just having a wee look through your heid. Ah wanted to check if you'd been wi' ma wife.'

'Mel, man! Ah wouldnae dae that tae you.' Jools felt hurt at the accusation.

'Johnny wants to see if you're really a poof. We heard you were but he wanted to check you out himself. He's gay. He says he fancies you. He wants tae…' The cartoon face licked its lips.

'Ah'm no gay, Mel man! You ken me. Tell um Ah'm no a poof. Nae offence, likes.'

'Ay says ay wants tae suck your dick,' Mel laughed.

'AY KIN FUCK RIGHT OFF!'

Mel hummed a tune to himself and Jools felt him prodding through his thoughts and memories.

'Hey! Cut that oot,' he shouted, as Mel prodded a sore spot inside his head.

'We can see all this on the monitor, Jools,' Mel said. 'Everything you think or remember is there to be accessed at the touch of a button. Ah see you've no shagged ma wife. Ah would've kicked fuck oot you if ye had. Ye better no have been having any sexual thoughts aboot her either.'

Jools couldn't remember if he ever had thought of her that way and tried to resist.

'Johnny's gonnie be disappointed tae. Yer no a poof really, are you?'

'Naw Ah'm fuckin no.' Jools was beginning to get annoyed at the probing. 'Ye ken me better than that, Mel!'

'Calm doon. You better no tell anyone aboot this, Jools. If ye do your family will get it,' Mel said.

'What the fuck are you threatening ma family for?' Jools asked. 'Ah thought we were mates.'

'Hold on just now,' Mel said. The cartoon face pulled down a shutter like a roller blind.

'They're arguing and we don't want you to hear what they're saying.'

'Don't say anything else!' Bulldog interrupted suddenly. 'That is not who you think it is. These people sound like others. They are very clever people. Ignore what they are saying. We are tracking them. I must warn you, whoever you are, that I'm working for the government and the police are on their way. You will be caught whoever you are. Jools I must advise you to say nothing. Do not give them any more information than they already have. The police will be with them shortly.'

'Fuck off!' Mel snapped. The vision vanished and Jools was alone with Bulldog.

'They seem to have gone,' Bulldog said. 'You can't trust what they say, Jools. They could be anyone. You don't want them to know anything else about you or they'll just exploit it.'

Jools felt pretty foolish falling for it. He tried to think if he'd told them anything important. 'But that was Mel's voice Ah heard,' Jools reasoned. 'Ah ken him. Ah know his voice.'

'They've sampled the voices from your own memory bank, Jools,' Bulldog informed him. 'That was not your friend. It was them. They are very clever people.'

Jools got up and went to the window. Jimmy Love's light was off. He took the safety catch off the window and opened it wide. He sat in the silence and listened to the rain, wrapping himself in the duvet. His cigarette burned down slowly and he put it out and rolled over, closing his eyes. Greg upstairs started to bang around. Jools grew restless and turned over, covering his ears with the pillow. Jools heard the door slam upstairs and someone run along the balcony. He thought it must be another tape finished. Tomorrow was his birthday. He'd be 31. He felt he was getting old. The last few years had flown by. He wished things were back to normal. Greg thumped on the ceiling. Jools was too hot and kicked the duvet off. He lay there listening to the noise from upstairs and he began to grit his teeth. He tossed and turned for a while and finally had to get up for the bathroom. He came back to bed and tried again to relax. The sky started to turn dark blue and got lighter quickly. Birds started to sing and he found it irritating. Jools could hear Greg's tumble dryer as it spun upstairs. The sound vibrated through the walls. He gave up trying to sleep a little while later and sat up. He was dead tired but found it impossible to drop off. He started to think of escape again. Would he be able to outrun the signal?

'Happy birthday, son,' Rob said.

'Cheers, man.'

'Don't worry, son. There'll be other birthdays. You won't always feel like this. Next year you'll be on top of the world. They'll all be saying "There's the one. There's that guy that went through all that stuff." You'll be famous. Everyone will know who you are.'

'Ah canny wait, Rob. Ah canny wait to meet Anastacia,' Jools said.

'There's a few people want to talk to you after this is over. Tanaka sensei wants to meet you. We have a great party to look forward to.'

'Ah'm a year older the day, man. This could be when ma life kicks off. Ah've no been too busy the last few years. Things have sort ay went a bit stale. Ah stay in too much. Ah should definitely go oot more. Ah'm glad you're here, Rob. Ah knew you lot wouldnae forget me.'

'I'm glad to be here too, son. I really am. Have a really good birthday, Jools. You deserve it. Even if you are sick. Just you enjoy yourself today, it's your day. Is your family coming today?'

'Ah think they'll be doon later. Ma auntie and ma sister.'

'Don't tell them anything. It's best they don't know what's going on for their own good. They wouldn't understand.'

Greg banged down again.

'This is fuckin brutal, Rob. Ah canny sleep.'

'Me neither. But happy birthday again. I feel daft tonight. I'm in a silly mood.'

'Ah'm past the silly stage, Rob. If Ah dinnae get some sleep soon Ah'll crack up. Greg's a noisy bastard this morning. It's too clammy. There's no air.'

Jools lay back down and closed his eyes.

'Ah canny sleep. There's a big daddy-longlegs climbin up the wawwwww,' Rob squeaked, sounding like he'd breathed in helium from a balloon.

Jools started to laugh. 'You're a fuckin sixth dan in Ninpo. Ye're feared ay a wee daddy-longlegs. You're mental, man.' Jools got the tired giggles.

'But Ah canny sleep cause it's climbin up the wawwwwww,' Rob squeaked.

Jools was in fits of laughter. 'You're off yer heid, man.'

'Aw nawww. It flew up the curtains an Ah canny find it. It's got big, long, hairy legs an it wis climbin up the wawww.'

Jools lay and tried to fall asleep. Greg banged down. A seagull squawked loudly outside. He heard the first bus drive slowly along the road. The first rays of sun reflected off neighbouring blocks.

'This is fuckin hopeless,' Jools said to himself and got up. He went downstairs and got dressed. He decided there and then to try and outrun the signal. He got some clothes together in carrier bags and left the flat. He walked up the main bus route, hoping for a bus to take him into town. He would try and make it to his aunt's house in Manchester. She'd take him in for a while until this blew over. Surely they wouldn't be able to track him that far. He counted his money out. He had a couple of hundred left, enough to do him a week or two. He walked up the cycle track. It took him into Haymarket and he made his way to the train station. When he got there the gates were padlocked shut. He was way too early. A taxi driver sat and listened to a radio with an ear piece in. Jools wondered if he could hear him. He sat on a wall and smoked a cigarette while he waited. The roads were still empty except for a bus at the terminus and the odd taxi.

'We're watchin you!' the voice said. 'Where the fuck do you think you're going?'

Jools was startled. 'Naewhere,' he replied.

'If you dinnae go back hame now, Ah'm gonnie have to hurt ye.'

Jools felt nervous.

'If you dinnae go hame now Ah'll hurt ye, Ah'm no kiddin',' the voice said.

Jools stood his ground. 'Ah'm no goin hame. Ah'm goin away for a while.'

'Hame!' the voice commanded. 'If ye dinnae Ah'll have tae hurt ye. Ah kin make you shite yourself. Dae ye want me tae make you shite and pish yourself right here in the middle ay toon?'

'Aye right,' Jools said, and he felt his bowels rumble.

'Take that!' the voice said and Jools felt a needle jab his leg.

'Aaargh! Fuck off!'

His bowels rumbled again and Jools thought he might follow through. He straightened up and tried to resist.

'Ah'll turn it up if you resist. Ah'm gonnie make you shit your troosers. Take that!' Jools felt another needle, this time in his side.

'Fuck off, ya fuckin mongo!' Jools howled.

The taxi driver looked over at him. Jools felt his bowels loosening. He couldn't resist and got to his feet double quick. He started to head for home at top speed. Across the road in front of a hotel he saw a silver car pulling up. A young man got out of the Mercedes Benz. He looked over at Jools.

'There's yer lift,' the voice said sarcastically.

The young man closed the car door and went into the hotel. Jools wondered what they had to do with it all. He'd had a good look over at him then limped off down the street. A car passed him.

'Shut your mouwf!'

They were following him. Jools looked at a street sign.

'Emmm, wait a minute. Orchard Brae you're at. Ah'll send one ay ma people doon tae spot you.'

A van passed. 'Shut the fuck up!' he heard.

It sounded like the sound came from underneath the van. Some mechanical device.

'Emmm… Wait a minute. You're at the Western General. Ma people will be there the now,' the female voice said.

Jools cut through the hospital. He headed through Telford and Drylaw and was soon back home. Rob's light was still on. Jools went in and went straight to bed. He fell asleep right away.

⊙

Jools woke up an hour and a half later, fevered and soaked with sweat. His foot had been bleeding and stuck to the sheets. The sun shone through the window, heating the room like a sauna. He got up and went downstairs. There were a few birthday cards in the mail. He read them and stood them on top of the TV. He sat in the chair and dozed a while. He thought of his mother and wished she was here. He always missed her more on occasions like this. The bin lorry came for the rubbish, disturbing the silence. He thought of escaping again. He wondered if he could keep his mind blank or at least think of something else until he slipped away. They wouldn't notice him gone until it was too late. He decided he would try again. Maybe that's why Bulldog made him stare at the wall. So he could keep his mind blank and Jimmy Love's people couldn't hear or see his thoughts. He needed cigarettes and decided to go to the shop. He limped along the road to the corner shop. A transit van circled the car park at the bottom of the multi-storeys. They seemed to be watching him. The back window of the van was tinted and Jools wondered if they might be filming him from behind it. The van turned around and headed up the street. Jools went to the corner shop and bought some cigarettes, a few tins and cat food. He returned home and ate. Bread and cold beans, for your birthday! He was starting to nod off again when the front door tapped. It was his sister Sarah.

'Happy birthday!' she said.

She came in and sat in the living room.

'Have you had a good day?' she asked.

'No bad. Ah'm a bit tired. Ah never slept much last night.'

'You don't look too well. Are you alright?'

'Ah'll be awright,' he said.

'Ah just dropped in on my lunch hour. Are you sure you don't want to go out for a meal later?'

'Naw. Ah'm no really up for it tonight. Ah just need to rest.'

'Say nothing!' Bulldog whispered in his ear. 'Don't tell her about us.'

'You look really pale. Maybe you should go back to bed for a while.'

She gave him some money. 'Here, get yourself something when you feel better. That's from me and your brother.'

'Cheers, sis.'

'It was just a flying visit. I better go and get something to eat before I go back to work.'

He saw her to the door.

'I'll phone you at the weekend to see what you're up to. See you later.'

She got in her car and drove off. Jools came in and flopped on the chair.

'What a way to spend your birthday,' he thought out loud. He felt a mess. He could hardly keep his eyes open. He felt depressed at his situation. His body ached from head to foot.

'Assume the position, if you would,' Bulldog said.

For once Jools looked forward to the practice today. It would come in handy when he escaped. He went upstairs and sat cross-legged on the futon matress. He focused his eyes on the tack head in the wall and cleared his mind.

'Concentrate,' Bulldog said.

◉

Jools limped fast. He tried to picture himself in his mind walking to the shops in Muirhouse, hoping to throw them off. He crossed the dual carriageway and waited at the bus stop. He pictured himself walking into the supermarket and doing some shopping. He grew impatient waiting and decide to walk back a few stops. He kept his mental journey going as he pictured himself going to the cigarette counter and stocking up.

'What are you doing?' the voice asked suspiciously.

'Nowt. Ah'm doing a bit ay shopping, that's aw,' Jools lied. He tried to keep his mental vision moving.

'You're trying to get away!' the male voice shouted.

'Ah'm no. Ah'm at the fuckin shops, man!'

Jools pictured himself standing at the checkout.

'You don't fool us. You're trying to run! We'll spot you. There's a car on its way to check on you. Where are you?'

Jools blanked his mind so they couldn't see.

'You're up to something. You better go back. Now!' the voice screamed.

A bus approached the stop. Jools got on it and went upstairs to the back seat. He looked out the back window to see if he was being followed and tried desperately to keep his mind blank.

'You're on a bus,' the voice said.

Jools said nothing and crouched down behind the seat so no one would spot him. He tried to think of taking a quiet walk along the beach. He remembered a visualisation exercise he'd read about, the three senses out of five rule and he added the sound of the waves to his picture. He tried to feel the sun and the sea breeze on his face as he'd done many a summer. The bus jolted him and he took a peek out the window. He was nearly at Crewe Toll. He tried to get back to his vision. The bus stopped on Ferry Road outside an office block. The driver turned the engine off and the bus went quiet. He looked out the window. The driver was off the bus stretching his legs. Jools got up and went downstairs. He got off the bus and started to run. He had to get away from the main roads if he wasn't to be spotted. He ran around the corner and across the road. He found a set of steps and ran up to the cycle path above then walked along the disused railway. He stopped for breath under a bridge.

'Wait there!' the voice shouted.

Jools froze.

'We're sending someone down for you. We know you're on the old railway.'

Jools's heart started to pound. He started to run along the path. He scrambled down the embankment and hid behind an elder bush. He could smell the earth as he lay motionless in the undergrowth. He could hear someone passing on the path above and tried to slow his heavy breathing. A large bee buzzed inches from his face and he tried to swat it.

'Think of anything except where you are,' Jools thought to himself and tried to stare at the ground. He tried to blank his mind and tried not to give away his position. Someone on a moped approached. The engine buzzed along the track past him.

'We've seen you!' the voice laughed. 'You can't escape.'

Jools tried blanking it out.

'We've caught you. You might as well go home. We've got people everywhere.'

Jools stood up. He thought he might as well give in and surrendered gracefully. If only he could keep his mind blank they wouldn't have caught him. He climbed the embankment and started to limp homewards with his head down. The sun shone and it was hot and windless.

⊙

Jools sat in his bedroom. It had just got dark and he decided to go to bed early. He'd lain awake for a couple of hours, unable to drop off. Greg started to bang around upstairs.

'Bulldog! Rob! Are you there?' he asked. There was no reply. He sat up.

'Rob! Bulldog! Is anyone there?' No one answered. Jools felt deserted.

He listened to the silence and felt totally alone. He went to the window. Jimmy Love's light was on. He went to the front door and checked Rob's window. His light was off. Jools began to panic. What if they'd left him?

'Rob! Bulldog! Answer me!' There was still no reply. Jools didn't know what to do. He started to cry. 'Where are ye?' he shouted.

Silence.

'Aw, man. That's aw Ah need,' he moaned. 'They've left me. What am Ah gonnie dae now?' He started to get hysterical. He'd been holding it back for a while but the floodgates opened now.

'This is fucked up, man! What did ye leave me for? Ye're there when you want me tae dae yer walking. As soon as it gets tough ye desert me. Ye're leaving me tae Jimmy Love's gypsy mates. Ah'll no take much mair ay this. Ah'm on ma last legs, man. Dinnae leave me, please!' he cried.

There was no answer. Jools bawled into his pillow. His body shook as he sobbed.

'The polis will probably get me for that hammer and the knife now. Ah never done nowt but ye're no here to watch me!' he howled. 'They're gonnie get me!'

Jools lay and sobbed for what seemed like hours. His throat hurt and his eyes swelled up. He had reached his limit. He started to think that this would never end. They would keep on at him forever until it killed him. He decided not to prolong his pain any longer. He went to his bedroom and looked through his tool box. He took a spool of blue polythene rope from the box and measured out a few feet. He took a Stanley knife from the box and cut the length of rope. He tied the end around a handle in the false cupboard door near the ceiling, then tied a noose in the other end. He dragged over a small table and stood on top, putting the noose around his neck. His mother came into his thoughts.

'Ah'll see ye soon, ma. Ah'm comin', he said out loud. He stepped off.

Jools hit the ground with a thump. The handle he'd tied the rope to had snapped off, unable to take his weight. The rope had burned his neck, taking the skin off. He sat on the floor against the wall and bawled hysterically.

⊙

Jools awoke the next day. His neck hurt from the way he'd fallen asleep sitting against the wall. He'd only had a couple of hours sleep. He went downstairs and sat in his chair staring blankly out the window. He passed most of the afternoon just sitting quietly gazing. He started to hear a hiss in his head. The sound grew louder and started to crackle like radio interference.

'Jools! Jools! Ye're a poof! Ye're a Jew! Shut yer mooth!' the voice shouted through the hiss of static.

The sound grew louder. White noise started to build up. Jools held his head in his hands as it began to hurt. He started to feel dizzy and sick as the crackle of the static pierced his head.

'Shut the fffffuck up! Ye're a poof!' the voice hollered.

'AAARRGH!' Jools screamed.

'Ya weeee Jeeewwww!'

'Fuck off! Turn it off! That's fuckin hurtin ma heid.'

The static continued.

Jools curled up into a ball, holding his head.

⊙

Jools sat on a bench at the edge of the field at the top of Muirhouse. The sun shone and a breeze blew. He sat smoking a cigarette.

'Jools, what are you doing? Why did you try to hurt yourself last night?' Bulldog said in a gruff voice.

'Bulldog! Where the fuck have you been? Ah thought you'd aw deserted me,' Jools said excitedly.

'We were listening. We heard what went on. Are you OK?'

'Ah'm awright. This fuckin static. It's daein ma nut in. Can you turn it down?'

'We'll try. Emmm… wait a minute.' Bulldog sounded distracted.

The white noise died down.

'There, that's better.'

'Thank fuck for that, man,' Jools said. His ears were still buzzing. He'd been hearing it for hours.

'Where are you going?' Bulldog asked, sounding strange.

'Ah thought Ah might try and walk to the train station. If Ah kin keep ma mind blank Ah kin get away oot the road ay aw this.'

'What way are ye gonnie go?'

'Ah might walk up the old railway.'

'The auld railway, aye? Emmm, wait a minute… where's that again?'

'You sound funny, man. Are you awright Bulldog?'

'Aye. See when you get to the station, where are you gonnie go?'

'Ah might go doon and stay wi' ma auntie in Manchester. Dae you think that's far enough away?'

'Emmm, wait a minute… here we are. Where aboot in Manchester does she stay?' Bulldog asked.

'What's aw the questions for? You sound funny, man.'

'Emmm, wait a minute…'

'Naw. You wait a minute. You're no Bulldog! Who the fuck are you?'

'Ah'm… emmm, wait a minute… Ah'm emmm…'

'You're no Bulldog.'

'Ah'm… Awright, Ah'm a gypsy.'

'Fuck off, ya sick fuck! Leave me the fuck alone!' Jools raged.

'Ah ken what you're up tae. Ma people will stop ye. Ye better go hame. Ye canny escape!' the female voice said. 'Ah pure tricked you. You thought Ah wis Bulldog.'

Jools started to walk up the road. He felt stupid for being taken in.

'Ye canny escape. Emmm... wait a minute. Ah've got yer manual here. That's right, it says you're the one that fancies Anastacia.'

'Manual? Ye better fuckin no have a fuckin manual on me!'

'It says ye dinnae like ma people. Ye're no allowed oot ay Edinburgh where we can keep an eye on ye. Wait till Anastacia finds oot what we ken aboot ye. Jimmy Love showed us the videos ay you in yer hoose. We were aw laughin like fuck. Ye're a dirty pig!' she laughed.

Jools was mortified.

'Jools, do not say any more! They are dangerous people. Do not tell them anything else. The police are on their way,' Bulldog said sternly.

'Bulldog, man!' Jools exclaimed hopefully.

The gypsy girl stayed silent.

'Jools, I would like you to assume the position. You know what to do. Tell them nothing. I repeat, say nothing. Just continue walking towards the police station. These people are dangerous. They associate with known murderers and paedophiles. The police have all our information. They are on their way.'

Jools smiled grimly. Finally they were doing something. He walked through Drylaw and into Telford.

'Keep walking. Keep the One,' Bulldog said.

Jools concentrated hard on not thinking.

'Do not picture anything. Keep walking towards the police station. Do not say anything. Just keep walking.'

Jools cut through the hospital. He reached Carrington Road and walked up the path to Fettes Police HQ.

'Ask to speak to the duty officer,' Bulldog said. 'Tell him that in the interests of national security you need to be put somewhere safe. He'll know what you're talking about. They've been fully briefed.'

Jools was happy. He'd be glad to get away somewhere quiet. He imagined they'd find him a safe house somewhere out of the way. A hotel maybe. He went in and walked up to the desk.

'Can Ah speak tae to the duty officer please?' he asked the guard.

'What is it in regard to?' he asked.

'Ah canny really say much, pal. Ah need tae speak with the duty officer,' Jools said.

'OK. Take a seat just now.' He picked up the phone and dialled.

Jools sat on a chair in the foyer. He gazed out the window into space.

'Someone will be right down to see you,' the guard said.

Jools waited nervously.

'Are you gonnie tell the polis aboot us?' the gypsy girl asked. 'Ye better fuckin no, cause Ah ken aw aboot aw they drug dealers you ken. Ah read that part ay your mind when ye were sleepin'. Ah'll stick them aw in and blame you for grassing. You'll get fuckin chopped up. You ken aw aboot smack and everything.'

Jools tried to blank it out.

'Say nothing,' Bulldog said.

An older policeman with a beard came through the double doors and walked over to Jools.

'Can I help you?' he asked. He led Jools over to a table and some chairs and they sat down.

'In the interests of national security...' Bulldog prompted him.

'In the interests of national security can you put me somewhere safe?' Jools asked. 'They said you'd know what Ah meant.'

'I don't understand,' the policeman said. 'Do you have a complaint?'

'SMACK!!!! HE KENS AW ABOOT SMACK!!! AY KENS WHO'S DEALIN SMACK!!!' the gypsy girl screamed.

Jools's heart pounded. His face flushed. He couldn't look the policeman in the eye.

'They said if Ah talked to you, you'd put me somewhere safe. They said Ah wis tae keep oot ay Leith.'

'AY'S intae FUCKIN HEROIN!!! SMACK!!!'

'Well, I'm sorry, but without a specific complaint there's nothing I can really do for you,' the policeman explained.

'Can ye no put me somewhere safe? They said ye would.'

'You said Wood! Kevvy Wood, fae the Grove! Daein smack!' the woman screamed.

'Not unless you make a specific complaint. Sorry,' the cop explained.

'Right. OK then.' Jools felt deflated. He got up and walked to the reception area as the cop watched him, looking puzzled. He left the station and headed home.

⊙

The hiss of static returned to Jools's head. It crackled loudly, making him flinch and he covered his ears to no avail. The sound grew louder and louder and

Jools gritted his teeth. He had to escape. He couldn't take this. Maybe he could block the signal. He ran down to the kitchen and rummaged through the cupboard. He took a box of tin-foil and tore off a large sheet. He ran back upstairs to the dark bedroom and started to wrap the tinfoil around his head. It moulded into a cap and he pulled on a black wool hat over the top to secure it. Silence. The foil seemed to block the signal. Jools lay listening to the quiet. He thought of escaping. He could sneak away early in the morning. Maybe he should go somewhere out of the way where they'd never find him. He decided to try and escape again next morning. He lifted the tinfoil hat. The white noise returned.

'Stop that, you!' a male voice said. 'Ditch the hat. You're not blanking us out. You're just making the signal stronger. The foil's a conductor, Jools. It's metal. I was just watching you make plans to nash. Foiled again, what?'

'Away and fuck yourself!' Jools said. He pulled the hat back on. He set his alarm clock for six-thirty then bundled some clothes in a bag. He checked out the window. Jimmy Love's light was on. He checked out the spyhole on the front door. Rob's light was off. He didn't know if he could risk falling asleep with no one watching his door so he sat on his bed and smoked a cigarette. He kept almost nodding off and sat up straight, stretching and yawning. He had to get away this time. He'd never felt so run down in his life. His body ached. His head throbbed and his foot was raw and blistered. He hadn't slept since God knows when and hunger was making him feel weak. His mind drifted. He thought of how things would be when it was all over. He'd get to meet the stars. He'd be famous. Maybe he'd even write about this one day. He could get away from this poverty. He could leave behind this bad life he'd been living for the last few years. Maybe he could find a soulmate and settle down. The future looked positive and he almost felt happy. This couldn't last forever. He'd been stupid. He'd nearly thrown it all away last night. He lay semi-conscious dreaming of the possibilties. He imagined being interviewed on TV. He'd finally get to set the record straight. He'd go to showbiz parties and mix with the rich and famous. He'd be the one, the one they were all talking about. He could form a group to make sure this never happened to anyone again. He'd go to Amnesty International. They'd like to hear about the way he'd been done up. It was surely against the Geneva Convention to use gadgets like they'd used on him. He pictured the Amnesty International logo in his mind. A lit candle surrounded by barbed wire. Someone blew the flame out.

'Fuckin dirty bastards,' Jools said.

The Queen herself had been following his story and had wished him well. Maybe she'd honour him. He'd stuck to his guns in not going to the IRA for help even though his own side weren't taking that good care of him. He wondered where Rob and Bulldog had got to. They'd been quiet for ages. He tried to get a little sleep. Greg started to bang around upstairs.

'Shut the fuck up!!!' he shouted and banged on the wall with his fist. He felt restless and his head buzzed from the static. He could hear a faint voice shouting at him to remove the tinfoil hat but he ignored it. The sky outside turned from black to blue and Jools lay trying to relax. If he couldn't sleep at least he'd rest. The dawn chorus started.

'YA WEEEE JEEWWWWWW!!!' a bird whistled shrilly. 'Keep oot ay Leith!!!'

⊙

The alarm woke Jools from a semi-conscious state. It was 6.30am. He went downstairs and dressed. He fed the cat and got his things together. He pulled the rucksack onto his back and left the flat. He blanked his mind the best he could as he limped up through Craigroyston school and crossed the road to Drylaw police station. He went into the reception and asked the woman if he could see the duty officer.

'Take a seat,' she told him and disappeared through the back. Jools saw his reflection in a mirror on the wall behind the desk. He looked like he'd lost a couple of stone in weight. His face was pale and his lips dehydrated and his eyes seemed to have sunk into his head. He was shocked at his appearance. He noticed a light and some movement behind the mirror and saw that it was a two-way mirror. He sat and stared down at the black and white lino. He grew edgy and stepped back outside for a cigarette. They were taking their time. A car sped past on Ferry Road.

'Shut your mouwf!'

They'd spotted him already. Jools ducked behind a brick pillar. He stubbed out his cigarette and walked through the tunnel to the car park at the back of the station. A police van and three pandas were parked out back. He stood for a few minutes out of sight of the road and decided to go back inside. He walked around the front and went into reception.

'Someone will be right down,' the woman at the desk said.

A policeman came through from the back.

'Yes. What can I do for you?' he asked.

'In the interests of national security, could you put me somewhere safe?' Jools asked. 'They said you'd know what Ah meant.'

The policeman looked at Jools. 'Who are "they"?'

'They just said Ah was to tell you that in the interests of national security Ah wis tae be put somewhere safe.'

'OK. Right... er, I'll be back in a minute, you just wait here.' The policeman went back through the door. Jools stared at the black and white checked lino. The pattern attacked his bleary eyes. A few minutes passed and he grew restless. He went back outside and stood behind the pillar, lighting a cigarette. A couple of cars passed. Jools ducked in away from the road. Another car passed.

'SHUT YOUR MOUWF!!!'

A police car drove from the car park and stopped in front of him. The cop got out and held the back door open for Jools.

'Come on, then,' he said. Jools noticed he wore a ring on his little finger and wondered if he was a mason. He got into the car warily. The policeman shut the door and Jools ducked down on the back seat so he wouldn't be spotted. There was a policewoman in the passenger seat. Jools's mind wandered as the movement of the car rocked him to the verge of sleep.

'You ken the main man who does smack! If ye grass us we'll grass aw yer mates up and blame you. You better keep yer mooth shut,' a voice said in his head. 'Yer drug dealin pals are aw fucked tae. Ye'll get fuckin chopped up. Yer family will get it tae. It'll never stop. NEVER!'

'Ah'm oot ay it aw now,' Jools thought. 'They canny touch me now.' He wondered where they were taking him.

'Are you alright back there? Not falling asleep?' the policewoman asked.

'Ah'm awright,' Jools replied. He wondered if the policewoman had heard of him. They were driving someone around who was going to be famous. One day soon he'd sign autographs for people like her. Jools closed his eyes. The sun was out and he let his mind drift. The car's motion rocked him gently. He wondered if he was being followed. Doubtful. They wouldn't tail a police car. They drove on for a while and no one spoke. The heat in the car made Jools drowsy. He dreamed of his ex and how if only she'd stuck around she could have been there with him. He wished his mother was still alive to see him. She'd have been proud of him.

The car drove on a while and Jools had almost fallen asleep when he felt it slow down and stop. The engine turned off and Jools sat up. The two officers got out of the car and let him out. He stood in front of a grey stone building and they walked through the automatic doors to a reception area. A sign read ROYAL EDINBURGH HOSPITAL. Jools sat on a fold-down wooden seat on the wall. The two police officers talked to a woman behind a glass window.

'Mikey Porter, 160/9 Muirhoose Broadway. Does three kilos a week!' the voice plucked the address from Jools's mind.

'HASH! DRUGS! SMACK!'

Jools tried hard not to give anyone away. He concentrated as hard as he could on blanking his mind. An old man sat and smiled at him across the room. Jools started to nod out.

'Are you alright?' the policewoman asked. 'Do you want to come with us?'

Jools followed them up the corridor. They stopped at a lift and waited. The lift came and they went to the second floor. He was led to a room full with beds along each wall.

'We'll just book you in. You just sit there and rest,' a woman said to Jools, showing him to a bed. She and the two police officers left him alone. He lay down and lost consciousness.

Jools heard the bed next to him squeak loudly. He opened his eyes to see a young man sitting there. The man had a skinhead haircut and wore black jeans and a tee shirt.

'Eddie Anderson! SMACK! He's a smack dealer… Mikey Porter's sellin hash 'n' eccies. He's dealin tae half ay Muirhoose.' The female voice pulled the names from Jools's mind.

The bed squeaked as the skinhead shifted his weight around. Jools fought hard to stop his thoughts being snatched. The skinhead seemed to be trying to warn him when a name was popping out. The bed squeaked again. Jools stopped in mid-thought. He bit his bottom lip hard to make sure he wasn't talking out loud. The salt taste of blood filled the back of his throat.

'DRUGS!!!' the voice screamed.

Jools nodded out again.

A loud rumble shook the walls. Jools's eyes opened slowly. A large black silhouette entered his line of vision. It moved slowly closer to the bed. The shape seemed to float and Jools started to feel fear creeping into him. Its face came into view and Jools was horrified to see its large beak-like nose and huge hairy eyebrows. The nose extended from its misshapen forehead to its top lip and its beady eyes were set in two dark sockets. It stopped and slowly turned to look at Jools. He couldn't bear to look at it and froze. It stood at the foot of the bed and stared at him. He could hear its heavy breathing. Jools felt a mixture of fear and disgust. The thing turned slowly and started to glide away from him. Jools wondered if it was even human. He wondered if it was an inbred and nodded out again.

⊙

Jools woke up as someone shook his shoulder. A woman asked him to go with her. She was moving him to another bed. Jools staggered along the corridor to the next room.

'This is your bed,' the woman said.

He lay down. The woman sat in a chair by the door talking to a man. Jools drifted off.

⊙

Jools opened his eyes. The evening sunlight filtered through the window. The man and woman were still sitting by the door. Jools's eyes began to flicker. He began to see the dials on a fruit machine spinning around in his eyes.

'What's happening?' Jools asked.

'We've wired you up to a machine,' a male voice answered.

Jools tried to struggle but couldn't move.

'We've wired you up to a lottery machine,' the voice said.

'Fuck off!' Jools tried to wriggle. The symbols spun fast in Jools's eyes. Cherries, bars, clubs revolved round and round.

'Why are ye daein this tae me?!!'

'We need to make more money,' the voice said.

Jools closed his eyes. He drifted off again.

⊙

'It's me, Chris!' the voice said.

Jools recognised it as his old friend whom he'd not seen for a few years.

'How are you doing, man?' He was glad to hear a friendly voice.

'I'm doing great, Jools. I've made it big in Australia. Got plenty money. I'm a millionaire now. I moved to Oz a couple of years ago and made it big. Now all I do is surf, man.'

'It's great to hear from you, man. We'll have to meet up when this is over, man. What the fuck are they daein tae me, Chris?' Jools hoped he'd shed some light on his situation.

'Don't worry, man. When this is over you can come and stay with me in Oz. You won't need anything. I get plenty of great weed over there. This is my scam, Jools. I'm sorry I couldn't let you in on it earlier but we had to keep it quiet. Don't worry, you've got plenty cash coming to you. It's a sting. It's a big computer fraud. We're skimming Mackenzie's money. We've got our hands on some pretty specialised equipment. We're going to take this all the way.'

Jools laughed. 'Ah knew you'd be in for me, man,' he said.

'You ought to see the drugs I'm getting, Jools. The best of everything,' Chris said.

'Ah'm glad to hear you're daein so well, man.'

'Jools, I want you to help us,' Chris said.

'Aye, sure man. What do you want me tae dae?'

'Do you know what I look like now?'

A picture of Chris in a long black coat and a top hat flashed through Jools's mind.

'I'm not far away, either,' Chris said. 'Guess what I am now? I'm a mason!'

Jools closed his eyes in horror and nodded out.

$\odot$

'I'm still here,' Chris said.

Jools came to. He noticed the man and woman still sat at the door. He started to feel a tingle in the top of his scalp. It felt like pins and needles at first and started to spread down through his head and neck. The tingle grew more intense and Jools felt the steel threads passing down through his skull and into his body. They wrapped around his armbones and he could feel them start to coil round his ribs. An electric current started to pass through him. It grew more intense and Jools couldn't move. He seemed to be pinned to the bed by his elbows by some invisible force. The current grew stronger and waves of pain travelled up through his feet to his scalp. He felt like he was being slowly electrocuted, the electricity increasing steadily. The steel threads contined to wrap around his bones under his skin. He could feel them creeping inside him, attaching themselves to his insides.

'AAARRGHH!!' he screamed. 'This hurts, Chris!'

'Just hold on for a while, Jools. We're running the computer through you. It's wired up to the national lottery's main machine. We're screwing the system. We need another few million. Just hold on. No pain! No pain!'

Jools gritted his teeth. The pain was getting unbearable. 'Turn it off, Chris! Ah canny handle it!' he said through clenched teeth. The wires continued to coil around him. The current made his body shake.

'Ah'm no kiddin Chris, turn it off! Now!' Jools growled.

'Just a while longer. Stop moaning!'

'It fuckin hurts bad!' Jools was getting annoyed. 'How much longer?'

'Another hour and a half should do it,' Chris said. 'Just another six million.'

'No way, man! This hurts too bad. Another five minutes is aw Ah can take.'

'Stop whining!'

'Aw you care about is yourself. You're only interested in the money. You're no ma mate!' Jools shouted.

'Please yourself then!' Chris sniffed.

The pain started to recede and Chris retreated. Jools's elbows came unstuck. They throbbed badly but he found he could move again. He looked at the man and woman by the door. Hadn't they heard him shouting? He closed his eyes and nodded out.

⊙

Jools jumped as three loud bangs came from behind the partition.

Knock… knock… knock!

'Who's that?' Jools asked.

'I'm here. In the next bed,' the voice said. 'Do you want to join us? I'm a mason.'

'Naw!' Jools shouted. He began to feel scared.

'You must say "Certainly not" three times or you'll be in forever. Once in, you can never, ever leave!'

'CERTAINLY NOT! CERTAINLY NOT! CERTAINLY NOT!'

The presence retreated. Jools tried to fight sleep. He lost.

⊙

He awoke with a woman shaking his arm.

'Jools. Are you awake? I'm the lobotomist and I'm here to take a blood sample.'

She came towards him with a large needle.

'CERTAINLY NOT! CERTAINLY NOT! CERTAINLY NOT!'

The woman frowned and marched off. Jools nodded out.

⊙

'Jools. Are you awake?' The man shook his shoulder.

'What is it?' he asked, half asleep.

'We're moving you to another ward. Can you collect your things and come with me?' the man said.

Jools looked at the man. He was a ringer for Ali G. He got his things and stuffed them into a carrier bag. The man led him along a corridor and up a flight of stairs. They walked down another corridor to a reception area with a large glass window. A blonde woman came out of the office.

'This is Jools McCartney,' Ali G said.

'Would you like to follow me?' the woman asked. She led him to another room with beds. His cubicle had a curtain around it.

'This is your bed,' she said. 'If you need anything I'll be in the office.' She left Jools and he lay down on the bed. He fell into unconsciousness.

⊙

Jools awoke to find it dark in the room. He could see by the light coming in from the corridor. He could hear someone playing the bongo drums. The sound echoed up the hall.

'They're playing that for you, Jools,' the male voice said. 'Jimmy Love's nephew's in the ward upstairs. You've all been brought here for safe keeping. They want to welcome you.'

The drums got louder. Jools lay back and listened. The drums stopped and Iron Maiden started to belt out 'Can I Play with Madness'.

Jools appreciated the gesture. At least they were trying to be friendly. He could hear a lot of thumping and banging going on upstairs. The Stone Roses started to play 'Waterfall'.

'They must be playing that one especially for me,' Jools thought, remembering the Botanic Garden. 'For ma Ma.'

'Wee man! Wee man! Are you intae a smoke?' the voice asked.

'Aye man, you got any?'

'Wee man. Ah've made ye a joint. It's there on the bedside cabnet. Under all yer gear. Dinnae faw asleep. The cleaners will find it, or the doctors.'

'Doctors?' Jools asked.

'Wee man. Ye're in the hospital for safe keepin'.'

Jools got out of bed and searched for the joint.

'Wee man, it's there! Under the towels.'

Jools looked everywhere. He could find nothing.

'Wee man, it's there! It must have fell doon the back.'

Jools shifted the cabinet. There was nothing.

'Ah canny see it,' he said. He got back into bed and lay back.

'Wee man. Dinnae leave that joint lying aboot. It's there. Under the stuff on the cabinet,' the voice said.

'Ah'll find it later.' Jools was nodding off when a woman came in with a tablet and a little glass of juice.

'Your medication,' she said.

He took the tablet and she left. He decided he needed a cigarette and got up in search of a smoking room. He shuffled up the corridor bleary-eyed and found the room. Inside the seats were arranged around the edges of the room. There was a TV on in the corner and a large glass window looked through to the office. Two women worked in the office. There were two men sitting reading newspapers in the room, smoking. Jools lit a cigarette. He hadn't had one all day and it made him feel light-headed. No one spoke in the room. One of the men got up and switched the TV off.

'Stay off the TV!' the voice said. 'No watching telly! You're not allowed any news!'

Jools sighed. He finished his cigarette and went back to bed. He pulled the curtain around him and got into bed. He expected they'd move him to a hotel tomorrow. He quickly fell asleep.

⊙

The sun streamed through the window. Jools could see the Pentland Hills from the window at the end of the room. He noticed a large aerial mast on a hill closer to the building. He thought that must be where the radio signal was coming from. He left the room and walked up the corridor. He noticed another corridor leading from the hallway and wandered up, finding a kitchen at the end. He made himself a cup of tea and wandered back to the smoking room for a cigarette. He sat in a chair and lit one. The room was full of people. They were all ages and seemed to be from different backgrounds. They sat together talking and smoking. Two children ran around, bored. The TV was off and a radio blared.

'What's your name?' a man asked.

Jools looked at him. He had medium-length fair hair which was sticking up all over, and a goatee beard.

'Jools,' he replied.

'Can Ah get a cigarette off ye, Jools?' the man asked.

Jools gave him one. A woman came in and walked over.

'The doctor would like to see you,' she said. 'This way.'

Jools got up and followed her along the corridor. She knocked on the door of a room in the hallway and went in. Jools took a seat in the room.

'Hello, Mr McCartney,' the dark-haired Irishman said, extending his hand. 'I'm Dr Malloy. I'm to be your doctor while you're here.'

Jools shook his hand.

'Can you tell me a little bit about what's been happening to you, Mr McCartney?' the Irishman asked in a heavy accent.

'Ah'm a bit run doon. Ah've been a bit depressed,' Jools said.

'Can you tell me where you were going when the police brought you in yesterday? They said you were just wandering around.'

'Ah was just out for a walk. Ah couldnae take any mair ay the hoose so Ah went for a walk. Ah've been feelin bad since Ah lost my ma.'

'The polis mustnae have let them in on what was going on,' he thought.

'And how do you feel now?' the doctor asked.

'No too bad. How long do Ah have to stay here?'

'We'll keep you in for seventy-two hours initially.'

Jools got up to leave.

'I'll see you again in a few days. It's just to keep an eye on you just now.'

Jools went back to the smoking room and had another cigarette. He wondered if they would move him to a better place after the seventy-two hours. Surely if he was going to be famous they would put him in a decent hotel. He must just be in here for security reasons. People would go mad if they knew he was being kept in here.

'Wee man! Wee man!' the voice said. 'You're in the blue team. Remember that. True blue.'

'Awright.'

'Ye're in the Tory ward.'

'Ah'm no a fuckin Tory.' Jools was insulted.

'Naw. Ye're in the blue team. Tory Liberal.'

'Awright. Ah'll play along but Ah'm no too happy aboot the Tory bit,' Jools laughed.

'Aw these people in here. They're all ex-Navy and armed forces.'

Jools didn't like the sound of that.

'Where's Bulldog and Rob?' he asked.

'The SAS are off the case since Mackenzie copped it. There's some Special Branch in here mixing with the people. They're all psychologists and actors. They're just training for when the ward opens up later in the year. Don't try and figure out their game.'

Jools looked around. A lot of them could have been ex-forces. He wondered who was Special Branch.

'Ah'm upstairs if ye need me.' The voice retreated.

The blonde woman from the day before came in. She mixed with the other people and finally came over to Jools.

'How are you today?' she asked.

'PERIOD BLOOD!' a voice said. Jools was embarrassed.

He found her very attractive. She looked in her late thirties, slim and blonde. Just his type.

'Ah'm fine, thanks,' he replied.

'PERIOD BLOOD!'

'Quit it!' Jools thought. 'Stop trying to make me sick. She's a nice woman.'

'Can you come with me? We'll get you weighed.'

They walked up the hall to the office. He stood on the scales and she adjusted the weight.

'That's fine,' she said, marking it down in a book. She took his blood pressure.

He knew he'd lost a bit of weight. A couple of stones, he reckoned. He'd hardly eaten in the last few weeks. He left and went into the smoking room. There were a few people sitting around the room. Jools said nothing as he glanced around. A short girl with long black curly hair and a pot belly danced around to the radio. Jools sat cross-legged in the chair. He wondered if any of them recognised him from the TV.

'Jools, Jools. Can Ah get a cigarette off ye?' It was the man from last night.

Jools handed him one. The girl danced over to him.

'Awright? When did you come in?' she asked.

'Last night.'

'Where are you fae?'

'Muirhoose.' He closed his eyes. He couldn't be bothered talking.

'Stay away from that girl!' the voice said.

'Who is she?' he thought.

'Stay away from her!' the voice warned.

Jools started to drift. He stubbed the end of his cigarette around the rim of the ashtray. Travis came on the radio.

'Go to your room!' the voice commanded. 'Go directly to your room! Do not pass go! Do not collect £200...'

Jools got up and went to his room. He pulled the curtain around his cubicle and sat on the bed.

'Assume the position!' the voice said.

He couldn't believe they still expected him to do this.

'Don't picture anything. Just be!'

Jools tried to clear his head.

SLAM! He jumped. A door slammed up the hall.

'Shut up, Jools. Literally, shut up!'

Jools focused on a screw in the wardrobe door. He widened his eyes and stretched his back then settled down, blanking his mind. He stared and stared some more.

⊙

An alarm sounded and Jools jumped. Some people scrambled down the corridor then the alarm switched off.

'That was nowt tae dae wi' me!' he thought, as peace returned to the room.

SLAM! The door up the hall closed with a loud bang and he jumped again. He got up and went to the room door. Looking up the hall he could see a man and two women in the office. A bell rang in the hall.

'That's dinner time, folks!' the nurse shouted. Jools followed the line of people coming out of the smoking room along the corridor to the kitchen. A line formed in front of a large metal food trolley. Trays were racked inside and everyone helped themselves. He took a tray and sat at a table on his own. Beef stew and mash. So much for vegetarianism. He got it down him anyway, he was so hungry. He ate quickly and tucked into his dessert. He looked around the room. People sat around tables eating, though not many people spoke. A nice-looking girl caught his eye at the food trolley. 'She must work here,' he thought. He noticed she wore a badge on her belt and carried a little box that looked like a walkie-talkie. 'That must be for picking up signals,' he supposed. He wondered if that's how they could hear his thoughts. He'd noticed a few of the staff carried them.

He finished his dinner and went for a cigarette. The smoking room was empty exept for an old woman eating her dinner off a tray on her lap. He smoked a cigarette quickly and went to his room before everyone came back from dinner. He lay on his bed and drifted. The sun beamed through the dorm.

SLAM! He jumped.

'Shut up, Jools!' the voice said.

'Awright! Fuck! Ye've told me.' He was getting angry.

'Just literally shut the fuck up!'

'Where's Rob and Bulldog? You're a nippy fuck,' he protested.

'We're looking after you now.'

'Where are you?' Jools asked.

'In the office,' the female voice said.

'You mean this is hospital staff Ah'm talkin tae?'

'The hospital got your application from your psychologist. She said you would be the right man for the job. But you have to learn to shut up!'

Jools didn't believe her. 'Shite!' he said.

The presence retreated. He lay back and drifted some more. He heard footsteps approaching up the hall.

'Jools. A visitor to see you,' the blonde nurse said.

It was his auntie.

'How are you feeling?' she asked. 'What's happened?'

'Shut up, Jools. Don't say anything. NOT A FUCKING WORD!' the voice warned him.

'Ah'm tired. Ah'm awright.'

'I've brought you a few things,' she said, handing him a carrier bag.

'Thanks.'

'Ah'm no kiddin', Jools,' the voice said. 'If ye dinnae shut up, we'll have to hurt ye!'

Jools felt a needle stab him in the side. He flinched.

He sat cross-legged on the bed. His head began to feel heavy and his eyes closed. His mind drifted and he nodded out.

⊙

'Jools! Jools! Medication time.' A woman shook his arm.

He sat up and she handed him a plastic cup with a tablet in it. He swallowed the tablet and she handed him a small plastic cup of juice. He drank it and gave her the cup back. He lay back and started to drift.

He awoke to find it dark in the room.

'Jools. Are you feeling any better?' the voice asked. 'I'm Dr Love. Remember I was sitting on the bed next to you when they brought you in?'

'You're the guy wi' the skinheid?'

'That's me. You were in a bad way when you came in. I just thought I'd check on you. I'm from Leith so you know you can talk to me. Us schemies stick together. You'll be fine with us as long as you're not into drugs. We're all dead against drugs in here. It says you're in for rehabilitation. What drugs are you taking?'

'Nowt. Ah only smoke a wee bit hash.'

'Well, we won't hold that against you. Most of us are into a smoke. It's hard drugs we're against. We've all lost family members to smack. That's how we're on the team. We all went to uni together. I lost a brother to smack. I really hate that drug. Jimmy Love was his name. One Love. That's what we called the project. In his memory.'

'Jimmy Love was your brother?' Jools was confused. 'They told me Jimmy Love had been watching me. That he'd been working for John Mackenzie.'

'There is no Jimmy Love. He's dead… That's really pissed me off. He was my brother.'

'Ah'm sorry. Well who have Ah been running fae then? The gypsies?'

'Dinnae say anything about gypsies. We're all fae folk. We're all Jock Tamson's bairns, as they say. You're in for rehab. That's what it says here.'

'But Ah'm no on drugs.' Jools was getting worried. 'How can you hear me?'

'You were wired up when you came in. We just magnetised your head so we can talk to you and find out what your problem is from the inside. We're in the lab upstairs. We're looking through your head at night when you're asleep,' Dr Love said. 'We'll keep you safe. It's kind of funny,' he laughed. 'You were a little shit when you were wee. Some of the things we've seen have had us pissing ourselves laughing.'

'Ah wis a bit wild when Ah was wee.'

'The Special Branch are having a good laugh with us too.'

'What one's the Special Branch?' Jools asked.

'I'm not allowed to say.'

'Do you think Ah'll be alright to meet Anastacia?'

'I don't know about that. We'll have to see how long it takes to groom you. That's where we come in. That's what the One Love organisation does. We take people like you and put them through rehab and try and bring out their best qualities. Teach them how to be more effective in life. We take people like you and mould them into useful citizens. The cutting edge in personal development. You've never really worked, have you?'

'Ah've been ill for a long time. Ah canny move forwards nor back. It's like, cause Ah'm sick, Ah'll always be poor.'

'Well, the One Love organisation will make a new man of you. Wait till you see how you feel when this is over. Listen, I have to go now but if there's anything you want, just ask. I'll be in the lab watching your progress.'

The presence retreated.

Jools went for a cigarette. The smoking room was full. He couldn't find an empty seat so he sat on the unit on the wall. The other people sat and smoked, watching TV. He began to feel self-conscious and thought everyone was looking at him so he smoked his cigarette quickly and went back to his room.

He lay on the bed with the curtain pulled halfway around and started to drift.

SLAM! Jools jumped.

He took it as a 'shut up' and cleared his mind.

'Jools! Jools! It's me, Chris!' the voice said.

Jools tried to move but couldn't.

'What's happenin, Chris?'

'I need your help. It's part of the sting.'

Jools started to feel strange. He was totally paralysed. His eyes closed involuntarily. He felt an energy creeping down his spine and into his arms and legs. His body pulsated and his breath grew deep. His mind lit up like a computer screen. Letters began to form in his mind's eye in time with his breathing.

jfewyusifioudrerigi+

"99'hpppo6oay '3505. . GRY'Z'O`. . . . .   'fkkkcrrt.

/tlKRHGEZELKMOVOI. ' . . . . . . EFGVYU788AWeTV52I. . . . .

FROM: ChrisJennings@Gartnavelmilitaryhospital.Submarinediv.com

SENT: 10 Jun 01

TO: Chief petty officer Lee Bowen.

Lee you fucking prick. . . . .

We finally caught you with. . . . . . .

your pants down you corrupt cunt. . . . .

We know all about the plutonium 525. . . . . . .

your dirty little base has polluted the enviroment. . . . .

around Garnavel for the next. . . . .

2000 years. I hope you are damn proud of the needless suffering you fucking. . . . .

nasty little piece of shit as . . . .

your dirty little backhand deals have been. . . . .

secretly filmed. By the way we know all about your homosexual activities. . . . . . .

you dirty little slag. . . . .

See how your computers deal with this. . . . .

You are the biggest threat to national...

Jools coughed

...front...

'Aw fuck! Sorry, man.'

'Jools, don't fuckin move!' Chris screamed. 'This is the end of two fucking years of work! Don't fucking breathe! This next part is vital. Don't move a fucking muscle!'

10

9

8

7

6

5

   'Don't fucking move, Jools!'

4

3

2

1

   An electric current started to flow through Jools.

trxwyubyuyjiho yotlÚønyj46 0o4-oo0 'kyblcekcjtJewrj. . . . .
bycyfhcv g5y24p5-';'rg[;ty;. . . . .
'DOWNLOADING!'
7823YVYR782855 V85GU6709Y0UU968Y0-UI-8859 OI6III3B'I3'WUOU
ODRP-O. B'U'BPUU3£W[YP[IO\U5OIOIO7I8ONUKLLIOFOOL. . . . . . .

   'Don't fucking move a muscle!!!' Chris bawled.

   Jools lay frozen stiff. He was scared to move his arms and he started to need the toilet.

   A short fat man came into the room and walked to a bed across from him. He started to bang around in his cubicle.

   'There's someone in the room!' Jools said. He was scared the man would come over and make him move.

dgtgj jy894. . . . .tty47y4nyuv8u8u95uk/;lkokajhuhgyg\si0
ihrlk;lkgp0iv9uy. . . . .

   The letters spilled out behind his eyelids.

   The electric charge started to get stronger. His elbows started to burn as if they were being held down by invisible energies.

   'Don't fucking dare move!' the voice screamed. 'This bit is dangerous!'

   The voice sounded different.

   'You're no Chris!' Jools said.

   'Chris has gone,' the voice said. 'He's took off for Australia. Won't be back.'

   The electricity was starting to burn his extremities.

   'Who are you? What are ye daein?' he asked.

   'We're here to connect up the satellite. Don't move! We're putting 50,000 volts through your body. If you break the connection you'll get an almighty shock,' the voice told him.

Jools was scared to breathe. The pain from the electricity was getting bad and he really needed to pee.

'Stop it! You're hurting him!' He heard his cousin say in her Canadian accent.

'SHUT THE FUCK UP!'

'Jen? Is that you?' Jools asked.

'Look, he's terrified!' his cousin pleaded. 'Leave him alone!'

Jools moved his hand, keeping elbow contact with the bed. His cousin held his hand.

'Get away, Jen! Dinnae let them catch ye!' Jools said. 'It's too dangerous for you. Dinnae get involved!'

The pain made him grit his teeth and tense his whole body.

'Will you leave him alone?' Jen asked.

'Shut the fuck up, ya silly wee cow!' the voice snapped.

'Dinnae fuckin talk tae her like that!' Jools bawled.

'We're putting the whole telecommunication satellite through your body so you better be still and shut up. That's 50,000 volts.'

A loud buzzing began to fill his head, vibrating his brain inside his skull, and the electric current started to decline slowly.

'Can Ah move now?' Jools asked.

There was no reply. The current wound down.

His body tingled all over and he thought he might lose control of his bladder at any minute. He slowly moved his elbow, sliding it across the bed. His arm ached. He lifted it from his lap. No shock. He moved the other one.

'Is it awright if Ah move now?' he asked.

No reply.

Jools staggered to his feet and raced to relieve himself. A door slammed and he jumped.

'Shut up, Jools!' the voice laughed. 'Literally, shut up!'

⊙

Jools noticed the clock in the hall read 2.00am. He went into the smoking room. The room was dimly lit with two lamps. There was no one around so he lit a cigarette and sat in one of the chairs. He sat in the silence, smoking, pondering what to do. A man came into the room and sat in a chair opposite. He began rocking his body back and forward in the chair and humming to himself. Jools closed his eyes. He wondered where Chris had gone. He didn't like this place. A woman with a name-tag on popped her head round the door then disappeared again. Jools looked out the window. He could see the silhouette of the Pentland

Hills beyond. The plants on the window sill looked in need of a good watering. The two women talked to each other in the office behind the glass window in the wall. He picked up a newspaper.

'PIT IT DOON!' the voice said.

Jools sighed and threw the paper back down.

'Finish that cigarette and go to your room!' the voice commanded.

He did as he was told. He went to bed and lay in the semi-darkness of the ward.

BANG! He jumped. Someone slammed a door up the hallway.

'Pit it doon!' the voice said.

Jools tried to blank his mind.

'Don't picture anything,' the voice said.

'Fuck this for a laugh,' Jools thought in a moment of rebellion and started to picture himself flying through the air on a surfboard.

BANG! He jumped again.

'Pit it doon, laddie!' the voice shouted.

Jools's nerves were raw. He seemed to flinch at every loud sound. He lay back and tried to relax.

A needle jabbed him in the side.

'If you dinnae shut up, we'll have tae hurt ye,' the voice said.

'WHAT THE FUCK DO YE MEAN? AH'VE SAID FUCK ALL!' Jools raged. 'How can Ah no think? Ah have to think sometimes, eh? Ah'd be deid if Ah didnae. And stop fuckin hurtin me, ya cruel bastards!'

'Simply shut up, Jools. If you dinnae shut up, we'll have to hurt ye.'

'FUCK OFF!' Jools shouted. He rolled over and tried to sleep.

The needle jabbed him again and he bent double.

'AAARRGH! FUCKIN STOP IT! See if Ah find oot who you are Ah'm gonnie boot fuck oot ay ye!' Jools fumed. 'FUCKIN WEIRDOS!'

He lay awake for a few hours, seething, unable to sleep, then drifted off restlessly.

⊙

Jools awoke with a nurse shaking him. She handed him a tablet in a plastic cup and a small glass of juice. He took the tablet and lay back down to sleep.

⊙

He got out of bed and went to the smoking room. People sat around the wall of the room smoking and chatting. The girl with the long black hair shuffled around the middle of the room. She came over to Jools.

'Awright, doll?' she asked.

'Hiya.'

'You look like ma brother.'

Jools pulled out his cigarettes.

'Can Ah get one?' she asked.

He handed her a cigarette and gave her a light.

'What ye in for?' she asked him.

'They said it was rehab.'

'That's what Ah'm in for. Ah'm a registered junkie,' she laughed.

Jools noticed all her top teeth were missing.

'Ah've been in and oot ay here the last ten years,' she said. 'Ah'm fuckin radio rental, by the way.'

'Stay away from that girl!' a loud voice said in his head.

The girl started to go around the room emptying ashtrays into a metal bin in the corner.

'Don't go near that person!' the voice warned.

'How?' Jools thought. 'She was awright. A bit fucked up, but she wisnae bad.'

'She's the fixer-upper,' the voice replied.

Jools looked around the room. He tried to spot who were the psychology students. His gaze caught an older man in his late fifties. He was short and plump with black hair. Jools thought he looked like the actor Walter Matthau. He sat in the chair smiling at the other people.

'That's the Professor,' the voice said. 'He's in charge of the students. He's teaching a psychology class.'

Jools studied the man. He looked a bit eccentric. He wore a red baseball cap and had sandals on. Jools thought he looked funny, as if his company would be great fun.

The black-haired girl fiddled with the CD/cassette player in the corner. She put on a collection of songs from the sixties and started to dance around the room.

'Get out of here when other people are playing their messages!' the voice said.

Jools finished his cigarette and went back to his room. He lay on the bed and wondered how long they would keep him here. He still half hoped they would move him to a hotel. He wondered when he would meet Anastacia. There was the party to go to and he still had to meet Tanaka sensei.

'Jools, don't picture anything.' The voice said. 'Shut up.'

BANG! He jumped. A door slammed.

'Stay out of the smoking room while other people play their messages. Two till four every day. And shut up. If you don't, I'll have to hurt ye.'

Jools felt a needle jab him in the stomach and the pain made him wince.

'Assume the position!'

He sighed loudly and swung his legs over the side of the bed. He stared at the door handle on the wardrobe and cleared his mind.

'Concentrate! Simply... sssshut up. Shut the fuck up, Jools! Don't picture anything...'

⊙

Jools looked out the window. He scanned his eyes across the Pentland Hills and spotted a tall aerial mast on a nearby hill.

'That must be where the signals are being sent from,' he thought.

'Keep off the Pentlands!' the voice warned. 'Stay off the Pentlands.'

Jools went back and sat on his bed. He was beginning to feel miserable, he wasn't allowed to do anything. A bell rang twice in the hall.

'That's dinner time, folks!' a woman shouted.

He shuffled up the hallway to the kitchen and took a tray off the metal trolley. He sat at a table on his own and started to eat. Red meat again. He tucked in. A guard stood at the side of the room. Jools could see his name-tag and what looked like a little mace spray hanging from his belt.

'At least the security is satisfactory,' he thought.

He finished his food and went to make a cup of tea. He grabbed a cup and went to the water boiler on the wall. He didn't trust the machine and he had visions of it exploding in his face, scalding him with boiling water. He made a brew and went along to the smoking room. Everyone was still at their dinner so the room was empty. He smoked a cigarette double quick and immediately lit another.

Back in the dorm it was dark when he woke from a short nap. He went to the bathroom and noticed a door to the bath cubicle. He went to his room and got a towel then went back and ran a bath. He locked the door and started to undress. He noticed a picture on the wall. It was of a flying seagull, an anchor and a lifebelt. Jools thought it was a reference to his dad being a trawlerman.

'All the people in this ward are from a marine background,' the voice said. 'Mostly ex-Navy. They're all in here to tell their story.'

Jools got in the bath. The water was lukewarm.

'Each one of you has his or her piece of the puzzle. You'll all get a chance to give your message.'

'So you mean all the people in here are going through the same as me?' Jools asked.

'There are only a couple of you in each ward. The rest of them are psychologists and doctors. Then there's the security. Special Branch. You're here for safe-keeping. Dr Love has brought you all together to put together all the pieces of a puzzle. He's a world famous psychiatrist from New York. I don't know what he's got planned for you lot but I'm sure it'll be spectacular. You see, he takes young people like you, people that have maybe strayed from the path a bit, and he moulds them into responsible citizens. He turns their lives around. After this you'll never look back.'

'But what aboot the gyppos and Jimmy Love? What happened to them?'

'That was before you came in. You were already wired up so we just use the same frequency. We magnetised your head when you came in.'

Jools could vaguely remember seeing some equipment in the room when he first came in.

'You're in the Royal Ed. Dr Love's organisation will look after you. But a word of warning. Don't use any racist language when you're on the course. Dr Love hates racism. He lost a lot of family during the war. He was a child in the concentration camps,' the voice informed him. 'Don't ever act in a racist manner or you'll get the max.'

'What's the max, likes?' Jools asked.

'Believe me, you don't want the max. It's like the worst pain you can imagine and it goes right through your body like an electric charge. You'll probably lose control of your bowels and bladder. Dr Love is very strict on racism.'

'Ah'm no sure Ah want this. Why can Ah no just go hame? Can they no put me in a hotel or something? Ah'm meant tae be meetin Anastacia and that.'

'You're in no state to be meeting anyone. You'll all meet her if, and only if, you complete the grooming programme. Dr Love's invested a lot of money in you lot. You didn't think Anastacia and all those other stars were only there for you, did you? They were hired by Dr Love's organisation. The Love organisation is very powerful. That's how you all got so much coverage on TV. All your walking with the wind was sponsored. For charity. That charity is the Love organisation. You paid for your own treatment. Dr Love is world-famous. He helped some of the stars get where they are today. He moulded people like Scary Spice, for example. He took them off the streets and turned their lives around. Made them into somebodies.'

'Ah'm no sure Ah want this treatment, aw the same,' Jools said. 'Ah jist want to go hame.'

'Once you start the course, Jools, you can't back out.'

'How no? Ye canny keep me here. Ah just want oot.'

'Jools, there is no out. You're all wired up now. It's too late to back out. I really feel for you, I do, but once you're in, that's it. There's no use in getting down about it. You've just got to accept it. You were a prime candidate for the jail the way you've been acting the last few years. The masons did this to you because they thought you were a threat to society. Dr Love can help you pay and he can help you get back your self-respect. You've a new life ahead of you, Jools. Now I'm going to go now, but just try and accept it. I'm going to leave you to get used to the idea.'

Jools's eyes began to well up with tears.

Someone banged on the door. 'Jools! Jools! are you in there?!' a woman called.

'Aye,' he replied.

'Come on out. I have to see you. You're on fifteen-minute checks. Come on out, I have to see you're OK!'

'Fuck off,' he muttered to himself. He got out of the bath and dried himself and put on some clothes. He unlocked the door and a fat woman gave him a quick look up and down, then waddled off.

'Fuckin nippy cow.'

He went back to his bed and put his stuff away, then took a walk along to the smoking room. A line formed outside the office. People queued up, waiting for their nightly medication, which was dispensed from a trolley in the room.

The smoking room was empty apart from a man he'd seen earlier, the Professor and a big guy with a beard.

'Jools, Jools, kin Ah get a fag off ye?' the man asked.

Jools gave him a cigarette. The guy looked in a bit of a mess with his scraggy hair and nicotine-stained fingers. 'He must be in for the same as me,' Jools thought. His eyes had the same tired, dark rings around them.

Jools felt conspicuous knowing the Professor and students were watching him. He looked down at the floor. The yellow tiles seemed to jump at his eyes. The pattern in the grout was made up of dozens of crosses. Jools could see nothing but crosses. He had a quick thought invade his mind's eye as if a slide was being shown. It seemed to be a cross made up of lights set on a dark background.

'It's an aerial photograph of Prestonpans taken at night,' the voice told him. The vision disappeared. Jools continued looking at the floor. The shabby man got up and switched the radio on. There was some trancey dance music on. The yellow tiles started to play on Jools's eyes again. The crosses reappeared.

'Prestonpans!'

'Jools, you better stop going on about that. You're going to get into trouble.'

'Prestonpans!' Another cross appeared.

Jools shivered and tried to clear his mind.

'Prestonpans!'

'Jools, will you shut up? You're getting me worried now,' the voice said.

'Prestonpans!' Jools tried to stifle it. 'It's no me, man! Ah'm no daein it!'

'Jools, that photograph was top secret, now cut it out! Stop going on about it!'

'Prestonpans!' Another cross.

Jools drew deeply on his cigarette, then stubbed it out. He scuttled back to the safety of his bed away from crosses.

A man brought him along a tablet and a glass of juice a short while later.

'They'll no get rid of my problems with tablets,' he thought, but he took the medication and lay back and dozed.

'Jools, Jools! Are you awake?' a voice asked.

'Who's that?'

'Ah'm a pal ay your sister's. Ye don't really know me. Ah'm more a pal of her pal's. So how ye doing? Ah work here in the hospital and Ah just thought Ah'd drop in and see how you're doing.'

'Ah'm a bit pissed off,' Jools said. 'They'll no let me off the programme.'

'Don't worry, Jools. Wait till you get out. Wait till you see what it's going to be like when you get out. Your money worries are over. Me and Shaun, your sister's mate, were into some heavy shit. Ah can't tell you too much about it till you get out but wait till you see the money we're making. The drugs, man. You've never seen so many drugs. Ah can get you literally anything. Coke, ye want charlie? Ah'll get you as much as you need.'

'Ah dinnae take coke, man,' Jools said. 'Ah'm just into a wee smoke, really.'

'Just wait till ye get oot but, Jools. Yer sorted for life, man. This Dr Love's no tae be pished around, though. He reports all the way up to the White House. It's a new plan the government's trying out. It seems to have had results in America.'

A picture of the US president slid into his mind. Jools imagined the cartoon profile to be snorting a line of cocaine from a big pile and they both laughed.

'You're gonnie get in trouble for that,' the voice laughed.

'Fuck them, man. What can they dae tae me?'

'Ah'll have to get going just now. Now you stay in the blue team and you

can't go wrong. Ah'll drop in on you again soon, OK? Remember, true blue!'
Then the voice was gone.

Jools got undressed and went to bed.

⊙

Next morning Jools was woken up by a man with his medication. They'd
changed it to a yellow tablet. He swallowed it and fell back asleep.

⊙

Jools opened his eyes.

'Jools, Jools, Yours Truly wants to talk to you today. You're in trouble for
last night,' the voice said.

'What have Ah done now?' Jools sighed.

'Dr Love's furious with you about last night. Dr David Love is totally against
drugs. He saw what you did with the president's picture. He rang Yours Truly
this morning and told him to discipline you.'

Jools sensed another presence listening in.

'AYE, AH'M LISTENIN'!' another voice growled. 'Ah'm Yours Truly. Ah'm
your doctor on the rehab course and Ah umnae too fuckin well pleased with
your shite, let me tell you. Now you better get your fuckin finger out and
stop fannying aboot! Have you any idea what trouble that thing with the
president could have caused? You do know that the president supports the
David Love organisation? Now Ah umnae too fuckin pleased with you, Jools.
The sooner you get doon to some hard work, the sooner you'll get oot of
here.'

'Ach! It was just a joke, eh?' Jools protested.

'Your joke could have caused a lot of trouble. Do you realise that the
president could have seen that? The David Love organisation is a world-
famous institution. You can't do things like that and expect no one to say
anything.'

Jools felt ashamed. 'Ah didnae mean any harm, eh?'

'The trouble with you is that you don't think. You're ignorant.'

'Awright, Ah'm sorry!'

'If Ah ever catch you bringing our name into disrepute again, Ah umnae
kiddin', Ah'll knock fuck oot you! Be warned, son!' Yours Truly disappeared.

Jools felt like a scolded child and part of him felt like rebelling. He got up
and dressed and went to the smoking room.

⊙

'Wee man, ye ken Ah dinnae like you eh?' a loud voice said.

'What for?' Jools asked.

'Yer gettin fuckin leathered.'

'What have Ah done, likes?'

'Ye're a fuckin beast and Ah dinnae like ye. Ye better stay away fae ma wee brother an aw. Ah'm upstairs and Ah've had a wee look through your manual. You're a dirty wee bastard.'

YLT, the letters flashed on the inside of his eyelids like they'd been slashed with a knife. The Young Leith Team marked his card.

'Ah'm Gary Love and Ah've been watching you fae upstairs. You're a fuckin beast. It says in your file you got a hard-on over two wee lassies. Ye're a racist wee cunt an' aw. It says ye dinnae like gypsy folk. Well Ah'm fae folk an Ah dinnae like you. Wait till ma big mate gets a hold ay ye.'

Jools's heart sank. 'Ah'm nae fuckin beast! Ask anycunt that kens me! Ah've never been accused ay anything like that!'

'Ah dinnae fuckin like ye. And when ye get oot, ye better keep oot ay Leith. Yer gettin fuckin tanned when you get oot. Ah'm gonnie tan yer jaw, ya dirty wee bastard. Yer gettin ripped fae earhole tae arsehole!'

YLT

'Yer manual says ye tried tae shag a cat when ye were a bairn. Ya dirty wee cat-shaggin bastard.'

'Did Ah fuck!' Jools shouted.

'Ye're a dirty wee deviant. Ah hate cunts wi' big mooths fae Muirhoose. If Ah catch ye in the kitchen yer gettin boilin water in yer coupon. Yer gettin fuckin stabbed. Aw these cunts in here are ma pals. They're fuckin choking tae set aboot ye. Ah telt them ye like wee lassies. They're gonnie knock fuck oot you the first chance they get. Every cunt in here. Even the staff will turn a blind eye. They hate beasts an' aw. Even the fuckin screws'll be at it.'

Jools was scared. 'Ah'm nae fuckin beast!' he said stubbornly. He stubbed out his cigarette and went back to his room.

'Ye better stay the fuck oot ay the smoking room two till four. They people are playing their messages. Remember, Ah fuckin run this place!'

YLT

Gary Love was gone. Jools sat on his bed, shaking. A woman pulled back the curtain and checked him out, then left. He wondered what she thought of him. Did she think he was a beast? He couldn't tell from her face. Suddenly a loud shrieking filled the air. An alarm sounded in the corridor.

'Right folks, can you make your way to the landing!' a woman shouted down the hall. Jools was still shaken. He shuffled out into the corridor and followed along with the crowd.

'Yer gettin a sair face when you get oot ay here!' Gary Love said.

Jools was trembling. He tensed his jaw as he approached the crowd gathered on the landing. A man walked past him and he prepared his jaw for a punch. He flinched as someone touched his shoulder.

'Jools McCartney,' the woman called out, marking his presence down on the register. The fire alarm was switched off and a man came running upstairs. 'False alarm,' he told the nurse.

'OK folks! You can go back in now!' she shouted and the crowd started to return to the ward.

Just then the lift door opened and a man wheeled the lunch trolley towards the kitchen. Two bells rang in the hall.

'That's lunchtime, folks!' the nurse shouted.

Jools walked up the hallway towards the kitchen. An Asian nurse sat by the door on a bench talking to a colleague.

'NIGGER!' a voice said as he passed. He felt his arm do a Nazi salute and had to look and make sure his arm wasn't really moving.

'That wisnae me,' Jools protested. 'Ah wouldnae say that tae a lassie. She looks nice.'

He felt really embarrassed. The woman paid him no attention and he went to the trolley and grabbed a tray. He sat at a table on his own and began to eat. His eyes flitted around the room as he checked the faces of the other diners for signs of malice. They generally seemed to ignore him. He shovelled down his food quickly and shuffled back to the smoking room for a quick cigarette before everyone came back. As he passed the Asian woman his arm did the invisible Nazi salute.

'Nigger,' the voice said. 'S… s… s… say nigger. N… n… nigg…'

Jools could feel an electric charge building up in his body and he tried to blank his mind from finishing the word.

'S… s… s… say n-i-g-g-e-r! David Love doesn't like racism. You'll get the max if you do say the N-word!'

His mind started to blank and the electricity decreased. His heart pounded. He felt he'd been pretty close to getting the max and his hands shook. The smoking room was empty except for the elderly woman who sat and ate her lunch. Jools lit a cigarette and smoked it fast. He returned to the dorm and sat on the bed. He thought about going home, he hated it in here. The people thought he was a pervert and they were out for his blood. How did it ever come to this? This whole experience was a nightmare. He pulled the curtain around his bed for some privacy. The sun streamed in through the window and the room was stifling.

BANG! Jools jumped.

'Shut up, Jools!' the voice said. 'Ye're a poof, ye're a Jew! Shut yer mooth!'

He tried to blank his mind but the pressure was becoming painful.

BANG! The door slammed again. He felt his sensitive nerves flinch.

'Shut yer mooth! Literally, shut the fuck up! Ah'm tellin ye, shut up! sssshutuuuup!'

'Ah'm tryin', fer fuck's sake!' Jools lost his patience. 'Ah'm no sayin a fuckin word!'

'Ye're a dirty wee bastard. Ye got a hard-on over two wee lassies it says in yer manual. Shagged a cat when ye were wee? Ye ken Dr Love'll go mental when ay reads this. Aw well, as long as ye dinnae dae anything racist. You'll end up gettin the max if you're no careful, ya dirty wee cunt. How auld were the wee lassies? They werenae pre-pubescent were they?' the voice giggled.

'Fuck off, ya sick cunt! Ah'm nae fuckin nonce!' Jools was raging.

'I never called you that! Did I use that word? No I did not! It's because ye're sick. You're sick in the head. Remember what the man in the Botanic Garden said? You have a yellow nose and forehead. It's in your forehead! You aren't well.'

'If ye ask me, you're the one who's sick. Goin on aboot wee lassies like that. Yer fuckin obsessed. Ah bet it turns ye on, ya fuckin bam!'

'Don't ever, ever say that to me.' The voice became threatening and Jools felt he'd gone too far.

'Don't ever! I'm not like that. It's you, Jools. Dr Love will find out. He will see all of your old thoughtwaves. It'll be Carstairs for the criminally insane. You with all the others.'

'If Ah was a beast, Ah'd put maself in Carstairs.'

'We'll see, Jools. We'll see.'

Just then a guard popped his head round the curtain.

'The doctor would like to talk to you, Jools. Do you want to follow me?' he said.

Jools pulled his trainers on and shuffled along the corridor.

Suddenly his vision started to go black and his head spun. He staggered and dropped to one knee, fighting to stay conscious. The crew-cutted guard had his back turned to Jools and was laughing with a colleague.

'It's the Royal Ed's new gadget. How do you like it? If they don't behave, we just zap them,' the voice laughed.

Jools got slowly to his feet. 'Fuckin bastards,' he mumbled, as he tried to shake off the dizziness. He tried to act normal. There was no way he'd let this cunt see it bothered him.

'Come on then, Jools,' the guard said, and led him to a door. He knocked and went in.

'Jools McCartney here to see you, Doctor,' he said, and left, closing the door behind him.

'Have a seat, Mr McCartney,' the dark-haired Irishman directed him.

Jools sat down.

'Don't say a word, Jools!' the voice said. 'He's just a student and he's got to find out what's wrong with you. You're playing the part of a paedophile. Just feed the pigeons. Play along.'

'Mr McCartney, I brought you along today to give you these. These are your section papers. I'm required by law to read this out to you.'

The doctor produced a photocopied sheet. Jools spotted the coat of arms on the top of the page. He read the words Edinburgh Sheriff Court and rolled the paper up while the doctor spoke.

'Don't say anything. He thinks you're a paedophile. He's just training. Don't talk. Say nothing. Say absolutely nothing,' the voice instructed him.

Jools hadn't really heard the doctor's words. He'd heard something about being held for twenty-eight days and something about his rights but he hadn't heard any more than that.

'Is there anything you want to ask me, Mr McCartney?'

'Say nothing!' the voice told him.

Jools said nothing and blanked his mind. He stared down at his hands not even blinking.

'Mr McCartney. Mr McCartney. Are you all right?' the doctor asked.

Jools said nothing and continued to stare.

'OK, Mr McCartney. You can go back to the ward now.' The doctor stood up and held the door open. Jools got up and shuffled out without a word. He shuffled back to his dorm room and lay on the bed. He looked again at the photocopied sheet and form and sat on the bed. He noticed that they'd spelled his name wrong. He wondered if they'd done that on purpose so the section wouldn't be legally binding. Why did he have to play the part of a paedophile? Why were they using him to train doctors? 'Ah'm nae fuckin beast.'

'Don't call them that, please. We don't refer to mentally-ill people as beasts.

They have serious mental problems, that's why they do what they do. We have to train our doctors to get it out of them. That's why you're here. If you have anything to hide our doctors will get it out of you. Just play the part for the student doctors.'

'Why do Ah have to play a paedophile, likes?' Jools asked. 'How can Ah no just be a sick person or something?'

'We needed someone to play the part for us. We allocated the parts to the actors and they all thought you were the best suited to play the part. To tell the truth, I think it's because you're a schemie. Most of the other actors are from Morningside and places like that. You're from Muirhouse. They needed someone rough so they gave you the part.'

'Actors?' Jools asked.

'Yes. Basically, the hospital is closed for the summer. We're using the building to train our students and doctors. We drafted in some actors to act as patients. It was the ideal place to put you for the summer. They're testing out the new control gadgets on you.'

'That's oot ay order, likes. There was nae need tae knock me oot.' Jools still felt a bit woozy.

'That's just a simple little control device for difficult patients,' the voice laughed. 'It's an American idea. We just got all this machinery from the David Love organisation and we're testing it out. We're trying to find out what the max is like. We've only done it once before and not everyone was there to see what happened. We know it leaves you in intense pain and you piss and shit yourself but we need to do more trials on it. This is the blue team. You're in a Tory ward. Most of the controllers in this ward are strict so you'd better behave yourself or you'll get the max.'

'That's aw Ah fuckin need,' Jools thought. He looked in the drawer for his cigarettes and lighter and found they were gone. He was sure he'd left them there. He searched through his jacket pockets but there was no sign of them.

'Thieving bastards!' he muttered to himself. He went to the office at the end of the hall and asked the blonde nurse if anyone had taken his cigarettes and lighter but they hadn't. He went into the smoking room and slumped down in a chair. The radio was on loud and Travis played. Jools scanned the room for anyone looking guilty. The room was full and he couldn't tell who was an actor or a psychology student. He looked down at the floor. The crosses in the grout of the tiles jumped at his eyes.

'Prestonpans!' he heard.

A tall man sat near the radio, crying.

'Prestonpans!'

He blanked his mind.

BANG! The door slammed and Jools jumped.

'Shut up, Jools. Just shut up!' the voice said.

The blonde nurse he'd spoken to earlier came over to him.

'I've asked in the office about your cigarettes but no one's seen them,' she said. 'Here's a couple to do you just now.' She handed him two cigarettes.

'Period blood!' the voice said loudly in his head.

Jools tried to ignore it. 'Thanks a lot,' he smiled.

'Period blood!'

She left him to attend to the man who was crying.

Jools looked at the floor. There was a streak of red paint splashed across the yellow tiles.

'Period blood!'

He looked away and focused his eyes on the air conditioner.

'Dinnae say nothing, Jools, but Ah've got a wee bit ay a fancy for you,' the female voice said.

He recognised the blonde nurse's voice but she was talking to him mentally, inside his head. She'd vanished from the room.

'Dinnae be scared, Jools. Ah'm in the office. The lassies are away the now so Ah can have a wee chat wi' ye. Ah'm an auld pal ay yer auld man's,' she said.

'She's an auld pro!' a male voice chipped in, laughing.

'Shut up, youse,' the nurse laughed back. 'They're dirty bastards, Ah swear it,' she went on. 'Ye ken ma sister. She steys in your street. Mary McFadden.'

Jools recognised his mother's old friend.

'That's ma sister,' she said.

'She's an auld pro and she's shagged yer auld man!' the male voice interrupted, laughing.

'Shut up youse, that was years ago!' the nurse laughed. 'Ah fancy the arse off you. You're gettin shagged when you get oot,' she said to Jools. 'Ah think you're tidy. Ye're a wee mod. Ah like the way ye dress. Ye've got a tidy wee erse on ye, dae ye ken that?' she giggled.

Jools found her attractive and was excited by her straightforwardness.

'Did you really used tae be a pro?' he asked.

'See youse,' she said. 'That was years ago, Jools. Ah'm no now. Ah work in here now. Ye're no bothered, are ye?'

'Naw,' he laughed.

The door of the smoking room slammed shut and he jumped again. The blonde nurse came in with a small plastic cup filled with liquid and gave it to him. He drank it and thought it tasted like whisky. She went back to the office.

'That was just a wee drop ay the good stuff for ma wee special patient,' she said.

'Cheers, doll.' Jools had perked up.

'Just you wait, Jools. Ah'm gonnie ride you!' she teased him, laughing.

Jools blushed and lit up a cigarette.

'Awwww!!! Ay's shy!' she laughed. 'Dinnae worry, doll, Ah'm gonnie take good care ay ye.'

The door slammed again and he jumped. Another nurse came over to him.

'That's your sister here to see you, Jools,' she said.

'What do you think ay her?' the blonde nurse asked in his head.

'UGLY!' the male voice hollered before Jools could answer.

Jools blushed again. 'That wisnae me,' he said, embarrassed.

'That's a shame,' the blonde nurse said. 'She fancies ye tae. Dinnae be nasty.'

'Honest, Ah dinnae think she's that bad,' Jools tried to explain. 'That wisnae me.'

Jools followed the nurse to the corridor where his sister and her boyfriend stood. He went over and gave his sister a hug.

'Hiya,' he said. 'Do you want to go for a fag?'

They all went into the smoking room and sat around a coffee table.

'How are you feeling today?' his sister asked.

Jools just shook his head. 'Ah want oot ay here,' was all he could say. 'Did ye bring me any fags up?' he asked.

'Ah didn't know you needed them,' she said.

Jools told her about his missing cigarettes and she gave him her packet. She'd get more later.

'What have the doctors said?' she asked.

'Nowt much,' he replied.

'Shut up, Jools! You better not tell them anything or we'll have to hurt them too. You don't want your sister wired up like you, do you?' the voice said.

'Do you feel any better on the medicine?' she asked.

He started to get a lump in his throat and his eyes began to fill with tears. He shook his head in reply.

'That's enough! Get rid of them, Jools. You better not say another word!' the voice threatened.

'Are you all right, Jools? Do you want me to go?' his sister asked.

'Shut up, Jools, I'm warning you!' the voice yelled.

Jools didn't know who to listen to. He blanked his mind and stared into space.

'Just you wait till they go away!' The voice sounded cruel.

'Jools, are you OK?' his sister asked again.

He stared blankly into space.

⊙

Jools lay on his bed with the curtain pulled around. He was thinking of his ex-girlfriend and how proud she'd be if only she knew what he was doing now. He'd helped the SAS, he was going to meet the stars, he'd helped catch a paedophile ring and now he was being trained by a world-famous psychologist. He could see her face in his mind's eye as he thought of the times they'd shared together.

SLAM! Jools jumped.

'Pit it doon!' the voice said.

He blanked all images out of his head.

'It's time. Assume the position,' the voice commanded.

Jools sighed loudly. 'What is this shit for?' he moaned. 'Ah always have tae dae this.'

'Shut up, Jools, just shut up.'

Jools took a cross-legged position and stared at the cupboard door handle. He blanked out all thoughts and soon his breathing had shallowed. A stray picture flashed across his mind's eye.

'Pit it doon!' the voice said.

Jools straightened his back, stretched his arms above his head and settled back, clearing his head again. His fixed gaze began to hurt his eyes and his eye-lids began to feel heavy. He fought hard not to blink and soon tears were rolling down his cheeks and his eyes burned.

'Keep it up. Every day, two till four,' the voice said.

'Aye fuckin right!' Jools huffed. 'Two hours a day? How long am Ah meant tae keep this up for? Ah have tae think, ye ken. If Ah didnae, Ah'd be deid. Ah'm a fuckin human being!'

'Once you can do it for twenty-four hours, then you'll get out of here.'

'No fuckin danger, man! Ah can barely dae it for an hour. How the fuck am Ah meant tae keep it up twenty-four hours? Ah'll never get oot ay here.' Jools felt it was hopeless.

'When and only when you don't have a thoughtwave for twenty-four hours, you will be allowed to leave this place.'

'But that could take years! That's if it's possible. Ah might never get oot.'

'You better start now, then. The sooner you do it, the sooner you'll get out. Concentrate. Don't picture anything. Just be.'

Jools blanked his mind as best he could and settled into it.

SLAM! He jumped.

'Pit it doon!'

Jools stood up and stretched. 'That's aw Ah'm daein today,' he said, yawning. The effort had worn him down. He needed a cigarette and shuffled along the corridor to the smoking room. He noticed the clock in the hall read twenty to five.

'Ah've done longer than Ah thought,' he told himself as he went in and sat down. The girl with the long dark hair stood shuffling her feet in front of a black woman. An older man in a long coat and glasses sat and read a paper. Jools lit a cigarette and drew deeply. The rush of nicotine made him slightly dizzy. The Professor sat in a corner by the radio.

'Jools! Jools! Can Ah get a cigarette off ye?' the scruffy-haired guy asked him.

Jools gave him one and watched as he tried to light it with shaking hands. He looked like he was getting an electric shock through his arms. Jools wondered if he was going through the same as him.

'Keep out of other people's business!' the voice told him.

'Stop scrannin fags, Archie!' the black-haired girl shouted over, smiling with no top teeth.

She danced her way over to Jools.

'He's ma wee darlin', eh?' she grinned, kicking Jools's foot playfully. 'Ah felt um Ah fancied um yesterday, eh?'

Jools smiled at her. He really just wanted to be left alone but played along anyway.

'You remind me ay ma brother. He looked like you. A wee hard man. Ay's in the jail, likes. Ay stabbed somebody. Ay's fae Niddrie. Dae ye ken um?'

'Naw,' Jools replied. 'Ah dinnae ken anyone fae Niddrie.'

The girl shuffled her feet and then started to go around the room emptying ashtrays again.

'Stay away from that girl!' the voice warned.

'How? She seems awright tae talk tae.'

'You've been warned!'

Jools finished his cigarette just as two bells rang in the corridor.

'That's dinner time, folks!' a nurse shouted round the door.

Jools got to his feet and shuffled up the hall.

'NIGGER!' the voice said, and he felt a phantom arm do a Nazi salute as he passed the Asian nurse sat outside the kitchen. As he passed he noticed her eyes were level with his sexual organs and he caught her giving his crotch a glimpse.

'She's checking to see if you've got a hard-on,' the voice said, matter of factly. 'She thinks you're a paedophile. It's part of your cure. No sexual thoughts. Especially about the staff. We will be checking.'

Jools felt embarrassed and grabbed a tray and sat on his own. Soon his table filled up so he ate faster to get away quickly. He scanned his eyes around the room to check for anyone looking at him but everyone seemed to be getting on with their meals.

'Do you want any extra, darlin'?' one of the kitchen staff asked him.

'No thanks,' Jools declined. He finished up and rushed back to the smoking room for a quick one before everyone came back.

⊙

Jools sat in the smoking room puffing on a cigarette. The radio blared in the corner and the old woman sat with her meal on a tray on a coffee table. A fair-haired man spoke in a cockney accent to a young woman.

'Stay away from the left!' a voice said.

He wondered if they meant the left side of the room and moved seats. He finished his cigarette quickly and went back to the ward.

Jools went to the sink at the end of the ward and got a cup of water. Two teaspoons lay on the sink.

'That's fuckin out ay order!' Dr Love shouted. 'Are you taking the piss or what?!' he bawled.

'What? What have Ah done now?' Jools asked

'That's my brother you're slagging off. Jools, Ah thought you'd be a bit more compassionate towards other people's feelings. Ah'm a pretty sensitive guy you know, that could've really hurt my feelings.'

Jools didn't know what he'd done.

'The tea spoons. You know my brother died of a smack overdose? He used the spoons to cook up a shot.'

'Wait a minute. Ah didnae put them there.' Jools felt ashamed but blameless.

'Did you not?' Dr Love paused in thought. 'If you didn't it must have been one of the team. They're all pretty sick when it comes to joking around the building. They must have left the spoons there so you'd see them and they know I watch all your thoughtwaves. They knew I'd see you looking at them.'

'Thank fuck for that. Ah'm glad ye ken it wisnae me.' Jools felt relieved. 'Your workmates sound a bit sick.'

'Oh they are. But you have to be, in this job. They've all lost people through drugs too. It's our way of making light of things.'

'A bit screwy, but wherever turns ye on.'

'We better stop mucking around. Special Branch have been on at us to stop the horseplay. They're in here to guard you lot.'

'Special Branch?'

'Yes, they're in here mingling so you don't get nosey and blow their cover. Try not to look for them and don't think too much about them in case you can still be picked up on the outside. We seem to have disrupted the outside signal,' Dr Love said.

Jools felt safer knowing Special Branch officers were guarding him.

He lay back on his bed and relaxed a bit. He felt really drained and he soon began to drift.

Jools awoke to a dark ward. He turned on his bedside lamp and rubbed his eyes. Suddenly the electric current paralysed him, sticking him down by the elbows.

'Naw! No again!' Jools tried to struggle.

'Oh yes! We must!' the voice said laughing.

The current grew stronger and the soles of his feet began to burn.

'AAARRGGHH! DINNAE!!!' Jools screamed as a hot steel wire pierced the top of his head and started to spiral around his skull and neck bones. The hot wire descended into his torso, splitting at the shoulders and corkscrewing around his arm bones and muscles. The steel penetrated his spine and sent wires up into his brain, writhing around the contours of his grey matter. The wire continued to spiral around his leg bones and down into his feet and the ends began to heat up with the current. Pressure began to build in his head and he felt a wire curl around inside his brain tissue. The wires started to coil inside the walls of his skull, just above both ears. Jools could feel where they exited his head, pulling the flesh of his scalp into peaks. He tried again to struggle but could not move.

'What's happening to me?' he asked.

'We're putting a little device in. Stay still,' the voice replied.

'Take it oot! It's hurtin ays!'

'We're putting a recording device in. Just be quiet.'

SLAM! Jools jumped.

The electricity started to burn his hands and feet.

'It's a virtual implant. Stay still and keep quiet. We're nearly done.'

'This hurts!' Jools shouted. 'Let me go. Ah can feel it in me. Take it oot!'

The current began to die down slowly.

'TEE HEE!' the voice mocked him.

Jools could still clearly feel the two wire coils behind his temples.

'They stay for the time being.' The voice said. 'They're your implants. You have a spider in your head. They're there to help you. You know all that self-improvement stuff you were reading. It's all leftist spin. It's really screwed up your head. It's hurt a lot of people. Stay away from that book. You've put a spider in your head. When you read all that stuff you thought up a circuit inside your brain. That book just made it easier for the left to gain control of your head. I told you you've been sick. You are really not well. Let the virtual implants do their trick. It'll take all that crap out of your head. That Californian stuff you were reading. It's New Labour spin. It's not good for your head. They just use it to control the masses. You were totally caught up in it. You've had no mind of your own for a long, long time, Jools. Remember, stay away from the left. It's all about mind control.'

Jools thought about it. He thought all the self-development books had helped him, although he had been feeling ill for a long time.

'Do you think they'll get it oot ay me?' Jools asked.

'The coils in your brain will take it out before they dissolve. It'll take a while but we'll get it.'

The steel wires started to pull out, unwrapping themselves as they went. The skin on the top of his head nipped where the wires entered. Slowly they began to untangle themselves from around his bones and muscles and soon Jools was left with just the two coils above his ears.

'Can Ah move now?' he asked. There was no reply so he chanced moving. His elbows ached from the invisible force that had held him down.

'Ah take it we're finished?'

No answer. He got up and went for a cigarette. He felt groggy and was unsteady on his feet. He shuffled up the corridor and went into the smoking room. People sat around the TV and talked.

'Stay off the TV. Don't sit too close to it. It'll cause interference and static to get caught in your head,' the voice said. 'And stay away from the left.'

Jools sat down. There were no spare seats so he sat on a unit by the wall. He lit a cigarette and scanned around the room.

'Jools, Jools. Can Ah get a fag off ye?' scruffy-haired Archie asked.

Jools didn't have many but gave him one anyway.

The Professor was there. The cockney guy sat talking loudly to a woman and someone turned the TV up. The dark-haired girl sat slumped in a chair, snoring. Jools smoked fast. He still didn't feel too safe in here. He wondered who was the Special Branch.

SLAM! 'Pit it doon!'

Jools blanked his mind automatically.

'Shut up, Jools!' the voice said.

He looked down at the tiles for somewhere to stare.

'PRESTONPANS!'

Jools struggled to control his thoughts.

'Aw, no again! That's no me!' he explained. 'Ah'm no daein that.'

His eye caught the splatter of red paint.

'Period blood!'

He stubbed out his cigarette and left the room. Outside in the hall, two middle-aged women sat in chairs.

'That's the night staff,' the voice told him. 'They're watching every move you make. They'll turn a blind eye to you getting leathered. They're ma people.' It was a different voice. It was Gary Love again.

'Ah'm upstairs and you're gettin fuckin leathered! Ye're a fuckin beast! Ah heard ye got a hard-on over two wee lassies. Ye're gettin fuckin stabbed. Dinnae go runnin tae the staff for help. They dinnae like beasts either. Ah made sure they aw found oot what you done, ya fuckin dirty bastard!'

Jools was scared but annoyed too. 'Dinnae fuckin start aw this shit again. Where are ye gettin aw this shite fae? Ah'm nae fuckin beast!'

'It's in yer manual. Ye're a sick fuckin pervert. Yer thoughtwaves will show us if ye have or no and if you have had any sexual thoughts aboot bairns, you're gettin fuckin chopped up, Special Branch or no!'

'Right then, ya fuckin bam! Ye'll no find anything like that in ma heid!' Jools was boiling.

'Ye better fuckin keep oot ay Leith an aw!' the voice spat.

YLT: the letters slashed into the backs of his eyelids.

'Fuck off! Ah'm too auld for aw that gang shite. So what, Ah used tae run wi' the MCF. It's just cause Ah'm fae Muirhoose, eh? That's what it is. You've got yer mates wi' ye, yer feelin hard. Ah'm no a fuckin beast! Ah've never been under suspicion ay that in ma life. Ask anycunt!'

'Cunt, ye better shut up or Ah'll come doon and leather ye now!'

YLT

The presence retreated and Jools was scared and alone again. He buried his face in his pillow. He thought of home and began to sob. He just wanted to go home.

⊙

The lamp by the next bed switched on and the blonde-haired cockney guy from the smoking room pulled the curtain around him. Jools could hear him fumbling around in his bedside locker.

'How are you, mate?' the cockney voice said in the gloom.

'You can hear me?' Jools asked mentally.

'Yeah, I can hear you. Keep your thoughts clean and to the point. I'm from Special Branch. We're here to look out for you. Don't muck about on our time. We've no time for larking around.'

'Is that you in the next bed?' Jools asked.

'Yeah, well you're not really supposed to know who I am but I don't suppose it'll matter. Just don't blow my cover. You can talk to me late at night but you'll have to pretend you don't know me around the ward, OK?'

Jools was excited. 'Ah'm glad you're here,' he said, relieved to have someone on his side.

'Are you keeping alright?' the cockney guy asked. 'You sound a bit pissed off.'

'It's just aw this shit. Ah want oot ay here. It's daein ma nut in. They're aw weirdos in here. They think Ah'm a beast.'

'Yeah, I know. We heard. You stick to your guns. Don't let 'em push you around. Don't worry. We're watching after you. We need you to play the part for us. It's dangerous, I know, but just let 'em think the worst for now. You're doing great. Don't worry, I promise they'll know you're alright before you leave. We're more interested in catching the ones on the outside. There's not that many left, you know. I think you've been wired up too long, personally. You're starting to lose hope. I don't know what Dr David Love's got planned for you lot but it'll be pretty spectacular, I'll bet. Just hang in there.'

Jools noticed the cockney guy's voice was a little hoarse-sounding. 'How do you dae that wi' the voices? How come nae one else can hear us?' he asked.

'I'm wearing a throat mic. The kind of thing divers use. I don't actually have to talk out loud to be heard. This thing's sensitive.'

'What happened tae the SAS?'

'They had to finish up after they got Mackenzie but they left us some of their gear. Don't worry, there are a few of us staking this place out. We're sure they'll come here eventually. It's only a matter of time before they come to us. Then we'll nab 'em. This'll probably go on until the general election.'

'When's that? Ah've no been allowed any telly for a while.'

'Soon, soon. We'll get rid of all these New Labour head-shrinkers. All that leftist spin has got a lot of people sick, you know. They have to go. They've taken over people's minds. Dehumanised them and turned them to near slavery with their so-called work ethics. These people are dangerous. We as a nation have a duty to stamp out what's happening so this'll never happen again. No one should ever have to go through this. The message has been spread by word of mouth. The people will know who to vote for.'

'Is that why Ah've tae be a Tory Liberal? Is that how Ah'm in the blue team?' Jools wondered.

'The two main opposition parties as well as the SNP are banding together for this one ballot, then after that New Labour can be disbanded.'

'Only if we win.'

'That's right. It has to be done democratically. This is being backed by the Royal Family. Their hands have been tied by this too. This is your chance, Jools, to do something for your country. You're in the position to help us to help you.'

The Special Branch officer turned his bedside light off.

'You better get some sleep, Jools,' he said, yawning. 'Remember, don't blow my cover. Don't let on or try to talk when you see me around. And don't try and spot the other officers. We've got a hard enough time as it is with our cover. I'll contact you when I need to.'

'Awright,' Jools said. 'Night, man.'

'G'night, Jools.'

Jools lay back in bed and turned his lamp off. He felt restless and it was too warm in the room.

'Ah wonder how much the Special Branch can see of my thoughtwaves,' he wondered. 'Thank fuck Ah didnae think ay anything illegal,' he laughed. 'The amount ay dealers Ah ken. Ah could get half ay Muirhoose locked up. Ah wonder if they've peeked at that. They must want tae find out if Ah ken anything aboot smack or anything heavy. Polis are polis. They're aw nosey.'

'Yeah, I can fackin hear that, Jools. I ain't looked at that part of your mind. I'm not allowed. You got a special pardon on this one. But if you want me to get suspicious just keep thinking like that. I can see all your thoughtwaves on the computer in the morning.'

'Ah'm no intae anything heavy,' Jools said in his defence. 'Ah just smoke a bit hash now and again.'

'Well, that's not too serious. I'm sure I can turn a blind eye to that,' the Special Branch officer said.

'What, ye mean Ah've got a licence tae smoke and ye'll no bust me?'

'I wouldn't go that far. As long as I don't see it.'

'Cool. Jools M fae the Muirhoose posse! Home Office licence to lum!' he laughed. 'Fuckin untouchable!'

'Look, it's alright for you but I've got to get up early tomorrow so can you quiet down and let me get some sleep? The sooner this gets done, the sooner I can go home to my family. I'm missing me wife.'

'Right, man,' Jools said. He tried to blank his mind to keep quiet. He sat in the gloom staring at the door and the corridor beyond. One of the middle-aged women from the hall brought him in a tablet and a glass of orange juice.

'Medication, Jools,' she said.

He took the tablet and once again sat and focused his gaze on the empty doorway. The heat in the room started to make him feel uncomfortable and he tossed and turned. Soon he could hear the cockney Special Branch officer snoring. He started to want a cigarette and got up. The two women were putting the drugs trolley away for the night when Jools went into the smoking room. It was silent in the room. An old man with glasses sat in one corner reading a newspaper and a heavily built man with a beard sat rocking in a high-backed chair. Jools lit a cigarette and sat down on the right-hand side of the room. The bearded man got up and walked to the door. Jools noticed he walked like a monkey and laughed to himself. The man was in bare feet and his soles were filthy from the floor.

Jools sat back in the chair and closed his eyes. It was the most quiet it had been since he came in here and he was enjoying the tranquillity.

BANG! He jumped.

He opened his eyes. The old man had left the room and the door had slammed behind him. Jools sat alone in the silence. A dim lamp shone in the corner next to the radio. He closed his eyes again. The tension started to ease from his scalp muscles as he relaxed. He was still aware of the two coils in his head but the more he relaxed the more he seemed to accept them. His head began to feel heavier and heavier and he started to breathe deeply, almost nodding off. His eyes flickered then slowly started to open involuntarily. His eyes started to move slowly in tight triangles.

'Don't move, Jools!' the voice said. 'Stay still. Yours Truly's bag of tricks is in residence.' His eyes started to speed up, tracing tight triangles faster and faster. Jools tried but could not stop it.

'Just stay still for a while longer,' the voice instructed him. 'Ah'm just making a little adjustment for Dr Love. Don't tell anyone about my techniques. They are not to be discussed with anyone. This is top-secret stuff. These techniques are still at an experimental stage. They were being tested by the military until recently. Never, ever tell.'

His eyes spun faster, then began to slow down.

'Ah'm just uncrossing a few connections. Ah'm actually looking into your brain through your eye. Ah can see all the little knots of cells in there. There's a bit ay damage but Ah can sort out the connections and untangle the knots.' His eyes stopped and Jools became aware of a hook being pushed down behind his eyeball.

'AAARGHHH! What the fuck are ye daein?' He nearly jumped out of the chair as the hook hit a nerve, causing the muscles to spasm.

'Ah told ye to stay still. Ah'm nearly done. You know this procedure is normally done under anaesthetic but Ah umnae gonnie be long so we didnae think you'd mind terribly. Now hold still…'

Jools didn't dare move an inch.

'How are the implants settling in? Are they uncomfortable?' Yours Truly asked.

'No too bad,' he replied. 'Can Ah move yet?'

'Nearly done.'

His eyes flicked around in their sockets. They felt like they were being pulled by some magnetic force. Jools pictured them being dragged round by an electronic pen touching a computer screen.

'That's us now. That wasnae too bad was it?' Yours Truly sounded pleased.

'Is that us finished? Can Ah move now?' Jools leaned forward and lit another cigarette.

'Ah've just put a couple ay wee stitches in there so nae exerting yourself for the next day or two. Let things settle. And remember, nae talking about Yours Truly's bag OK ? Ah umnae kiddin'.'

'Will Ah have tae sign the Official Secrets Act?' Jools laughed.

'This is a bit more secret than that, Jools. Ah'm serious. Tell no one. Ever. You could get twenty years for it.'

'Ah've got a spider in ma heid and stitches in ma brain and Ah've no tae tell anyone aboot them. Ah hear ye.'

'Dinnae talk about the spider. It's never to be spoken of!' Yours Truly scolded. 'These techniques are worth millions ay pounds, Jools. You're one ay the first people ever to benefit from this new technology. It's top-secret stuff. They thought it would help ye. We don't want anyone outside listening in so you've got tae put it all away out of your mind. Do we understand?'

'Aye, Ah understand.' Jools was starting to feel tired. 'Ah'll no say nowt. Can Ah go tae ma bed now? Are ye finished?'

'You can go.' Yours Truly left him alone.

Jools finished his cigarette and shuffled off to bed. His head hit the pillow and he dropped off straight away.

⊙

'Jools, medication.' The blonde nurse handed him the plastic cups. He took the tablet and lay back. The sun shone brighly through the window and Jools could see the Pentland Hills from his bed. He got up and shuffled through to the bathroom. He went into the cubicle and stood in front of the toilet, pulling his dick out to pee. He felt a painful throbbing at the base of his shaft. He looked down to see an angry red boil on his member.

'Aaaaaaw naw!'

'Ah've got a spot on ma cock!' the female voice laughed.

'Away tae fuck! Can Ah no go for a pish withoot you stickin yer faces in?' Jools growled grumpily.

'We have to watch you all the time. It's our job,' the woman said.

'What, even when Ah'm havin a shite?'

'All the time.'

Jools squeezed at the boil but the pain was too bad. His knob throbbed as the spot grew redder.

'Stop that! That's disgusting. It's a stress boil. Leave it alone.'

Jools zipped up and left the cubicle.

'Now wash your hands!' the woman tutted.

Jools stood sleepily in front of the mirror. His eyes seemed sunken and dark rings circled them. His face was drawn in and his skin dull and grey.

He dried his hands on a paper towel and shuffled into the hall. An involuntary twitch squeezed his penis and he dribbled in his jeans.

'Ah've pished maself!' the woman laughed.

'That wisnae fuckin me!!! Stop it, ya cunts!' Jools bawled.

'EEUUGHH yuk! You've pished yerself,' she giggled.

Jools stomped up the hall to the kitchen and made a cup of tea. He took it into the smoking room and sat down with a cigarette.

'Jools, we're only having a laugh with you. Don't get all grumpy now,' she teased.

'Nae wonder, man! Ah'm just oot ma fuckin bed an yer at me. Fuck off and leave ays alone!' he huffed.

'Aw, Jools. Don't be like that. Don't muck about. Shut up, Jools, just shut up!'

'Fuck off!'

'Don't be like that. We've seen worse, you know. You should see some of them we get in here. We have to watch you having a shit. Imagine what it's like for us,' she said. 'It's just a spot, don't get upset.'

'Is there naewhere private at all?' Jools asked.

'We have to watch you all the time. We can see your thoughts on the screen. We see what you do. Do us a favour, will you? Try not to go for a shit at lunchtime will you? We're all eating at that time and it's bad enough. Don't worry, we won't tell anyone about your boil.'

Jools felt totally embarrassed and his face flushed. He felt truly disgusting and wanted to hide himself.

'You know, you ought to pay more attention to your personal hygiene. You're not a bad-looking guy but you've let yourself go a bit recently,' she said.

'Ah know. Ah've been ill,' Jools replied. 'Ah'll get a good bath today.'

He looked around the smoking room. The Professor sat in the corner by the TV and the black-haired girl sat talking to Archie, the scruffy-haired guy. The Special Branch officer talked to a tall, older man and Jools noticed a couple of faces he'd not seen before. A tall young guy in a Hearts top stood talking to a man and Jools overheard him mention something about Lockerbie.

'His mum and brother were killed in Lockerbie. You weren't meant to hear that,' the woman's voice said. 'Don't think about it.'

An animated picture of a plane exploding in mid-air flashed across Jools's mind.

'Stay away fae gliders!' the voice said.

Jools was mortified. 'That wisnae me! Honest, Ah never thought that! That's oot ay order! Slagging people off!'

'You must stop thinking about that, Jools,' the woman said. 'None of you are to know each others' business. That was a big mistake. Put it out of your head totally. He's a psychologist's son. His dad's one of our senior psychologists. He won't be too pleased if he finds out you know all his business. Please Jools, don't think about what you heard.'

'Stay away fae gliders!' the voice said, as the picture of the plane exploding flashed across his mind's eye.

'That's no me!' Jools pleaded his innocence. 'Ah never said that. It's oot ay order. Someone's fuckin aboot. Ah'm no takin the blame for that.' He felt embarrassed and tried hard to supress his thoughts.

'Jools, stop it now, you're getting worked up. Now calm down.'

'Stay away fae gliders!'

Jools's heart was racing as he tried to calm himself. The exploding plane invaded his mind again.

'I think you'd better stay away from him for a while, Jools,' the woman said, sounding worried. 'You do realise that he'll have to be told about your business in return. I'm really sorry about this. If you know about him he has to know about you. He'll be given the chance to get his own back. If you slag his life he gets to slag yours.'

'Awright, but Ah didnae mean it. It wisnae me that said that.' Jools finished his cigarette and left the room.

'Stay away fae gliders!' the voice said. The plane exploded.

SLAM! Jools jumped.

'I told Eddie you heard him talking about Lockerbie,' the woman said. 'And he said, "Ye're a poof and a Jew." That's it. That's him got his own back. You two better keep away from each other from now on.'

'Fair enough.' Jools shuffled back to his bedroom. He sat back on his bed and his mind began to drift. He thought of his ex-girlfriend and how he missed her. He missed Muirhouse and wished he was back there where he belonged. He started to feel hungry and shuffled along to the kitchen.

'NIGGER!' The voice filled his ears and his phantom arm gave a Nazi salute as he passed the Asian nurse sitting outside. A short line of people queued up in front of the water boiler on the wall, taking it in turns to fill their cups. Jools helped himself to some bread and put it in the toaster, then sat down at a table to wait. An old woman with a shrill voice squawked loudly to her friend as she stood in line for tea. The toast popped up and Jools buttered it with the only knife he could find. He was walking to the sink where the old woman stood when he felt his arm start to rise. He checked himself as he felt a phantom arm savagely plunge the butter knife in the old woman's back.

His heart pounded. 'That was a close one,' he said to himself when he realised he hadn't really done it. He left the kitchen with his toast, shaken.

'NIGGER!' his arm rose invisibly.

He shuffled down the long corridor back to his bedroom. He passed the smoking room and on his right was another door marked Quiet Room. The door was wedged open wide. Jools did a double take as he saw the tall older man sitting in a highbacked chair totally nude. The man was talking to someone matter-of-factly as if nothing was out of place.

Jools laughed to himself and went to his room. He sat on the bed and ate his toast.

'Jools, are you there?' the Special Branch officer asked.

'Aye, Ah'm here.'

'Jools, I need to ask you to eat with your mouth closed. If you think while your mouth is open you can be detected on the outside.'

'Awright, Ah'll try and remember,' Jools said.

'Listen, don't try and look for our guys around the ward. Don't break our cover. Remember we're watching after you.'

Jools got up and stretched. He walked to the window and looked out across the Pentland Hills.

SLAM!' He jumped.

'Pit it doon! Stay off the Pentlands!' a voice checked him.

He went back and lay on the bed. He sat gazing into space when the curtain pulled back and a dark-haired nurse looked in on him.

'Do you want to go for a walk, Jools?' she asked in a Canadian accent.

'Aye, please.'

'Well, you get dressed and we'll take you for a little walk around the grounds, how about that?'

'Sound.'

'OK. I'll be back for you in five minutes.' She left him to dress.

Jools pulled his socks and trainers on and put on a sweatshirt.

'Don't wear purple!' the voice told him. 'Purple's the Royal colour. You don't want them to know you're working for Her Majesty do you?' the cockney officer said.

He took it off and tied it around his waist. 'It's all Ah've got. It'll be awright like that, eh?'

'That's OK. Now when you're outside, be guided. They've been setting this up all morning. The people you see outside are all our people, so don't worry. We've got them all in place so they'll look natural and if anyone comes near we'll nab them. You just have to follow the staff. That nurse is the Royal Navy's finest. She's doing a pretty damn fine job undercover. She's one tough lady. She's a combat veteran.'

The woman came back for him accompanied by a man and they walked up the corridor to the hall.

'Don't try and pick out our people now. Just be normal. Don't look at them,' the voice instructed him as Jools and the two nurses descended the three flights of stairs. Jools thought it best to be safe and looked down at the ground to avoid anyone's gaze. The man and woman talked to each other and Jools followed along behind them. People passed them and Jools couldn't help wondering if they were all police officers.

'Some of them are Royal Navy,' the voice said, 'but don't try to spot them. If you spot them we'll have to take them off the case and replace them. It's a major headache.'

The two nurses led Jools out across the lawn. The sun was blazing down and a light breeze rustled the trees. Jools breathed the fresh air deeply. He been stuck indoors for God knew how long. They headed across to a huge cedar tree with an old park bench next to it. Jools sat down on the cracked wooden slats and pulled out his cigarettes, offering them to the nurses.

'No thanks,' the woman said. 'We've got our own.' She pulled out a packet of Marlboro. 'So how are you doing?' she asked. 'We hear you've been not so well. Can you remember the police bringing you in?'

Jools nodded. 'Ah'm awright,' he said. 'Ah just want oot ay here.'

'Yeah, it's pretty tough being stuck in here, especially with the heat we've been having. What do you do with yourself when you're not in here?'

'Nowt much really. Weight trainin'. Ah read a lot. Go tae the pub, and Ah practise ma martial arts. That's aboot aw Ah dae.'

'Trisha's just done her first parachute jump for charity,' the male nurse said.

'Aye? Was it scary?' Jools asked.

'No. I really enjoyed it. I'd like to do it again,' she said.

Jools was impressed. Not only was she tough, strong, fit and brave, he found her very attractive too. She could throw him around any day. 'Ah hope she's no got access tae ma heid,' he thought. That would be embarrassing. He wondered if she'd been the Canadian accent he'd heard a few nights ago and not his cousin after all. She had a radio stuck to her belt. Was it her hand he'd been holding? He looked around the long grass by the tree. His eye caught sight of something glinting in the sunlight. He looked closer. The pile of empty purple tinnies made him cringe and he struggled to hide the memory of his days bingeing on super lager. 'Ah'll be keepin that tae maself,' he thought, as he finished his cigarette. 'Ah wonder if they put them there to test me.'

He stood up and they started slowly back to the ward.

'She's yer cousin's best pal,' the voice said. 'She grew up with your cousin, they went to college together. That's why she's assigned to you.'

'Cool,' Jools thought. 'Maybe Ah'll get to know her later on. She'll want to know me when Ah'm famous.'

·

Two bells rang in the hallway. 'That's lunchtime, folks!' a woman shouted.
Jools made his way up the corridor to the kitchen.

'NIGGER!' The voice screamed as he passed the Asian nurse. The arm gave
a salute and Jools tried to ignore it.

He lined up in front of the food trolley as a heavily-built man with a black
beard passed out the trays.

'He's Navy,' Jools thought to himself. He stood out a mile in his white
sleeveless shirt and black slacks. His big shiny shoes were the biggest giveaway.

'Don't look for our people, I told you!' the cockney voice shouted. 'Fuck's
sake, Jools, I told you earlier, now will you fucking listen! I'm going to have to
replace him now. Jools, wake up for fuck's sake. Stop pissing about and get
with it. Stop trying to figure out our game.'

'It's no ma fault!' Jools protested. 'He's too fuckin obvious. Ay looks like a
busy.'

'Listen, if you know our game, they know what we're up to. They can still
get a signal outside, you know. Why do you think they're teaching you not to
think? It's to quiet your mind down so they can't eavesdrop.'

'Ah canny fuckin dae it! It hurts too much!' Jools shouted.

'Jools, you've got to get with it. They need you to be able to do it for twenty-
four hours. So far you've managed about an hour and a half. You've got to get
down to work. We're already running behind schedule, now get to it.'

'But Ah canny dae it for that long! It's impossible. A deid man could go
twenty-four hours without a thoughtwave. Is that what ye want? Dae ye want
me deid?' Jools couldn't see any hope.

'It's the only way! There are no other options. We've tried everything else!'

'Can you no just put me to sleep? Gie me a jag and put me under? Surely
that would work.'

'Jools, we need you awake. We need you almost catatonic. We need you quiet
for twenty-four hours. I'm sorry, but there's nothing else we can do for you.'

Jools felt hopeless. It was a daunting task. Even if it was possible it could
take him years.

'Aw Ah kin dae is dae ma best,' he said bleakly.

'OK, Jools. I'll talk a bit more later on. Now you stick to your two-till-four
sessions and you'll soon get there. I've got to get back to work.'

'Catch ye later,' Jools said. He finished his dinner and hurried along to the
smoking room.

Jools sat down on the right-hand side of the room with his back to the
office window. Two young men sat in the corner and the old woman sat

crying, being comforted by a male nurse with a skinhead. Jools felt he was intruding and hurried to finish his cigarette. He tried not to look at the woman.

'Period blood!' His eyes caught sight of the red paint.

'Prestonpans!' The cross in lights flashed across his mind's eye. One of the young men got up and put the radio on loud and a cheesy techno beat pumped out. Jools stubbed out his cigarette.

He sat back and closed his eyes.

SLAM! He jumped as the door banged shut.

'Pit it doon!' He automatically blanked his mind. Eddie, the tall guy with the ginger hair and the Hearts top, came back from lunch.

'Stay away fae gliders!' The plane blew up in his mind's eye.

Jools's heart raced as he struggled to block it out.

'Stay away from each other, Jools,' the female voice said.

He got up and went back to his room. 'Will ye stop fuckin orderin me aboot?' He was sick of being picked on.

'Ah've got a spot on ma cock,' the woman laughed in a squeaky voice.

Jools felt embarrassed. His stomach started to rumble and he began to need the toilet.

'Jools, not when we're eating,' the woman protested. He skipped quickly to the toilet cubicle and sat down on the pan.

'Jools, that's how none of us fancies you. We have to watch you having a shit. It's pretty digusting for us.'

Jools tried but could not go. He tried blanking his mind. Still nothing.

'Don't worry, I'm used to it. I'm a healthcare professional,' she said, putting him off again.

'Can ye no just leave me for two minutes?' Jools asked.

He tried to distract himself by reading the grafitti on the door.

He looked around the cubicle and his eyes caught sight of a pattern in the marble veneer on the wall. It was a cross with one spar out of alignment.

'Cygnus the swan,' he thought. 'They've left a sign for me.' The secrets of the masons entered his head and he struggled to blank them out.

'Cygnus and diarrhoea!' the woman said.

'Dinnae fuck aboot wi' that!' Jools shouted. 'The secrets. They stay wi' me. They could cause you a lot ay trouble. The masons wouldnae be too pleased to hear you're giein away their secrets.'

'Cygnus and diarrhoea!' The cross pattern jumped out at him. 'You know a lot of the Navy guys are masons,' she said.

'Well they'll no be too pleased if you start stealin secrets oot ay me, will they? Ye better shut up aboot that, Ah'm warnin ye. How did you hear about that anyway?' he asked, inspecting the boil on his dick.

'We watch your thoughts when you're in bed at night. We can see your thoughtwaves. You had a funny dream last night. That was us. We can make you dream about anything. It's easy, we just talk to you through a brainwave monitor when you're asleep. Your subconscious takes it in like auto-suggestion and you dream about whatever we say. We watch all your old memories when you're asleep. I'm in a room along the corridor. Upstairs has a computer in the lab.'

Jools farted loudly and blushed.

The woman tittered. 'They all heard that in the office,' she giggled.

It was no use. He couldn't go and zipped himself up.

'Now remember and wash your hands, Jools,' the woman said. 'We're here to make a new man of you.'

Jools did as he was told.

'What was that earlier about the purple tins outside, Jools?'

'Aw, nowt,' he covered up.

'Dr Love hates that kind of thing. You'll really get it if he thinks you're like that.'

He dried his hands.

'Brush your teeth and have a wash!' she commanded.

'Awright, awright, fuck.'

'We insist on cleanliness. HY-GIENE!' she sang.

'Is that you bein difficult?' Yours Truly's voice interrupted.

'Naw, Ah wis just sayin', there's nae need tae be on ma back twenty-four hours a day. She's been at it since Ah got up again.'

'Listen son, you and me are gonnie fuckin well fall oot if you don't stop fuckin around! Ah umnae going to tell you twice. Do as you're fuckin told! You fuckin better buck up your ideas, laddie, or Ah'm gonnie kick your cunt in personally. And what's all this about you drinking the purple tin? See if Ah find out you've been involved in alcohol abuse Ah'm warnin you, you'll be for it!'

'Ah've no done nowt!' Jools said, trying to blank his guilt.

'I heard about your antics with the two wee lassies. Ah mean it, Jools, you're skatin on thin ice. If Ah find oot you've been having sexual thoughts about wee lassies Ah'll kill you myself. Ah've got a daughter, Jools, and the thought of some piece of shite touching her makes my skin crawl.'

'Check if ye like!' Jools was adamant. He felt like scum and wanted to shrink out of existence.

'Jools, that kind of thing makes ma blood boil, Ah umnae kiddin'. Ah canny handle that. You've got to understand, we get the worst of the worst in here. We've got to treat them. How do you help someone like that when you really just want to cut their dick off and kill them? Now Ah've heard you got a hard-on over two bairns. What am Ah supposed to think? Ah'll have tae go through your thoughtwaves and see for myself.'

'Fair enough,' Jools shrugged. 'But ye'll no find nowt.'

'Now you better get with the Love programme. You know what's required of you so get on with it! You've wasted enough time. And you better watch yourself in the kitchen. One or two of the lads in the other wards have heard rumours. They're not too friendly, if you know what Ah mean. Make sure security's there whenever you go. It's best you stay off the ward as much as possible for your own safety.'

'Great. That's aw Ah need.'

'Now Ah'm going tae leave you for the day. Ah'll be back in touch later.' The presence left him.

Jools went back and sat on his bed with his head in his hands.

SLAM! He jumped.

'Pit it doon!'

He lay back and tried to unwind. The thought of home and his cat all alone brought a lump to his throat. He went for another cigarette. The radio was on loud in the smoking room and it was full of people. He smoked quickly as his eyes darted around for signs of hostility. The Professor smiled at him with his comical, saggy face. The tall older man stood laughing hysterically with a friend. A big wet patch spread out across the groin of his sand-coloured trousers.

'He's just had the max,' the woman's voice said. 'It's made him pish himself.'

SLAM! Jools jumped. A short fat man entered the room quoting passages from the Bible.

'How are you, my friend?' he asked Jools.

'Ah'm awright,' Jools croaked. He realised it had been a couple of days since he'd last spoken to anyone out loud.

'Don't worry, my friend. Jesus will help you.' He made a cross in the air. 'God bless you, my son.' Jools smiled. 'You know I was very upset earlier, I do apologise. They won't let me out to worship at my local parish church and I became very angry with them. I do not mince my words, I'm afraid. I must apologise for my language.'

The man caught sight of someone else and wandered away.

SLAM! Jools jumped.

A middle-aged balding man stood in front of the radio with tears rolling down his cheeks. A small plastic juice bottle and some sweets lay on the table in front of the radio.

'Leave the room when other people are playing their messages!' the voice said.

Jools stubbed his cigarette out and left the room.

'That man lost his daughter to a paedophile. She was sexually assaulted and murdered. That's the charity you did your walk for. It's for children who have been abused. And now we find out you had sexual thoughts about wee lassies. What kind of a position will that put our organisation in?' the voice hissed. 'Wait till Anastacia hears about that. Do you really think she'll want to meet you then? She'll probably sue us for damages. I doubt if any of the stars will want anything to do with this project. This is a multinational company we're talking about here. We really thought you were the right man for the job. All your family and friends nominated you for this treatment. You've let them down too. And your grandmaster will have a thing or two to say to you. I doubt you'll be able to go back to training if they hear about this. That's what everyone's so annoyed with you for. You were meant to be the one. The one that was good, genuinely. The one that made the grade. Then we find out this. You better keep a low profile around here or I can't guarantee your safety. Can you imagine what they'll do if they find out next door? They'll tear you apart.'

'But Ah've no done it!' Jools bawled. He started to cry.

SLAM! He jumped.

'Shut up, Jools, just shut the fuck up!'

Jools sat on his bed, blubbering to himself.

'Ah've got a spot on ma cock!' the squeaky voice goaded him. 'Shut up, Jools, shut up! Ye're a poof, ye're a Jew, shut yer mooth!'

'Fuck off!'

'OOOH! He's throwing a tantrum. Get up, Jools. Get up or Ah'll have tae hurt ye.'

'Fuck off!' Jools fumed through gritted teeth.

A stab of pain like a needle hit his eye socket. 'Get up!' the voice shouted.

'AAAARGH! Fuckin stop it!' He sat up.

'It's time. Assume the position!'

Jools fidgeted. His head throbbed and his back and buttocks ached. He stretched his spine and swung his legs over the side of the bed. He got up and shuffled up the hall. The wall clock read five-ten.

'There, Ah've done extra time today. Ah've earned ma fag.' He gave himself a pat on the back.

He went into the smoking room and the door slammed behind him making him jump. The black-haired girl sat by the radio. The Professor, Eddie in the Hearts top and a woman sat by the window. The old woman still had her lunch tray on the table in front of her. Jools sat on the right-hand side and lit a cigarette.

'Jools, Jools, can Ah get a cigarette off ye?' Archie asked in his slow drone.

Jools tossed one over and Archie grabbed for it with a shaking hand.

'Stop fuckin scrannin fags, Archie!' an old man with glasses shouted.

'Ah remember twenty year ago. Ah wis at Powderhall at the dug track. Ma brother-in-law wanted me tae put a grand oan a dug. Ah'd never pit a grand oan a dug.' He laughed. 'Dae ye bet, Jools?'

'Naw.'

'Would you put a grand oan a dug?'

'Naw.'

'Goan chuck ays that paper over, Jools.'

Jools threw him the *Sun*. He opened it at the racing pages and chewed the end of his pen while scanning the form. 'Ah'd never pit a grand oan a dug,' he mumbled to himself, smiling. 'Did you used tae go tae Powderhall, Jools? Tae the dug races?' he asked.

'Aye. When Ah wis young. Me and ma mates used tae skive in through a hole in the fence at the side ay the turnstiles. Ye go through a car park. It took ye intae the kennels area. We goat a chase off an auld guy one night for pingin tickets at him wi' elastic bands. This auld cunt must have been an ex-marathon runner or somethin'. He chased us for aboot a mile, man. Ah pinged him oan the back ay the neck a fuckin beauty. It must ay stung like fuck.' He laughed. 'Ah went tae the speedway a few times tae. Did ye ever go tae that?'

'Aye. A couple ay times.'

'It was loud as fuck, eh? The engines oan the bikes. It was the Edinburgh Monarchs.'

The black-haired girl shuffled over to them. She stood dancing in front of them, smiling a gummy smile. 'There's ma wee mellow man! Wee cool gadgie! Where you fae again, doll?' she asked, her speech slurred.

'Muirhoose,' Jools answered.

'Dae ye ken Billy Osbourne and that? He stands at the shops wi' Cammy and Smegs an that?'

'Aye. Ah ken them. Dae ye ken Donna Riley and Geggy and big Stu and that?'

'Aye Ah ken them aw. Ah used tae get ma DFs off ay Geggy. Dae ye ken John Doyle fae Boswall? That's ma ex-felly. He's oan the junk still but ay's awright. He's a good dad tae the bairns.'

'Ah dinnae really ken anyone fae Pilton,' Jools said.

'How long ye steyed doon there?' she asked.

'Aw ma life. Ah steyed in Davidson's Mains for a year when Ah was aboot two and Ah steyed in Leith for a while when Ah was aboot three. That's it.'

She picked up the ashtray and went to the bin to empty it.

Jools caught site of Eddie in the Hearts top.

'Stay away fae gliders!' the voice said. The plane flashed through his mind. He closed his eyes and tried to blank out all thoughts.

'Jools, he's going to lose the rag with you if you keep that up,' the voice said.

'It's no me! Ah canny stop it.'

'You do know he'll have to get his own back for this, don't you?'

'Whatever!' Jools was sick of arguing.

The sun went behind a cloud, casting the room in shadow.

'Was that me?' Jools started. He tried to think with a positive spirit. The sun emerged again. Jools's heart pounded.

'I'm afraid so, Jools. We've wired you up to a weather satellite. You have to control it with your thoughts,' the voice instructed him.

Jools panicked. The sun started to cloud over. He struggled to put on a happy attitude. The sun slowly started to shine through.

'They're monitoring you from RAF Turnhouse, Jools,' the voice said. 'Keep up the good work.' The presence left him.

Jools drew his legs up on the chair and sat cross-legged, too terrified to move. He closed his eyes and blanked his mind, forcing a positive feeling into his spirit. He could see the sun brightening up the room through his closed eyelids. He was aware of someone sitting next to him and opened his eye slightly to see the black-haired girl sitting cross-legged next to him.

'Ah'm jist daein yer Buddha wi' ye,' she gummed.

⊙

'Jools, this is Mrs McGuire.' A plump, dark-haired nurse introduced a curly-haired woman with glasses; she looked in her late fifties. 'She's here to talk to you. She wants to see you're OK.'

Jools sat down and the woman pulled up a chair.

'How are you?' she asked. Jools noticed she wore a ring. It had two hands linked together. He wondered if it was a masonic ring.

'Don't worry. I'm Jim McGuire's sister,' she said mentally. Jim was a good friend of his uncle's. 'It's better if we speak this way, Jools, so the rest of them can't hear us. I was sent by friends to make sure you're being treated OK.'

'Who sent you?' Jools asked.

'Remember, only in emergencies?'

'Slag!' a male voice shouted. 'Fackin murderin bitch!' an English voice added.

The woman wrinkled her nose and kept her cool.

'Do you want to do something?' she asked. 'What about a jigsaw puzzle?' she suggested. 'I'm with the Lodge. I'm a grandmaster in the Dublin lodge,' she said mentally.

'Yeah, she's a fackin murderin IRA bitch!' the English voice shouted.

'That's the Royal Navy for you,' the woman said calmly. 'Let him make up his own mind! Remember Jools, you do have friends.'

'Thanks,' Jools said, 'but that's a bit heavy for me.'

They started to line up the jigsaw pieces on a table.

'Look, someone's written on the back of the pieces,' she pointed out.

Jools didn't have a clue what he was doing and felt uneasy sitting there.

'Look, they're there for you,' she said, and tried to pass him something.

'Don't take it, Jools!'

'Yeah, tell her to fack off!' the Navy voice shouted. 'Get rid of 'er!'

The chopping noise of an engine grew louder and louder in the room. Jools heard a helicopter fly past level with them in the building. The vibrations shook the floor.

'That's security for you! Her Majesty's finest!' the English voice bawled out.

Jools stood up. 'Ah'm really tired, missus,' he said, nervously excusing himself. 'Ah'll have tae be going tae ma bed. Thanks for visiting.' He scuttled back to his room at top speed.

⊙

Jools sat on his bed in the semi-darkness. 'Maybe tomorrow Ah'll get oot,' he thought to himself. The curtain pulled back and a nurse brought him his tablet. He took it and lay back, closing his eyes and trying to relax.

SLAM! He jumped.

'Shut up, Jools!'

He blanked his mind.

YLT flashed up in red letters like blood.

'Ah'm up here watching you and Ah'm sick ay aw the noise comin fae you. It's settin the machine off every two minutes and daein ma nut in. Ye better fuckin settle doon, wee man, Ah'm tellin ye!' the voice said.

'Ach, Ah've got tae think sometimes, eh?' Jools answered back. He could hear the throbbing of the bass thumping on the ceiling.

'Wee man, you're that wee racist cunt fae Muirhoose, eh? Ma pal wants tae talk tae you.'

'You're that dirty wee cunt fae Muirhoose, eh?' a woman asked. 'Ah've seen inside your heid and ye're a manky wee bastard. Ye've got a big spot oan yer cock an' all, ya dirty wee cunt.'

'She had a shot ay lookin through yer thoughwaves earlier. She thinks ye should get yer cock cut off for that,' the male voice added.

Jools pictured the Young Leith Team in the lab.

'We're here tae look after ye when the doctors go hame at night. We're having a wee party and playin wi' all the brains. It's great fun. We made a wee cunt in ward three pish ays self in front ay everybody earlier. Zapped fuck oot ay um. So you're a Tory then?'

'Naw, Ah'm nae Tory,' Jools replied.

'Well ye're in a Tory ward. Ye ken Ah dinnae like you, eh? Ye better stay away fae ma wee brother tae, ya fuckin dirty wee cunt. Ay says ay's gonnie leather ye. He fuckin hates beasts.'

'Wee man, wee man!' another voice interupted. 'Wee man, Ah hear ye've got a problem wi' black folk?' the voice sniggered. 'Tellin racist jokes amongst yer pals. Ah heard ye ken a few beauties. Go on, tell ays yer best blackman joke,' the voice laughed.

The other voices giggled in the background and Jools could sense something was going on.

'Come on, ye ken a few nigger jokes, tell ays one. Nowt wrong wi' niggers, son. As a matter ay fact, Ah think everybody should have at least two! Aye, ya wee bastard! Ye can tell Ah'm black, eh? Ya fuckin wee racist cunt!'

Jools felt the electric charge building inside him and his heart almost leapt from his chest. The hair on the back of his neck stood on end.

'Gie me one fuckin reason why Ah shouldnae fry your ass right now?' the black guy growled. 'Ah could sit here and gie you the max until the doctors come in in the mornin. Naebody could say nowt aboot it. Ah dinnae like your type, Jools. Ye're a manky wee cunt. Ah'm gonnie look through your thoughtwaves and see if Ah find any racist stuff, Ah'll come back and fry your arse, Ah'm fuckin tellin ye.'

YLT: the letters cut into the back of his eyelids.

Jools was frozen stiff with fear. The current began to die down. He slid quietly under his covers.

⊙

The light in the next bed switched on, illuminating the ward. The cockney Special Branch officer brushed his teeth by the sink. He finished up and went back to his bed, pulling the curtain round.

'Alright, Jools? I'm just calling on you to see if you're OK.'

'Awright, man. Did ye catch anybody then?' Jools asked.

'No, but that was spot-on earlier. That IRA bitch. I didn't think they'd have the bottle to turn up here. SLAG! Fackin murdering cow! You did good to send her away, Jools. We're all proud of you. Actually, there was another reason why I wanted to talk to you. I need you not to think after twelve. A Chinese spy satellite passes over us at midnight every night and we need you to keep quiet for us while you've got the spider in you. It's highly secret technology and we don't want the Chinese getting hold of it from fifteen miles up.'

'Ah'll dae ma best,' Jools said.

'I'm going to bed now,' the officer said, yawning. 'It's been a long day.'

'Do you carry a gun?' Jools wondered.

'Why do you want to know that? Yes, I carry a firearm. It's my duty. You're always asking dumb questions. Now I've got to get some sleep,' he said. The light switched off.

Jools sat twiddling his thumbs in the dark. He got up and shuffled up the corridor to the smoking room. He pulled out a crushed packet and straightened a crumpled cigarette. The room was totally empty and he sat in the silence and smoked. He rested his head back against the wall and closed his eyes. He began to feel light-headed from the smoke and the blood throbbed around the coils in his temples. He opened his eyes to see an Asian man sitting in a chair opposite him. He hadn't heard the man come in. The man sat and silently stared over at Jools. His gaze seemed to go right through him as if he were invisible. Jools started to feel a bit wary but tiredness took over and his heavy eyelids closed.

SLAM! He jumped.

An old man with glasses shuffled over and sat down, lighting a cigarette. The Asian man was gone from the room. Jools shivered. He finished his cigarette and lit another. A tea trolley stood in the middle of the room. Jools put his hand to the teapot but it was cold. He helped himself to some digestive biscuits from a plate. The old man picked up a paper and started to read.

'Stay still!' the voice said.

'Naw, no again!' Jools tried to struggle. He could not move.

'I just have to put another stitch in,' Dr Love said. 'You've burst last night's one.'

Jools felt the hook go down behind the back of his right eye.

'Now don't move!' the doctor ordered.

He could feel invisible threads being pulled through his scalp and the two ends being drawn tight and knotted on top of his head. The skin on his face pulled tight.

'There now, that's us. Now don't strain, Jools. I want you to keep these stitches in. They lock off part of your brain so we can concentrate on the parts we want. Now it's vital you don't burst these stitches. I can't keep putting them in.'

'When am Ah gettin oot?' Jools asked.

'When you can do the One for twenty-four hours. Twenty-four hours without a thoughtwave, then you'll get out. This operation should make it easier for you.'

'But Ah'll never dae it!' Jools moaned.

'Of course you will. Other people get out of here, don't they? Anyway it's nearly midnight. You better go to bed.'

Jools finished his cigarette and left the room. The hall clock read eleven-fifty. He went back to his bed and blanked his mind as he looked out the window to a dark, starless sky.

He closed his eyes and tried to rest. A little white box appeared in his left eye. It moved over to the right and disappeared. Another box appeared in his left eye, moved over to his right and disappeared. Then another, and another. Jools began to make out a shape on his mind's eye. It was a carriage clock. The clock grew bigger as it started to come towards him. The clock melted into his head and stuck firmly in his brain. Jools could feel the wheels in the mechanism spinning and whirling round in the centre cavity of his skull. The clock's second hand ticked round and a counter-weight spun around clockwise then slowed and spun anti-clockwise. Jools gripped his head.

'Get that oot ay me!' he shouted.

The clock ticked on.

⦿

Jools awoke to find the clock still there. He lay there gritting his teeth until the curtain pulled back and the blonde nurse brought him his medication. He took it and tried to go back to sleep.

'Jools, Jools, get up, Jools!' the female voice said.

'Fuck off! Get rid ay the clock!' he shouted.

'Jools, dinnae be like that. Ah'm yer pal. Remember Ah used tae be a pro. Ye just missed yer chance. Ah was just in wi' yer medication. Ye could have geid me a wee bag off, Jools. Ah thought ye liked me,' she said.

A little white box moved from his left eye to his right.

'Can ye no get rid ay this clock? It's daein ma nut in. Ah can feel all the wee wheels whirring around in ma heid and it's crackin me up,' he said.

'Sorry, Ah can't. Dr Love put it there. But get up anyway.'

Jools got up and put his old jogging pants on. He shuffled up the hall to the smoking room. The old tall man, an old woman and hair bear Archie were in the room.

'Jools, Jools, can Ah get a cigarette off ye?' Archie mumped.

'Ah've only got a couple,' he replied. 'Is there anywhere you can get some?'

'Aye, there's a shop. But it'll no be open yet,' Archie said.

'Here! Dae ye want a fag?' the tall man asked Archie, and threw him a cigarette.

The radio blared in the corner. The Charlatans played. Jools had never heard this new track. It was the first track from their new album. He pulled out a broken cigarette and doctored it back together as he'd learned under the tunnels at school when he'd been one of the regulars at breaktimes having a fly puff. The door slammed and he jumped. A short guy with blonde shoulder-length hair came in sweeping and mopping the floor.

'Mind your feet a minute, blue,' he said in a cockney accent as he swept under Jools's chair.

'He's Special Branch,' Jools thought, as he watched the man disguised as a cleaner.

'Shut up, Jools! Stop figuring out other people's games!' Yours Truly said. 'He's no Special Branch. He's Royal Navy. He's here tae protect you lot so stop thinkin about that. Do you want everyone tae know who he is?'

'It was too obvious!' Jools said. 'He sticks oot like a sair thumb.'

'Ah'm no bothered. Dr Love's put a lot into this. We dinnae need the bother of replacing the guards because they've been spotted. Now stop thinking aboot what you saw!'

Jools tried to blank his mind. He could feel the mechanism of the clock spinning in his skull. He finished his cigarette and went to the toilet.

'Ah've goat a spot oan ma cock!' the woman squeaked in a high-pitched voice, laughing. The boil had grown redder and angrier and throbbed as Jools peed. He finished up and gave a careful shake.

'Hands!' the woman clipped.

Jools went over to the sink to wash them. His dick gave an involuntary twitch and he dribbled down the leg of his jogging pants, leaving a dark patch.

'Ah've pished masel',' the woman laughed.

'Fuck off!' Jools bawled. 'You cunts are fuckin crazy, by the way. Fuckin spastics!'

'Now brush those teeth!' the woman instructed.

'NAW!!! Ah'm no daein it,' Jools yelled.

'Ah've goat a spot oan ma cock!' she giggled.

'Can ye no leave me alone for two fuckin minutes? Ya fuckin radged cow!'

'Cleanliness, Jools! Hygiene! Don't be tacky.'

He looked in the mirror as he washed. The dark rings around his eyes seemed worse and another large spot was coming up in his earlobe.

He shuffled up the hall to the kitchen for tea and toast. A big dark-haired guard with tattoos sat outside on the bench listening to the radio. Jools went to the water boiler and poured a cuppa. A short queue waited behind him for the spoon. He had noticed they were short of cutlery, especially knives. He put a couple of slices of bread in the toaster.

'Only use blue cups!' the woman said. 'The other stuff belongs to ward five! You better avoid ward five! They don't like you because of the two wee lassies.'

Jools was wary but made his toast anyway.

'That's a load ay fuckin shite. Ah'm no like that. Ah'm no a fuckin beast, Ah telt ye!'

'Shut up, Jools! Just shut up!' the woman laughed.

Jools took his tea and toast back to his bedroom and sat on the bed munching, being careful to close his mouth while chewing.

A needle stabbed him in the side and he flinched.

'AAARRGH! What ye fuckin daein?!' he bawled.

'Ye're a poof, ye're a Jew! Shut yer mooth!'

Jools was sitting gazing out the window when the male nurse with the crewcut came in.

'We're going to move you to another room Jools, can you collect your things together?' he asked.

'He doesn't like you, Jools!' the voice said. 'He's a martial artist too. He's a wing chun kung fu teacher in his spare time. He heard about you and the two bairns and he's choking to kick fuck out of you! He fuckin hates paedophiles!'

Jools cautiously got his belongings together and followed the man. He took him down to the end of the hall to a single room. The room contained a bed and a small bedside cabinet. The walls had been stripped bare of paper and Jools thought it looked like a Romanian orphanage.

'I'll be along in the office if you need anything,' he said, and left Jools to unpack. The window looked out onto a small annex full of rubbish and dead potted shrubs.

⊙

He went up to the office and knocked on the door. A slim, dark-haired male nurse answered.

'Can Ah go for some cigarettes the day?' Jools asked.

'Can you give me a few minutes? I'll have to get someone to take you down, we're really short-staffed at the moment. I'll come and get you in a few minutes,' he said.

The clock in his head gyrated and spun. He went to wait in the smoking room.

'It's a sting,' the cockney Special Branch officer said. 'Now you have to act completely normal. We've set it up and the timing has to be spot on. Everyone you see today will be one of our people. They're all in place, so hurry up.'

Jools walked down the corridor and descended the stairs with the skinny male nurse. They got to the bottom and along past some paintings and photographs on the wall. Two men came towards them and passed with impeccable timing. His heart began to pound and he felt very nervous about being out and about. A woman passed them from behind and turned off down a side corridor. They passed a fat porter pushing a trolley and Dr Molloy, the Irish doctor, crossed the hall in front of them. They stopped at a small shop in the corridor and the nurse waited outside while Jools went in. A queue formed in front of the till. Jools bought a packet of cigarettes and they turned back to the ward.

'SEXY BUM!' a voice shouted to the male nurse as they climbed the stairs.

Jools went into near panic. 'That wisnae me! Ah never fuckin said that!' he pleaded his innocence. 'Ah'm no a fuckin poof!'

The weights in the clock spun around in his skull making him feel off-balance. They walked down the corridor and they passed a young fair-haired guy of around twenty-five sitting outside the office.

'Do you know they've got a gym in here?' he said to Jools.

Jools just smiled.

'He's one of you,' the voice said. 'He's got they eyes. The same eyes you've got. You're the one. You've got they eyes too. Do you understand? You're all related in some way. It goes way back, before you were born. That's Gary Love's brother. His grandfather came to this country during the war. He was on the same ship that brought your granny here from Egypt. You're all from the same folk. Dr Love is a New York Jewish psychiatrist. His family had to leave what's now part of Palestine during the war. Your granny was the interpreter on that boat. The Nazis wiped out most of his relatives. That's why he's so down on racism. Never, ever say the N-word. If you do, you'll get the max. It's all part of the puzzle. Dr David Love is the only one who knows what's really going on.'

Jools went into the smoking room. Emma, the dark-haired girl, was sitting in a chair asleep with her mouth open and her knickers on show. The Professor smiled over.

'Jools, Jools, did ye get fags? Ah'll go tae the shops for ye if ye want,' Archie droned.

'Ah got some,' Jools replied.

'Can Ah get a cigarette off ye?' Archie asked.

'Don't! He's not to get any cigarettes. He's in here to learn,' the voice said.

Archie's hand began to shake violently as he reached out for the cigarette. Jools wondered if they were giving him a shock.

SLAM! Jools jumped. Eddie came in still wearing his Hearts top.

'Stay away fae gliders!' the voice said as the plane exploded.

'That wisnae me. That's shan as fuck, slaggin the boy,' Jools began to panic. He finished his cigarette and nearly scuttled back to the wrong room.

'Eddie said ye're a poof and ye're a Jew for slagging him,' the woman's voice sighed.

Jools sat on his bed as the clock spun and ticked in his head.

⊙

Two bells rang in the hall and Jools started to shuffle towards the kitchen before the nurse announced lunchtime. He got to the kitchen before most of the ward and grabbed a tray and sat down by the window. The kitchen window looked across to some trees and a block of offices. Jools wondered if they were watching him from an open window on the second from top floor. He noticed a silver car driving out of the car park. It was a Mercedes Benz and he was sure it was the same car that had been at the West End a few weeks before. Who was the man in the silver car? Why was he following him? He lifted the lid on his plate. Liver. The sight made him gag.

'Period blood!' the woman laughed. 'Ah'm pure tryin to make you sick, Jools. You make us sick. We have to watch you having a shit when were eating so we're going to be disgusting while you eat. PERIOD BLOOD! Shut up, Jools just shut up!'

Jools tried to blank his mind.

'Two wee lassies!' she laughed. 'You're a disgusting cunt! They werenae pre-pubescent, were they?'

'FUCK OFF!' Jools choked. 'Ah'm no a paedophile. Ah'm no a fuckin beast!'

'Lick oot ma stringy discharge!' she giggled.

Jools started to retch. He dropped his fork on the plate and left the kitchen.

The smoking room was empty. Jools smoked a cigarette quickly and lit another. The door slammed and he jumped. The Professor shuffled in and sat over by the TV. Emma, the tall older man and a woman all came in together.

'Stay away from Emma!' the woman's voice said. 'She's the fixer-upper! Stay away from her, Jools! She knows all the local psychos. All the local faces. She's from Niddrie but she moved to Morningside a few years ago and now she's pretty well known. We use her to control the patients. If you don't do what she tells you she'll have you seen to. She used to be a patient but now she's trusted. She works for us now.'

Eddie came in.

'Stay away fae gliders!' The plane blew up.

Jools stubbed out his cigarette and went back to the kitchen for a cup of tea.

'S… s… s… Say nigger!' the voice said.

He tried hard to blank his mind. He could feel the electric charge building in his legs and spine.

The electricity peaked, then died down as he reached the kitchen. It left him shaking and his heart pounded. He poured himself a cup of tea from the water boiler and shuffled back to his room. He closed the door behind him and sat down on the bed, clasping the cup in his hands. He was aware of the heat radiating into his hands.

'See when this is over,' the female voice said. 'You're gonnie meet the Dalai Lama! He wants to meet you! He thinks you're a natural! He's interested in how you get on. Concentrate, Jools. Feel it inside you. Feel the energy!'

Jools concentrated.

'Feel the energy within you, Jools. Let it shine!'

Jools felt the energy expand from his navel. A gold light grew in him until he was completely enveloped and the energy radiated from his body, making his hair stand on end. The energy expanded with each breath, filling the room from wall to wall with a golden light.

'Ah'm a fuckin god! Ah'm the One! Ah can dae fuckin anything!' Jools was exhilarated. He felt the air rushing past him as if he were flying at incredible speed, a gold blur trailing out behind him like a comet.

Higher and higher he flew, his heart pounding as he became more and more excited. He closed his eyes and breathed deeply, inhaling the energy from the air. A computer graphic on the inside of his eyelids showed a human silhouette.

Jools concentrated the energy. He made it grow more intense. The head of the computer graphic silhouette split in half, the two sides opening apart with each burst of energy Jools expelled. He let the energy ebb a little. The two halves of the silhouette drew back together, making the head shape whole again. He expanded it again and the energy flared up more intensely. He thought this feeling would send him through the roof. He rushed inside and felt he understood everything.

Doubt struck him.

'Wait a minute. Dinnae be daft. Ah'm no a god. Ah'm gettin too carried away wi' maself. Ah'm getting too excited. What are you daein to me?' Jools gasped as his feelings plummeted back to earth.

The energy slowly started to subside. He tried to breathe deeply and calm himself but he was on the brink of hyperventilating. The gold light began to dim and fade and he started to come down. A feeling of deceleration began to fill him and a sense of disappointment came over him with the realisation that he wouldn't feel that good forever. He felt like he'd just been on a rollercoaster.

'Ha ha ha!' the voice laughed. 'We had you going there, eh? Thought you were a god and everything! Ha ha ha! It's time! Assume the position, ya wee bam. Remember, two till four.'

Jools got comfortable on the bed and began to clear his mind. Someone had written G-ROK 2000 in purple chalk on the wall. He focused on the O of ROK and drifted out of this world.

⊙

Jools's head hurt. He'd stayed blank for what seemed like hours and the effort had ground him down and left him with a splitting headache. He stood up and felt light-headed. He shuffled up the hall for a cigarette. The hall clock read six forty-five. He rushed to the kitchen but found he was too late for dinner. He hadn't heard any bell and no one had shouted. He walked back to the smoking room, mumbling to himself about the injustice. As he passed the office he saw a new face. A man stood talking on the phone on the other side of the glass. Jools looked him in the eye. He was filled with a sense of dread.

'That's Billy Love,' the voice said. 'He's got those eyes too. He's fae folk. He's no too happy wi' you so you better stay out of his way! He thinks you're a racist. His laddie told him about the two wee lassies and he's really not happy wi' you.'

Jools ducked into the smoking room and lit a cigarette.

'Dinnae let Billy Love see you smoking! Billy Love absolutely hates smoking!' the woman's voice warned him.

Jools turned his back to the glass to hide. He finished the cigarette and lit another. He puffed on it nervously.

The room was full and the TV was blaring. Smoke nipped his eyes.

SLAM! He jumped. A man and a woman came in, visiting. The cockney Special Branch officer sat talking to a woman in the corner. Jools finished his cigarette and scuttled back to the safety of his room. He passed Billy Love in the corridor. He wore a navy blue shirt and had piercing blue eyes.

'Aye, ye better fuckin git. Go on, fuck off tae yer bed oot ma sight!' the voice boomed.

Jools made his room double-quick and jumped straight into bed.

'Ah'm Billy Love and Ah'm no too happy wi' you, let me tell ye!' the voice shouted. 'Aye, Ah'm a mason! And what's this Ah hear aboot you and wee lassies?'

'It's no true! Ask anybody that kens ays,' Jools protested.

'Well that's what ma laddie telt me! And what's this aboot ma people? Aye, Ah'm fae the 'Pans. East Lothian. Ah'm fae folk. Ah dinnae like wee fuckin paedophile rapists who smoke! Ah hear ye dinnae like ma people?'

Jools started to cry. 'Ah'm no a paedophile!' he blubbed.

'SHURRUP! Stop fuckin blubberin. Ye're makin me fuckin seek!' Billy Love spat.

Jools tried to stop crying and pulled the cover over his head.

'You better stay away fae ma laddie! Ah'm goin doon tae ma local for a pint after this and see if Ah hear another peep oot ay you the night, Ah'll come along there and fuckin leather ye! Ah fuckin mean it! Ma laddie will tell me later and if Ah have tae come back here tae check on you the night, Ah'm no kiddin', Ah'll burst ye!'

SLAM! Jools jumped. He sat under the duvet and tried to keep his mind quiet. The coils in his head throbbed. He eventually fell into a restless sleep.

⊙

The room door opened and Jools woke with a start. He saw the silhouette of a woman coming towards him in the dark carrying a torch.

'Medication, Jools,' she said, handing him the plastic beakers. He downed them and settled back to sleep.

⊙

'Jools, Jools, dinnae say nowt.' The woman's voice woke him up. The early morning sky was dark grey and it looked like it would rain. Jools sat up and pulled his tee-shirt on.

'Dinnae worry, doll. It's me, yer pal Jane wi' the blonde hair. How are ye daein, doll? Ah just thought Ah'd gie ye a wee shout. Ah'm chokin tae ride you, by the way. Wait till you get oot, ya sexy wee bugger,' the woman laughed.

Jools sat on the side of the bed, rubbing his eyes. He got up and went to the toilet.

'Ah can see you, by the way. Ah dinnae mind watching you in the toilet. It's just part ay the job, so dinnae feel embarrassed about going in front ay me.'

Jools sat down and tried to blank his mind as he did his business.

'She's an auld slapper! She used tae be a pro!' a male voice laughed in the background.

'Cygnus and diarrhoea!' The marble effect jumped out at him.

He finished up and left the cubicle.

'Ye better wash your hands, Jools, before they all start all their moanin',' Jane told him, and he complied. 'Ah nearly came along tae your room last night, Ah'm no kiddin, Ah'm that horny for ye.'

'Ye should've,' Jools said.

'Wait till you get oot, it's gonnie be barry. Just me and you. Ah'm gonnie shag the arse off ay you, just you wait!' she laughed.

'She wants yer cock! She's a dirty auld cow!' the male voice shouted.

'D'ye hear that, that's terrible,' she sniggered. 'Ah'm no kiddin', Ah canny wait till Ah get a hold ay ye.'

Jools felt flattered and smirked to himself. She was about the only one who'd been nice to him and he felt quite attached to her. He shuffled up the hall. The clock read seven-twenty. He found the smoking room empty and sat and smoked cigarette after cigarette, enjoying the peace of early morning.

⊙

SLAM! Jools jumped. The skinheaded male nurse came in with two plastic beakers and Jools took his med. The sun had come out from behind the clouds and the smoking room buzzed with people. The radio was on loud and people sat around smoking and chatting. Jools shuffled up the long corridor to the kitchen and made some tea. He was walking back to his room when the nurse stopped him. 'Jools, Dr Bates would like to see you this morning. I'll come and get you later,' he said.

'Ah'll be in the smoking room,' Jools answered, and went in for a cigarette.

The TV was on and was turned up quite loud.

'Stay off the TV! No news!' the voice ordered.

Jools turned his seat away from the set.

'Stay away fae wee lassies!' the female voice laughed.

'Fuck off!' Jools spat. 'Ah'm no in the fuckin mood.'

'Ah've goat a spot oan ma cock!' she giggled. 'Dr Bates thinks ye're disgusting! Ye're a dirty wee paedophile wi' a big spotty cock!'

'Ah'm seek ay fuckin listenin tae you, ya nippy cow! Shut the fuck up!'

'Dr Bates has been watching you from the lab. We've seen all yer thoughtwaves, ye're a manky wee bastard!' she laughed.

SLAM! He jumped.

The male nurse came over to him. 'Dr Bates will see you now, Jools,' he said, and Jools followed him up the corridor to the landing at the top of the stairs. He knocked on the door and went in.

'Come in, Jools,' the young woman said. 'Have a seat.'

Two young women sat round a small table. Jools felt embarrassed. They'd seen inside his mind, watched him on the toilet and they knew about the boil on his dick. What must they think of him? He felt disgusting and wished the ground would swallow him up.

'We'd just like a word with you about the way things are going. How have you been feeling?' she asked.

'Awright. When can Ah get oot?'

'You're under section, Jools. We have to get you better first, then we can think about going home. Tell me, how are your thoughts? Have you been down recently? Is there anything on your mind? Any invasive thoughts?'

Jools blushed. 'Naw,' he lied.

'DINNAE SAY FUCKIN NOWT!' the voice boomed. 'SAY FUCK ALL! SAY FUCKIN NOWT! She's a student doctor. Say nowt. It's her job tae find oot what's wrong wi' you. Ye've no tae tell her. Just be blank, Jools. Ah need you to just be.'

Jools blanked his mind and ignored the women.

'If we could help you, Jools, what would you say are the biggest problems you have just now? How can we help you? Jools? Jools?'

Jools stared into space, his face expressionless.

'She kens aw aboot ye, Jools!' the voice said. 'The spot! The wee lassies, everything! Thinks ye're a disgustin wee paedophile!'

'Jools, are you OK?' Dr Bates asked.

Jools continued staring.

'That's it, Jools. We want you catatonic,' the voice said.

'OK, Jools. You can go back to your room now,' Dr Bates said. Jools shuffled back to the smoking room.

'Jools, can Ah get a cigarette off ye?' Archie held out a shaky hand.

Jools threw him a cigarette, although he was getting a bit sick of handing them out.

SLAM! He jumped.

A striking looking blonde girl entered the room. Jools watched her as she tended to an elderly woman. He'd never seen anyone like her and couldn't take his eyes off her. He watched her as she flitted from person to person. Then she left the room and went back to the office. Jools gazed at her through the glass. He felt ashamed to be seen in this state and decided he would clean himself up.

⊙

'Jools, it's me! How ye daein, buddy?' the voice said.

Jools recognised Terry Williamson's voice instantly. He was his brother's best mate.

'Jools, say nowt! Say fuckin nowt tae these cunts! Dinnae tell them fuck all!' the cheeky wee curly-top laughed.

'Terry, man! How the fuck are you in on this?' Jools asked. 'How can you talk to me?'

'Ah'm doon the road. In the scheme. Ah'm in for ye! Dinnae worry, Jools, wait till you get oot! Ma cousin works in there. That bird ye called ugly. She's ma cousin Sandra! She got ays on.'

'Thank fuck you're here, man. You're a wee shark, by the way. You can get in anywhere. Did ye hear aw they Leith cunts? They keep callin ays a beast, says they were gonnie set aboot ays,' Jools said.

'Dinnae worry, Jay man. Fuckin smelly Leith bastards!' Terry laughed. 'They want tae fuckin start wi' the ghettos we'll gie them it. Ah'll have half ay fuckin Muirhoose up here if they start.'

'It's one ay the Loves. Gary Love, Ah think it is. Ay's upstairs at night gien me aw sorts ay abuse. Ays wee brother's in here and ays dad works here. Ah'm gettin it fuckin tight fae aw sides. They say they'll get half the ward tae go against ays. Telt ays Ah wis gettin stabbed.'

'Fuckin Leith wankers! Is one ay them a nigger? Ah'm sure Ah ken who ye mean,' Terry said.

'Aye, that's them. They threatened tae zap ays for bein a racist.'

'Fuckin black bastard! Ah do ken who ye mean. If they dae anything, Jay, just gie's a shout. We're in!'

'Does yer cousin ken that bird that's workin the day? The blonde bird,' Jools asked.

'Who, Claire? Ah ken Claire.'

'Is that her name? She's fuckin beautiful, man. Is she goin oot wi' anybody?'

'She's fae Barnton. Ah dinnae think she is goin oot wi' anybody. Are ye intae her, likes? Ah'll get ma cousin tae put in a wee word for ye, likes,' Terry laughed.

'Naw, ya wee cunt!' Jools said. 'Ah mean it, ye better no say nowt, Terry!' Jools was blushing.

'Ma cousin says she's no seein anybody. Ah'm tellin ye, Ah could tell ye a story or two aboot Claire. Ask her what happened wi' the hairbrush!' Terry giggled.

'Nut! You better shut up, Terry, Ah'm no kiddin!' a female voice cut in. She sounded annoyed.

Terry laughed loudly. 'What's up, Claire? Ye gettin a beamer?' Terry goaded her.

'You're a little bastard, Terry, Ah'm no jokin'. That was years ago. Stop goin on aboot it!' she warned him. 'It wasnae true!'

'That's Claire, Jools. She's in the office and she's ragin wi' me!' Terry laughed.

'What happened wi' the hairbrush, likes?' Jools asked, sniggering slightly.

'Nowt! You better shut up, Terry, Ah'm warnin you!' Claire shouted.

'What? Ah wisnae sayin nowt!' Terry acted the innocent. 'It's him that fancies ye!'

'YOU'RE A WEE BASTARD, BY THE WAY!' Jools laughed, blushing again.

'She's intae ye, by the way, Jay. Fire in!' Terry blabbed.

'Ah'll talk tae her later,' Jools said, trying to be cool.

'Ah've got tae nash, Jay. Mind if ye need ays, Ah'm in. Ah'll see what these Leith cunts have got tae say before Ah go. Ah'll catch ye later, Jay!' Terry's presence faded and Jools was alone again.

Two bells rang in the corridor and he shuffled to the kitchen for lunch.

⊙

Jools puffed on his cigarette. The smoking room was full and the collective smoke burned his eyes. The radio was on full blast in the corner and an older man stood in front of it weeping silently.

'Leave the room when other people are playing their messages!' the voice said.

The Professor looked over to Jools and shrugged his shoulders. Jools noticed that the Special Branch officer was missing. He'd not been at lunch either. He finished his cigarette and left the room. He walked down the hall and went into the dorm. The Special Branch officer's bed was empty. Everything was gone.

'The Special Branch have left the building, Jools,' a woman's voice said. 'It's just the Navy guarding you now.'

Jools walked back to his room. 'They never even said he was leaving,' he thought.

'It's time, Jools. It's nearly two o' clock. Assume the position.'

⊙

Jools shuffled up the corridor. The clock read five-fifteen and he went into the smoking room and sat down.

'Jools, Jools, can Ah get a fag off ye?' Archie asked.

'Ah've only got one left, Archie,' Jools croaked. His head throbbed and he was losing his voice. It had been that long since he'd physically spoken to anyone.

'Ah'll go for mair if ye want,' Archie said, sounding desperate.

'Aye, awright then.' Jools handed him a ten pound note. 'Just get me twenty Regal Kingsize.'

Archie hurried to catch the shop. Jools sat back and closed his eyes, rubbing his temples. The coils in his head throbbed and the skin of his scalp felt tight since they'd put the stitches in him.

SLAM! He jumped.

Two women and a loud child came into visit someone. The kid ran up and down the room noisily.

SLAM! A nurse came in and tended an elderly woman. Jools inhaled deeply on his cigarette. He noticed Eddie sitting in the corner in his Hearts top. He tried to blank his mind but it was too late.

'Stay away fae gliders!' The plane exploded.

Jools sighed deeply. 'That wisnae me,' he said calmly. 'Ah'm no leavin the room. If he canny handle it, he can fuck right off. Ah've been oot the way aw day.' He turned his seat around so he couldn't see Eddie. Eddie got up and stomped out of the room.

SLAM! Jools jumped. He finished his cigarette and stubbed it out. Emma walked around the room, emptying ashtrays. She shuffled over to Jools.

'Awright, doll?' She gummed a smile. 'Ah telt um Ah fancied um. Eh, Ah telt ye yesterday? Aye, Ah did,' she told the thin woman sitting next to them. Emma got hold of Jools and cuddled him, much to his embarassment.

'You're tidy, likes!' she said, planting a sloppy wet kiss on his neck which he wiped on the sleeve of his tee shirt.

SLAM! He jumped.

Archie came in and handed Jools his cigarettes with a shaky hand.

'Just keep the change, get yourself a packet ay fags,' Jools said.

He opened the packet and threw Archie one, lighting one for himself.

'Ah'm Ah no gettin one?' Emma asked.

Jools handed her a cigarette and pulled his lighter out to spark it.

'Gie's!' she said, snatching the lighter off him. She walked away with it.

Jools just sat and shook his head.

Archie studied the racing form in the paper.

'Ah remember twenty year ago,' he said. 'Ma brother-in-law and me were at Powderhall at the dugs. Ay wanted me tae put a grand oan a dug,' he grinned. 'Ah widnae pit a grand oan a dug. Would you put a grand oan a dug, Jools?'

Jools shook his head.

'Pit a grand oan a dug,' Archie mumbled to himself. His shaky hand marked off a horse with a bookie's pen.

SLAM! Jools jumped.

'That's your auntie here to see you, Jools,' the nurse said to him. He stubbed his cigarette out and went to the hall to meet her.

A presence filled his head but stayed silent, on the side.

'Hi,' she said.

'Hiya,' he croaked. 'Do you want to come along here?' He led her to the quiet room with its varnished floorboards. They went in and sat down.

'I've brought you a few things,' she said, handing him a carrier bag.

'Ta,' he said, as he put it aside.

'So, how are you? Are you feeling any better?'

'SHUT UP, JOOLS!' The presence seized him. 'DON'T SAY A WORD! YOU BETTER NOT TELL HER NOWT!!!'

Jools clamped his jaw together, unsure what to say. He shook his head.

'What? Are you still as bad? Is the medicine not helping?' she asked.

'Shut up, Jools, Ah'm not kidding!' He felt the electric current building in his body. His heart raced. 'SAY A WORD AND YE GET THE MAX!'

'Can I do anything to help? Can I get you anything?' his aunt asked.

Jools said nothing, but clamped his jaw tight and shook his head slightly.

'Do you want me to go?' she asked.

He said nothing. His eyes welled up with tears.

'Get rid of her, Jools! Now!' the presence commanded.

'I'll come back another time, Jools,' his auntie said, putting her coat back on. 'I really just dropped in to hand in some things for you. Now if you need anything just say and I'll see what I can do, OK? I'll see you later.' She gave him a hug and left.

He went back to his room with a lump in his throat.

'Somebody fancies you in the office!' the female voice said.

'Who?' Jools wondered.

'Ah'm no sayin'. But somebody fancies you in the office.'

'Who is it? Is it ma pal, Jane? The blonde nurse?'

'It's no the one that used tae be a pro, she's an auld slapper. Ah'm talkin aboot somebody else,' the woman said.

'Is it Claire?' he asked.

'Might be. Anyway, ye're no allowed tae have any sexual thoughts about the staff. You could get the max for it. Dr David Love hates that. So does Yours Truly.'

'Ah've no had any sexual thoughts aboot any ay the staff. Certainly no ma pal. Ah'm no bothered if she used tae be a pro, she's a magic wee woman. Ah'd dae anything for her. She's the only one that was nice tae me. Ah think Claire's tidy but Ah've no had any sexual thoughts aboot her.'

'You better not. And Ah'd keep that aboot the hairbrush tae maself if Ah was you. That's Billy Love's daughter. Did you know Billy Love's having an affair wi' yer blonde bit stuff, Jane?'

'What, the wee blonde nurse?' Jools asked.

'The one that used tae be a pro. She's shaggin Billy Love!' she laughed.

'Maybe that's why he didnae like me,' Jools thought. 'Anyway, like Ah says, Ah've no been thinkin sexually aboot anyone. Jane's just ma pal.'

'We'll be checking!' The woman disappeared.

⊙

Jools lay in bed in the dark. The hall light shone through the small window set in the door.

'Jools, Jools, don't be scared,' a voice whispered. 'I'm an old friend of your auntie's. I'm here to help you, Jools. We're here to teach you to quiet down. We want you to join usssss,' the voice hissed.

'Who are you?' Jools asked.

'I'm here to quiet your mind. I'm a friend of your old Aikido teacher.'

'What, you know John Quinn?'

'He sent us to teach you to shut up,' came the whisper. 'We want you to be as quiet as us. Join us.'

'But who are you?' he asked again. He found himself whispering back.

'Jools, a lot's been going on since you've been in here. Do you remember that mural you saw when you were walking with the wind? "We must walk in the darkness to find the light." That was our people. You know, Jools, law and order has been going to the dogs recently. Street crime's hit an all-time high and we sit back and do nothing. Until now. Jools, this is secret. It's not to be told. We are starting a secret society. We might have to work outside the law but we do mean to clean up society. You have a good solid background in the martial arts and we need people like you. Join us.'

'What, is it some kind of vigilante group or something?' Jools wondered.

'We're starting a civilian police force, Jools. We need you. Join usssss.'

'Ah'm no sure what use Ah'd be tae ye. Ah'm nae angel maself,' he whispered.

'Think it over, Jools. Give us your answer soon. If you ever need to contact us in future, go to your old Aikido class and ask for Mr Short. Remember, Mr Short. He'll know what you mean. Remember, we need you. Now how are you doing with keeping quiet?'

'Ah'm managing a wee bit longer every few days but there's no danger Ah'll dae twenty-four hours in one go. It's impossible. Ah'd need tae be deid,' Jools told them.

'Your thoughts are very quiet just now, Jools. See, you are making some progress,' the voice whispered. 'Now concentrate, but relax too. That's it. Now breathe deeply and naturally. Don't clench your teeth. Now just be. That's it. Concentrate on being quiet. See to it no thought is born. Cut loose from thinking in words, that's it. Don't picture anything.'

Jools noticed his hearing getting super-sensitive.

'Take in all, but give out nothing,' the voice instructed. 'We want to train your consciousness to be silent. Concentrate on your breathing being natural. Don't count your breath in words. Now put your consciousness outside your body. Be aware of your surroundings. That's where to place your consciousness. Feel the timing of a breath.'

Jools practiced this new way of being blank. He noticed it was gentler than the brute force he'd been using. He sat on his bed and practiced and lost track of time. A woman came in with his medication some time later and he went to bed.

⊙

'Jools, medication,' the male nurse said, and handed him the plastic beakers.

He sat up drowsily and downed the contents. The sun reflected brightly off the facing block and made him squint.

'Shut up, Jools!' the female voice said. 'Don't muck about! Yours Truly's going on holiday soon so he wants you to start paying attention to the programme. He'll expect a great improvement in you when he gets back. He's off for a fortnight. He thinks it's time you got your finger out and improved up to his standard. Yours Truly used to be a Royal Marine, you know. He expects a high standard of cleanliness!'

'Is that what you want from me?' Jools asked. 'To act like Ah was a Marine or something? If that's what you want Ah can gie ye that. Ah'll start now.' He got out of bed and started to fold up his clothes and put them away in drawers. He made the bed, folding the covers tight in military fashion. When the room was spick and span he decided to have a bath. He went through the bag his auntie had brought him. Soap, disposable razors, toothpaste and a toothbrush. He wrapped the items up in a towel and went to the bathroom. The door to the bath cubicle was locked so Jools shuffled up the corridor and knocked on the office door. His heart almost leapt out of his chest when Claire answered.

'Hairbrush!' the voice giggled.

Jools couldn't look her in the eye and shuffled his feet shyly.

'Can Ah have a bath?' he asked. 'The bath door's locked.'

'I'll get someone along in a minute,' she said.

'Right, ta,' Jools mumbled, and shuffled back down the corridor at the double.

'Ah've got a spot oan ma cock!' the female voice laughed.

Jools's face went scarlet. How the fuck could he face Claire if she knew about that?

'Hairbrush!'

'Stop that, that's brutal. Leave the lassie alane!' Jools pleaded.

'Hairbrush!' the woman said, sniggering. He could hear another woman laughing in the background.

'That isnae me. Ah ken that's youse. Stop rippin the pish oot everybody. Ye're no funny. Ye're a bit sick yerself, if ye ask me.' Jools was beginning to get annoyed.

He went into a cubicle and had a piss. The spot was redder than ever and was developing a head. He tried to squeeze it but the pain brought tears to his eyes.

'Jools! Knock, knock!' the male nurse called in. 'I've opened the bath for you!'

Jools finished up and gave himself a careful shake.

He left the cubicle.

'You're not allowed to have razors in the ward, Jools,' the nurse said, spotting the bundle under his arm. 'Can I take those? I'll keep them in the office for you. If you need one, just ask, but you must hand the razor back when you're finished, OK ?'

His dick gave an involuntary twitch and he dribbled down his leg.

'Ah've pished maself!' the female voice laughed.

The nurse left and Jools stood in front of the mirror. His hair had grown and was greasy, sticking up in places. He lathered up the soap in his hands and had a rough shave. The stubble was almost too long to be cut with a razor and the skin stung. He inspected his teeth. They were brown, stained with cigarette smoke, and his gums were red and sore from gritting his teeth. Luckily his auntie had got smokers' toothpaste and he scrubbed until his gums bled. He went into the cubicle and ran a bath. He put his hand in to test the water. It was lukewarm. It came out of the tap at that temperature so he got in and washed briskly. He scrubbed at himself, being careful of his genitals. The water quickly became cold and he shivered as he rinsed the soap off his hair. He was beginning to worry about the spider they'd put in him. The electric charge. If they should zap him in the bath he could be electrocuted. He washed quickly and got out to dry himself. He changed into clean clothes and went back to his room to put his things away, then took the razor back to the office and knocked on the door. Claire answered again.

'Ah'm just handin this razor in,' he said, now a bit more confident.

'HAIRBRUSH!' the woman's voice laughed, but Jools tried to blank his mind.

'Thanks,' she said, smiling. She looked him right in the eye. Jools wondered if she was thanking him for handing in the razor or sticking up for her earlier. He went into the smoking room. It was nearly empty and a few people sat around in their night clothes.

SLAM! Jools jumped. The cleaner came in with his broom and started to sweep the floor.

'G'morning blue,' he said to Jools in his chirpy cockney accent.

'Hiya,' he replied, lighting a cigarette.

The cleaner whistled to himself merrily as he swept under the chairs. Every now and then he'd stop for a chat with someone.

SLAM! 'Stay away fae gliders!' the voice said, as Eddie came in, looking grumpy.

'Fuck off!' Jools thought. He turned his seat around so Eddie was out of view.

SLAM! He jumped. Emma shuffled in and sat down next to the Professor. Jools finished his cigarette and went to the kitchen to make tea.

⊙

Jools sat on his bed covering his ears.

'Shut up, Jools, just shut up!' the female voice shouted.

'Fuck off! Ah'm no daein anything ye tell me!' Jools was boiling. 'Ye've done nowt but nip ma fuckin heid for months now and yer daein ma fuckin nut in! Fuck off! Ye can gie me the max if ye want, Ah dinnae gie a fuck! Just get the fuck oot ma heid. This is surely against the Geneva Convention, daein this to people. What aboot human rights? The right tae yer own private thoughts in yer ain heid? Am Ah meant tae have went through life keepin ma mind pure so you cunts could test ma thinkin one day? You people are sick fucks and yer gettin nae mair co-operation fae me until ye tell me what the fuck ye're up tae. Ah'm no a paedophile! Ah'm no a Jew! Ah'm nae poof and Ah'll no shut up in ma ain fuckin heid! Ye can aw go and take a flying fuck tae yerself, ya sick fuckin cunts! Who's in charge ay this? Eh? Ah'm takin this aw the way tae the European courts if Ah have tae, by the way! You lot are in healthy trouble!' He sat cross-legged and concentrated on projecting a golden energy that filled the room.

'Aw naw, no the golden child again. Here we go, man,' the woman sighed. 'Jools! JOOLS! If you dinnae shut up,we'll have to hurt ye.'

'Hurt ays again and Ah'll have half ay fuckin Muirhoose up here and ye can fuckin tell that tae yer Leith mob tae! Fuckin aboot wi' peoples brains while the doctors are away hame! Who the fuck put them in charge ay human beings? They're no fit tae look efter a dug! Fuckin threatenin me wi' aw sorts! It shouldnae be allowed! That's ma fuckin mind their playin wi!'

A needle jabbed him in the neck.

'AAARGH! What're ye fuckin daein?! See if Ah ever find oot who you are, Ah'll cut your fuckin heid right off, Ah swear it! You're fuckin deid!'

'Shut up, Jools!' The woman was adamant.

'Ya fuckin sick, twisted fucks! Ah'm no sayin a fuckin word tae anycunt! Aw Ah'm daein is thinkin in ma ain heid. Fuck off!'

'Is that you playin up again, Jools? Ah'm warnin you, son. Ah umnae too pleased with you just now. Now, what's yer problem?' Yours Truly asked.

'It's aw they fuckin weirdos. Every two minutes they're at ays, fuckin humiliating ays, hurtin ays, actin like spastics! This is surely against the Geneva Convention! Ah'm no daein fuck all else till they start treatin me like a human being and stop hurtin ays! Ah want tae see ma lawyer.'

'Ah umnae too pleased with you, Jools. I told them to give you a hard time. It's the only way you'll learn. We found out about Billy Love having an affair with wee Jane, the nurse. We were raging when we found out but we discovered it wasn't your fault. Someone deliberately put that there for us to find. It was one of our staff and Ah'm not pleased about it. It wasn't your fault. Someone was just trying to cause trouble and blame you. I'm just annoyed with you and your racist pal last night. Your pal said the N-word and you agreed. You know that's what really makes my blood boil. I hate racism, Jools. Dr David Love would have given you the max for that last night.'

'Ah wisnae bein racist. Neither was Terry. He asked if one ay the Leith mob was black, Ah said ay was. What's racist aboot that? Ay's fuckin grandad was black!' Jools told him.

'Your pal asked if one of them was a nigger. You said yes, Jools.'

'Aw he meant was is one ay them black. That's aw. It's like if we say Ah'm goin tae the Pakis for twenty fags. It's no a racist remark where Ah come fae. It's just our language. It's just the way we talk. People's mas talk aboot goin along tae the Pakis. Are ye tellin me they're aw racists? No danger, man! Fair enough if Ah was goin up tae the boy and callin him the N-word. That's racist. Ah'm no demeanin the guy for bein black.'

'Jools, we've got your thoughtwaves of you telling racist jokes. It's not funny.'

'That's just a bit ay crack between the lads. What's wrong wi' havin a laugh? We make jokes aboot anything. There's nae malice in it, eh? It's just like tellin a mother-in-law joke or a fat joke. Ah hung aboot wi' black guys, man. Ah've goat a couple ay black mates. If anyone called them the N-word, we'd kick fuck oot them. Aw that PC shite might work in nice middle-class Morningside but yer missionaries dinnae cut the crap doon in the scheme. These cunts ye keep sendin in fae the toon tae try and change our attitudes. They're a waste ay fuckin space, never mind the taxpayer's money. Ye can change the scheme, knock doon hooses and stuff but you'll never change the people. Ah'm the cunt gettin discriminated against. Ye ever tried bein a schemie gettin intae a club in toon oan a Friday night? It used tae say nae dogs, nae Irish, but now it's nae neds. Aw Ah've had since Ah've been in here is shite cause Ah'm fae Muirhoose and Ah've ended up here in a Tory ward. Ah'm no wearin any mair ay this shite. Ye can aw fuck right off! It's you cunts that are the Nazis. Fuckin treatin a human being like that. Ah might be just some wee diddy fae the ghettos but Ah ken when Ah'm bein taken for a cunt!'

'I hear what you're saying, Jools, but there's no other way now. You see, once you start the Love programme, you have to see it through to the end. It can't be stopped once you're wired up to the machine. I'm sorry Jools, but you have no alternative. You must carry on.'

'How long for, likes?'

'Until you can go twenty-four hours without a thoughtwave.'

Jools was crushed.

'I'm going to leave you alone now, Jools. You'll need some time to get your head round this. I'm glad we've had our little chat and you've got things off your chest. I'll be back in touch soon. Keep your chin up, son.' Yours Truly disappeared, leaving Jools sitting quietly on the bed.

Two bells rang in the hallway and he shuffled off to lunch.

Jools finished his cigarette and went to his room. The clock in the hall read two-twenty but no one had told him to start practice so he sat gazing into space, daydreaming. Suddenly his body sat bolt upright and he felt a familiar tingle as static started to build in his body. His eyes started to revolve in tight triangles and they spun faster and faster.

'Naw, no again!' he shouted, as he tried to struggle but found he was paralysed.

'Stay still, Jools!' the loud whisper said. 'Dr Love's bag is in evidence!'

The skin on his scalp started to pull tight and he felt a sharp nip as the steel wires broke through the skin. He could feel the wires pulling upwards as they unwrapped from the tangle around his bones then pierced the top of his scalp. His arms and legs fully unwrapped, the wires pulled on his spine and up his neck, untangling from around his brainstem and vertebrae. Finally they traced round the contours of his brain and his body began to feel light without the burden of the steel spider they'd put in him. His scalp muscles could finally relax and it felt good. All he was left with were the coils behind his temples.

'The coils will have gone in a few weeks, Jools. Body heat will make them dissolve.' Dr Love retreated, leaving Jools free to move again.

⊙

Jools lay on his bed relaxing. It was the most relaxed he'd been for a while. He could hear the nurses talking in their little staff room next door as the wall seemed to be paper-thin. He could hear someone laughing and someone stirring a cup of tea and thought their voices sounded like the teacher from the Charlie Brown cartoons. He decided to go for a cigarette. He went to the smoking room and sat down. The tall man sat talking to a woman in the corner and Emma sat in a chair snoring, dribbling slightly from the corner of her mouth. The Professor looked over with a smile.

'Jools, Jools, can Ah get a cigarette off ye? Archie with the scruffy hairdo begged.

'This has got tae stop,' Jools thought. 'Ah've only got a couple, Archie,' he lied.

'Gie him a fag, ya tight cunt!' the voice said. 'That's Archie McNab. He's a homeless guy. He's a helper around the place. He's the finder-outer. You see, we let him live here while we're doing our training and he gets somewhere to sleep and three square meals a day. All he has to do is find out about people for us. He gets a bigger giro for being of no fixed abode and he can scran all the fags he needs. He doesnae need your fags anyway. He's got his own. He just doesnae like to pull them oot, if ye ken what Ah mean. Just watch him. Ah'll bet he pulls out twenty fags.'

Archie sighed loudly and chewed the end of a bookie's pen. His arm shook violently. He got up and went out of the room.

SLAM! Jools jumped.

'Six marks,' he heard the Professor say to someone. He seemed to be addressing the students.

Two bells rang in the hall. 'That's dinner time!' a nurse announced.

⊙

Jools was sat in the smoking room when a nurse came in and told him his sister was here to see him. He stubbed out his cigarette and went out to the hall to meet her.

'Hiya,' Sarah said, and gave him a hug.

Jools took her into the quiet room and they sat down.

'I've brought you some fags,' she said, handing him two twenty packs. 'So how are you feeling?'

'Say nothing, Jools,' the voice said. 'You know what'll happen if you do!'

'Ah'm awright,' Jools mumbled.

'So have you been able to sleep OK? You look really tired.'

Jools just shook his head.

'You know, you have to get yourself better, Jools, or they'll not let you go home.'

'How's the cat?' he asked. He missed his wee buddy.

'She's fine. I'm feeding her for you,' Sarah said.

'Ah just want tae go hame. Ah hate this place.' Jools's eyes filled up and he got a lump in his throat.

'Shut up, Jools! Don't say another fucking word! Get rid of her, now!' the voice screamed.

Jools clamped his jaw shut. He wouldn't say another word.

'Jools, are you alright?' Sarah asked. 'Do you want me to leave you? Just tell us what's the matter, Jools. We can't help if we don't know what's wrong with you. You have to tell your family or the doctors. That's what they're here for.'

Jools was on the edge of blurting it all out but feared the consequences too much. He wouldn't know where to start. He sat with his jaw clamped shut and tears in his eyes. His sister got up and put her jacket on.

'I'll be back up in a couple of days. I'll bring you some more smokes. Is there anything you need?'

Jools shook his head.

'I'll see you later,' she said, and left him alone.

⊙

Jools sat in the smoking room puffing on a cigarette. He finished one and stubbed it out, then immediately lit another. He rested his head back against the wall and closed his eyes. He started to inhale deeply and tried to breathe from his navel as he'd been taught in Ninpo. He pulled his legs up on the chair, crossing them under him, and set the breathing rhythm. Eight seconds in, hold for three and exhale for eight. He tried to imagine waves crashing onto the shore and retreating as another wave started to build.

'Stay off the navel!' the voice said. 'Stay off Gartnavel!'

Jools sighed. He just wanted to relax a bit. He opened his eyes to see Eddie sitting opposite him.

'Stay away fae gliders!' the voice said, as a plane exploded in his mind's eye.

'Look, Jools, you've got to stop this. He says ye're a poof and ye're a Jew. Now you two keep away from each other.'

'How can he no leave the room? Ah've kept oot the way aw day,' Jools said. 'Ye can fuck off! Ah'm steyin put!'

'Do you see the Professor, Jools? He's in charge of a team of students. Eddie's one of those students. They're studying you, Jools,' the voice told him.

'Maybe Ah dinnae want tae be studied. What if Ah want left alane?'

'Suit yourself, Jools. You can just keep out of the way if you like, it just means you'll get paid less.'

'Paid?' Jools asked.

'Oh yes. You were to be paid a sum of money after the course. It's a tidy little sum too.'

'How much are we talking, likes?' Jools asked.

'Oh, about sixteen thousand, something like that.'

'Sixteen grand? Ya fuckin beauty!' Jools had never had that kind of money.

'Only if and when you complete the course. You must finish the programme,' the female voice told him. 'Do you want me to let you in on a secret?'

'What?' Jools wondered.

The woman started to laugh. 'You're a wee bugger! You're too strong! You know they've all just had a meeting about you. You've managed to wear out the whole team. Jools I don't know how you'll take this but we've finished with you for the time being. You're to go on med research next.'

'Med research?' Jools asked.

'Yes. The team's been following you around for months now, Jools. You've worn them out. They've all had a turn at thinking up new scenarios to put you through but they've dried up. They have to leave soon. Jools, everything you've been through recently, it was the team that set it up. The Professor, Eddie,

Emma, Archie, all of them. They're all psychology students. They've been trying to keep you scared for months. It was them in the cars calling you Bigmooth. That one in particular was Dr Pickering's idea. He's the old guy with the glasses that's always reading the newspapers. He's actually a top psychiatrist, you know. It was them that zapped you with the swastika. You were getting too racist. They had to teach you a lesson.'

'But it couldnae be, what aboot the SAS and Rob? Ah seen the SAS a couple ay times. At the West End that night.'

'They were just Naval reserves, Jools. We had that set up. Bulldog was played by Big Davy Love. He's a big nutter, you'd like him.'

'What about Rob? Ah ken his voice. Ah ken it was Ninpo he was using. Under the pier at Granton that night. Master Tanaka was here.'

'Jools, Rob was played by a student that used to be in the Iga school in Leith. He's one of the second year psychology students. He was pishing himself laughing that night when you thought it was your grandmaster. He thought that one up. It was him that scared the horse on the beach that day, he ran right past you. He was the IRA guy with the shades on in the Botanic Gardens. You've been had, Jools,' she laughed. 'He's only a third dan. What a laugh we've had with him. He's taught the psychology students a few tricks too. He's a good sport, though. He says when you finish the programme you're more than welcome to come and train with them in Leith. He thought you were alright, just a wee bit gullible. He said you can earn yourself a year's free lessons when you pass. It was him doing all that with the animals.'

'Ah'm no wantin any lessons fae the Iga school. Ah'm fae the Koga ryu. That's a fuckin sneaky trick, likes,' Jools huffed, disappointed. 'The Iga and the Koga schools are rivals. Ah dinnae fit in there. Ah'm loyal tae Tanaka sensei.'

'OK, Jools but it was all arranged as a gesture of goodwill. I hope you don't hurt anyone's feelings,' the woman said.

'What aboot ma fuckin feelins?' Jools snapped.

'Jools, we've put you through intense psychological warfare. You're bound to feel irritable. This could happen in the future for real. Terrorists could use it on the population. The students and doctors are here to monitor what you go through. They're trying to find ways to counteract the effects of psychological warfare for the military. This is already happening to people in Palestine, Jools. We're trying to study the effects in case we ever get it over here. Modern warfare is a dirty game. Just think, you're one of the only people in the west to have been through psychological warfare. These techniques were used in Bosnia. Our government is doing everything possible to ban the use of such weapons.

You're right. It will be against the Geneva Convention. It's allowed under military research, though.'

'But why me? Why did you use me?' he asked.

'Jools, you've never had a job have you? People who've never worked all have to do some form of national service. You got picked for med research. It's like getting jury duty. Some people do, some don't. Besides, we picked you because you're used to handling long-term stress. No one ever tells about med research, though. If you do you'll get it again a second time. Once is usually enough for anyone.'

'But what aboot when Ah was walkin wi' the wind? That was real.'

'That was done from the university. It's really quite old technology now. They plot your course from a computer in Nicolson Square. It's just done with ions. They have a wind generator. It's connected to a virtual dummy which you're plugged into. The whole set up's really quite simple.'

'But what aboot when Ah was walkin wi' the wind? That was real!'

'That was done from the university, Jools. It's all done with negative and positive ions. They create a vortex, like a mini tornado, and plot its course with a global positioning satellite. It's all connected to the virtual dummy that you're plugged into. Quite simple, really. It's pretty old technology now. It was used in the Gulf War to guide special forces in Iraq.'

'But mind when they were slaggin ays off on telly. How was that done?' he asked.

'Composite. That was done from the back of a uni van. It was just university technicians. It was really simple to send the computer-enhanced videos through your cable box.'

'So naeone else saw aw that?'

'You were told it was foolproof.'

'But what aboot when Ah whistled at Vanessa Mae on the telly? Ah heard somebody whistle at her the same way Ah did. That was a live show,' he reasoned.

'That was one of the team. The show was put on for the charity workers. The guy from our team was listening to you through a radio mic in the audience. He just conveyed your message to her. I told you the stars weren't just there for you. They're there for Dr David Love. He's the one with the influence.'

'Will Ah still get tae meet Anastacia?'

The woman just laughed. 'Maybe. There's to be a big showbiz reception after this programme ends, Jools. She'll be performing at that.'

'But will Ah still get tae meet her?'

'We'll have to wait and see.'

⊙

Jools lay on his bed. The light from the hall shone through the small window set in the door. He got up and went to the smoking room. He lit a cigarette and sat down.

'Jools, can Ah get a cigarette off ye?' Archie asked.

'Ah've only got a couple, Archie' he replied.

The room was smoky and full of people in their night clothes. They locked the door at the end of the hall at 9pm and access to the kitchen was stopped. A nurse wheeled in a tea trolley and Jools poured himself a cuppa from a leaky aluminium teapot. He helped himself to a plate of digestives.

'Leave the biscuits!' the voice goaded him.

Jools smoked fast and lit another cigarette. He noticed his fingers were badly nicotine-stained. *News at Ten* started on the TV.

'Leave the room! No news!' the voice ordered.

Jools stubbed out his cigarette and left the room then queued up outside the office for his medication. He waited in line as the nurse dispensed medicines from a trolley and the patients helped themselves to juice from a jug. He looked around the office. A poster on the wall showed a syringe.

'SMACK!' the voice screamed.

'Jools, syringes are used for proper medical procedures, not just illegal drugs. That's what we want from you. Right-mindedness. We want you to start thinking as cleanly as possible. Your mind automatically goes to the worst possible scenario every time. We want you to start thinking cleanly,' the voice told him. 'Cleanliness, inside and out. In thought, word and deed.'

He took his tablet.

'Placebo!' the voice said. 'It may or may not be, but you still get paid for completing the course of tablets. Sixteen grand!'

Jools shuffled to the toilet and had a pee. He was walking to his room when his dick twitched involuntary and he dribbled down the leg of his jeans.

'Ah've pished maself!' the voiced laughed.

⊙

'Join usssss Joolsssss!' the whisper came. 'Have you made a decision yet? Will you join usssss? The civilian police force need you, Jools. Mr Short needs you. Will you walk through the darkness with ussss Joolsssss? Together we'll find the light.'

'Ah'm no sure Ah want tae get involved, man,' Jools whispered.

'Think about it some more, Jools. Take some more time. You know with your special training you could be a great asset to our group. We need you. You're trained in psychological warfare. You are to become the psychological warfare officer for the Muirhouse area. In the event that terrorists used this on the population, you would be called up to help deal with the casualties. You would lead them back to reality. You would guide them. Do you understand? We need your knowledge.'

'Ah'm no sure Ah'm no as bad as the folk you're after. Ah'm nae angel, Ah told you that. Ah could never grass oan anyone if Ah caught them daein anything. Never, ever grass.'

'Think about it, Jools. Remember, go to your Aikido teacher. Ask for Mr Short. He'll know.' The presence faded.

Jools rolled over and got into bed. He fell asleep fast.

⊙

'Are you up yet, Jools?' the woman's voice said. 'Shut up and put Anastacia doon for a minute! We need twenty-four hours without a thoughtwave. Will you start today? It's a good day to begin the One.'

Jools opened his eyes and sat up, yawning. The rain poured down outside and he could see three pigeons huddled together on the roof of the opposite block. The blonde nurse Jane came into the room and handed Jools his medication.

'How are you feeling today?' she asked. 'If the weather clears up we can maybe go out for a bit later. Would you like that?'

'That would be sound,' he replied, knocking back his tablet.

'I'll come and get you later.' She left him alone.

'She totally fancies you, Jools!' the woman laughed in his head. 'Would you go with her, even though she used to be a pro?'

'So what? She's no now, though. We've aw got our skeletons. Ah think she's a sound wee woman,' Jools answered. 'She's pretty nice, aye.'

'She said she's going to ride the arse off you when you get out!' the woman laughed. 'But dinnae think sexually about the staff. It's not allowed. Don't picture anything. You know, she was going with Billy Love so I'd keep out of his way if I was you. He won't take too kindly to someone stealing his woman.'

'Ah've no done nowt,' Jools said. 'It was her that went for me, Ah never did nothin'.'

Jools got up and went to the bathroom. He stood in the cubicle, bleary-eyed. The boil on his knob throbbed and looked angry. He finished up and gave a thorough but gentle shake.

'Now wash those hands, Jools! Cleanliness!' the woman called.

Jools's dick gave an involuntary twitch and he dribbled down the leg of his shorts.

'Ah've pished maself!' the voice laughed.

Jools shook his head. 'Will ye just fuck off?' he huffed, not in the mood. He stood in front of the mirror and scrubbed his hands. He shuffled up the hall to the smoking room. The cleaner was in mopping the floor and Emma sat talking to Archie and the Professor.

SLAM! He jumped. Eddie came in. Jools blanked his mind instantly and nothing happened. He smoked a cigarette and immediately lit another. Emma got up and put the radio on. Dido was on.

SLAM! He jumped.

A nurse came in with two more people. They sat in the corner talking.

'Jools, can Ah get a cigarette off ye?' Archie asked.

'Ah've only got a couple,' Jools replied.

'Stop scrannin fags, you!' Emma shouted over with a gummy smile. She got to her feet and shuffled over. 'How are you, ma darlin?' she said to Jools.

'Ah'm sound,' he replied, a bit flat.

'He's ma wee honey,' she said to Archie. She picked up an ashtray and went to the bin to empty it. Jools noticed she wore only socks on her feet and she walked across the freshly mopped floor leaving dry footprints.

SLAM! He jumped.

A heavily built man with dark hair came in and walked over to Emma. They both sat by the TV and they began chatting and smoking. Jools got up and left the room. He went up the long corridor to the kitchen to make tea. A guard sat outside the kitchen on a bench listening to a radio. Jools noticed his arms were covered in tattoos.

'He's fae folk!' the voice said. 'He's a gypsy!'

He went to the water boiler on the wall and poured himself a cup. There were no tea bags left so he made do with coffee. He looked out the kitchen window across the car park to a group of trees. They were fully in leaf now and Jools wondered how long he'd been in here. It seemed a long time. He needed to get out and feel the fresh air on his skin.

◉

'You're a sick wee cunt, Ah swear it, Jools!' the voice said. 'Ah was going through your thoughtwaves last night when you were sleeping and Ah found a few belters.'

'Like what?' Jools asked.

'When you were wee, especially. D'you remember killing your hamster when you were a bairn?'

'Aye, sort ay,' Jools sniggered. 'Ah didnae mean tae kill it, though. Ah was only a bairn. Ah must've only been about four or five. Ah remember Ah was standing on the couch with this wee fat hamster in ma hands. Ah gave it a wee squeeze to make its eyes pop out and it sank its teeth intae ma finger. Wee bastard. Ah just dropped it and caught it oan the volley,' he laughed. 'Ah booted it clean across the room, man. Ah just mind ay getting up the next morning and it was stiff as a board!'

'You're a sick wee bastard!' she laughed. 'Was that when you jumped out your auntie's window?' she asked.

'Naw. That's when Ah was two. Ah was at ma auntie's in Muirhoose Medway. Ah thought a was Superman and tried to fly oot the windae. Twenty-five feet straight doon. Ah landed in the soft mud and grass below. There wasn't a mark on me. They were going to keep my Ma in hospital for shock and send me home. It was oan the front page of the *Evening News*.'

'And the time you burst out crying watching *Dumbo*, when they locked his mum up for being a mad elephant? You're a sensitive wee soul. And what about that time when you stuck your finger up your arse? You have hidden depths!' she laughed. 'That's why all the guys were calling you a poof. They all saw the video of your thoughtwave on that.'

'Aw fuck's sake, man!' Jools said, a bit embarrassed. 'Ah was only a bairn. Ah was just… exploring things. Aw bairns dae daft things like that. Ah bet you even done things when you were wee.'

'One of my favourites is when you had diarrhoea when you were about three. You shouted your mum and told her your bum was being sick! Do you remember trying to shag the cat?'

'Fuck off, man! Ah never done that!' he choked.

'Just testing for adherence. Stay away fae wee lassies!'

'That's shite tae! Ah'm no intae wee lassies! Ah'm no a fuckin beast!' He was adamant.

'Jools, you know your stuff,' the woman sniggered. 'Two wee lassies. One was true, the other one wasn't. One of them was just a set up. It was just for the students to train on. You know they'll not even find out till October when they come back from holiday. They'll go on thinking you're a racist paedophile until the Professor tells them next term. That's the part you're playing for the Royal Ed. A racist paedophile. They're all trainee psychologists. They'll have to get used to dealing with people like that in their work. It's to desensitise them. That's why the security. A few of them are finding it hard to deal with. A couple of the guys are getting a bit angry and we have to protect you. Wait till they find out the truth about you,' she laughed. 'That'll teach them not to make assumptions. They're there to help people. They have to learn not to let their personal feelings into it no matter how bad the patient. You know they might actually have to treat people like that one day, for real. We see the very worst cases here in the Royal Ed. It is the main psychiatric hospital in Edinburgh.'

'Well as long as they find oot Ah'm no really a pervert. It's getting hard tae keep this up, the way they've been treatin me,' Jools reflected. 'If any one ay they students start wi' me, Ah'll fuckin smack them one! They'll need the security.'

The room door opened. It was Jane, the blonde nurse.

'The rain's stopped, Jools. I was wondering if you still want to go out?'

'Sound! Aye,' he replied.

'I'll come along and get you in a few minutes,' she said, and left the room. Jools changed into his jeans and pulled his boots on.

'We'll be watching you when you're out, Jools,' the voice said. 'This is your chance to practice doing the One out in society. You have to blank your mind or anyone within a mile of the Royal Ed will be able to pick up your signal on their radios. It's not stifled. Anyone could have access to your private thoughts. We don't want just anyone listening in, do we?'

'Ah'm no ready for that!' Jools said anxiously. 'Ah thought it was stifled, only the Royal Ed could hear inside ma heid. What if ma thoughts get oot? Anyone could hear them. It's oot ay order! Every cunt'll think Ah'm a racist beast who likes wee lassies when it's no even me! Ah'm no wantin tae go oot.'

'This is just a practice for when you rejoin society, Jools. We'll be there with you every step of the way. Now get ready.'

He tied a purple sweatshirt around his waist in case it was cold and sat on the bed to wait. A few minutes passed and Jane returned carrying an umbrella. 'Come on then, Jools,' she said, and she led the way down the corridor. They decended the stairs and turned down the hall past the lift into a corridor hung with paintings and photographs, part of an exhibition of patients' work.

'You better check him, Jane, I think he's got a hard-on!' a woman's voice said. The nurse looked Jools up and down, giving him the once over.

He shook his head with his most innocent face on. 'No me!'

They carried on down the long corridor of the main hospital and Jools stopped in at the shop for some cigarettes. Jane led him out of the building into the fresh air. He inhaled deeply. The sun started to come out from behind the clouds and he felt the warmth of its rays on his face. It felt great to be out. They started to walk slowly through the beautiful landscaped grounds and Jools lit a cigarette. Two large magpies hopped across the lawn and a squirrel darted up a tree as they approached.

'Jools, we can all hear everything you're thinking,' the voice said, laughing. 'You better start blanking out. You know one day you'll be on your own and there'll be no one there to stifle you. You better get the practice in. Yours Truly set this part of the programme. He'll expect you to be able to do this by the time he gets back from holiday.'

Jools blanked his mind with a sigh. They walked along past the church and up by the bowling green. Jools was having a tough time staying blank. There were too many distractions outside.

'Ah'll never dae this,' he thought, as they approached a group of parked cars. His right eye blinked involuntary and he heard a click like a camera shutter.

'Stay off car number plates!' the voice commanded.

Further on a brand new Jaguar had been parked on the kerb by the greenhouses. Jools's right eye blinked again and he felt the camera shutter click.

'Fuck off!' he snapped. 'Ye're no takin pictures through ma heid!'

'Shut up, Jools! This is Dr Love's idea. We're taking a few photos through you for our sponsors. They stand to make a lot of money out of this. All the companies want to be photographed with the One. You've become an icon, Jools. You should be flattered. We're using this technology on you. Just think, you'll be famous. You're the One!'

Click! another picture of the Jag was taken.

'Will Ah see any ay the money for this, likes?' he asked.

'Jools, the money is raised by the students to finance their year. That's how they raise funds for the uni. Through sponsorship. You'll be the face on billboards all over the western hemisphere. It's part of an advertising campaign.'

Jools felt uneasy. 'Maybe Ah dinnae want tae be famous. Maybe Ah just want ma auld life back. Ah just want tae go hame. Ye can keep the money. Ah just want tae be anonymous.'

'What, not even for Anastacia?'

Jools sighed. 'Awright.'

'I promise you, in the end you'll be totally anonymous again,' the voice reassured him. 'It's foolproof.'

Jools and the nurse walked across the car park towards the building. Suddenly a light breeze whipped up. It caught some fallen leaves which spiralled around in a mini whirlwind by the corner of the building. Jools smiled at Jane. 'Mad, am Ah?' he smiled. She must have seen that. The wind wanted to play. They entered the building and walked through the maze of corridors back to the ward. Jools was just in time to see them wheeling in the food trolley and he followed it to the kitchen. Two bells rang out in the hall.

⊙

Jools sat in the smoking room while everyone was still at lunch. He smoked a cigarette quickly then lit another.

'This chain smoking has got tae stop,' he thought to himself. He rested his head back against the wall and allowed his eyes to close. He sat there listening to the silence. Suddenly he felt the sensation of someone sucking his dick. His eyes sprang out on stalks. It ended. He was alone in the room. He stood up wide eyed. 'WOW! What the fuck was that?'

Suddenly he began to be aware of a pair of woman's breasts and genitals. He could feel, between his legs, his lack of a dick. 'WOW!' He stood up and the sensation ended. 'Somebody's playin silly cunts!'

'It was one of the lassies!' a female voice laughed. 'She's in the lab having a laugh. She gave your virtual doll a blow-job for a laugh, just to see what you'd do. She's from Leith, she's mental. She was just trying to cheer you up. She feels sorry for you. She put the headset on to let you see what it feels like to be a woman. She wanted to know what it felt like to be a guy. You could feel what it was like to be in her body. Just think, you're one of the few men who know what it's like to be a woman.'

'That was pretty cool,' Jools said, amazed. 'Weird. It felt dead real.'

'Dinnae worry, we'll look after our wee gomer. You're our gomer for the blue team. We're not all bad,' she reassured him.

'A gomer?' he asked.

'You're a gomer for med research. That's what we call you people we get to practice on. Gomers. Somebody in the office fancies you, by the way! Ah don't know how. No one can ever fancy a gomer. We have to watch them having a shit and playing with their spots and stuff. We have to look through all their thoughtwaves, all their filthy habIts. It puts us right off. No one ever fancies a gomer, she must be mad.'

'Who is it? Is it Jane, the nurse? Or Claire?'

'Maybe,' the woman said. 'I'm not telling you.'

Jools felt excited.

SLAM! He jumped. People started to come back from lunch. He got up and went to his room.

⊙

'You did OK today, Jools,' Yours Truly said. 'Ah just thought Ah'd have a word before Ah left on ma holiday. How have you been feeling about the Love programme? You're making some progress but you need to get your finger out, do some serious hard work. Ah'll expect a new man to meet me when Ah get back. Ah'm taking the wife to Tenerife for ten days. Ah'll be back at work in a fortnight so you best get cracking. When Ah get back Ah umnae wantin to hear any stories of you mucking about, Ah umnae kiddin. Do Ah make myself clear?'

'How long do you think it'll take me to finish the course?' Jools asked.

'Oh, Ah don't know. First of August maybe, if you practice.'

Jools's heart sank. 'What?! The first ay August's months away! Ah'll never stand this till August! Ah'm at the end ay ma rope wi' it now! Are you tryin tae kill me? Ah'll fuckin die before then!'

'It's the only way, Jools. The students go on holiday on the first of August. Twenty-four hours without a thoughtwave is what we want. It'll take you till then at least,' Yours Truly told him.

'Fuck that, man! Ah'm no wearin it. Ye can fuck right off!' Jools felt tears welling up in his eyes.

'You can always talk to the doctors. See if they'll get you out quicker but you can't tell them anything about the programme. They are final year students. It's their job to find out what's wrong with you without being told. It's how they learn to diagnose people. They really think you're a racist paedophile.'

'Ah'll see the shrink! Ah'll see if he'll let me oot. Ah just want tae go hame.'

He marched up the hall to the office and banged on the door. A male nurse with a crewcut answered.

'Can Ah speak tae the doctor the day?' he asked.

'He'll be in this afternoon, Jools. I'll leave a note in the book that you want to see him, OK ?' the nurse said. Jools went into the smoking room and had a quick cigarette. He finished it and went back to his room and lay on his bed.

⊙

'Dr Malloy is in now, Jools,' the skinheaded male nurse said. 'Do you want to follow me?'

They walked up the corridor to the hall, stopping at an office on the right. The nurse knocked, then entered.

'Jools McCartney here to see you, doctor,' the nurse said.

'Come in, Mr McCartney. Have a seat,' the dark-haired Irishman said. 'Now, you wanted to speak to me. What can I do for you?'

Jools stayed standing.

'When can Ah get oot?' he asked. 'Ah want tae go hame.'

'You're still on a section, Mr McCartney. You can go home when you start to improve. We can't just send you home in this state, can we?'

'But there's nothin wrong wi' me. It's this programme ye've got me on. It's killin me. Ah need tae go hame. Ah canny take any more ay this place.'

The doctor just looked at him blankly.

'Aw, it doesnae fuckin matter! What's the use?' Jools stomped out in the huff, leaving the doctor puzzled.

⊙

Jools lay on his bed listening to the silence. Suddenly a small grey ball appeared in his mind's eye. It started to move slowly, hit the top of his skull and bounced. The ball rebounded off the bottom of his skull and continued to bounce around his brain cavity.

'QUIT IT!!!!' he shouted. 'Get that fuckin thing oot ay me! Now!' The discomfort made Jools feel dizzy and sick. The ball continued to bounce around his head.

'It's a negative thought displacer, Jools,' the woman said. 'It bounces around your brain and sticks to any negative memory cells. They all fall off and sink to the bottom and we can collect them for analysis.'

'Take it oot, please,' Jools pleaded. 'Ah canny handle it! It's daein ma nut in.' He clasped his head in his hands.

'I'll turn it down a bit. There, how's that?' she asked.

The sensation faded a little but was still really uncomfortable.

'We put it into the computer. We have a computer model of your brain. Don't picture it. Don't picture anything! Stay blank.'

Jools watched the ball in its continuous movement. He lay back and did his best to relax.

⊙

Two bells rang in the hall.

'That's dinner time, people!' a male nurse shouted.

Jools had been lying down for a couple of hours. The ball still bounced around his skull and it made him stagger slightly. He shuffled up the long corridor to the kitchen.

'Nigger!' a loud voice said as he passed the Asian nurse sitting outside the kitchen. A phantom arm gave a Nazi salute. Jools ignored it and got a tray from the trolley.

'S… s… s… say nigger! Nig… Nig… Nig… ger!

He sat at a table on his own and tucked in. Meat again. He ate quickly and went back to the smoking room which was empty except for the old woman. He smoked a cigarette then went to his room to get his toiletries and wrapped them in his towel. The bath door was unlocked so he ran the taps and got undressed. The water was cold and he washed briskly. He inspected the boil on his dick. It was red and angry and had formed a yellow head. He gave it a squeeze but the pain made him stop.

'YUK! Stop that, Jools!' The female sounded disgusted. 'You're a minging wee shite, Ah swear it! That's how no one ever fancies a gomer! Go and dinnae do that on my shift, eh? That's minging. We have to watch you doing that.'

'Well fuck off and gie me some privacy then!' Jools hollered.

'I can't, Jools. We have to watch you all the time. Shut up! Stay away fae wee lassies!'

'That's no true!'

'One was true, one wasn't,' she said.

'Shite!' Jools got out and dried himself. He got dressed and came out of the cubicle. He stood in front of the mirror and brushed his teeth.

'That's it, cleanliness Jools!' she laughed. He finished up and went into the toilet for a pee.

'Now wash those hands!' she prompted him.

'Ah know! Ah'm on it. Just shut up, will ye? Ah'm fuckin sick ay hearin your voice. Just give me two minutes peace.' He scrubbed his hands and shuffled back down the corridor to put his things away. His dick gave an involuntary twitch and a dribble of pee ran down the leg of his jeans.

'Ah've pished maself!' the woman giggled.

⊙

Jools stood in his room in the centre of the floor and took up the martial arts stance *ichimonji no kamae*. He stepped forward putting his whole bodyweight behind a punch and followed up with a stomping kick with the sole of his foot. He gave a couple of short jabs and followed with an elbow smash to the ribs of his imaginary opponent, then applied *omote gyaku*, a reverse wrist break.

'Stop that!' a loud male voice boomed. 'You're not allowed to practise. Anything Japanese is strictly forbidden!'

'What for? Sounds a bit racist tae me,' Jools said, still practising.

'There are many geriatric patients in this hospital. They fought the Japanese in the war. It upsets them. Stop practicing! Now!' A needle jabbed him in the ribs, knocking the wind out of him.

'AAARGH! WHAT ARE YE DAEIN, YA FUCKIN RADGE?!' Jools bawled, holding his side. He picked up his cigarettes and stomped up the hall for a cigarette. The smoking room was full and there were no seats so he sat on the unit by the wall and lit a cigarette. The room was full of new faces—visitors, Jools supposed—and the atmosphere was thick with smoke. An old air-conditioning unit buzzed uselessly in the corner.

'Missus, missus, can Ah get a cigarette off ye?' Archie asked a woman who was visiting. The Professor sat in the corner smiling and Eddie talked with an older woman, probably his mum by the look of her. The fair-haired guy with the piercing eyes talked to another man who bore a family resemblance, maybe his brother. They looked over at Jools and smirked at each other. Jools started to get the feeling they were staring at him and it made him feel uncomfortable. The tall man was missing and Jools felt comforted knowing that if he'd got out they'd have to let him out one day. The two fair-haired brothers with the eyes glanced over again, smirking snidely. Jools stubbed his cigarette out. He got up and left the room. He started to shuffle down the corridor when the short fat man walked up to him.

'How are you, my friend?' he asked. 'Let Jesus help you, my friend. I must apologise for my language earlier. They still will not let me out to worship in my own parish. I have to go to church here in the hospital and I'm afraid I do not mince my words. Let Jesus help you. Let him guide you.' He handed Jools a Bible. 'Take comfort, my friend.' He waddled off up the hall. Jools went back to his room and sat on the bed. He opened the Bible at the first chapter, Genesis.

'Pit it doon!' the voice said. 'You're not allowed any religious books on the ward.'

'Why no?' Jools asked. 'Surely Ah'm allowed tae read the Bible. What harm can Ah possibly dae readin that?'

'It's not allowed. No reading! There are many students from all religions.

We can't allow anyone's religious preferences to be involved. It may upset some of the other students.'

'Ah'm no in the least bit religious though,' Jools said. 'Ah just want something tae read. Something harmless. Ah'm bored silly. Ah'm no allowed tae dae nowt!'

'No reading!'

'Fuck's sake, man.' Jools put the Bible on the bedside cabinet.

'WEE MAN! SETTLE RIGHT DOWN!' another voice shouted. The presence totally took up Jools's mind. It felt close.

'Settle down, wee man! Stop takin bennies every two minutes! Ah'm upstairs watchin you. Ye ken Ah dinnae like you, eh?'

YLT: the letters slashed into the backs of his eyelids.

'Ah dinnae like you much either, come tae think ay it,' Jools said apprehensively.

'Dinnae be fuckin wide, ya wee cunt, or Ah'll come doon and fuckin leather ye now!' the voice said, annoyed. 'Ah ken what ye look like. Ah was doon earlier for a look at ye. That was me talkin tae ma wee brother in the smoking room. Ah'm Gary Love. Aye, Ah've goat they eyes tae. So's ma wee brother Danny. Aw ma family's goat they eyes, so's ma brar, Billy. Ye thought there was somethin special aboot yer eyes! Ye better stay away fae Claire tae, ya wee beast, or yer gettin fuckin tanned! You're gettin fuckin stabbed when ye get oot! That's ma wee sister. Wait till Danny gets ye. He's oan the course and ay kens aw aboot ye. Ay kens ye're a beast. Ay's goin fuckin mental, man. Wait till they get a hold ay ye oan their ain, they'll fuckin kill ye! And what's this aboot Billy's bird?'

'Who? Jane?' Jools asked.

'Aye, ye ken what Ah mean. That's ma brother's bird, awright? And see if Ah find oot ye've been thinkin sexually aboot her, yer fuckin gittin it.'

'Ah've no thought anythin like that aboot anyone in here. Ye can check for yerself. She's just ma pal. Ah've nowt but respect for the woman.'

'Aye, well remember we've goat ye every night when the doctors go hame and we can dae anythin we want tae ye! See if ye grass, ye'll get fuckin wasted. Now you better shut up and stop settin the alarm off every two minutes. Ah better no hear ye again the night or Ah'll come doon and fuckin dae ye tight! Remember, ma family runs this place! We can have a word wi' the doctors and get you sectioned for as long as we want. Ye'll never get oot. NEVER! The doctors listen tae us. We're major players. LOVE HURTS!'

YLT

The presence faded.

Jools got into bed and pulled the cover over his head. He lay quiet and almost dozed off.

⊙

'Jools, are you awake?' the woman's voice asked.

'What?' he croaked.

'They're away now. You can get up.'

It had got dark outside and the hall light shone through the window on the door.

'They were a bit mental, eh?' the woman said. 'Seem tae have a problem with you. Are you alright? I'm from the scheme, you can talk to me. Big Steve and all your neighbours are asking for you. Natty's asking for you tae, she's really missing you, you know.'

Jools thought of his ex-girlfriend Natty and a lump formed in his throat. How he missed her and wished she was here. That was back when the world was normal. Before they'd done this to him. It seemed a lifetime away.

'I'm over at Telford College's Muirhouse campus. In the shopping centre. The auld bookie shop with the computers. We've got you online so we can talk to you. People have been asking for you around here. You've been missed. They wanted someone to check on you. I'm Carol, by the way. Aye, and Ah'm black, so they wee bastards that are gein you the hassle better fuckin back off or I'll have half of Muirhouse up there. Ay's no a fuckin racist, right! Anyone that says ay is can argue wi' me! Yer wee pal Terry told us what they were treating you like. Toffee-nosed bastards. Big Steve's fuckin raging, by the way.'

'Shurrup ya silly fuckin cow!' the voice shouted. It was Gary Love.

'You, ya wee bastard! Leave him alone or you'll be the one that gets wasted! Tell yer black pal that tae. He's got a major chip oan his shoulder, that guy! Youse have got that poor laddie terrified!'

'Ay's a fuckin wee beast!' Gary Love argued. 'Ay's gettin fuckin leathered!'

'Naw ay's fuckin no! People roond here have kent him aw his life and he's got a spotless record! Everybody kens him and ay's done a lot ay work in the community, specially when he was younger. Ah've kent him since ay was wee and Ah knew ay's mother. Ay's a barry wee guy!' Carol stormed.

'Listen, dinnae fuckin…'

ZZZZIIIIPPPP!

A roller blind was pulled down over the proceedings and the voices were turned down low.

Jools lay quiet. He thought of Natty. She could make eveything alright. A tear trickled down his face. He felt totally miserable.

⊙

Jools heard the tea trolley rattling as it was wheeled down the corridor and got out of bed for a cuppa. He went into the smoking room and poured himself a cup from the leaky teapot. He helped himself to a plate of biscuits and sat down to smoke a cigarette.

'Jools, Jools, can Ah get a cigarette off ye?' Archie called over.

Jools pretended not to hear and nibbled nervously on a digestive.

'Can Ah get a fag, Jools?' Archie asked again.

'Ah've only got a couple,' Jools fended him off. He got up and when through to the quiet room. The wooden floorboards creaked and it sounded amplified in the silence.

SLAM! The smoking room door banged shut making Jools jump again. He was beginning to feel like he had shell-shock. He'd been a nervous wreck since he came in here.

He sat down at a table and picked up a deck of cards, half expecting to be told off. No warnings came so he started to sort the deck into suits.

Suddenly he became aware of a static-like tingle in the top of his head.

'STAY STILL!' a voice told him. 'We're sending the signal out!'

The static built up then suddenly emptied upwards from his head.

I FUCKED A CAT!! The message zapped from him into the air.

'What the fuck was that?!' Jools asked, his heart pounding.

'We're doing a radio test, Jools. You know, that message is being bounced off a satellite and picked up by a ship in the Pacific. They're relaying it from the naval base in Portsmouth.'

ZAP.

I STUCK A FINGER UP MY ARSE!

'Hold still, Jools,' the voice said merrily, 'they're about to clear another message.'

ZAP.

I LIKE WEE LASSIES!

Jools froze stiff.

'The boys have had a field day watching you on their monitors. They've been watching your thoughtwaves. They all think your ex is pretty lovely. She's become a real pin-up among the lads. We took some snaps from your memory bank. Of course they're only interested in the dirty bits. They've got one of your thoughtwaves of her topless. I hope you don't mind.'

'Natty's ma bird, ya dirty cunts! Fuck off!' Jools bawled.

ZAP.

I'VE GOT A BIG SPOT ON MY COCK!

'There now, we've zapped that lot to the ship. We just wait on it being sent back.'

ZAP.

IFUCKEDACATISTUCKAFINGERUPMYARSEILIKEWEELASSIESI'VEGOT ABIGSPOTONMYCOCK!

The words zapped back into him.

'Do you realise that message was relayed six thousand miles across the planet via a satellite in Portsmouth and back again? That's pretty damn good. The ship's computers hold so many million megabytes. They've just zapped them right through you. It's state of the art technology. That was a test to see if we could download info from a field operative on black ops.'

ZAP.

IFUCKEDACATISTUCKAFINGERUPMYARSE...

The messages zapped out of him faster and faster. They became a blur.

'C'MON MAN! ENOUGH!' Jools tried to shake himself free.

'Settle down! You'll damage the ship's computer! This is state of the art spy technology,' a cockney voice said.

ILIKEWEELASSIESI'VEGOTABIGSPOTONMYCOCK... The messages zapped back into him.

'This is the Royal Navy signing off for the night. We'll be watching, Jools. Bye bye from the lads in Portsmouth!' A cheer rose in the background. 'Tell Natty we love 'er!'

'Amazing Jools, modern technology,' the voice said. 'You can go for a fag now. We're finished for the night.'

The Canadian nurse came into the room with his medication and he knocked it back.

'You, ya dirty wee pervert! Stay away fae wee lassies,' a voice laughed in his head.

'Ah'm no a pervert! Ah was abused when Ah was wee. A cunt got me in the stair in Martello Court when Ah was about five. Tried to touch me up! Ah never, ever told anyone. Ah just ran away!'

'Tell her,' the voice suggested.

'How are you feeling Jools?' the nurse asked. 'Are you OK?'

'Ah was abused when Ah was wee!' he said blankly. A tear rolled down his face.

The nurse came over and hugged him. Jools soaked up the body contact like a sponge. It was all he needed.

⊙

Jools lay in bed unable to sleep. He got up and went for a cigarette. Two nurses sat on chairs in the hall outside the office door. He went into the smoking room and sat down in the corner. Everyone was in bed and he sat in the silence smoking peacefully.

'Secrets of the masons!' the voice said.

'Dinnae start aboot that!' Jools growled.

'Masons!'

Jools started to feel anxious. 'Shut up! Ah was warned no tae say nothing aboot that!'

'Masons!'

A tingle started in his head. He felt something being whipped out.

'What was that? What did you just take?' he asked.

'The secrets of the masons!' the voice answered, laughing.

'Fuck you! Ye've no tae touch that! Billy Love's a mason! He'll go spare!' Jools tried to reason although he'd begun to panic.

'Masons!'

'Jools, you better get that out of your head!' another voice said. 'You know you're not allowed to talk about the masons.'

'Ah know! Ah'm tryin!' He tried desperately to blank his mind. 'It's no me! Ah'm no thinkin that. It's them!'

'Masons!'

'Jools, stay off the Ms!' the voice warned him.

'Masons!'

BANG! BANG! BANG!

Jools nearly hit the ceiling. His heart nearly jumped out of his chest.

A huge dark-haired male nurse had come into the room and knocked on the window to his colleague. Jools stubbed his cigarette out and scuttled to bed.

⊙

He lay in the dark, unable to sleep. He felt restless and it was too warm even with the small vent window fully open.

'Jools, are you still awake?' It was Jane's voice.

'Aye pal, Ah'm awake,' he whispered.

'Jools, doll, Ah'm sorry about the way things are goin'. Billy Love was goin mental at me earlier. Gary told him about us and he went mental.'

'But we've no done anything,' Jools said.

'Ah know, that's what Ah've been trying to tell him but he'll no have it. Me and Billy's finished anyway. It's been over for ages. He just doesnae like the fact that Ah found you. He says it's unprofessional. He just doesnae like to think Ah can be happy without him. That Gary's a shit-stirring wee get! Wait till Ah see him. Aw Jools, Ah saw the wind earlier, Ah believe you. The wind people Jools, they want you out of here. Back to the scheme were you belong, so ye can play with the wind again. They can see how you're doing in here, Jools. They want you away from this place. It's killing you.'

'Ah know,' Jools said. 'But they'll no let me oot.'

'You need to escape. Ah can help. Ah just want to be with you,' Jane told him.

'Ah could probably get oot ay here if Ah wanted. Aye, awright then. Ah'll escape.'

'You'll have to stay blank Jools, in case they read your thoughtwaves when you're sleeping. Do you think you can keep it up till morning?'

'Ah'll gie it a bash.'

'Ah'll see you on the outside, babes. Ah'll be waitin for you. Ah canny wait till we're together,' she said huskily.

A pair of red lips blew him a kiss in his mind's eye and Jane left him. Jools kept blank the best he could and fell asleep as it got light.

Jools shuffled slowly down the hall. He did his best to keep his mind blank and to act sedated. He slowly shuffled up to the balding male nurse guarding the top of the stairs and the lift.

'Claire said she wants you in the office,' Jools said, slurring his speech slightly for effect.

'Thanks, Jools,' the nurse replied, and started off down the hall to the office.

'Sucker!' Jools said under his breath as he scampered down the stairs two at a time. He reached the bottom and turned left into the corridor with the photographs on the walls. He turned into the main building and went through a set of automatic doors into the car park. He ran up the grass verge onto the driveway and followed it out the hospital gates onto a quiet side street. He glanced back over his shoulder nervously to see if he was being followed and continued up the hill, crossing the main road at the top. He knew he'd be spotted if he took the main road so he stuck to the side streets heading north towards the Forth.

'What are you doing?!' the male voice asked suspiciously.

'Nothing!' Jools said innocently.'I'm just sittin oan the bog, see!' He pictured himself sitting on the toilet.

'You're trying to escape!'

'Naw Ah'm no. Ah'm sittin here havin a crap, see.' He kept the visualisation going.

'Where are you, Jools? We know you've escaped. Where exactly are you? Stop! We'll find you. What street are you in? West Tollcross! We're sending someone for you! Stay where you are!'

'Fuck off, ya fuckin bam! Ah'm no comin back!' Jools growled. He looked at the ground as he walked to stop himself looking at the street names. He changed course and headed up Lauriston Place and cut down a backstreet towards Edinburgh Castle rock. He turned down a narrow side street that brought him out on the Mound and headed to Market Street. He took a short-cut through the back of Waverley Station onto Princes Street. A silver people-carrier drove towards him at speed on Princes Street and he wondered if he'd been rumbled. He crossed and ducked into the crowds of shoppers. The sun burned down and he took off his conspicuous red jacket, tying it around his waist.

'Safe!' he thought. They'd never find him in the crowds. He stood at the Georgian Records Office building at the East End and stopped to light a cigarette. He put a hand on the stone balustrade of the building and vaulted it like a gymnast.'Ah wonder if anyone saw that,' he thought.

'That was us helping you,' the voice laughed.'You were like spiderman there!'

'How did Ah do that? Ah felt light, like a spring,' he said.

'We've got you on the superslide. It enhances your natural abilities,' the voice told him.

'How does that work?'

'It's just an adrenalin burst. We just enhance your adrenals by computer. It's all that's been keeping you alive, Jools. You would've crashed and burned weeks ago if we hadn't been zapping you with shots from this baby. You're chemically enhanced.'

'It feels good. Ah feel strong. Gie me another blast.'

'I can't. That feeling in your stomach recently, your adrenal glands are swollen. We can't hit you again for a few hours. It's too dangerous,' the voice told him.

Jools walked along Queen Street and headed down into Stockbridge. He started to limp again on Raeburn Place and turned into Inverleith Park. He sat down by the edge of the pond to rest and lit a cigarette. A group of pigeons pecked at the pavement and Jools noticed one pure white bird in the group.

'One dove,' he laughed to himself. He got up and cut through Broughton High School to Carrington Road past Fettes police headquarters. He ducked into a bus shelter as a police car passed him slowly and for a second he expected them to jump out and grab him but the driver seemed to be adjusting his seatbelt and they carried on. He cut through the back of the Western General Hospital into Drylaw and down finally into Muirhouse. He limped down Pennywell Road and was just approaching the bottom of the shopping centre when the voice stopped him.

'Stop Jools! Don't go any further. Stay away from the pub! Big Jim, the manager. He's not been caught yet.'

'What dae ye mean?' Jools asked.

'The whole place is playing a game just now. It's been going on while you've been away. Do you remember when you were catching the cars on Telford Road? Well you caught about one hundred and twenty people that night. All those doors you stopped at when you walked with the wind, that was the same. The whole country is playing a big psychological game just now. It's a dummy run in case terrorists ever try using it on the population. Big Jim's the captain for this area. He's not been caught yet. You better stay away from the pub. He's got a lot of money staked on this game so you better not get him caught or you'll get your arse kicked. Big Jim doesn't like people losing him money. You were in the blue and yellow team, Tory Liberal, until you went to the Royal Ed. Now you're in the blue team. They're a Tory ward. You'll not be too welcome in there now. You know, they could spy on everybody through your head. You're like one giant bug just now. You best stay away!'

'How long for?' Jools asked.'

'Until after the general election.'

Jools took a detour and walked across into Pennywell to his flat. He reached his door and realised he didn't have his keys. He'd given them to his sister and auntie to look after the cat. He sat on the doorstep and wondered what to do.

'Don't worry, I've phoned your auntie,' the voice told him. Jools looked over at the facing block. Bulldog's house was empty.

'That was the Iga ninpo guy's house. The one you thought was your grandmaster!' the voice laughed. 'He's away back home, he's finished up for the summer. He's studying for his psych major. What a laugh he's had with your neighbours while you were away. Iga man's mental.'

Jools lit a cigarette and sat back against the wall. His auntie's car drove round the corner and pulled up. His grandmother and aunt walked up the path, surprised to see him.

'How did you get here?' his auntie asked.

'Ah just walked,' he answered.

'What? All the way from the hospital? How did you get out?'

'Ah just walked oot,' Jools said. 'Ah wanted tae see the cat.'

She opened the front door and the cat came running. Jools picked it up and it purred loudly in his ear.

'You're lucky we came down,' his auntie said. 'We just came to feed the cat. Sarah's going out tonight so she asked us to do it.'

Jools sat with his cat on his knee. It felt so good to be back in familiar surroundings.

'Jools, I'm going to have to take you back,' his aunt said.

'No danger! Ah'm no goin back there! Never!'

'You'll have to, Jools,' his grandmother said. 'You can't just walk out of there, they'll be looking for you.'

'They'll send the police out to get you, Jools,' his aunt said. 'You have to come back. Come on, I'll take you.'

Jools huffed. 'Ah canny go back there. That place is killin me.' Jools refused to move.

'Look, Jools, do you want them to send the police out?'

Jools thought they were taking the game a bit too far. This psychological warfare game was getting a bit too serious. It must have been Billy Love who'd threatened to send the polis for him. He felt his aunt and grandmother were playing the part too well. Billy Love must have tricked them.

'Jools, come on, let me take you back now before they come for you,' his aunt pleaded.

Jools sighed.

'Jools, I don't need to point out that something very sinister is going on!' the loud voice whispered. 'She's going to drive you to a safe house, out of Edinburgh!'

'Ma sister's hoose!' Jools thought.

'Don't think, Jools! Don't picture your sister's address! Stay blank!' the voice warned.

Jools blanked his mind as they left the flat and walked to the car. He climbed in the back seat and they drove off. Jools ducked down on the back seat, blanking his thoughts. His auntie drove erratically and Jools was thrown from side to side in the back. He dared not look out of the window for fear of giving his position away.

'Your auntie's nervous!' the whisper said. 'She's trying to get you away, somewhere safe where they can't find you! Don't think, Jools! Don't picture your sister's address! Whatever you do, stay blank!'

The car jerked round another bend and Jools was thrown aside. They finally came to a halt and his aunt turned the engine off and opened the door.

'Twenty-seven Hopetoun Rise, Kirknewton!' the voice spat out.

'Shit! Fuck! Dirty grassin bastards!'

His aunt opened the door and his grandmother got out.

'Come on, Jools,' his auntie said. 'We're here.'

He sat up and looked around. They were parked in the Royal Edinburgh Hospital car park.

'Ah'm no goin back!' Jools refused to budge.

'Come on, Jools, you have to go back!' His aunt started to cry.

'Ah'm no goin back in there!' he said stubbornly.

'Jools, they'll send the police out, you have to go back. They'll be looking for you.'

'Come on, Jools,' his grandmother said. 'We'll come with you.'

Jools shook his head.

'Look, I'm going to have to call someone,' his aunt said, pulling out a mobile phone.

Jools sighed deeply and got out of the car. He headed anxiously towards the building with his head down. His aunt and grandmother followed behind. They walked through the main building and took the lift up to the ward. Jools's mouth was dry with anticipation as they walked down the corridor to the office. His aunt knocked on the door and Jools took a deep breath to steady himself. Billy Love answered.

'Jools, where have you been? We were looking for you,' Billy Love said, taking Jools by the shoulders. 'You must tell us if you need to leave the ward,' he said firmly.

Jools stared at him, wide-eyed. His leg was on a hair trigger ready to knee Billy Love in the balls should he try to hit him. Billy Love backed off.

'He went home to see the cat,' his aunt explained.

'Thanks for bringing him back,' Billy Love said, smiling like a crocodile.

Jools felt sick watching him crawling to his aunt. This charade he was putting on for their benefit. If only they knew what he was really like they would never have made him come back here. He headed to his room with his head down.

SLAM! The smoking room door banged shut and he jumped.

⊙

Jools got up late next morning as the walking he'd done the day before had tired him out. He'd taken his medication at eight and went back to sleep until nearly noon.

'Jools, Jools, someone in the office fancies you!' a female voice said.

'Away tae fuck!' he growled.

He got up and shuffled to the toilet. The boil on his dick was still angry and sore, throbbing with every heartbeat. He gave himself a gentle shake and left the bathroom. Halfway up the hall his knob gave an involuntary twitch and he dribbled in his shorts.

'Ah've pished maself!' the woman laughed.

Jools huffed and went to the kitchen for a cup of tea.

'STAY OFF THE WARD!' the loud voice told him as he poured himself a cuppa. Two men entered the kitchen followed by a male nurse.

'Those guys are from ward five! Word has got around that you're a racist paedophile. Some of the students must have been talking and a few of the guys in ward five are annoyed with you. Stay off the ward as much as possible. Stay out of the kitchen. The security will have to follow you around so don't give them a hard time.'

Jools left the kitchen warily and went back to the smoking room. The room was nearly empty so he lit a cigarette and sipped his tea in peace.

SLAM! He jumped. The male nurse with the crewcut came over to him.

'Jools, someone's just come in and we need that single room. Can we move you to the dorm?' he asked. 'I'll let you get your things together and I'll come and get you in five minutes.'

Jools shuffled back to his room and packed his belongings away in bags. He sat on the bed and waited a while.

The nurse came in and picked up a bag. 'Follow me,' he said, and they walked out across the hall. Jools was led to a cubicle in the corner by the window. One wall of the cubicles was made up of a wardrobe unit with drawers and there was a curtain across the foot of the bed. He looked out of the window to a panoramic view of the Pentland Hills. A large ash tree grew directly beneath his window and he watched the black and white magpies hopping around on the lawn below.

'Stay off the Pentlands!' the male voice boomed. 'Stay off...' A picture of a pair of legs in plus fours and golf shoes dropped into his mind. It looked like someone had projected a slide onto his mind's eye.

Jools ignored the voice.

'STAY OFF THE PENTLANDS! PIT IT DOON!' the voice boomed.

He sighed and closed the curtain. He began to unpack and two bells rang in the hall.

'That's lunchtime, folks!' a nurse called down the hall.

⊙

'What are ye scared ay the masons for?' a male voice asked Jools, who was sitting on the toilet.

'Ah didnae want to betray Rob, ma sensei. He taught me the secrets ay the masons,' Jools said.

'But that wasnae Rob, it was Iga man or whatever you call him. It was probably just some wee radge that got drunk and blabbed all his old man's masonic secrets. Do you think they're worried aboot the masons?' the voice asked.

'Ah dinnae suppose so.'

'Well then, stop bein so feared ay the masons.'

Jools thought about it and smiled. 'True, when you think about it that way. Is that aw Ah've been worried aboot?'

'Jools, the young generation now have nae respect for anything. Naebody's feared ay the masons anymore. They've nae power. They're a bunch ay bams.'

Jools got up and flushed the toilet. He automatically scrubbed his hands and went up the hall for a cigarette. He blushed as he passed the office. The thought that the female staff had just watched him have a shit on their monitors made him cringe. He'd find it hard to face them. He sat down and lit a cigarette.

'Jools, Jools, can Ah get a cigarette off ye?' Archie begged.

'Ah've only got a couple,' Jools said automatically.

SLAM! The door banged shut and he jumped.

A nurse came over to him, smiling. 'Probably embarrassed about the shit,' he thought.

'Jools, can you come and get weighed?' the nurse asked.

'Ah'll be a bit lighter after the load Ah just dropped,' he sniggered.

Jools followed her to the office and he stood on the scales. She adjusted the bar and took a reading, marking it down on her chart.

'You've gained weight,' she smiled. 'Now let's get your blood pressure.' She attached the velcro pad around his arm and pumped it up. She listened to a vein through a stethoscope and released the pressure valve which hissed as it deflated.

'Good,' she smiled. 'That's us.'

Jools went back to his room and lay back on the bed.

'Is that you fuckin lying aroond again?!' Billy Love's voice boomed. 'Ah'm no gonnie tell you again aboot lying there daydreamin'. You're meant tae be daein the One, two till four every day. Wait till Yours Truly gets back fae holiday and finds ye've been fuckin aboot. Ah'm no gonnie tell you aboot it again! Now what do ye want me for?'

'What are ye on aboot?' Jools asked.

'You contacted me. You thought aboot the top of your heid. That triggers an alarm in my hoose. Ah've got tae answer it every time it goes off. Dinnae think ay the top ay yer heid unless ye need me for something. Ah'm no happy wi' you.'

'What have Ah done now?' Jools asked.

'It's aboot ma daughter, Claire. Ah'm no happy wi' you sniffin aroond her. Dae ye understand?' Billy Love said.

'Fair enough. Ah'm no that interested anyway,' Jools lied.

'Ye better no have been thinkin ay her sexually,' Billy Love said. 'And what's aw this aboot a hairbrush?'

'Ah dunno what yer talkin aboot,' Jools coughed.

'Anyway, dae you remember that hoose you visited wi' the wind in Barnton? The hoose with the lions on the gates?'

Preston pans

'Ah remember,' Jools said.

'That's ma hoose. Ah'm originally fae the 'Pans but now Ah run the Scots Tories fae ma hoose. Keep that tae yerself. Ah've no been caught yet. Anyway, since ye dinnae really want anything, Ah was just aboot tae get my tea so Ah'm goin away now. Stay off the top ay yer heid. Ah'm no wantin bothered again the night.' Billy Love's connection terminated.

Jools sat trying not to think about the top of his scalp. Something tweaked involuntarily.

'What is it? You again! What are ye wantin now?!' Billy Love sighed impatiently.

'Nowt, it was a mistake. It wisnae me,' Jools said.

'Ah'm tryin tae get ma tea. Ah've been oan ma feet aw day and Ah'm knackered. Ah'm no wantin tae keep gettin up tae answer tae you. Now stop thinkin ay the top ay yer heid and stay away fae Scots Tories,' Billy Love moaned.

A nurse came into the dorm. 'Jools, Dr La Plante would like to see you now. Can you come with me?' she asked.

Jools followed her up the corridor to an office at the top of the stairs. The nurse knocked on the door and they went in.

'Jools McCartney to see you,' she smiled.

'Come in Jools, take a seat,' the man said, pointing to the chair by his desk.

'Say nothing, Jools!' a female voice told him. 'Don't tell him anything. He believes you're a racist paedophile and it's his job to get it out of you,' the woman said. 'Don't tell him anything.'

'I'm Dr La Plante. I'm a consultant psychiatrist,' he said, extending a hand. Jools shook hands.

'Now do you remember when you came in, Jools, do you remember saying something to Dr Malloy about invasive thoughts? I wonder if you can tell me more about these thoughts,' La Plante said, pointing to the area just behind his temple where Jools's coils were. Jools noticed the computer and pack of slides lying on the table and put two and two together. 'He must be in on it,' he thought. 'He must be the one playing the slides.'

'SAY NOTHING!' the voice said, now closer than before. It felt as though the presence took up the whole of Jools's skull.

'Ah canny mind. Ah really dinnae remember,' Jools said truthfully. 'Ah'm awright, there's nothin wrong wi' me. Ah just want tae go hame.'

'Say nothing! Jools we want you almost catatonic! Say nothing! Not a word!' the female voice told him.

Jools clamped his jaw shut. He blanked his mind and adopted a faraway gaze. Like looking at a distant mountain, as they said in the the martial arts.

'Jools, could you tell me just how these thoughts manifest themselves? Are they bad thoughts? Are they making you feel depressed? Scared or anxious?'

Jools said nothing and sat motionless staring into the distance, taking in all around him.

'Jools, are you OK?' the doctor asked.

Jools stayed blank.

The doctor wrote something down.

'OK. You can go back to the ward now, Jools,'

'SMIFFY! He looks like Smiffy from the Bash Street Kids!' the woman laughed.

Jools shuffled back to the ward. He went into the smoking room. Emma sat with a large heavily-built man. She had an arm around him and they shared a seat.

'Stay away from Emma!' a loud whisper came. 'She's the fixer-upper! That's her minder! If you get on the wrong side of her she'll send him to break your legs! She's not too happy with you! One of the students told her about the wee lassie. You'd better stay out of her way!'

Jools lit a cigarette and glanced around the room nervously. Eddie sat with Danny Love and Jools stared over at them. They seemed to be watching him and every now and then would turn to each other and smirk. Jools began to feel uncomfortable. Archie sat with a shaky arm checking the racing form in the paper and chewing a bookie's pen. The Professor smiled wisely at everyone.

Jools thought the Professor looked like a down and out with his old leather bulldog face.

'Don't think about the Professor like that!' the voice said. 'He's a very intelligent man. He only looks scruffy. He's not normally unshaven. He's been working very hard.'

'But he looks like an auld jaykey,' Jools said.

'That's the part he was playing. You see, Jools, the students are practicing helping a racist paedophile. Now the Professor and his colleagues have sort of beefed up all your negative traits on the computer. They've magnified them about ten thousand times and the students have to practice on this virtual patient. They don't know it's a computer mock-up. This thing has been created to be really evil. It rapes and murders young children and has been known to be cannibalistic. It's the worst thing you can possibly imagine. It makes people literally sick, and see when it laughs… it's totally evil. It gives you the creeps. It's like your laugh but really distorted and evil. It's the sickest thing in creation. The first year students in the smoking room all think you're really like that. That's why they're all getting so angry with you. They think you're a racist, child-murdering paedophile. The project is called "IT". Do you remember that horrible thing you saw that floated past your bed with the big beak? That's what "IT" looks like. It's an inbred psychopathic paedophile and it's on the loose. The students have to practice catching it and treating it. Because you escaped, "IT" escaped. It does what you do. If you laugh, it laughs. We put the programme in your head as you slept. The programme takes on all your traits but the negative ones are amplified. It even coughs and sniffs like you. It's really annoying.'

Jools could feel pressure in his head above his left eye. 'So this thing's in ma brain, alive? What if it takes over?'

'It's safe. We'll destroy it before it comes to that.'

'Ah thought they could hear inside ma heid,' Jools said.

'Only third and fourth year students are allowed on the inner game. You'll never be allowed to meet them. That's how we maintain confidentiality,' the voice told him. 'The first year won't be allowed till the end of term. It's their job to take you apart and treat you. They have to turn you into a new man by the end of term. That's what they get their marks for. It's all part of the Love programme.'

Two bells rang in the corridor.

'Dinner time, people!' a male nurse called.

Jools stood in line by the food trolley in the kitchen. Danny Love was in front of him and kept turning round to look at Jools warily.

'That wee cunt's shitting himself. He's skiddy aboot me,' Jools thought to himself, smiling inwardly. Danny Love sat down at a table beside Eddie. Jools took a tray and sat on his own with his back to a wall but soon his table started to fill with the most lost of souls. Jools seemed to attract the quiet, nervous people of the ward. He wondered if they felt safe next to him. Did he give out a protective vibe, he pondered. A young Oriental girl in particular always seemed to sit near him. He wished he could reach over and give her a cuddle. She seemed so in need of someone. He began to feel very protective of her and although she never spoke he enjoyed her company. He found her cute in her baseball cap and jacket that had an Oriental tiger on the back. He watched her nibble nervously and tried to think of something to say to break the ice but couldn't and stayed silent. He finished up his dinner and made a cup of tea, keeping Danny Love in view. He doubted they had the bottle to attack him as there were too many guards in the room. He went back to the smoking room and had a quick cigarette before everyone got back from dinner. The Oriental girl came into the room and sat down. She looked over at the ashtray and picked up a large butt end, put it in her mouth and lit it.

'Do you want a fag, pal?' Jools asked her, handing out his packet.

'Thanks,' she said nervously. 'I'll give you one back tomorrow.'

'Take a couple for later,' Jools said, smiling gently. 'Have you been in long?' he asked.

'I'm in for the week,' she said. 'I lost my brother and sister in an accident. Have you been in long?'

'A wee while.'

Jools's heart went out to her. She looked so fragile. He wanted to hug it all away, make it all better for her. He knew what it was like to lose someone close and a lump came to his throat. If only he could get closer to her. Maybe he could help.

She sat nervously puffing on her cigarette. The room started to fill up as people came back from dinner. Danny Love swaggered into the room with Eddie and they sat opposite him.

'Takin the fuckin brave tablets again,' Jools thought. The students looked over and smirked at each other. The girl finished her cigarette and left the room. Jools noticed a new face. A man in a wheelchair talking to Archie and the Professor.

'What about all your wheelchair jokes, Jools?' the voice said seriously.

'Aw come oan, man. Ah was just havin a laugh, eh? Ah've got a cousin in a wheelchair so dinnae start! Ah wis only muckin aboot!'

'He's a psychology professor you know. Wait till he looks through your thoughtwaves on the computer, he'll fuckin zap you! You'll get the max for sure.'

Jools avoided looking at the man in the wheelchair. He fought hard to conceal his memory. He nervously left the room and went back to the dorm.

'We told him about your jokes and he said ye're a poof and ye're a Jew!' the woman said. 'That's him got his own back so no more disabled stuff, OK? Dr David Love hates that kind of thing. Any more of it and you'll get the max.'

'Fair enough,' Jools said, relieved.

'DEFINITION OF A SWASTIKA! A SPASTIC WELDED TO A SUBMARINE!' the voice screamed.

A wave of panic hit Jools. He fought hard to blank his mind. 'That wisnae me! Honest! Ah never said that!' Jools gibbered.

An electric charge filled his body. His heart pounded and he cowered in the corner of his bed.

'Do you want the max?!' the voice bawled.

'Naw!'

'The Professor says ye're a poof, ye're a Jew and you're the crippled cunt! He knows you're on disability benefit.'

The electricity subsided but Jools's heart continued to pound.

'Ah'm just some wee diddy fae Muirhoose, man!' he said. 'Ah'm Ah meant tae have been perfect aw ma life? How was Ah meant tae know you'd be takin ma fuckin heid aff me? Ah never knew aboot this!' he babbled. 'Fuckin revenge ay the bodysnatchers! Fuckin Burke and Hare! Gie's ma heid back! And ye can tell that Gary fuckin Love that Ah'm no John Merrick either. Fuckin comin doon for a look! Ah'm no the fuckin Elephant Man! This fuckin place is

Dickensian! He'll be chargin cunts admission next! Come and see the schemie! Come and play wi' the brain! That's ma fuckin mind yer playin wi'! Ye can aw fuck right off!'

'CALM DOWN, JOOLS!' the voice ordered.

'Fuck you, ya fuckin', petty, touchy motherfuckers! Ye can gie me yer max! But see if Ah ever find oot who you are Ah'll fuckin kill ye! Ah'll boot fuck oot ye! Ah'll kill aw yer fuckin family an' all!'

'Shut up, Jools! I'm warning you!' the voice said.

'Suck ma fuckin dick! Ya fuckin mongo bastards!'

'Jools, shut up! Give him the schizo voice, that'll shut him up,' a man's voice said.

'Jooolllllsssss! Jooooollllllssss! SSSSSSShut uuuuup Jooolllssss!' a demonic voice gurgled.

'That's a schizophrenic voice you're getting. That's what schizophrenics hear, Jools. If you don't calm down we'll turn it up and leave you like that!' the voice threatened.

'Just gie me ma heid back,' Jools pleaded. 'Even just at night so Ah can get a decent sleep.'

'Twenty-four hours without a thought wave!' The presence left him.

⊙

Jools lay on his bed with the curtain pulled around his cubicle. The evening sun shone through the window and he could hear a group of people playing with a football on the lawn below.

'Jools, it's me, Carol. Ah'm over at the Telford computer suite in the shopping centre. Listen, everyone sends their best wishes and all your neighbours are asking for you,' the black woman said. 'Big Steve asked me to have a wee word with you and see how you're bein treated.'

'No too bad, pal. Ah just wish they would gie me ma heid back,' Jools said.

'Ah know, it must be terrible. You shouldnae even be on med research either. You should be back doon here in Muirhoose where you belong. You're meant to be doing psychological warfare from your own hoose. It was when you crossed the Dean Bridge that night when you were walking with the wind. You got caught that night. The Royal Ed took you over when you went into the town. They're saying you're their gomer. All that walkin you done. It was all sponsored. The money was meant to go to charities in Muirhoose but the Royal Ed have taken the money. They say you're their gomer so the money goes to them. We're fightin it aw the way.'

'Dirty bastards! They better fuck off!' Jools said. 'Ah'm daein fuck all for the Royal Ed. The only one worth talkin tae in here is Jane.'

'Your pal Kev's asking for you. Dinnae be too hard on him, Jools. He didnae want to treat you like that. They had to scare you into getting rid of him while you were on psych warfare. He was told what you'd go through. He didnae want to go along with it but he knew you'd be alright in the end. We told him how much money you'd be getting paid for it.'

'So Kev never done nothing? Ah thought he'd sold me oot tae the papers.'

'Jools, he understands and he's still there for you so you better hurry up and get out. Wait till you get back home! You should have been having the time of your life, not stuck in that shit hole. Natty's asking for you tae. That lassie really loves you, you know. She's really missing you,' Carol said.

Jools felt a warm glow inside and he cheered up. He missed Natty more than he was letting on and news of her gave him renewed hope. 'Tell her Ah miss her tae,' he said.

'Listen, Jools, this link's about to crash. Ah'll have to go now, they only allow me a few minutes. Now dinnae worry. Me and Big Steve are doin our best to get you out of there. We'll keep at it and you stay strong, OK? We're gonnie have the party of all parties when you get out! Ah'll see you later, pal,' she said. Her presence faded and Jools was left alone.

It had got dark in the dorm and the room was illuminated by a wall light in the next cubicle. Jools heard the tea trolley rattling and got up for a cuppa. He went into the smoking room and poured a cup, helping himself to toast from a plate. He sat down and filled his face. There was another new face, Jools noticed. A tall man in a checked suit with an earring in sat opposite the TV.

'Stay off that man!' a loud whisper hissed.

Jools wondered who he was. He looked like a gangster.

'Do not picture that man's face!' the whisper warned.

'Who is he, likes? A smack dealer or something?' Jools asked.

'No, Jools, that is exactly the sort of thinking we are trying to train you out of! He is a high-ranking Scottish Executive official! He is here to see conditions for himself in the ward since your friends in Muirhouse started to cause concern about the way you've been treated in the Royal Ed. Do not picture his face! Stay off that man!'

Jools tried to blank all thought of the man from his mind but something about him attracted his attention.

'Stay off that man!' the whisper warned.

Jools finished his toast and reached for a cigarette but he'd run out. He got up and went back to his room. He took a pack of cigarette papers from his rucksack and went back to the smoking room. He went to the ashtray and picked a few butts and broke them up to make a roll-up. The black ash stained his fingers and he lit the cigarette. Suddenly a sharp agonising pain hit him like a knife in the stomach and he dropped to one knee, holding his side. His heart pounded as he struggled to regain his breath.

'You digusting little piece of filth! Leave the room! NOW!' a male voice bawled.

Jools stubbed out the roll-up and scuttled from the room. A queue had formed outside the office and a nurse called to him to come and get his medication. He stood in line shaking, boiling inside. He fought back tears of rage as he took his tablets, then went to his room. He got undressed and got into bed, pulling the duvet over his head. Thoughts of Natty ran through his head and he started to cry. How he missed her. He wished his family were there and he was back home in his own house.

'Jools, Jools, dinnae worry, son. Jools, stay strong,' his dead mother's voice called out to him from the distance.

'Mum!' Jools shouted. 'Mum, it's really you!'

'Jools, Jools, dinnae give in,' she called, clear as day.

Jools broke down hysterically. 'MA!' he wailed. 'MA! dinnae leave me!'

'Jools! Ah'm here, son!' his mother called, her voice getting further away.

'MA! Dinnae leave me, please! Ah miss ye, ma! Ah miss ye!' Jools cried. His body shook as he sobbed, the tears streaming down his face.

Suddenly Jools stopped crying, like someone had flicked a switch and he calmly said 'Love you, Forever': the words on his mother's gravestone. He lay back down quietly.

'Good, Jools,' a sympathetic sounding voice said. 'That was your part of the puzzle. You've given your message.'

'Was that really my ma?' Jools asked. There was no reply.

'If it wasnae really my ma, at least Ah heard her voice again.'

He fell asleep peacefully.

⊙

Jools's eyes flickered open and the cleaner stood sweeping his cubicle.

'G'morning, Blue,' he said in his cockney accent. 'I hope I didn't wake you.'

'It's awright,' Jools said, sitting up.

The cleaner picked up a mop and gave the floor the once over. He whistled as he worked and moved onto the next cubicle.

Jools got up and shuffled to the bathroom.

'Walk for us, Jools!' the voice said. 'Walk for the Royal Ed! We want you to do a sponsored walk for Safegates, the supermarket. It's all taken care of. The students have fixed it up. All you have to do is as before. Be guided.'

'Fuck you! Ah'm goin naewhere!' Jools refused to budge.

'You must, Jools! We have it all organised. You do your walk for the Royal Ed students to make money for their term work.'

'Ye can get to fuck! And Ah want aw ma sponsorship money returned tae Muirhoose. You greedy fuckers had nae right tae take that money. Ah did the walkin for ma own area.' Jools left the toilet cubicle and scrubbed his hands. He left the bathroom and shuffled down the hall. Halfway down, his dick gave an involuntary twitch and he dribbled in his jogging pants.

'Ah've pished maself!' the voice laughed.

'Fuck off, ya nippy bastards!' Jools gritted his teeth.

He went back to his room to get dressed. When he got there he found a post-it note stuck to his wardrobe door.

The note read,

> Dear Rodney,
> I'll meet you at 8.00 outside the building.
> See you later,
> Claire.

'Rodney?' he wondered. Had she got his name wrong or was it a pet name for him? Like Rodney from *Only Fools and Horses*. He was a plonker. Was that what she was calling him? She was just being playful. He tucked the note in the drawer and smiled to himself smugly. She wanted to take him out. He was pretty chuffed. He couldn't wait. This was going to be cool. He dressed and went to the smoking room. It was nearly empty. He had no cigarettes so he asked a nurse if she'd take him to the shop. 'We're severely understaffed at the moment, Jools. I'll see if I can take you in a minute,' the nurse said. She went away then came back for him and led him down the stairs and through the corridors to the shop in the main building. He bought a hundred cigarettes to last him and they went back to the ward.

He went into the smoking room and lit a cigarette.

JAB!! He flinched as a needle jabbed him in the side.

'What the fuck was that for?!' he asked.

'Shut up, Jools! It was your virtual dummy. I just jabbed it to see if you'd feel it,' the voice said, sounding bored. 'I'm in the lab and I thought I'd try it out. That feeling of pressure in your left temple is where the antenna's bolted on. Have another.'

JAB! He flinched again.

'Fuck off, ya wee bastard! That's fuckin sore! What ye daein?!' Jools was boiling.

'Take that!' JAB! Jools jumped. 'And that!' JAB! 'And that!' JAB!

'Aaargh! Fuckin stop it!' Jools bawled.

'There! You've been stabbed, what more d'you want?' the voice said. 'That's what we meant by getting stabbed. You see, everything is like you're told, just not in the way you think. It's not what you expect it to be. TEE-HEE!' the voice laughed.

JAB! He flinched.

SLAM! He jumped.

Jane came over to him.

'Hi, Jools,' she said. 'I'm just wondering if you feel up to going out today? Would you like that?'

'Aye, sound,' Jools said.

'It'll give you a chance to get out of the ward for a change. You must be feeling pretty cooped up. I'll come for you after lunch, OK?' She left him to tend an elderly woman.

Two bells rang in the hall.

'That's lunchtime, everyone!' a nurse called.

⊙

Jools finished his meal and went to the smoking room. The Oriental girl was in. She came over to Jools and handed him some cigarettes from a ten pack.

'It's awright, pal,' Jools said, smiling gently. 'You dinnae have to gie me them back.'

'You gave me some fags,' she said.

'I'll take one off ye,' Jools compromised.

He gave her a light and lit his own and they sat together saying nothing for a while. The girl slipped out of the room when she'd finished her cigarette. Jools never saw her again.

'Jools, Jools, can Ah get a cigarette off ye?' Archie asked.

'Ah've only got enough to last me,' Jools evaded him.

'Ah'll gie ye a line for the bookie's if ye gie me a fag,' Archie relented.

'Ah'm no wantin it,' Jools fended him off.

'It's for Man United tae win the cup,' Archie persisted.

'Ah'm no wantin it!' Jools said again.

Archie snatched up a paper and turned to the racing page. His hand started to shake badly.

Jools threw him over a cigarette. He couldn't stand to watch this any longer.

'Dinnae keep askin'. Ah've only got enough tae dae me,' Jools told him.

'Stop buckin scrannin fags, you!' an old man with glasses shouted to Archie.

'Ah'm no, Ah was only askin for a fag,' Archie mumbled.

'Ah'm sick ay you buckin beggin fags off people!' the old man shouted. 'You're a buckin scrannin cunt! Ah've been gien you fags all day, now enough! You better go and buy some! Ye're no gettin any buckin mair off me!'

'They'll no gie me any money,' Archie said. 'They've cut ma social. Ah only get fifteen pound a week for ma giro. Cause Ah've been in here over six weeks. Ah got intae debt wi' ma catalogue money 'n' eveythin'. They're takin ays tae court.'

'Well you should keep yer buckin money and buy fags!' the old man argued.

'Ah do buy fags!'

'Well ye never buckin seem tae offer me one! As soon as ye get them ye must go intae hiding!' The old man would not back down. 'Dinnae dare ask me for another fag tonight. That's it buckin finished!' He pulled out a pack and lit a cigarette, drawing hard on it. 'Yer takin the pish, now enough!'

Archie chewed a bookie's pen and got back to his racing form. The man in the wheelchair came in with the Professor. Emma and her minder followed. Jools finished his cigarette and lit another. Emma sat cuddling the burly minder.

'Stay away from that person!' a loud whisper said.

Emma got up and danced over to Jools.

'Awright? Is yer sister comin up the night?' she asked.

Jools got the feeling he was being grilled. 'Ah dunno.'

Emma shuffled her feet. 'You're fae Muirhoose, eh? Dae ye ken Rob Hatchett? What aboot Stevie Macintosh? Ye must ken him.'

'Naw, Ah dinnae ken them,' Jools said.

'She's checking your rep!' the voice said. 'She knows you're hiding something, Jools. She's been hearing rumours about you and wee lassies. It was Danny Love and Eddie that told her.'

Emma's minder growled over. Jools felt extremely nervous. Everyone seemed to be watching him. He finished his cigarette and went to his room. He passed the short man who'd given him the Bible. The man stood crying in the hall.

'That's Jimmy!' the voice said. 'He's an actor. All the people in here are either students, professors or actors.'

Jools thought he looked pretty convincing. He went and sat on his bed. His mind drifted and he began to think of Natty, his most recent ex. His heart fluttered as he pictured himself in her arms. He cuddled his pillow.

'PIT IT DOON!' the voice said. 'Don't picture anything! Stay off the sexual!'

'Ah'm no daein nowt,' Jools said.

'Ye're a poof, ye're a Jew! Shut yer mooth!'

'Shut up? Ah've hardly spoke tae anyone in two months,' he told them.

'You tasted your own spunk! Ye're a poof, ye're a Jew, shut yer mooth!' the voice laughed.

'Did Ah fuck!' Jools spluttered. 'Ah'm no a fuckin poof!'

'Shut yer mooth, Jools! Just literally shut the fuck up!'

'Ah'm no fuckin sayin nowt!' Jools bawled.

'Shut… yer… mooth! Shut up, Jools, just shut up! SSSSSSShut the ffffffffffuck up!'

'You're a nippy fuckin bastard, Ah swear it! Leave me the fuck alone!' Jools boiled.

'Shut up!' the presence disappeared as Jane entered the dorm.

'Hi Jools, are you ready?' she asked.

'Ah'm ready,' he said and they walked down the hall. They passed the man in the checked suit. Jools watched his demeanour, his form. The man seemed completely relaxed. At one with his surroundings. Jools had seen this before in Aikido practitioners. He wondered if the man was a martial artist. They walked down the stairs and through the main building, coming out in the car park. She led him through the main gates and into Morningside.

'Do our walk for us, Jools! Just be guided!' a loud whisper said.

Jools ignored it and they went into a coffee shop and sat down at a table.

He scanned the shop nervously. Someone in a wheelchair sat opposite them and he turned his chair so they were out of view. Jane gave him a reassuring look.

'Are you OK?' she asked.

'Sound,' Jools said.

'What would you like?' she asked, handing him a menu.

'Just coffee, thanks.' He felt good being out with Jane. He found her very attractive and she was nice to talk to. He hoped she'd talk more about them seeing each other but she didn't. They drank their coffee and she asked him if he thought the medication was working. He hadn't really noticed any difference.

'So what do you do with yourself at home?' she asked.

'Not a lot. Lift weights and practice the martial arts. That's about it, really,' he said.

'But you get out, go for a drink with friends, don't you?'

'Aye. Ah like a pint.'

'Where do you go usually?' she asked.

'Usually just along tae my local in Muirhoose,' he said. 'Ah've no been in for a while.'

Jools hurried nervously to finish his coffee.

'Do you want anything else?' she asked.

'Naw, Ah'm sound,' he said.

She stood up to go and pay the bill.

'Ah'll get it.' He stood up.

'No, I'll get it. I get the money back from the hospital,' she told him.

Jools stood outside and waited, keeping his mind blank. The heavy traffic on Morningside Road made him feel nervous. It had been a while since he'd been in crowds. They walked the short distance back to the hospital in the sunshine.

⊙

Jools sat in his cubicle. He was still buzzing from the excitement of the crowds. He lay on his bed and congratulated himself on keeping together outside. He hadn't really thought he was ready to face the world yet.

The curtain at the foot of his bed pulled back and a fat woman stood there.

'Did you find the note I left here earlier?' she asked, her large jowls wobbling as she spoke.

'Aye, was that you?'

'Where is the note? I put it in the wrong cubicle,' she said.

Jools got it from the drawer.

'Thanks' she said, grabbing the note in a pudgy hand. She left him alone.

'That's Claire? Ah thought the blonde one was Claire,' he said to himself.

'There are two Claires. One of the girls in the office fancies you!' the voice said.

'Anyway, Ah've been thinkin', Jools said. 'Maybe Claire isnae the one for me. It would cause too much hassle wi' Billy Love and the two brothers. Tae tell the truth, Ah've still got a lot ay feelins for my ex. Ah think Ah'll go back tae Natty. That's who Ah'm really interested in.'

'She's in the office. You've upset her. She fancies you.'

'Ah dinnae believe ye. Ah bet it's another hook. Yer takin the piss oot me. Yer just tryin tae fish me in again. Ah'm no wearin it!'

'Claire's upset. She generally gets what she wants around here, you know. She won't be too pleased,' the voice told him.

'Ah'm sorry, but no this time. Ah want Natty back.'

'She says ye're a poof! Ye're a Jew and ye've tae shut yer mooth! She didnae fancy ye anyway. She says you're a wee dog and she'd never go oot wi' ye! She says have you still got that big spot on your cock?' the woman laughed. 'She thinks you're disgusting! You're getting leathered off her brothers! Ya dirty, smelly, pishy wee dog! Naeone ever fancies a gomer! Eeeugh! Yuk! You used to have a wank in your sock!'

'Fuck off, ya mingin bitch! Ye can tell her tae shut her fuckin spoiled mooth an' all. It's just cause she's no gettin her own way,' Jools said.

JAB! He flinched as a needle stuck him in the back.

'Fuck off, ya wee boot! What ye daein, ya fuckin fuckpig?! You're fuckin skankin', by the way!'

'Shut up, Jools! Just shut up!' the woman giggled.

Jools got up and stomped to the bathroom. He ran the bath taps and got undressed.

He climbed into the lukewarm water and started to scrub.

'Yuk! You're a dirty, mingin wee bastard Jools!' the woman laughed. 'Is that big spot still on your cock? You make us sick! You canny even go for a pish without pishing yourself!' she giggled. 'Claire says you're a dirty, clarty, ugly wee bastard.'

Jools started to get wound up.

'Suck ma dick, slutfuck! Ya fuckin dirty-moothed wee hoor!'

'Wash yourself, ya dirty wee filthbag! Remember and wash behind your foreskin, cheesyknob! Ya smelly wee get!' she laughed. 'Yer breath's stinkin ay shite!'

Jools let out a growl as he scrubbed hard at his skin. He'd lost his grip and scrubbed neurotically, harder and harder. He almost rubbed the skin right off and the flannel left raw red patches on his body.

'Jools! Dinnae do that,' the woman gasped, sounding shocked. 'We've never seen you like this, Jools, are you alright? It's just standard gomer treatment. Don't take it all so seriously.'

Two bells rang in the hall.

'Dinner time, folks!' a male nurse called.

Jools sat at a table on his own. The dining hall started to fill up and the same lost faces appeared around his table. Danny Love and Eddie, still in a Hearts top, sat together and would glance over now and then, smirking. Jools ignored it and ate quickly. He finished his meal and helped himself to seconds. He was pretty self-conscious of the weight he'd lost and wanted to put it back on as quickly as possible. His table soon started to empty and he finished his food in peace. He made himself a cup of tea and went down the corridor to the smoking room. The Professor, the man in the wheelchair and the man in the checked suit sat together talking. Archie filled in a betting slip on a coffee table. The TV blared in the corner and Emma shuffled over to him.

'Awright, doll?' she gummed. 'What have you been daein the day? Ah was arguin wi' ma felly earlier. Ah'm gonnie get ma other brother tae waste um. The cunt was talkin aboot pullin the machetes oot 'n' that. Ah'm no wantin tae hear aw that shite so Ah telt um tae nash. What you in for again?'

Jools froze, his heart pounding. He looked at her minder.

'Ah've goat depression,' he lied.

'You better watch her, Jools!' the voice said. 'She knows there's something up. There's something about you, like you're trying to hide something!'

Jools pulled out a cigarette nervously.

'Gie's!' She snatched it. She took his lighter from him and lit his cigarette.

She gave the cigarette back and sat down next to him. Jools began to feel like a rat in a trap.

'C'mere,' she said, grabbing him around the waist. She lifted his tee shirt and pulled it up over his head. Jools sat half naked with his arms folded covering up his skinny ribs.

'Can Ah get ma lighter back?' he asked. She handed it back and shuffled off. Jools put his shirt back on, scanning around to see who was watching. The sun shone through the window. The room was hot and smoke stung his eyes. Jools heard the familiar sound of a helicopter and ran to the window to see it. A train ran past on tracks at the back of the building and he laughed at his mistake. He'd really thought it was a helicopter giving him a fly past.

JAB! He flinched. A needle stuck him in the groin. He sighed and shook his head. He heard footsteps approaching and turned to see his sister Sarah coming into the room followed by Kev, his mate.

'Awright?' he greeted them.

'I've just had a word with the nurses, Jools,' Sarah said. 'They said we can take you out for a walk. Do you want to get out for a while?'

'Aye, sound,' Jools said.

'We can take a wee walk.'

They headed down the corridor.

'So how's it goin, Jay?' Kev asked.

'Ah'm no too bad. Ah just want oot ay here,' Jools mumbled.

'Ah've gave your sister that hundred quid Ah owe you,' Kev said.

'Do you want me to look after it for when you get out?' Sarah asked.

Jools nodded. 'Kev kens me,' he thought. 'He'd tell them Ah'm no a paedophile.'

'You've still got a couple of orders on your benefit book to cash too. You'll have a few quid when you get out,' Sarah said.

They walked through the main building past two Navy security guards and out through some doors to the car park. Jools felt too nervous going out any further so they stood in a doorway and smoked a cigarette.

'Shut up, Jools. They have to go. Now! Get rid of them,' the voice ordered.

'We'll have to be going,' Sarah said. 'It's just a quick visit tonight, I've not been home from work yet.'

'I'll come back up and see you again, Jay,' Kev smiled.

They walked to the car and Jools went back to the ward. He went along to the dorm and sat on his bed thinking of Natty. He pictured her laughing.

'PIT IT DOON!' the voice said. 'Stay off the sexual! Pit it doon laddie, pit it doon!'

'Ah'm no thinkin anything sexual, for fuck's sake!' Jools said.

'Stay off the sexual! Nae wanking!'

'Mate, Ah've no had a wank since Ah came in here. Ah've no had a wank in months!'

'Stay off… Aw… Aw just shut the fuck up, eh? Literally shut the fuck up!'

Jools turned over and looked up the dorm. He saw a skinny, scruffy-looking guy next to the bin that was hung over the door handle. He watched as the guy raked through the rubbish. The creepy wee guy dribbled down his chin and nervously looked around for anyone coming. Jools watched the disgusting creature as it rummaged in the garbage and then scuttled off down the corridor. He went to the bin to see what he'd been doing. A pile of empty purple tinnies showed through the clear plastic bin bag and Jools's heart skipped a beat.

'Dinnae fuckin start aboot the purple tinny! Ah've paid enough for ma past! Leave me alone!' he hollered.

JAB! He flinched. A needle stuck him in the leg.

'Aaargh! Get tae fuck!' he screamed.

'We've sort ay shot ourselves in the foot there. You caught us. You weren't meant to see him. He put those tins in the bag to booby-trap you. He works for us. He does the more… unsavoury jobs for us. Disgusting, isn't he? You were meant to think about the purple tinny when you saw the empties. Dr David Love hates that sort of thing. Alcoholism! It's disgusting. It makes people neglect their children! It leads to child abuse!'

'Ah've no goat any kids!' Jools shouted. 'How the fuck Ah'm Ah responsible for child abuse?'

JAB! He flinched as a needle stuck in his armpit.

'You'd better not be! We'll be checking your thoughtwaves on that and if you are, you'll get the max!'

'Ah'm easy!' Jools said. 'You'll find fuck all ay that nature in ma heid! Ye can check all you want! Ah was good tae bairns! Ah have a magic laugh wi' them! Bairns love me!'

'Stay away fae wee lassies!' the voice laughed.

'That's no fuckin true! Ah'm no a beast!' Jools was getting angry. 'Ye can check! Ask anybody that knows me! Ye can ask Kev if Ah'm a nonce. Ah've never once been accused ay anything like that!' Jools started to cry. 'Not once, ever! Ah'll get half ay fuckin Muirhoose tae vouch for that.'

The presence left him and Jools lay back sobbing. Some time passed and it started to get dark. Jools got up and shuffled to the smoking room. The room was full and everyone looked round as he came in. The air was thick with smoke and the old air conditioner coughed in the corner. The TV was turned up full blast and people talked loudly over the sound.

Danny Love sat talking to Eddie. They looked over with a smirk and continued talking. Jools smoked a cigarette quickly.

'They don't want you in here, Jools,' the voice said. 'The students have taken a vote and they've decided that you're not welcome to sit with them. It's because of the wee lassies. And they don't want you watching what they're up to at night. Your head is like a giant bug, Jools. It picks up every last detail. They don't want you around when they're trying to relax after work. Hurry up and finish your cigarette.'

Jools smoked fast and left the room. He went into the quiet room and turned the light on. A tall bookcase stood in the corner and Jools looked through the titles. A large pile of National Geographics caught his eye and he thumbed through them, selecting an issue with an article on feudal Japan.

'Stay off names and faces!' the voice said. 'That means no repping names and stay off faces, that means hard men. Nae repping! Stay off other people's business!'

'Fair enough,' Jools said, and took his magazine back to his cubicle.

'Pit it doon!' the voice told him as he flicked through the pages. 'No reading!'

Jools sighed. 'Can Ah no just look at the pictures then? Ah'll no read nothing, honest.'

'PIT IT DOON!'

Jools threw the magazine aside, huffing loudly.

JAB! He flinched. The needle jabbed him in the eye socket.

'What ye daein?! Ah've put it doon!' he bawled.

YLT

'You're gettin stabbed!' Gary Love said. 'Ah'm upstairs and Ah'm watchin you. You better stay away fae ma wee sister, ya fuckin degenerate!'

'Ah'm no fuckin interested in yer sister!' Jools shouted.

'Ah'm gonnie leather you, ya wee beast. Danny told me aboot they wee lassies and wait till him and his mates get ye, yer fuckin dead!'

YLT: the letters slashed across his eyelids in red.

'Ah'm fuckin easy, come and stab me!' Jools raged. He'd totally blown his lid. 'Fuckin come ahead! Me and you right now! In the toilet! Let's fuckin do it!' Jools stormed to the bathroom. A nervous looking Danny Love stood looking at himself in the mirror and another man stood washing his hands. They saw the demonic look on Jools's face and Danny Love scuttled like a cockroach from the room. The other man locked himself in a cubicle. Jools stood there fuming.

'C'MON THEN!!! LET'S FUCKIN GO!!! Fuckin shitebags!' he growled and went back to his room.

⊙

Jools lay in the darkened dorm. He heard the tea trolley and got up. He went to the smoking room and poured himself some tea. He sat on the unit as there were no seats and smoked a quick cigarette. Danny Love looked over nervously and Jools swaggered inwardly to himself. 'Fuckin wee prick!' he thought. The Professor smiled over and Jools gave him a nod. *News at Ten* began on TV.

'Jools, leave the room! No news! Stay off the news!' the voice said.

Jools finished his cigarette and left the room. He stood in line outside the office as the nurses dispensed the medicine. Jools took the plastic beakers. He noticed that they'd changed the medication. Now he had a blue capsule. He swallowed it. As he was turning around he noticed a piece of card that had been drawn and doodled on standing up on the window sill. 'Vote Love!' had been scrawled on it and Jools's heart sped up. 'There's no fuckin escaping these people!' he thought as he went to bed. They were everywhere!

⊙

Jools lay in the hot bedroom. He felt drowsy and a high-pitched whine began in his head. It got louder and louder, then vanished.

'That's them sending the signal, Jools,' the voice said. 'It's picked up by the antenna on your virtual dummy. It's your instructions for tomorrow. We send the signal out at midnight every night.' Jools fell into a restless sleep.

⊙

Jools opened his eyes.

'Jools, shut up, dinnae say nothing,' the voice said.

Jools cringed. 'When are they goin away?' he thought as he turned over and sat up. The sun shone through the window and the room baked.

'Jools, keep quiet, see if you can make today your twenty-four hours without a thoughtwave,' the woman whispered.

A nurse brought his medication and he swallowed the blue capsule. His head felt adrift of his body and he got up drowsily and staggered to the toilet. He stood over the toilet and had to reach for the wall as he felt a dizziness come over him. He left the cubicle and scrubbed his hands in the sink. His dick twitched involuntarily and he dribbled in his jogging pants.

'Ah've pished maself!' the woman laughed.

'Will you just fuck off and leave me alone?!' Jools said.

'I'm along in the cupboard by the kitchen. I'm only mucking about with you, Jools. Don't be so grumpy. I'm talking to you through a brainwave monitor. It's confidential. It's just me sitting in a wee room talking into a brainwave monitor. The mic's plugged into the top. There's no one else can hear us. I thought I'd have a blether.'

'Can you no just gie me ma heid back?' Jools said. 'Every day Ah get up and you're still there. When will this ever end? Ah canny handle it much longer. It's killin me.'

'You must complete the treatment!'

'Ah canny!'

'Not even for Anastacia?'

'Aye, awright then,' Jools sighed. 'Ah'll try, fuck.'

He went along to the kitchen, poured some tea and took it to the smoking room. The cleaner was mopping the floor and whistled cheerfully. A nurse came in. 'Jools, Dr La Plante wants to see you this morning. I'll come and get you later, OK?' she said eagerly. Jools lit a cigarette, rested his head against the wall and closed his eyes. He nodded out.

⊙

He opened his eyes. His cigarette had burned down to the filter and a long stack of ash fell to the floor as he stirred. He lit another cigarette and sat up. The room was half full and thick with smoke. The radio blared in the corner. Jools closed his eyes. He nodded out.

⊙

Jools started. His heart pounded and he gasped in a deep breath. He was still in the smoking room. He'd nodded off. He felt like he'd stopped breathing and awoke with a fright. He looked around to see if anyone had been watching. The Professor smiled over. Eddie, Archie and Emma sat talking in a corner. Jools got up and went to his room. He lay on the bed and nodded out.

⊙

'Jools, Dr La Plante will see you now,' the nurse said. Jools got up groggily and followed her along the corridor. She knocked on the door and they went in.

'Come in, Jools,' Dr La Plante said. 'This is Bill Rae. He's a mental health officer and a social worker. He's here to act on your behalf. He'll be sitting in at our meetings from now on.'

A smartly dressed, stocky man with grey hair sat opposite the desk.

'Shut up, Jools. I've got ma finger on the stifle button and if you say a single fuckin word to this guy Ah'll put ma boot up your arse!' the man said mentally.

Jools looked down at the man's feet. He wore big shiny brogues. His arsehole tightened up at the thought of it.

'Aye, it's me,' the man went on. 'The doctor canny hear us. Ah'm a mason and Ah used tae dae the boxin so dinnae pish me aboot. Say fuckin nothin!'

Jools sat tensely. 'So can you tell me, Jools, about any difficulties you've been having with your day-to-day life? How have you been managing to get out? Do you do your own shopping? Your sister said she'd been helping,' La Plante said.

'Say fuckin nothin! Ah'm no kiddin', Jools! Ah dinnae like paedophiles! And neither does Big Jim fae the pub! He's ma pal fae the boxin and he'll boot yer fuckin hole if he catches you. Ah'll no take any ay yer shite!'

'Jools?' La Plante said.

Jools clenched his jaw shut and blanked his mind.

'Say nothin! Nowt!' the man ordered mentally.

The two men looked at each other as Jools stared blankly into space. His eyes started to water and tears rolled down his cheeks.

'OK, Jools, you can go back to the ward now,' the doctor said.

Jools got up and shuffled out.

⊙

Jools sat in the smoking room. The sun shone through the window and the room was stifling.

SLAM! A skinny nurse came in and tended to an elderly woman.

'Jools,' a voice said.

'What? Who's that?'

'I'm upstairs in the lab. I'm your computer operator for the day. I'm here to make sure you behave. Yours Truly left us to watch you. You better get doing the One. Yours Truly will expect you to be a lot further on than you are. You've just been mucking about the last while. Remember, you were supposed to be doing the One, two till four every day. You'll get hung, drawn and quartered if you don't pull your finger out!' The man's voice laughed.

Jools already dreaded Yours Truly coming back. He'd not been doing too well keeping the One.

'Watch this!' the voice said.

Jools's eyes moved involuntarily like they were being dragged across a computer screen by a mouse. His eyes settled on the skinny nurse's small breasts. The nurse looked about fourteen. Adrenalin sped through Jools like a freight train. He started to panic as a picture of him masturbating dropped into his mind's eye. Jools flinched in blind terror and tried hard to blank his mind. A picture of a schoolgirl in uniform dropped into his mind's eye. The familiarity of the image betrayed his guilt. Again the picture of him masturbating. He remembered the day it happened. The picture of the schoolgirl in uniform. The subject of a fantasy. He shuddered and gasped for air as he began to hyperventilate. He fled from the room and half ran down the corridor to his dorm. His went to his cubicle and got into bed, shaking.

'PAEDOPHILE!' the voice screamed. 'You abused yourself over a child!'

'Ah never done it!' Jools tried hard to cover his thoughts.

'You're a paedophile!'

'Ah'm no a paedophile!' Jools stuttered. 'Ah never done it!'

'It was when you'd been drinking! Alcohol abuse! Child abuse!' the voice screamed.

Jools felt the electric current build in his body. It became more intense and he sensed he was on the very edge of recieving the max. He cowered in the corner of his bed and pulled the duvet over his head. He fought desperately to blank his mind.

'You dirty little pervert!' the voice said. 'Wait till Dr Love finds out about this! Yours Truly will have your balls for this!'

'Ah'm no a paedophile! It isnae true!' Jools bawled. He'd started to cry.

'It's in your mind, Jools. You are a paedophile! Our equipment doesn't lie!' the voice screamed.

'Do you understand what this means? Your charity work. Who'll want to work with a known paedophile? It'll make the Love Organisation a laughing stock. All that good work, gone! You'll never be able to go back home now. They'll kill you! And wait till your family find out. They'll disown you! Yes, you've really done it this time! People had faith in you, Jools, and you've let them down. They really thought you were the right man for the job and we find this out! Caught with your pants down, literally.'

'Ah'm no a paedophile! Ah'm no a beast. Ah've never touched anybody in ma life! Ask anyone that kens me!' Jools blubbed.

'You've let us all down so badly, Jools. Wait till your sensei hears what happened. They'll never let you go back to training, ever!' the voice told him. 'You'll be lucky if they ever let you out of here now. They'll throw the book at you. You see, word got around about your escapades on the super lagers.' The elecricity built up again, winding Jools. 'I really really want to fry you when I think about it. How you could use a young girl like that? Go on! Say something! I dare you! Give me an excuse to give you the max!'

'Ah canny even remember it,' Jools cried. 'It wasnae like that. Ah'm no a creep.'

'So how was it, then? Are you admitting it?' the voice asked.

'Ah never done it. If Ah did Ah canny remember! Ah'm no a beast. Ask ma doctor, ask ma neighbours if ye dinnae believe me!' Jools sobbed.

'Stay away fae wee lassies!!!' The presence faded. Jools lay sobbing on the bed. He eventually nodded out.

⊙

Two bells rang in the hall. Jools got up.

'That's lunchtime, folks!' a nurse called.

An image of the blonde schoolgirl flashed through his head involuntarily. Jools shuddered. He nervously shuffled up the long hallway to the kitchen. He sat at a table on his own and his eyes darted nervously around the room. Jools could feel a violent tension in the air and was glad the Navy guards were there. He took a few mouthfuls of food.

'They've all spat in that!' the voice said. 'They don't like beasts. Wait till the ward on the ground floor get hold of you. They're going to kill you! You better stay out of the kitchen. Ward five next door are after your blood. The students have been whispering! They all know what you did! You're a dirty little paedophile!'

Jools got up and scuttled back to his room, terrified.

'Stay off the ward!' the voice warned.

An image of the blonde schoolgirl popped into his mind's eye and left again. Jools cringed. He lay on his bed and began to sob. He nodded out.

⊙

'Do you remember this?' a voice asked.

A picture of Jools dropping his trousers on a night out with the lads flashed into his mind's eye. 'You exposed yourself! There were women there! You're not only a paedophile but you've also exposed yourself on several occasions! You need locking up. Do you still think you're in here for nothing?' the voice asked.

'Ah'm no like that, honest!' Jools mumbled. 'Ah was just havin a laugh. Nae one got offended. It was only a bit ay fun, eh?!' Jools tried hard to defend himself.

'Still think you're not sick? You've been sick for a long time, Jools. We're here to treat you. We're putting you on a programme.'

Suddenly three-quarters of Jools's head went tight. His left eye was covered by what looked like a slide of the blonde schoolgirl. Jools shuddered and his heart pounded.

'TAKE IT OOT! PLEASE!' Jools hollered.

'Stay away fae wee lassies!'

⊙

Jools awoke and got up for a cigarette. He nervously went into the smoking room. Emma left her minder and shuffled over to him.

'Awright?'

Jools tried to steady his shaky hand to light a cigarette.

'STAY AWAY FROM EMMA!' a loud whisper said. 'She's the fixer-upper! She's trying to find out your story.'

Jools felt very wary and looked over at her stocky minder. He seemed more interested in the TV.

'Ah'll light it!' Emma said bossily, snatching the lighter from him. He felt he was being leaned on. She lit his cigarette and he had to ask for his lighter back.

'It's the only one Ah've goat,' he explained nervously.

'Ma wee lassie's coming up the morn,' she said. 'Ma wee blonde lassie.' Her eyes narrowed.

Jools's heart skipped a beat. She was fishing big time and he tried to show no outward signs of guilt or fear. He stubbed his cigarette out and scuttled back to his bed.

⊙

A picture of the blonde schoolgirl covered his left eye and three-quarters of his head had been taken over, leaving just his right eye free.

'Ah'm no a paedophile, honest. Just look in ma heid. Check for yourself. There's nae child porn in there. Ah dinnae sit thinkin aboot wee bairns aw day, Ah'm no obsessed wi' schoolies,' he tried to explain. 'If Ah done it, it was just a throwaway image. Ah'm no intae bairns! There's nae thoughtwaves ay anything tae dae wi' bairns in ma heid is there? Not now, not ever! Ah'm no like that. Ah'm well trusted.'

'Exploiting children for your own sexual gratification? You don't think exploiting under age girls is OK, do you!'

The electric charge built up in him suddenly, stealing his breath. 'Just one more word, just one more filthy little word!!! I'm so tempted!' the voice said angrily.

'But Ah've no done it!! Ah dinnae dae things like that. Put me in front ay aw ay Muirhoose. Ask anybody if Ah've ever been under suspicion ay that. Ah'll fuckin shout it fae the Gunner roof!'

'That was before you were put in here for child abuse! You are being treated for sex crimes. It was either here or the next step's prison. We can always have you transferred to Carstairs for the criminally insane if you become a handful to us. You'll get a warm reception in there alright!'

The blonde schoolgirl dropped over his eye for a split second and Jools flinched.

'Stay away fae wee lassies!' a voice cut in.

'Ah'm no a beast!' Jools cried.

'Stay off the ward. Wait till the students get you. Emma's minder's going to kill you,' the voice said. 'She's going to have your legs broken for that. Emma knows the lassie's family, from Pilton, She's heard all about what you did. She's just playing you along, to see what you say.'

Jools was terrified. He missed his family. He thought of Natty and started to cry again.

'No point in blubbing now,' the voice said. 'No one in Muirhouse will want to know you! Specially Natty. You did the crime, now you must pay! Don't be looking at the staff to protect you. They don't like paedophiles!'

The schoolgirl dropped into view and Jools flinched.

Three-quarters of his head tightened up again and he peered, terror stricken, out of his right eye.

'S... s... s... say paedophile,' the voice said.

Jools fought hard to blank it all out. He lay drowsily on his bed and nodded out.

⊙

Jools awoke and shuffled groggily up the hall to the bathroom.

'Stay off the ward!' the voice said.

'Ah'm just goin tae pish,' Jools said.

'There are no security guards to cover you! Get out of there, Jools!'

Jools tried to hurry up and finish. He gave himself a shake and left the cubicle. His dick gave an involuntary twitch and he dribbled in his jogging pants.

'WILL YE FUCKIN STOP IT?!!!' he bawled.

'Ah've pished maself!' the female laughed.

A picture of the blonde schoolgirl dropped into his mind and left. Jools flinched. His heart skipped a beat.

'Ah'm no a paedophile,' he mumbled.

'Have you ever felt sexually aroused when touching or being touched by a child,' a voice asked.

'Naw! Dinnae be a sick cunt! Ah'm...'

'Do you now or have you ever used child pornography to get aroused?'

'Ah've telt ye! Ah'm no like that! Ah'm no a...' Jools tried to answer.

'Have you at any time had sexual relations with a minor?'

'Naw!!! Ah've never even done stoat the baw! Fuck this man, Ah'm no answerin any ay this shite! Ah want ma lawyer!'

Jools scuttled back to bed.

'Have you at any time ever touched a minor in a place you weren't supposed to?'

'Fuck off, ya sick cunt! You're the fuckin pervert! What are you askin me all this for?'

'Do you find pre-pubescent children sexually arousing?'

Jools lost his temper. 'FUCK YOU, YA FUCKIN SICK FUCK!!! Are you gettin turned on by askin me all this? Ah'll bet you're a fuckin paedophile! Is that what it is? Dae you like the wee girlies?'

'There's no point in arguing, Jools,' a voice cut in. 'It's just a tape. We've got you on a machine. It's a paedophile monitor. It's an American invention. Dr David Love designed it. You see, it asks you the questions on tape then it gauges your answer, sort of like a lie detector, but it also extracts anything you've ever pictured and it'll give you an electric shock through your genitals if it catches you out. The pain should be enough to knock you out. It's to retrain paedophiles. You're testing it for med research.'

'Ah'm no a paedophile,' Jools mumbled. It was beginning to sound like a mantra.

'S... s... say paedophile.'

A picture of the blonde schoolgirl dropped in. Jools flinched.

'Stop it! Take it oot! Please!' Jools pleaded.

'Have you at any time ever exposed yourself to a child?' the tape went on.

Jools tried to blank his mind.

'Have you at any time swapped or distributed literature of an unsavoury nature?'

Jools stopped answering. He totally refused to carry on with it and sat with his jaw clamped shut. He sat with his head back against the wall and soon nodded out.

⊙

Jools woke up. Three-quarters of his head was still taken over and he had a feeling of pressure running through the side of his head. A slide of the schoolgirl dropped into his mind's eye and Jools flinched.

Two bells rang in the hall.

'Dinner time, folks!' a male nurse called out.

Jools shuffled up the hall drowsily. He was wary of the people around him and nervously peeked out from his normal right eye. He took a tray from the trolley and sat on his own. He peeped around the room and noticed Eddie staring at him.

BANG! BANG! BANG! Jools's heart nearly leapt out of his chest. Danny Love came in. He'd banged on the top of the metal food trolley.

'Enough!' a nurse told him off.

'That's the students really annoyed with you, Jools! They want to tear you apart,' the voice said. 'They've been having a lesson about you today. They know about the schoolgirl. They're not too happy with you. They don't even want you to eat in the same room as them. You make them sick. From now on you'll eat after the students have finished and left the room.'

Jools's table started to fill up and he tried to eat fast so he could get a cigarette before everyone came back from dinner.

He finished up and made a cup of tea. He took it to the smoking room and smoked a quick cigarette. The room was still empty except for the Professor and the old woman who ate from a tray in her lap. Jools lit another cigarette.

'The Professor is watching you!' the voice said. Jools felt he was being studied so he stubbed out the cigarette and went to his room. Three-quarters of his head started to hurt with the tightness of his muscles and he tried to relax. He lay on his bed and nodded out.

⊙

Jools awoke to find it dark in the dorm. He became aware of someone sobbing in the next cubicle. 'None ay ma business,' he thought to himself. 'Maybe they had him on the paedophile monitor. Maybe he canny handle it either.'

Jools got up and shuffled to the bathroom. He stood over the toilet and everything started to turn black. He threw out a hand to steady himself. He thought he would pass out and went straight back to bed. He nodded out.

⊙

'Jools, Jools, medication,' the nurse said, crouching down by his bed.

He took the large blue capsule and went straight back to sleep.

⊙

Jools woke up with a craving for a cigarette. He shuffled up the hall past the two nurses who sat in chairs in the hallway outside the office. The clock read 2.40am. The smoking room was empty and Jools sat in the silence, smoking a cigarette. He leaned his head back against the wall and nearly drifted off.

'How did it come tae this?' he thought. 'How have Ah ended up like this in here?' He reflected on a time when everything was normal. He thought of Natty. Would she ever speak to him again? A thing like this could ruin a man for good. True or not. Once you get accused of something like that, it sticks. Jools was miserable. Three-quarters of his head felt heavy. He finished his cigarette and immediately lit another. He felt drowsy and closed his eyes. He started to nod out again and went to bed.

Two cartoon men appeared in Jools's mind's eye. The one on the left opened a drawer and started to rummage through some files.

'Hmmmm,' his uncle's voice said, pulling out a file. 'What's this? Had a wank over… Oh ye did, did ye?! Ah didnae ken ye fancied her!' he laughed. 'Here Jim, check this oot, likes. Stoat the baw!'

The other cartoon character looked at the file. 'Ya wee shite! You'll get ma boot up your arse!' Big Jim, the manager of his local said. 'Well would ye credit it? Ah ken her mother, tae!'

Jools nodded out into a deep sleep as they rummaged through his thoughtwaves.

⊙

'Jools, medication,' Jane said.

He sat up and took the plastic beakers. 'That blue tablet isnae agreeing wi' me,' he told her.

'I'll tell the doctor,' she said. 'Just take the other one.'

Jools swallowed the yellow tab and Jane left him. It was another sunny day and he got up, dressed and went to the bathroom. His head was still swimming and he staggered into a cubicle.

'Stay away fae wee lassies!' a voice said.

"Ah'm no a beast!' Jools croaked. 'Leave me alone.' Suddenly the pressure in his face returned and three-quarters of his head was taken over by the machine. He peered through his normal right eye.

A picture of the schoolgirl dropped into his eye and his heart started to race.

'Two wee lassies, one was true, one wasnae!' the voice said.

'Stop this!' Jools shouted. 'It's killin me. Ah canny handle it!'

'One… had a wank!' Jools recognised the voice of Dr La Plante. 'S… s… say, paedophile. PAED… PAED… PAEDO-PHILE!'

'Ah'm no a paedophile!' Jools bawled. 'Ah knew La Plante had somethin tae dae wi' this. Ah saw the slides in his room,' he thought.

'Ah've goat a spot oan ma cock!' a woman's voice laughed.

Jools came out of the cubicle and scuttled back to his room. His dick twitched and he dribbled in his shorts.

'Ah've pished maself!' she giggled.

'One is… a paedophile!' La Plante said in a loony voice. 'Had a wank?'

The schoolgirl dropped in, then disappeared. Jools flinched. A wave of panic washed over him.

He gripped his head in his hands.

Jab! A needle stuck him in the side and he jumped.

'S... s... say paedophile.'

'Leave me alone!' Jools shouted. He gritted his teeth hard.

The schoolgirl.

He started to panic. His heart pounded. He lay back down on the bed and pulled the duvet over his head. He started to cry, then nodded out.

⊙

Jools awoke. The heat in the room was stifling. Three-quarters of his head was still taken over.

'What have they done tae me?' he thought. He got up and shuffled to the smoking room. It was half empty so he sat and lit a cigarette. He rested his head against the wall and nodded out.

⊙

Jools woke to find his cigarette burned down to ash. He lit another.

SLAM! He jumped. The Professor came in. He smiled at Jools and sat down.

A picture of the schoolgirl dropped over his eye and he began to panic. He stubbed out his cigarette and went to his room. He sat on the edge of his bed and began to sob. 'How have Ah ended up like this?' he bawled. 'In a mental hospital bein treated as a sex offender.' His life was never meant to turn out like this. 'Ah never thought Ah'd be punished for thinkin'. Ah thought ma private thoughts were mine. Ah never thought anyone would ever see them,' he reasoned. 'Ah never thought Ah was doin anything wrong. If Ah did dae it, it was years ago. Ah could only have been about twenty-two or something.'

'Twenty-seven, Jools,' the voice told him.

'But she wasnae that young. She must have been at least sixteen!' Jools offered.

'Fifteen!' the voice said.

'But she looks a lot older than that, eh?'

'She is a minor, a child!' The electricity built up in his body and his heart pounded.

'What's this for?!' Jools bawled. The machine brought him to the brink of an electrical shock then started to ease off.

The slide of the schoolgirl dropped in, then vanished.

'Jools, the machine nearly zapped you there,' a male voice laughed. 'Try not to think of anything sexual. Either that or you could just take the max. Just say nigger or think about wanking over that schoolie. You'll get the max and you'll probably piss and shit yourself in front of everyone but at least you'll get it over with. The machine will reset itself.'

'Naw!' Jools struggled to clear his mind. He tried to blank it out.

'Two hard-ons and a schoolie nightmare!' the voice laughed. 'Two wee lassies, one was true, one wasnae!'

'YUK! They werenae pre-pubescent, were they?' the woman asked.

'Fuck off, ya fuckin sick hoor!' Jools raged.

'Just testing for adherence!' she quipped. Her presence left him.

Jools lay fighting his thoughts and tried to keep his mind blank. Three-quarters of his head throbbed painfully.

The tape began again with its grilling.

'Have you ever been aroused by the sight of a young child being bathed?'

'AAARGH! FUCKIN LEAVE ME ALONE!' Jools cracked. He kicked out at the wardrobe. 'Ah canny fuckin handle this!' He gripped his head and pulled at his short hair.

He stood up and looked around in a panic for a way out. He looked at the vent window. It was about a forty-foot drop from there. 'Not enough to kill me outright,' he thought. He looked at the curtain track. Would it hold his weight? He doubted it. He couldn't even hang himself. He would have to break his own neck. He took hold of his head in both hands, took a deep breath and yanked it around as hard as he could. He felt a sharp pain in his neck and a loud crack. He tried again. His neck would not break. The questions on the tape faded and he was alone again.

Jools lay in bed under the covers. He'd taken the belt from his jeans and wrapped it around his neck. He pulled tighter and tighter but every time he felt close to passing out, the belt would automatically slacken.

'Don't you dare try to kill yourself while we're on duty!' the voice boomed. 'I'm Professor Love, Danny Love's grandfather. Do you realise you could be screwing up his career! If you died when we were on duty he'd fail his exams! I'm not prepared to let a little piece of slime like you do that! You lack discipline, mental toughness! It's all a matter of self discipline! My grandson will not fail for the likes of you! I personally don't care if you live or not as long as Danny doesn't fail because of you.'

Jools fell asleep, weeping silently.

⊙

Jools got out of bed and shuffled up the ward to the smoking room. Three-quarters of his head was still taken over. The picture of the schoolgirl dropped into his head. Jools didn't flinch but the electricity built up inside him and he frantically tried to blank his mind. His heart pounded as he fought. The current faded and he began to calm a little. He lit a cigarette and puffed on it desperately.

'Stay off the ward!' a male voice told him. 'You've been told. There aren't enough security guards to watch you. They don't like paedophiles in here. They're all going to kill you when they catch you and I'd stay out of the kitchen if I were you. Ward five is full of people who hate you. They're all after you.'

Two bells rang in the hall.

'Dinner time, everyone!' the nurse called.

Jools shuffled nervously up the hallway.

'STAY OUT OF THE FUCKING KITCHEN! You've been told!' the voice said angrily. 'The students don't want you sitting with them. You make them sick! They've had to watch "IT" all term. They think you're really like that. Then we find out you really are a paedophile! That's why you were picked, Jools. People trusted you, especially with children, then we find out this. You've really let everyone down.'

Jools turned around and went back to his room with his head down. He went back a while later but the food trolley was gone so he made a piece of toast and a cup of tea. He sat on his bed and quietly ate. He heard footsteps approaching. His auntie came in.

'How are you?' she asked.

'Shut up, Jools!' the voice warned. 'Don't say a fucking word! Get rid of her!'

'Ah want oot ay here,' Jools croaked. His eyes glazed over and he held back the tears.

'Are you feeling any better? Is the medication doing any good?'

Jools just shook his head. 'Ah want tae go hame,' he mumbled again.

'The doctor won't let you, Jools. Have you managed to find anything to do during the day?' she asked.

Jools shook his head. His eyes closed and he nodded out.

⊙

Jools woke up. The dorm was dark.

'Jools, stay away fae bairns!' a voice said.

Jools cringed. 'Ah just fuckin woke up. Leave me alone!'

He got up and went to the bathroom. Two black nurses, a man and a woman, sat on the chairs outside the office. He scampered back to his room at top speed.

'WHOA, YA CUNT, YE!'

He took a run and jump into bed, ducking under the duvet.

⊙

Jools woke up early and shuffled up the hallway to the smoking room. A big guy with a beard sat rocking his body back and forwards in a chair. Jools lit a cigarette and smoked it nervously. The other three-quarters of his head felt normal again.

'Jools, stay away fae wee lassies!' the voice said.

Jools gazed into space.

The sun came up and the room was bathed in sunshine. Jools noticed the morning staff coming into the office to start their shifts. He shuffled down to the bathroom and inspected his spot. It was still red and angry but was beginning to heal. He had a pee, gave himself a shake and scrubbed his hands. The same three-quarters of his head was taken over again as a slide of the schoolgirl dropped into his mind's eye. Jools flinched and his heart skipped a beat. 'No again! Ah'm no a paedophile!' he mumbled nervously.

He went back to bed and hid under the duvet.

'Medication, Jools,' the skinheaded male nurse said, handing him the plastic cups. Jools took the yellow tablet and the nurse left him. He got up and shuffled to the kitchen.

'S… S… SAY PAEDOPHILE!' the voice said loudly in his head. 'Stay out of the kitchen. Ward five are after you!'

Jools looked around warily as two guys came into the kitchen and stood behind him. He got ready to throw the boiling water over them should they start anything but they seemed to ignore him. He took his tea back to his room.

⊙

Three-quarters of Jools's head hurt. He peered through his right eye and shuffled to the smoking room. The room was nearly full and Jools sat on the unit near the door. He lit a cigarette and smoked it fast. Emma shuffled over to him.

'Awright?' She gummed a smile at him.

Jools blanked her completely.

'Ye no talkin the day?' she asked.

Jools stared into space.

She shuffled off back to her minder. Jools finished his cigarette and went back to bed.

⊙

The curtain pulled back in Jools's cubicle. The lumbering frame of Emma's minder stepped in and sat down slowly on the bed beside him. The minder breathed heavily. Jools felt the adrenalin pumping through his veins. The minder sat there in silence. Jools didn't dare move. The minder sat for a few long, agonising minutes then stood up and slowly lumbered away. Jools breathed a sigh of relief. 'That was a close one,' he thought.

'That was Emma's minder. She sent him through to scare you!' the woman laughed. 'He was brilliant! That got you going, didn't it? Psyched you right out!'

'Fuckin hilarious,' Jools said sarcastically. He still shook.

A picture of the schoolgirl dropped into his left eye and he flinched.

'Ah'm no a paedophile!' he bawled.

He gritted his teeth and kicked out at the wardrobe. 'Aaargh! Fuck off!' he screamed. 'Yer fuckin killin me!'

'Jools, it's not us. It's the machine. It's actually killed people in America. It's an American invention. We want it banned. We don't agree with it. It's been responsible for too many deaths. It was meant to be sponsored for charity to see how long you'd last. Once it's switched on you can't turn it off. You have to complete the programme until it re-sets itself.'

'Turn the fuckin thing off! It's killin me! Ah canny handle it!'

'I'm sorry Jools, it can't be turned off. The machine is in a drawer in Yours Truly's office and he's taken the key away on holiday with him. We can't get in to switch it off. The only way is to let it give you the max and it'll reset itself. It's just like a box with a magnetic loop that turns around. It sticks to your negative thoughts and won't let go until the thought pattern is changed. It's a piece of shit. We want it banned.'

'Kick the fuckin door in or Ah swear it, you'll have a death oan the ward. Ah canny fuckin take this, now stop it!' Jools was reaching new levels of desperation.

The schoolgirl dropped into his eye and out again. He flinched and began to panic.

'Jools, try to blank your mind. Try not to think of that wee lassie. It might reset and pick up something else instead,' the woman suggested.

Jools tried again to blank his mind. The picture of the schoolgirl flicked across his mind's eye and the electric current built up in his body, taking him ever closer to the max.

⊙

Jools sat in bed under the duvet. A picture of the schoolgirl ran across his mind's eye. He didn't flinch. He didn't have the mental strength left in his body to fight.

'This is the end,' he thought. 'What a way to die. A sex criminal. How did it all come to this?' Suddenly a white light shone brightly in his mind's eye and then it went dark.

'Jools, we had someone break open the machine,' the voice said. 'They've taken the slide out, that's all it was, a slide. Don't worry. It's gone. One of the doctors noticed how ill you were getting and broke the side of the machine open. He took out a slide. It's just a transparent blob of colour, Jools. Nothing to worry about any more.'

Jools lay gibbering incoherently. He was pretty far gone.

'Jools, stay with us now,' the voice said. 'Don't lose it now.'

Jools sat staring into space, mumbling to himself.

'Jools, Jools? Are you in there, Jools?'

JAB! A needle stuck him in the genitals. He didn't flinch.

Two bells rang in the hallway. Jools didn't move.

'Lunchtime, people!' a nurse called.

He sat with a faraway look in his eyes.

'Do you really think you're a paedophile?' the voice asked.

'Ah don't know,' he replied numbly.

'Don't ever let me hear you say that again. You are not a paedophile.'

'Ah was sure Ah wisnae, then...'

'Jools, you better get that out of your head. It was like that film with the middle-aged man who has the affair with the fourteen-year-old. It was just a moral dilemma. Remember that, Jools. A moral dilemma.'

The presence disappeared. Jools stared some more.

⊙

'Jools, I'm along in the cupboard talking into a brainwave monitor. What's up? You look terrible,' the woman's voice said.

'They said Ah'm a paedophile. They said Ah had a wank over a schoolie.'

'Aw, is that all? That doesnae make you a paedophile. It was just a moral dilemma. Christ, the way you were acting, we thought you'd touched up a bairn or something. Listen, Jools, you never touched anyone, right?'

'Naw, never,' Jools answered.

'What you did was perfectly normal. We've all done it. It was just a fantasy. All you've done, Jools, is have a thoughtwave. That's all it was. A thoughtwave. Now how can a thoughtwave do anyone any harm? Now never, ever let me hear you call yourself that again! You're not a paedophile. It was nothing!'

Something clicked with Jools. 'Ah dinnae sit thinkin aboot wee lassies aw day. Ah'm no like that, honest. Ask anybody. Ah'm no a beast.'

'Jools, what actually happened, truthfully?' the woman said.

'Ah canny really remember. Ah'd been roond at ma uncle's. We had a couple ay cans. Purple tinny, likes. Then oan the way hame Ah went for a packet ay smokes. A goat tae the shoaps and this wee bird Ah ken came over tae me askin for a fag. She gabbed oan tae ma arm, aw flirty, likes. Ah ken her fae aroond the scheme. Ah knew her older brother. Anyway Ah started gettin the signs off her. Flirtin', likes. She's a tidy wee bird and she looks a lot aulder than her age. There's a sort ay electricity between us, like wi' ma first love when Ah was younger. It was chemical. Ah could feel the vibes off her, teasin me. Anyway, Ah gave her a couple ay fags and she gave me a cuddle. Ah could feel her body against mine. Ah dunno, it sort ay turned me oan. Ah went hame and the telly was shite so Ah turned it off and Ah went tae ma bed. A goat a touch ay the horn and… Ah just rolled over and went tae sleep efter it. Ach, Ah was pished, man. Ah've never even thought ay that since. Ah've fantasised aboot aulder women tae, what does that say aboot me? Like Ah says, Ah dinnae sit aroond thinkin aboot bairns. Ah'm nae beast. Ah've never even done stoat the baw.'

'Just thoughtwaves, Jools,' the woman said. 'That's just normal. A wee bit misguided, maybe, but you're not a sex criminal. Get it through your head.'

'Anyway, that was years ago. Ah've no been like that since. Ah dinnae even drink the purple tinny any more. That's before you lot warned me off it. Ah gave it up off ma own back. Surely that says something for me.'

'Tell me, Jools, in this fantasy, did the girl make love like an adult. Was she sexually experienced?'

'Aye, Ah think so,' he replied. 'Ah was, at that age.'

'Well, that proves that it was just fantasy. In real life that probably wouldn't be the case. It was make-believe.'

'So Ah'm no really a beast?'

'Far from it, Jools. I defy anyone to say they've never fantasised about forbidden fruit. It's human nature,' she said. 'It was only a thoughtwave. How can a thoughtwave harm you unless you choose to let it? It can't harm you. Actions harm people. If that's the worst that's in your mind, you'll go far.'

'Ah'm glad we had this talk,' Jools said. 'It's helped me a lot. Ah was really beginning tae think there was something seriously wrong wi' me.'

'That's why I'm here. We're trainee counsellors. It's our job to counsel you back to health. That's why I'm in a cupboard talking to you through a brainwave monitor. So it's confidential. I'm not supposed to ever know which one you are. It's kind of hard not to know who you are. You have a very distinctive cough and sniff. That's you been counselled.'

He lay back and quietly thought about it.

'Just a thoughtwave,' he smiled to himself.

'Dinner time, people!' the nurse shouted.

Jools shuffled up the hall to the kitchen. There were plenty Navy guards around so he took a tray and sat down on his own. The room started to fill up. He could sense a tension in the room and almost expected it to explode at any second. He stuck out his chin and ate ravenously. If it kicked off he was ready. His eyes scanned the room. Eddie and Danny Love sat opposite him. Emma and her minder were up the back near the wall and had their backs turned.

'Stay out of the kitchen when the students are eating!' a voice said.

'Fuck off! Ah'm starvin for nae cunt!' Jools was determined.

'Do not trifle with me! I will not be trifled with!'

Jools ignored it and kept eating.

Archie came in looking thin. Jools finished up and made a cup of tea.

CRASH! He jumped about a foot in the air.

Jools spun around, fists ready. A woman had dropped her tray.

He went back to the smoking room shaking with jelly legs. It was empty so he smoked his cigarette and tried to calm down.

The door opened and his sister Sarah walked in.

'Awright,' he said.

'You're looking a bit better. How's things?' she asked.

'There's nowt wrong wi' me. Ah just want tae go home.'

'You certainly look a lot better. Have you been talking to the doctors?'

Jools shook his head. 'Ah've never told them nowt. Ah'm sure that Dr La Plante doesnae like me. He'll no let me oot.'

'You have to talk to them, Jools. Or talk to us. Tell someone what's the matter with you,' she said.

'Ah'm awright.'

'Norrie and Terry were asking for you. They want to come up and see you.'

'Ah'm no really wantin tae see anyone in here,' Jools murmured.

A presence filled his head. It felt close.

'Shut up, Jools! Ah'm listenin to every word you say! Tell her nothing! Get rid of her,' it said.

'Naw, why should Ah?' he thought. 'Ah'm fuckin sick ay listenin tae you lot.'

'GET RID OF HER, JOOLS! NOW!' the voice told him.

'Naw!'

The presence hung around, listening in.

'I was going to ask if I can take you out again,' Sarah said. 'Do you want to go up to Nana's on Sunday? The doctor thinks it would be good for you to get out and about.'

'They're still trying tae get me tae dae their walk for them,' Jools thought. 'Naw,' he shook his head.

'You have to get used to going out, Jools. You can't sit here all the time. It's up to you if you want to go on Sunday. Just let me know if you change your mind.'

'How's the cat?' he asked. He was really missing his wee pal.

'Fine. She's a bit lonely. She wouldn't come out for the first few days but now she comes running to meet me,' Sarah said. 'I'll see if I can get you home for a visit.'

Emma shuffled into the room and made a beeline for them.

'Here we fuckin go,' Jools thought. She just wouldn't leave him alone.

'Hiya,' she gummed. 'You've goat barry hair. It's dead long, eh? Have ye been growin it for ages?'

'A wee while,' Sarah said, humouring her. Emma sat on the floor and picked up Sarah's handbag. She opened it and started to rummage through the contents.

'Whoa, that's my bag! There's nothing much in it.' Sarah snatched the bag back.

Jools just shook his head. 'Do you want to go through to the quiet room?' he suggested.

They got up and went next door. The quiet room was empty and the silence helped Jools relax a bit.

'Was that your bird?' Sarah laughed.

'She's a fuckin pest! She'll no leave me alone.'

'Have you been getting to sleep at night?'

Jools nodded.

'You look a lot better. You've put on some weight since you came in. What's the food like?'

'Stodge,' he said.

She looked at her watch. Jools sensed she found it hard to think of anything to say.

'I better be going,' she said. 'I'm meant to meet my pal Denise in a wee while. We're going out for dinner. I'll visit again soon. Is there anything you need?'

Jools shook his head.

'What about clean clothes? Have you any washing to be done?'

'Aye, Ah'll get it.'

Jools got his washing from the dorm and put it in a carrier bag. He went back to Sarah who was coming out of the office.

'They said I can take you out for half an hour next time,' she told him.

'Sound.' He gave her the washing and she gave him a hug. 'Remember what I said about Sunday. Let me know if you change your mind.'

'See ye later,' he said, waving as she went down the hall. He went back to his room.

⊙

Jools lay on the bed thinking of Natty. He missed her and he pictured them sitting in a pub in Stockbridge as they'd done a hundred times in the past.

'Uh-uh! Them upstairs say you're subversive!'

A little dog in a red baseball cap pointed up at the sky and shook its head. The little animation played across his mind's eye.

Jools laughed. 'You're fuckin crazy, you lot.'

'No sexual thoughts. Wait till the Labour administration leave the building!' the voice said.

'Ah'm no thinkin nothin sexual,' Jools said. 'Ah was just… sort ay…'

'Keep off the sexual!'

JAB! A needle stuck in his side. He didn't flinch. He'd started to get used to it.

'What was that for?' he asked.

'One… is a paedophile!' La Plante's voice said loonily.

'Aw dinnae start that again, eh?! Aw Ah done was have a throwaway image in ma heid. It was only a thoughtwave.' Jools started to get on his high horse.

'Jools, shut up… Just literallly ssssssshut the fuck… up!' the voice said.

'Ye're a poof, ye're a Jew, shut yer mooth!'

Jools sighed deeply. 'Can you no just fuck off and leave me alone?'

'Shut up!'

'You shut up.'

'SHUT UP! Jools shut up!' The voice came right up to the microphone. 'SSSHUT UUUP!'

'Fuck off, ya fuckin weirdos! Ah'm no sayin fuck all!' Jools bawled.

'Simply shut up, Jools. Don't say a word! Just…'

'Aaargh!' Jools tugged his hair. 'Get tae fuck! See if Ah ever get you Ah'll fuckin kill ye! Ah swear it, you're fuckin gittin it!'

'Shut up.'

The presence left him.

⊙

'Jools, Jools, it's me,' the female said. 'I'm along in the cupboard talking into the brainwave monitor. How are you feeling today?'

'That cunt earlier! Tellin ays tae shut up. Over and over again. Nippy fuck! Ah'll boot the shite oot ay um when a catch him,' Jools said.

'Jools, you know these feelings of anger you've been having? Your strategies for dealing with anger are in need of attention. I heard him earlier. I don't know what his problem is but he sounded annoying. You've got to learn to deal with your anger more positively and try not to lose the rag all the time. It's all about what you're saying to yourself when something annoys you. Can you think what goes through your head when someone annoys you?'

'Usually Ah want tae rip his heid right off,' Jools said.

'No, that's not what I mean. Slow it down a little. What are you saying to yourself, before you blow?'

'Ah usually feel like he's takin the cunt oot me. Like he thinks Ah'm a right fuckin radge or something. Ah'm no wearin that.'

'Good, that's what I meant. You see, in your mind you see this person looking at you like you were stupid. Treating you like you were an idiot. But how do you know that's really what he's saying? Maybe he doesn't see you that way. Maybe you jumped the gun a bit. You tell yourself that he's saying such and such about you and your anger rises. You have to think positively, Jools. You have to catch yourself. Stop before you become too annoyed. What else could you say to yourself instead of something negative?'

'Ah dunno,' Jools said. 'Maybe something like… Ah'm no going tae get annoyed by this person. He's no aware that he's sae nippy. Ah'll just ignore it.'

'Good, Jools. What other positive stategies can you find? What else could you tell yourself?'

'This is trivial. Ah'll no let such small things get to me? He's only daein it tae annoy me so if Ah dinnae get annoyed he's no winnin'. Ah'm better than that?'

'Great! That's it, Jools,' she said. 'Now that's you been counselled about anger.'

⊙

It had got dark and Jools heard the tea trolley rattling down the hall so he got up. He went to the smoking room and poured some tea. He lit a cigarette and sat down on the unit. The man in the wheelchair went past and gave Jools a dirty look. Eddie talked to the Professor.

'Jools, Jools, can Ah get a cigarette off ye?' Archie asked.

'Ah've only goat a couple.' Standard reply.

The news started on TV.

'Leave the room. No news! Stay off the news!' a voice said.

Jools stubbed his cigarette out and went into the hall. A queue had formed outside the office and the nurses dispensed the medication. Jools stood in line. He took his tablet and went to bed. He sat in the gloom by his bedside light. Natty flashed through his mind. He wished he was home in his own bed. Maybe tomorrow they'd let him out. He turned off the light and lay back, closing his eyes. He thought of Natty, blew her a kiss and turned over.

'STAY OFF THE SEXUAL!!! OFF THE SEXUAL!!! Stop thinking sexually. I'm going to have to ask you to put her down while you're on the med research. We've had the pervables, now we need the nonpervables,' a distinctive voice said. It sounded like a comedian's voice. He was sure he'd heard it before, on TV maybe. There was something about the timing, the way the man spoke, the delivery of his speech.

'I used to be a comedian before I became a professor,' he said.

'Professor! Is that you?'

'We were just listening in before we go to sleep. I've given the students an earpiece each so they can hear what's going on. How are you feeling after the counselling?' the Professor asked.

'Better. A bit.'

'That's good. I wanted the students to know a bit more about you. Can you tell us what you do in your spare time?'

'Ah have a wank over children!' a voice laughed in the background.

'Fuck off!' Jools bawled. He recognised the voice. 'That was Eddie!'

'Now, Jools. The students are studying you for their psychology major. They'll be with you till the end of term so it's best if you try and get along. We see our work on the racism has changed your view. You were a bit light on your toes the other night with the two black nurses, eh?' the Professor chuckled. Jools, it is our aim, over this term, to take you and mould you into a complete new man. You're here for grooming. We want to take you and completely rework you from top to bottom. Now I'll switch off the earpieces just now so they can't hear us.'

Click.

'Now Jools, they still don't know that you're not really a racist paedophile. They won't know the truth until after the October break. I need you not to talk to anyone about this, OK? Remember, you'll be paid a lot of money. Sixteen thousand at least. Now a few of the students have been getting a bit angry with you. They really think you've tortured and murdered young bairns and it's got to a few of them. I'll have to ask you to stay off the ward as much as you can. You see, you're doing so many jobs for the Royal Ed. You're doing the machines, drug testing, the inner game, quite a few jobs to be getting on with. The most important one was the racist paedophile, "IT". You're doing a good job with the counsellors too. Now you try and get some sleep. I'll see you around the ward. I'll contact you, OK?'

Jools lay in the dark, staring at the ceiling. A high-pitched whine grew in his head.

'That's the signal!' the voice said. 'The signal for tomorrow.'

The whine faded. Jools rolled over and soon fell asleep.

Jools's eyes flicked open. A male nurse brought him his medication. He took it and lay back down.

'We'll get you out and show you around today, Jools,' the nurse said. 'I'll show you around the hospital.'

'Aye, awright,' he replied, yawning.

He pulled the duvet over his head and dozed for a while.

Jools got out of bed and shuffled to the bathroom. He stood in the cubicle and inspected his spot. It was finally beginning to heal. He gave himself a shake and went to wash his hands.

He looked at his reflection in the mirror. He noticed another deep spot coming up on his cheek bone and gave it a squeeze. Yellow pus oozed from the blemish.

'YUK! You're a disgusting wee swine, Jools, Ah swear it!' a woman's voice said. 'I have to watch that! Stop doing disgusting things on my shift, eh? That's how no one ever fancies a gomer! You're mingin!'

He washed his face and hands and went up the corridor to the smoking room. The Professor stood by the unit and the students sat in the chairs around the room.

'He's just finished giving a lecture,' the voice said.

Jools looked at the scruffy old Professor. The Professor dragged his sandalled foot across the floor as if drawing an imaginary line.

'The Professor says you're a skater,' the voice told him. 'He says you skate close to the edge but you don't cross the line.'

Jools smiled sheepishly and lit a cigarette. The students watched him and he began to feel uncomfortable. A female student smiled mildly at him.

'That's June,' the voice said. 'She's originally from Drylaw. She doesn't think you're too bad. She just thinks you're a wee shite.'

The man who'd worn the checked suit sat resting his head against the wall. He now wore an Iron Maiden tee-shirt and jeans and looked completely different.

'He's not really a Scottish Office official,' the woman said. 'That's Big Davy Love. He's Billy Love's nephew. He's doing his psych major.'

Jools finished his cigarette and lit another. Eddie looked over and smirked at Danny Love.

'Fuck's sake man, how many ay these fuckin Loves are there?'

'The whole family are in the mental health service, Jools,' the woman said. 'The grandfather is Professor Love. He's the top of the tree. They all followed in his footsteps.'

Jools finished his cigarette and went up the hall to the kitchen. He went up to the water boiler and poured a cup. Two men came in behind him. Jools got ready to throw the boiling tea at his attackers but they hung back like they were waiting in line. Jools took his tea back to his room.

'Stay off the ward!' the voice told him. 'Ward five are after you!'

Jools sat gazing from the window. A train went slowly by. He still thought it sounded like a helicopter. The male nurse pulled back his curtain.

'Are you ready to go out?' he asked.

Jools followed the nurse along the corridor and down the stairs. They emerged from the building into the warm sunshine. They walked slowly through the grounds and Jools lit a cigarette. The nurse led him by a modern building with a large stained-glass panel set in a huge plate-glass window.

'This is the church hall,' the nurse said. 'You can get a coffee and a game of pool here. They do art and other stuff here. You can sit and watch a video or listen to sounds.'

They went into the hall. He walked up to the counter that separated the kitchen from the hall and ordered two coffees.

'That'll be 24p, please,' the woman on the till said.

Jools took the coffees to a table and they sat down.

'TWELVE PENCE!' the voice said as he looked at the nurse.

Jools's face went red. 'That wasnae me!' he thought. 'Ah never brought it up, honest. You're just tryin to embarass me!'

Jools looked at the nurse.

'Twelve pence,' the voice said.

They drank their coffee and Jools picked up a free newspaper that was on the table.

'No reading!' the voice said.

'Ah'm no readin it!' he thought. He blanked out his mind and looked at the pictures. They finished their coffees and left the church. They walked further up the roadway.

'That's the bowling club in there,' the nurse said. 'You can get a beer in there. They've got a bar. Just as long as you don't get too drunk.' They continued round the grounds past a row of greenhouses.

'This is the garden project,' the nurse told him.

'Ah like gardenin',' Jools said. 'Ah've done a bit ay gardenin for a livin'. Oan the side, likes.'

'Maybe we can get you involved in the hospitals garden scheme. I'll find out about that for you.'

'Sound.'

They carried on round the hospital and came back into the main building through the car park. Jools thanked the guard at the top of the stairs and went to his cubicle.

◉

'Jools, I'm in the cupboard talking to you through a brainwave monitor. I'm here to counsel you,' the woman's voice said.

'Ah dinnae need counselling. Is that what you were trying to wind me up for? Goin on aboot 12p in front ay that nurse?'

'We've sort ay shot ourselves in the foot again. Alright, Jools, I'll level with you. You see, we got you scared about the paedophile thing. The students needed a model of a paedophile so we had to make you seem the part. That's why we had you on the paedophile monitor. All it really was was magnets. We've got a sort of silhouette of your head and we stuck magnets to it. It attracted all the negative thoughts to it. Don't you remember when you first came in, we magnetised your head? Well, all the thoughtwaves stuck to the top of your head. We put the magnets on it. You're not really a paedophile. It's just so we could all fix you again. That's how we learn.'

'That's fuckin oot ay order! You mean you put me through that so you could practise counselling me? <u>Youse</u> are aw fuckin <u>radged</u>!' Jools bawled.

'Now remember, what are you saying to yourself? Don't let that negative thought make you jump the gun,' she said cheerily.

'Fuck off, ya fuckin barmy cow! Ye nearly fuckin killed me! Ye're no fuckin counsellin me! Ah'm no listenin tae anymair ay your psychy shite!'

'Now Jools, it's not so bad, I'm sure…'

'AH'M NO FUCKIN LISTENIN! AH DINNAE WANT TAE HEAR IT!' Jools shouted. He put both hands over his ears and started to hum to himself.

'Jools, I'm just trying to…'

'HMM HMM HMMM!!! …' He skept humming loudly, drowning her out.

'Alright, Jools, I'll come back when you're in a better mood.' The presence disappeared.

Two bells rang in the corridor.

'Lunch, everybody!' the nurse called out.

⊙

Jools finished his lunch and went to the office. He knocked on the door and a nurse answered.

'Can Ah see Dr La Plante?' he asked.

'I'll make a note of it in the book, Jools. He'll be in this afternoon,' the nurse said.

'Ta.'

He went into the smoking room, which was empty. Someone had left the radio on loud. He smoked a cigarette then immediately lit a second. The band REM came on. Jools jumped up and shot across the room in a panic. He didn't want to jog anyone's memory about that night on the TV. He switched the radio off and silence returned to the room. He sat a while with his eyes closed. The man in the wheelchair came into the room. Jools got up and left.

⊙

'Dr La Plante's in his office, Jools,' the nurse said.

Jools walked up to his office at the end of the hall, knocked and went in.

'Take a seat, Jools. What can I do for you?' La Plante asked.

'It's this programme you've got me on. It's… too hard,' Jools said.

'What exactly do you think is wrong? Is it the content? The medication?'

'When am Ah gettin oot? Ah want tae go hame,' Jools said.

'We can talk about that at the meeting, Jools. We'll be having a meeting on Friday. I'll be asking your doctor and Jan Raymond, your Community Psychiatric Nurse to a meeting. I'll be there with your co-worker and maybe a couple of other people. Dr Bates will also be attending, and your GP. We can talk then about getting you some passes off the ward.'

Jools sighed loudly. He went to the door and left. It was no use talking to La Plante. He had something against him and there was no way he was going to let him out. Jools wondered why they were punishing him. He hadn't committed any crime. He went back to his cubicle with his head down.

'It's time you got back to work, Jools!' the voice said. 'Yours Truly will have expected you to have mastered the One by now. He'll not be too pleased with you when he gets back from holiday and finds out you've been mucking about. You'll get the max!'

'Aw fuck, naw! No that again!' Jools moaned.

'Oh yes! Assume the position! Two till four every day! Twenty-four hours without a thoughtwave!'

'Was that La Plante put ye up tae this? Because Ah asked when Ah'm gettin oot?' Jools reasoned.

'Assume the position! Concentrate!'

He took a tack from the wall and drove it into the fabric panel on the unit. He sat cross-legged on his bed, straightened his back and emptied his mind. He focused on the head of the tack and began to stare and stare.

Two bells rang in the hall.

'Dinner, everyone!' the nurse called.

Jools stood up stiffly. He walked up to the kitchen. He got there first and took a tray and sat at an empty table. He ate fast and was already out of the kitchen before most people got there.

'Stay off the ward!' a voice told him.

He took a cup of tea to the smoking room and lit a cigarette. The old woman was brought her tray by the Canadian nurse.

'Everything alright, Jools?' she asked.

'Sound,' he replied. He stood by the window. He watched a magpie chase a squirrel up a tree on the lawn below. It was a sunny evening and Jools wished he was outside in the fresh air. Why had he come to this place? He remembered his nights of walking with the wind. At least it had been exciting. He'd been outdoors all the time but they'd kept him crammed in like a sardine since he'd come to the ward. It made him think of home and all he was missing.

'Uh-uh! Them upstairs say you're subversive!' The animation of the dog in the baseball cap played across his mind's eye.

People started to come back from dinner. Jools finished his cigarette and went to his room.

⊙

Jools lay on his bed. He heard a loud click come from the bone under his top lip.

'That's them,' the voice said. 'That's the students in the smoking room, listening in. Whenever you hear that clicking sound it means they're switched on.'

Jools blanked his mind.

CLICK

'That's them turned off again. If you hear them switch on, watch what you think about because they can hear you thinking. They're all relaxing after work. Stay out of the smoking room till the Labour administration has left the building!'

'What time will that be?' Jools asked.

'After the news!'

'Fuck that, man!' Jools said, annoyed. 'Ah canny get a fag until ten?'

'Stay off the ward!'

⊙

Jools lay in bed. He thought of his cat. A lump came to his throat. His mind drifted and he thought of Natty.

'Pit it doon!' the male voice said. 'Stay off the sexual!'

'Ah'm no daein nowt!'

JAB! The needle stuck him in the ribs.

'Aaargh! Fuck off!' Jools bawled.

Jools became aware of a dead feeling creeping up his body. He tried to sit up but was held down by an invisible force. The energy enveloped his body and he tried to scream but nothing came out.

'Hold still!' the voice bawled. Suddenly his mind's eye began to grow dark. Jools could see the blackness spreading like ink in water, filling his head, blotting out all pictures. The black fog grew thicker, choking out all light and colour from the picture screen.

'Hold still, Jools! Don't move! We've put a visor in your mind's eye. That should help you do the One. You won't be able to picture anything in your mind for a while,' the voice told him.

'What are you daein tae me?!' Jools asked. 'Who are you?!'

'We're from the University of Edinburgh, Jools. I'm a med student. I'm practicing on the systems of the brain. I'm training in neurosurgery. This is the first one of these I've done. How do you feel?'

'Take it oot! Everything's black. Ah canny think right!' Jools panicked.

'Relax. It's just an oxide in your mind's eye. It'll take a while to wear off. It's semi-permanent. It should all dissolve by the time your coils have gone,' the voice said.

Jools closed his eyes. There was nothing but blackness.

⊙

Jools got up and went to the smoking room. The man in the wheelchair talked to the Professor, Eddie, Emma and Archie. Jools watched as Big Davy Love passed what looked like a joint to a young guy with dark hair. Jools lit a cigarette.

'Leave the room! The students don't want you in here after lessons,' the voice ordered.

'Ah'm just gonnie finish ma fag…'

'LEAVE THE ROOM NOW!'

Jools stubbed out his cigarette. The young man with the black hair passed the joint to Jools.

'Naw, thanks,' he said.

'Good, Jools! It was a test. If you'd taken it you would have got the max! You see, you are changing. The treatment's working!' the voice rejoiced.

Jools left the smoking room and joined the queue outside the office. He took his medication just as *News at Ten* started next door. A nurse wheeled in the tea trolley.

'Right, it's ten now. Can Ah go for a fag?' Jools asked.

There was no reply so he went in and poured some tea.

Jools turned his chair away from the TV and smoked a cigarette.

'Jools, Jools, can Ah get a cigarette off ye?'

Jools knew it was Archie, although he had his eyes closed.

'Ah've only goat a couple,' he said, not even lifting his head.

Someone turned the TV off and put a CD on. Cheesy techno blared out, filling the room. The young guy with the dark hair turned to Jools. 'What do you think?' he asked holding up a watercolour painting.

Jools's heart skipped a beat and his face flushed. It was a painting of the standing stones at Stonehenge. They'd whipped it straight from his mind.

He left the room in total embarassment. He tried to blank out his thoughts.

'Can Ah no keep nothin tae maself in this fuckin place?' he bawled.

A loony voice laughed in his head. 'We caught you out there, Jools!'

'That's fuckin bang oot ay order, likes!' Jools huffed as he sat in the dark on his bed.

'We were particularly fond of that one, Jools. That little… dreamscape of yours. Who's been fantasising about Anastacia then?!' the voice laughed.

Jools's face glowed scarlet.

'Fuck off, ya dirty bastard! How come is it you cunts are only interested in dirty stuff? Ah'm sick ay fuckin hearin it! Leave me alone! Ma dreams are mine!' Jools raged.

'So you thought we wouldn't find it, did you? You're in no fit state to meet Anastacia. She'd be disgusted! Look at you! You're a piece of filth. Do you think she'd want to meet a worm like you? She'd laugh in your face while she pushed past you to the limo. Stay off the sexual!'

The presence left him glowing scarlet in the dark.

⊙

Jools lay in the dark, unable to sleep. He saw a glint of light shine in from the hallway and he caught sight of the big man with the beard silently walking past the dorm door.

'He's a doctor,' the voice said. 'He's Eddie's dad. A psychology professor. That flash you saw was him signalling with a mirror. He's signalling to someone outside in a car. They're still watching you outside, you know. Stay away from the windows at night. They can see you at night. It's time they changed shift. Iga man taught them some ninpo tricks. They learned all about stealth and signalling. They know a few handy moves too, just in case a patient gets out of hand.'

Jools saw another glint. The man passed the door again silently. Jools sat up and looked out the window. A car started up and drove away in a nearby street.

Jools lay in the darkness. The high-pitched signal grew in his head. The sound seemed to resonate through the coils behind his temples. It reached a peak and started to fade. Jools wondered if there was any way to block it. It would leave him a day without a signal. Without instructions. Enough time to escape. Enough time to leave Edinburgh. He'd outrun the signal.

⊙

Jools awoke to the curtain being pulled back at the foot of his bed.

'Morning, Jools,' the male nurse with the skinhead said.

He took his medication and the nurse left him alone. The sun poured in through the window and he got up and went to the bathroom. His spot was healing up finally and he blanked his mind as he went about his business.

'Now wash those hands!' the woman's voice said. 'Hygiene.'

Jools did as she said, then went up the hall to the kitchen for a cup of tea.

'Stay off the ward!' the voice warned him. 'Ward five are after your blood! I'm telling you, for your own safety.'

Jools made his tea and warily went back down the ward to the smoking room. The room was nearly empty. A nurse tended a female who sat in a chair crying. Jools turned away from them as he felt he was intruding. The old man with the glasses read a paper in the corner. The sound of a floor polisher filled the ward as the cleaner went to it in the hall. The man in the wheelchair came in. Jools noticed a large scar on his head and quickly looked away.

'It's not polite to stare!' the voice snapped. 'Leave the room! That man is a highly respected psychology professor! He will not be mocked!'

Jools stubbed out his cigarette and left the room.

⊙

Jools sat on his bed quietly. He still could not picture anything in his mind, and a black soot covered his mind's eye. He got up and went to the toilet. He went into a cubicle and stood in front of the toilet unzipping himself. His eyes zoomed in involuntarily onto a plastic tube and a pair of soiled rubber gloves lying on the toilet cistern. His heart began to race as the electric current belted through his system, knocking the wind out of him.

'DO YOU WANT THE MAX?!' the voice screamed. 'Stay off the man in the wheelchair!'

'Ah wasnae sayin…' Jools said.

'Don't! Don't ever! That man is disabled. Don't you think he's entitled to some dignity?!'

'Ah never said nowt!' Jools bawled, shaking uncontrolably. 'It wasnae ma fault he left them there! Ah just went for a pish! Ay's a dirty bastard!'

'Look, Jools,' the voice sighed. 'The man in the wheelchair says you're a poof and you're a Jew!'

Jools left the cubicle and used the other one.

'Hands!' the woman said, but Jools was already on it.

⊙

'Jools, it's me,' the woman's voice said. 'I'm in the cupboard talking into a brainwave monitor and I'm here to see if I can help you.'

'Ah dinnae need any more counsellin', thanks!' Jools said sarcastically. 'What's the matter, have they no wound me up enough for ye? They were stealin ma fuckin dreams there earlier on. Why no counsel me oan that?'

'Who stole your dreams?' the woman asked.

'That cunt in the smokin room,' Jools said. 'He showed me a paintin ay Stonehenge. Goin on aboot a fantasy Ah had once. They dreams are private! Can Ah no keep anything tae maself? Fuckin stole the dream right oot ma heid!'

'Maybe you should tell me about your fantasy. Who does it involve?' she asked.

'Ach, it's nowt really. Do you know how when you go to your bed you sort of dream and fantasise? You see yourself doing all sorts of exiting things, meeting famous people… That place ye go where you're the hero ay the day? Well, Ah always fancied Anastacia, the singer. Ah'm no some weirdo fan stalkin her or anythin', Ah just think she's really tidy. She's just someone who sings and writes songs, eh? Anyway, one night she was on telly. The programme finished and Ah went tae ma bed. Ah was lyin there dreamin ay what it must be like tae have a woman like her. Ah fantasised aboot her.'

'And what exactly did you think?' the counsellor asked.

'Ach, it wasnae creepy or anythin'. Ah dreamed we were at Stonehenge, just the two of us and we're sort ay half naked. We're standin goin to it, kissin each other in the rain and there's a howlin wind blowin'. Ah'm standing behind her, wi' ma arms aroond her waist and we're gettin it on. It's a warm rain, like in summer. There's thunder and lightning and we're standin wrapped around each other. There's a powerful energy aboot us. As if nature itself flows right through us, through our bodies. We're alive!… It's electric!… Ah'll no go any further cause Ah believe in bein a gentleman but Ah've fantasised aboot that two or three times. But it was private, no to be shown tae anyone else. That fucker stole it right oot ma heid. Drew a fuckin picture ay ma dream.'

'There's nothing wrong in having a dreamscape. To fantasise is only natural. It's healthy for the mind to visualise our desires. It sets our goals and brings them closer to us,' she said.

'Like when Ah meet her for real, right?'

'Maybe. That's for Dr David Love to decide. It's certainly within your grasp to meet someone you find equally attractive. You could just as well fantasise about the nature of your future wife whoever she may turn out to be. The fact that you're visualising how you would treat her, it's like a sort of practice run. It'll make you a more capable, experienced lover in the end.'

'It's just… Ah feel he shouldnae be stealin what's in ma mind and showin it tae people. That's ma private thoughts. How come they're only interested in the dirty stuff? They say they're studyin psychology.'

'He was probably winding you up so we could counsel you,' the woman laughed. 'You see, they're all from posh areas. They don't really know what a schemie's really like. They've been treating you like that because they don't really know how to deal with you,' she said. 'They think that's what you're really like. Like "IT".'

'Well how can they no just treat me like a human being? Leave oot the private stuff. Stop bein so obsessed wi' the dirty bits. There's a lot more tae me than that, ye ken? Ma heid isnae generally filled wi' shite like that. Ah'm no a mingin bastard! Ah dinnae sit aboot pullin ma puddin aw day!' he laughed. He saw a funny side to it. 'Just treat ays like a human being.'

'It's just human nature, Jools. They've never seen inside a schemie's head before. Anyway, that's you been counselled on embarrassment.' The woman's presence disappeared.

JAB! A needle stuck him in the eyeball.

'Aaargh! Get tae fuck!' Jools bawled.

'Do not smoke!' a mean-sounding voice said.

'Aw naw, no that! Ah can put up wi' anythin but no that,' Jools said.

'Do not smoke! I warn you, I will not be trifled with!'

'How long for?'

There was no reply. Jools sat in his bed. Miserable.

Two bells rang in the hall. Jools was halfway to the kitchen before the nurse called 'Lunchtime, folks!'

He took a tray and sat at an empty table with his back to a wall. The dining hall started to fill and Jools tried to hurry his food. Eddie came over and sat at Jools's table. Jools stuck out his chin. He refused to be intimidated by Eddie. Eddie started to chew his food noisily. He slurped loudly, not looking up. Jools thought he was taking the piss and started to get annoyed. He finished up and walked away, giving Eddie a dirty look.

'Stay out of the kitchen when the students are eating!' the voice said.

Jools refused.

'Do not smoke! I will not be trifled with!' the voice said.

Jools put his cigarette back in the packet. 'Fuck's sake, when can Ah smoke then?' he huffed.

'It's almost time! Assume the position!' the voice commanded.

'Naw, fuck that! Ah want a fag first!' Jools said stubbornly.

'Take up your position! It's time! I will not be trifled with!'

JAB! He flinched as a needle stuck him in the chest.

'Aaargh! Fuck off, ya fuckin spastic!' he bawled.

'I will not be trifled with! ASSUME THE POSITION!'

'Trifled with? Where did ye get that one fae?' Jools mocked. 'You sound like some 1970s Open University cunt! Aye, Ah'm fuckin triflin'. Ah'm fuckin triflin wi' yer rice puddin', ya fuckin spaceball! Get tae fuck!' he started to giggle. It was a tired laugh.

JAB! a needle stuck his thigh.

'AAARGH! FUCKIN STOP IT!'

The presence disappeared. Jools got up and had a cigarette.

'Assume the position, Jools,' a woman's voice said. 'Twenty-four hours without a thoughtwave. The sooner you do it, the sooner you go home.'

Jools thought about it. It made sense. He took up his cross-legged position on the bed, focused on the tack head and cleared his head. He began to stare...

Two bells rang in the corridor.

'Dinner time, people!' a male nurse called round the dorms. Jools got up and stretched his back. He had to sit back down again as his head spun and he felt dizzy. He got up and shuffled stiffly to the kitchen. He stood in line for a tray and nervously scanned around for attackers.

'You're a wee shite, Jools!' the woman's voice laughed. 'You're meant to stay off the ward. You're meant to stay out of the kitchen when the students are eating. Do you not understand? They're going to kill you when they catch you! They all want to beat the shit out of you. Does nothing scare you?'

Jools smiled. 'There's nae way Ah'm stayin in that dorm. Ah couldn't give a fuck. They can come ahead!'

'But Jools, ward five are after you too. They think you're a paedophile. The daddy of ward one keeps coming up here looking for you. He wants a square go with you. Have you seen the size of that guy? He's huge!'

'If it happens, it happens. Ah'm no backin doon anymore. Ah'd rather be deid than exist like that another minute. Ah'm really ready tae die if Ah have tae.' Jools meant it. 'Ah've goat tae the stage where Ah've almost accepted death.'

He ate his food at an empty table. Some quiet people joined him. An old woman cackled loudly with Emma at another table. Everything seemed alright.

⊙

Jools sat on his bed. He heard women's footsteps coming up the corridor. Sarah, his sister, put her head round the door.

'Awright?' he said.

'They said we can take you out for a walk,' she said. Her boyfriend stood beside her.

'Cool!' Jools said. He got up and pulled his boots on. They went along the corridor and down the stairs. He pulled out his cigarettes and put one in his mouth.

'Do not smoke! I will not be trifled with!' the voice warned him.

Jools was feeling brave. He was with family. They couldn't touch him. They walked through the main building and out through a side door into the grounds. It was a warm, sunny summer night. They walked slowly across the lawn and Jools led them to a seat built around the trunk of an old hawthorn tree. He'd be out of sight of the office window there. His sister and her boyfriend lit their cigarettes and gave Jools a light.

'Do not smoke! I'm warning you!' the voice said meanly.

Jools ignored it and kept smoking. Suddenly his head began to spin. Everything started to turn black and Jools thought he was going to drop. He felt the neck of his tee shirt start to tighten and constrict, shutting off his jugular.

His eyes rolled back in their sockets and his eyelids fluttered as he put down a hand to steady himself. He threw down the cigarette in disgust.

'Are you alright, Jools?' Sarah asked.

'Here,' he said, thrusting his packet of cigarettes at her. 'Take them.'

'You'll need them, Jools. You keep them.' She looked at her boyfriend, slightly puzzled.

Jools fought hard to stay on his feet and stay conscious. His heart pounded fast as he took some slow deep breaths and tried to pull himself together. His hands shook and his legs were like jelly.

'Ah think Ah'll just go back up the ward now,' he croaked.

⊙

Jools lay on his bed listening to the sounds in the ward. Every now and then the smoking room door would slam shut and he'd jump. Cheesy techno beats pumped from the boogie box in the smoking room. Someone paced up and down the corridor. Jools peeped out from behind the curtain. The big guy with the beard was pacing the hall. Jools's mind's eye was still black and he still couldn't picture anything. He longed to be able to have a good long private think to himself. He really craved a cigarette but he was scared to smoke again.

He thought back to his days in cognitive therapy. His psychologist had taught him to fight anxiety and panic attacks. He must accept the fear and still dare to do it.

'Whatever happens, you can take it!' he said to himself. 'Override the negative thoughts with positive ones.'

He started to chant to himself:

'I will not back down

I will not back down

I will not back down.

I can take whatever they throw at me!'

Over and over again he repeated it.

'BRING IT ON, MOTHERFUCKERS!!!'

He heard *News at Ten* starting on the TV and got up. He joined the queue outside the office and took his medication. He went nervously into the smoking room. The room was smoky and there were no seats so he sat on the unit. A nurse wheeled in the tea trolley and he helped himself. He pulled out a cigarette and lit it with a shaky hand.

Nothing happened. He cautiously puffed away. He finished the cigarette and immediately lit another.

⊙

The high-pitched whine began on the stroke of twelve. It grew louder and louder until it reached a peak, then died down. Jools tried to cover the coils in his head with his hands. The signal seemed to be partially blocked. He fell asleep in silence.

⊙

Jools opened his eyes as the curtain pulled back at the foot of his bed.

'Morning,' the nurse said, handing him his medication.

He swallowed the tablets and went back to sleep.

⊙

'Jools, you're a little shit, by the way!' the voice said as Jools awoke. 'You blocked out the signal last night and our technicians are pretty pissed off with you. They had to come back into the uni today to send out another signal. Now don't cover the coils!'

The high-pitched signal began to whine through his head. It peaked, then fell.

'Now that's you been done again. Stop mucking about. You've already been hung, drawn and quartered, what more do you want?' the voice said.

'What do you mean?' Jools asked.

'Well, you were hung, like last night when we choked you, drawn, like when we drew you out so we could counsel you, and quartered: three-quarters of your head was on the paedophile monitor. You know it's the students who think up all these tests. Them and the professors.'

Jools got up and went to the bathroom. He blanked out his mind as he sat there. His spot was getting a little smaller. He left the cubicle and scrubbed his hands, then shuffled up the corridor to the kitchen and warily made some tea and toast.

'Stay off the ward! Ward five are after you! He's not all there!' the voice laughed. 'He's still getting up to go to the kitchen. Are you not scared of anything, Jools? You're mental.'

Two men from ward five came in and sat at a table, talking. Jools eyed them up. If they were trying to act menacing they weren't doing a very good job of it. He took his toast and tea and swaggered back down the hall to the smoking room.

Jools sat in the smoking room sipping his tea. A nurse came in. 'Jools, Dr La Plante would like to see you,' she said.

Jools followed her to a room on the kitchen corridor. She knocked and they went in.

'Come in, Jools,' La Plante said. 'I think you've met everyone here.' Jools recognised his GP and Jan Raymond, his old psychologist. Dr Bates also listened in.

'This is Grant Smith. He's your co-worker,' La Plante said. Jools remembered the skinheaded nurse from the ward. 'And you've met Bill Rae, the MHO. That's Mental Health Officer.' The mason smiled over.

His eye caught sight of a pile of brightly coloured plastic toys piled in the corner of the room.

'Jools, don't say anything!' the female voice said anxiously. 'They're trying to trick you! They want you to admit you're a paedophile! That's what all the toys are there for. To see if you get agitated or turned on. They want to keep you in because of the wee lassie! Jan Raymond went mental at them. She's not too happy with them. She's just been arguing with them. Don't say anything, Jools! Tell them nothing! Don't look at the toys!'

Jools started to feel anxious. He clamped his teeth together tightly and blanked his mind.

'So how are you feeling?' La Plante asked.

Jools said nothing. He blanked the man completely and stared at the wall.

'Jools?'

He stared.

'Well, we've decided that passes would be good. They'd get you off the ward for a while. We're going to start you on half-hour passes but you must come back to the ward. We've been discussing a plan as to where we take your treatment from here. We'll be letting you go home for a night, then two. Ideally we'd like to see you back home permanently with support.'

HOME

Jools's concentration broke.

'Ah'm awright. There's nothing wrong wi' me,' he said.

'Jan is going to be visiting you when you get out. She'll be popping down regularly to see you,' La Plante said.

Jools smiled at her.

'Watch them, Jools! Don't tell them anything else. Don't look at the toys!' the voice screamed. 'STAY OFF THE TOYS!!!'

Jools blanked again.

'Is there anything you would like to ask us, Jools?' La Plante asked.

He shook his head.

'OK, then. You can go back to the ward.'

⊙

Jools stepped out of the bath, dried himself and dressed. Two bells rang in the corridor.

'Lunchtime, people!' a male voice called up the hall.

He shuffled up the corridor.

'STAY OFF THE WARD! Ward five are gonnie leather you! Honestly, he's not all there!' the voice laughed. 'If that was me I'd be shitting myself.'

'I'll take whatever they throw at me!' Jools repeated over and over. 'Ah can handle it!!!'

He went in and grabbed a tray. He sat at an empty table and began to eat. He heard a familiar voice laughing and joking around and turned to see Billy Love talking to Eddie and Danny.

Jools froze. He nibbled his food nervously then left the kitchen.

⊙

Jools walked along the corridor to the smoking room. He went in and sat down. Someone was visiting and the men talked over a cup of tea and a cigarette.

BANG! He jumped. The door bumped open. A young child pushed his buggy into the door and into the smoking room.

'Come here Kieran! Dinnae go away now. We're going home in a wee while,' the father called to the child.

'See!' Jools thought. 'Ah'm no a beast! Ah'm awright wi' bairns! Ah could never hurt a bairn! Ah love kids.'

'DON'T!' the voice bawled.

The electric charge hit his mid section and his heart pounded.

'Don't ever test yourself!'

'But Ah wasnae!' Jools said, winded. 'Ah was just sayin…'

'GET OUT OF THE ROOM!!!' the voice ordered, 'before I become angry with you! You're going to get the max if I ever see you test yourself like that again!'

Jools stubbed out his cigarette and went to bed shaking.

⊙

'Assume the position!' the voice said. 'It's time! Twenty-four hours without a thoughtwave is required! Just be!'

Jools sighed deeply. He took up his position cross-legged on the bed, blanked his mind and focused on the tack on the wall. It seemed easier since they'd blacked out his mind's eye. He stared and stared.

⊙

'Dinner time, folks!' the nurse called.

Jools got up stiffly. His back ached and his head throbbed. He shuffled up the corridor to the kitchen. Billy Love stood by the queue talking to someone. Jools stood warily in line. He took a tray and sat down with his back to a wall. He kept an eye on Billy Love while he ate.

⊙

Jools went down the hall for a cigarette. He caught sight of Billy Love through the office window.

'Stay out of the smoking room! Billy Love hates smoking!' the voice warned him. Jools sighed. 'Naw, fuck him!' he thought, and went in anyway.

⊙

Jools sat in the dorm. He heard a woman's footsteps approaching. His aunt put her head round the door.

'Hi,' she said.

'Awright.'

He led her along to the quiet room and they sat down.

'I've brought you a few things,' she said, and handed him a carrier bag.

'Cheers,' he said.

'So, how are you feeling?'

'Ah'm awright. Ah just want oot ay here. It's crackin me up.'

'Is the medication not doing any good?' she asked. 'Are you getting enough sleep?'

Jools shook his head.

His aunt told him his cousin in Canada had emailed her. She was asking for him.

'Don't say a word, Jools!' the voice told him. 'Get rid of her, now!'

'Naw, fuck off! She's ma auntie!' Jools thought.

'Your auntie's got sussies on!'

Jools started to laugh.

'What are you laughing at?' his aunt asked.

Jools shook his head and tried to control himself. He had an urge to giggle but held it in.

'Your auntie's got sussies on for Billy Love! She used to go about with him years ago, before you were born. They've been pals for years,' the voice told him.

'Aye? Who'd have thought?' Jools said mentally. 'What's he so down on me for then?'

'He thinks you're lazy. You've never worked.'

'Aye, but Ah've done plenty voluntary work and Ah've had jobs oan the side. Labourin and that,' Jools, said, defending himself.

'He was expecting her nephew to be… a bit more straight, I think. He thinks you need someone to make a proper man of you. He thinks you lack mental discipline. He was expecting someone of your aunt's calibre but he's ended up with a schemie.'

'Have you heard from your brother?' his aunt asked.

'Ah've no seen him.'

'What have you been doing to fill your time then? Have you managed to find something to do?'

Jools shook his head. He sensed she was looking for something to say. He was struggling too.

'Well, it's just a quick visit tonight. Me and Nana are going out tonight,' she said, putting her coat on. 'Now is there anything you need?' she asked.

Jools shook his head.

'I'll visit again in a couple of days,' she said.

He walked her up the corridor and she gave him a hug.

⊙

Jools lay in bed. It had started getting dark outside and he heard the tea trolley being wheeled down the hall. He got up and walked up the corridor. Two nurses sat outside the office on chairs.

'Thank fuck that's Billy Love's shift finished,' he thought. He went into the smoking room, poured some tea and lit a cigarette. *News at Ten* came on TV and Jools turned his seat away.

'Stay off the news!' the voice said. 'The students are trying to relax after work. Leave the room. They don't want you in here.'

JAB! A needle stuck him in the side and he flinched.

Jools sighed loudly, stubbed out his cigarette and went to bed.

⊙

The curtain moved and a nurse brought Jools his medication in bed. He swallowed the tablet and lay back down. The nurse went back to the office.

Jools lay in bed unable to sleep. He'd lain there for what seemed like hours and decided to get up for a cigarette. He went up the corridor to the smoking room. Big Davy Love sat in the corner by the lamp talking to the young guy who'd shown Jools the picture of Stonehenge. They turned round to look at him then looked away again. Jools sat down and lit a cigarette. Davy Love started to laugh and Jools wondered if he was laughing at him. He stared over. The young guy sat by the coffee table rolling a joint.

'Psychologists like to relax too, Jools!' the voice said. 'Leave the room!'

Jools stubbed out his cigarette. He hadn't meant to intrude and hurried back to the dorm.

'Don't think about what you just saw! It could get them into trouble!' the voice said.

'It's cool, man,' Jools said. 'Ah'll no say nowt. Ah'm nae grass.'

'Don't think about it! You must forget what you saw!'

'Mate, how am Ah meant tae forget somethin Ah saw two minutes ago? Yer askin the impossible,' Jools reasoned.

'Get it out of your head! Don't think! Forget that thoughtwave!'

'Aw naw! Ah get enough ay that shite during the day. Ah'm no daein it again,' Jools said. 'Ah'll no grass them, honest.'

Jools lay in bed in the dark. The high-pitched signal sounded midnight then faded to silence. He fell asleep soon after.

⊙

The nurse brought Jools his medication and he got up and went to the bathroom. He shuffled up the corridor to the kitchen and made himself some tea then walked back to the smoking room. The cleaner was mopping the smoking room floor and Jools lifted his feet so he could get under the chair.

'G'morning, Blue' he said cheerily.

'Hiya.'

'Looks like we're in for a spot of rain this afternoon,' the cockney cleaner said.

Jools nodded, looking out the window. He had half-hour passes off the ward. 'Ah might go oot the day,' he thought.

Jools dressed and put his boots on. He went up the corridor to the top of the stairs.

'Ah've got passes oot,' he told the guard.

'That's fine, Jools,' the guard said, ticking him off on his sheet. 'Be back in half an hour, OK?'

'Ah'm just goin tae the shops,' Jools replied. He walked to the foot of the stairs and down the corridor. He left the building and walked through the grounds of the hospital taking in some fresh air. A strong wind whipped up and the sky was dark. The wind caught Jools from behind and blew him along.

He nearly lost his balance as a gust caught him by surprise, almost blowing him into a plate-glass window.

'The wind people are angry with you, Jools,' the voice said. 'They think you did something bad with a wee lassie. The students have been whispering.'

Jools ducked nervously back into the main building. He went to the shop and stocked up on cigarettes then went back to the ward.

⊙

Jools sat on his bed. He began to feel some discomfort in his pubic area. The discomfort turned to pain.

'Aaargh!' he screamed, as he started to burn. He felt a cigarette burn smouldering on his groin.

'Stop fuckin burnin ma balls!' he screamed.

The pain throbbed on.

Jools checked but there were no marks to be found.

⊙

'Jools, Dr Curry would like to see you this afternoon sometime,' the nurse said. 'He's taking over from Dr Bates. She's finished her six months placement with us.'

'Aye, awright,' he said.

Two bells rang in the hallway and Jools went for lunch.

⊙

Jools walked down the corridor. He reached the hall at the top of the stairs when a girl called to him.

'Your mum phoned, Jools,' she said, totally straight-faced.

Jools frowned at her and shook his head in disgust. He noticed a badge hanging from her belt with the word 'STUDENT' printed across it.

'She's lucky she's no a man,' he thought, 'or Ah'd rip her fuckin heid right off. Fuckin wee hoor, using ma ma against me!'

He stormed off to his bed.

⊙

'Jools, it's time! Take up your position!' the voice said.

Jools sat cross-legged on the bed. He tuned out all thoughts and focused on the tack head. He stared for a time.

Jools snapped out of it as the curtain pulled back at the foot of the bed. A tall, thin man with dark hair and glasses stood before him. Jools thought he looked like an older Harry Potter.

'I'm Dr Curry,' he said, extending a hand. 'I'm here to examine you. We'll take your blood pressure first, shall we?' He wrapped the velcro pad around his arm and pumped it up. 'I'd like to listen to your heart next,' he said, putting a stethoscope in his ears. 'Just lift up your shirt for me, could you?'

He placed the cold instrument on Jools's chest then moved around and listened to his back. 'That's fine,' he said, putting the stethoscope away. He scribbled on his chart then looked up. 'So how have you been feeling generally?' he asked. 'You've not felt unwell at all?'

Jools shook his head.

'Don't worry. You can trust us,' the doctor said.

'Ah'm awright. Ah just want tae get oot ay here.'

'Well, everything seems normal here,' he said, standing up. 'I'd better be getting on. Remember, if you want to talk, that's what we're here for.' The doctor left him alone.

Two bells rang in the corridor and Jools went for dinner.

⊙

'Ah'm goin back oot for a while,' Jools said to the guard at the top of the stairs. 'Ah'm away for a walk.'

'That's fine, Jools,' the guard replied. 'Be back in half an hour.' Jools went down the stairs and through the corridors. He left the building by a side door and walked across the lawn in the evening sunshine.

TAP TAP TAP

Jools looked up to see an old man with a white beard knocking and waving at him from a window. He waved back.

'Ah'm gonnie get you raped!' a bird twittered in a tree.

Jools started to feel wary. He lit a cigarette and forced himself on though he was starting to get nervous.

'Ah'm gonnie get you raped! Ya dirty wee cow!' the bird twittered.

'Jools, dinnae worry!' the voice said. 'It's just the students. They're using a thoughtwave generator on the birds. It makes them sound like they're talking. They're a bunch ay bams!'

'GET IT UP YE!' the bird laughed as two girls squealed and flapped around on the lawn like they were swatting a wasp.

'It's the two university fraternities. The Magpies and the Blackbirds. They're all trainee doctors and medics. That's them talking to the lassies using the birds. They're immature bastards, really. They should go over and talk to the lassies instead of chasing them around with the birds.'

Jools smiled.'They sound freaky when they dae that,' he said. He carried on.

Jools had completed his circuit around the hospital grounds. He started to turn back to the ward.

'See that wee schoolie ye had the wank over?' the male voice laughed. 'Did ye think she was tidy?'

'Ach, she looked a lot aulder than her age,' Jools laughed. 'She was pretty tidy though.'

The voice started to laugh again and Jools joined in. Suddenly the electricity hit him and turned his legs to jelly. His heart pounded.

'SO YE THINK IT'S FUCKIN FUNNY DAE YE?!!!' the voice screamed.'WAIT TILL YOU GET BACK TO THE WARD!!! YE'RE GETTIN FUCKIN LEATHERED!!! YE'RE GETTIN YER FUCKIN CUNT KICKED IN!!! Emma's minders gonnie boot fuck oot ay you! She kens that wee lassie's family! Yer fuckin gettin it!'

Jools started to panic. He looked around for a way out. Should he run away? He could just leave, go home over the wall. He almost started to run, then stopped.

'Naw!' he thought. 'Whatever happens, Ah'll handle it. But if anyone does start, Ah'm goin doon fightin!' He stuck out his chin and clenched his fists. 'The first cunt that comes near me gets it!'

He put his head down and marched back to the ward.

⊙

Jools got to the top of the stairs and was welcomed by the sight of Emma crying.

'You're brave!' the voice said. 'That's why Emma's crying. She was upstairs in the lab just now when they zapped you. She thinks you're so brave for coming back.'

Jools went through to the smoking room, his heart pounding. It was full of people and their visitors. The air was thick with smoke. No one paid him much attention so he sat and had a cigarette and tried to calm down.

⊙

Jools sat on his bed thinking about escaping. He wondered if he could outrun the signal. Maybe if he reached his aunt's in Manchester he'd be out of range.

'Uh-uh, them upstairs say you're subversive!' the animated dog in the baseball cap said, pointing at the ceiling.

'That's all I've heard all week in the office, Jools,' a woman's voice laughed. 'Uh-uh, them upstairs say you're subversive!' she mocked. 'That's not you thinking of escaping again, is it?'

'Ah'm no daein nowt!' Jools said.

It had started to get dark in the dorm so he turned on his bedside lamp. He felt grubby and got up and went for a bath.

'Cleanliness, Jools! A clean body and a clean mind! Cleanliness is next to godliness.' The woman laughed as he ran the taps and got undressed.

'They were brutal earlier, eh?' she said, sounding sympathetic. 'That guy's just a technician. He works on the top floor. He doesn't like you, Jools. I don't know what his problem is. Maybe he's got something to hide but it seems to have got to him.'

Jools got into the lukewarm bath and started to scrub. Suddenly a pain hit him in the balls, knocking the wind out of him. A can of shaving foam had been lobbed over the cubicle wall and had found its mark. Jools got out of the bath and hobbled to the door but they'd gone, whoever threw it.

'Ah'll bet it was either Danny Love or Eddie,' he thought to himself.

'It was the Professor who had them do it,' the woman said. 'He wants you to get all this paedophile nonsense out of your head. He's told you, you're a skater. You skate close to the edge.'

Jools got out and dried himself. He dressed and went back to his room.

Jools heard the tea trolley being wheeled up the hall so he got up and went to the smoking room. The students and actors sat around the TV. Jools lit a cigarette and poured some tea. He caught sight of the TV screen. Stephen Seagal, the martial arts film star, flashed onto the screen wearing a red Aikido uniform.

'He's there for you, Jools!' the woman said. 'He's out in support for you. He wants to meet you when this is all over. You're to fly to LA and meet him. He wants to give you Aikido lessons at his dojo in Hollywood.'

Jools was thrilled to bits. He was going to meet his hero.

Jools took his tablet and left the office. He was tired and went to the toilet before going to bed.

He stood in front of the toilet and began to pee.

'Shut up, Jools!' the voice said. 'Just simply shut the fuck up!'

'Look, Ah've tried to help you people. Are ye just gonnie leave me alone and gie me ma heid back? Ah canny take any mair ay this,' Jools appealed to him.

'Just gonnie gie's ma heid back?' the voice mimicked from his arsehole.

'That's no funny,' Jools said grumpily.

The voice moved around front. 'Are you gonnie stop stickin me up so many skanks?' his dick said. 'Nae wonder Ah've got warts! Get a shag, ya plooky wee ride!'

Jools had to sort of laugh, but he didn't want to.

'Ah can make ma voice come out of anywhere, Jools,' the voice laughed. 'This machine's easy to work. Ah just click on it with the mouse where Ah want the voice to go.'

'And ye can stop pullin me off so much!' his dick said. 'Leave the wee lassies alone!'

Jools went to bed and lay in the dark. He just drifted for a while.

The signal started to whine on the stroke of midnight then faded to silence. Jools fell into a deep sleep.

⊙

'Medication, Jools,' a voice said.

Jools opened his eyes to see Billy Love come into the cubicle. He sat down on the bed and handed Jools the plastic beakers. Jools swigged them back. He lifted up a hand to scratch his head and Billy Love flinched.

'AAAHH!' Jools thought. 'This cunt's feared ay me!'

He grinned to himself as Billy Love went back to the office.

⊙

Jools lay in bed thinking about escape. He wondered if they'd ever let him out.

'Ask to see the OC, Jools,' the voice said. 'The OC will let you out. He's meant to be coming to see you sometime today.'

Jools got up and went to the office. He knocked on the door and a male nurse answered.

'Can Ah get tae see the OC today?' he asked.

'Who?' the nurse asked, puzzled.

'The OC,' Jools repeated.

'Sorry, Jools. Never heard of him. Do you mean the doctor?'

'Naw, it's awright,' Jools said, and went back to his room.

Jools lay back on his bed.

'HA HA HA!' the voice laughed. 'You fell for it. The OC means your own counsel. You have to get better by yourself round here. Twenty-four hours without a thoughtwave! Ye're a poof, ye're a Jew! Shut yer mooth!'

Jools walked up the corridor for a cigarette.

'Stay out of the smoking room!' the voice warned. 'Billy Love hates smoking!'

'Fuck Billy Love!' Jools said. 'He's a fuckin radge! If he's goat anything tae say, Ah'll be in there havin a fag.'

Jools went in and sat down. Emma made a beeline for him.

'Awright?' she said, shuffling over.

'Aw, fuck,' Jools sighed. 'Ah wish she'd just fuck off. She's aw mooth wi' her minder sittin there.'

'Is yer sister comin up the night?' she asked, toothlessly.

'Get out of the room, NOW!' the voice screamed. 'STAY AWAY FROM THAT PERSON!!!'

Jools got up and moved to the other side of the room.

'Ma wee lassie's comin up tae see me the morn,' Emma said to a woman, but Jools thought she was really just talking out loud to anyone that could hear her. 'MA WEE LASSIE, WI' BLONDE HAIR!' she said, her eyes narrowing to slits.

Jools started to panic. 'Ya fuckin evil bitch!' he thought. 'If that minder cunt starts Ah'll rip ays fuckin face off!' He stubbed out his cigarette and stormed to his room.

Jools sat on his bed, head in hands. Two bells rang through the hall.

'That's lunchtime, people!' Billy Love called.

'Assume the position!' the voice said, but Jools was already waiting cross-legged on his bed. He blanked his mind and began to stare.

Two bells rang in the corridor.

'That's dinner, everyone!' a nurse called out.

Jools walked up the hall. The clock read 6.15 but it was surely wrong. Jools reckoned it was only around five. A notice on the wall confirmed the time. Dinner: 6.15, it said.

'Ah must have been doin a lot longer than Ah thought every day,' Jools realised. He went to his meal contented.

⊙

JAB! a needle stuck him in the ribs. Jools didn't flinch.

'Aaah… dead sore! Is that the best ye've goat?' he laughed. 'Ah love pain! Bring it on, ya fuckin mongos!'

He heard the nurse approach.

'Jools, your brother's here to see you' she said.

He went into the corridor and met James, his brother.

'Awright,' James said, as they walked up the hall. 'D'you fancy goin oot for a while?' he asked. 'The nurses said Ah could take you for a drive.'

'Aye, sound,' Jools said. 'Where tae?'

'We can take a run doon the beach,' he said.

They went through the main building to the car park and got into the car. James drove out of the main gates and they headed into the traffic. His brother put a hand up to his ear.

'He's got an earpiece in,' Jools thought. 'Ah better watch what Ah say.'

'Are they no daein your nut in?' James asked. 'Aw the mongos in there? Ah couldnae handle it in there, Ah tell ye. Ye've just goat tae get yer heid together and they'll let you oot.'

'Get ma heid together?' Jools thought. 'It's no me that needs tae get it together. It's these spastics runnin the Royal Ed.'

They drove in silence for a while and soon reached the hotel car park on Marine Drive. They left the car and headed down the gravel path to the seafront. Jools watched the surf. He tried to time his breathing to the waves rolling in, then retreating. They walked along a distance.

'Smoke?' James offered.

'Naw, ta,' Jools said. They walked along as far as Gypsy Brae with the two huge blue towers of the gasworks in the background. It looked like it might rain so they turned back to the car.

⊙

Jools sat ready for bed in his jogging pants and tee shirt. He was bored and wandered up the hall to the quiet room. He went in and switched the light on. He noticed a pile of board games on a shelf in the corner and thumbed through them. He pulled out solitaire and took it to the table. He laid out the black and white marbles on the board and started to play. He suddenly had the feeling he was being watched. A presence sat inside his head. Jools jumped a black marble with a white. The presence watched.

'I used to play this game when I was in the 'Dam. They had it in a coffee shop,' the voice said. 'You better not let the white balls win. It could be seen as racist,' the voice laughed.

'Aye, Ah was thinkin that,' Jools joked. 'So you were in Amsterdam, were you? Is it no pretty heavy over there? Ma mate was over. He got chased off a Moroccan wi' a knife,' he told the presence.

'Aye, it's pretty wild in the red-light district alright,' the voice said.

'Ah've heard it's aw the immigrants that cause the bother wi' the tourists…'

He was cut off mid-sentence by a bolt of electricity zapping through his body. His heart skipped a beat.

'What?! What have Ah done?!' Jools asked, shaking.

'Go to your room. NOW!' the voice said. 'I've never heard anything so racist in my life! You make me sick! You're one step away from the max, let me tell you! Dr David Love hates racism!'

Jools got up and left the room, shaking.

'It's what ma pal says! Ah didnae ken. Ah wasnae bein racist!' Jools tried to calm the scene.

He went back to his bed and tried to calm himself down.

'Awright, son?' the old man's voice said. 'It's me. Dinnae worry, it's just us. We're ootside in the van dismantling the gear for the university. It's me, Whiskers! Ah banged on the window tae ye yesterday.'

'Awright.' Jools recognised the old man with the white beard. 'How's it gaun?'

'Me and ma pal were just takin a break. We've just had a couple ay cans ay beer and a pipe. Ah'm just aboot tae start dismantlin a machine we used tae relay ye tae the uni. What's up wi' ye the night?' Whiskers asked. 'You look awfy doon.'

'Ah just goat zapped. They said Ah was bein racist.'

'Aw, the dirty… Ach, dinnae let them get tae ye, son. They're aw a bit snooty up this neck ay the woods. Where are you fae?' Whiskers asked.

'Muirhoose,' Jools replied.

'Is that doon by the gasworks? Aye, Ah ken where ye are. It's a bit rough roond there, is it no?' Whiskers asked.

'It's awright. Ah've stayed there aw ma life, so Ah dinnae get any hassle.'

'What were they goin on aboot ye bein racist for? Do ye no like the darkies?' Whiskers laughed.

'Naw, it's no that,' Jools said. 'They've goat it intae their heids that Ah'm a racist paedophile. Ye ought tae see the way they're treatin me.'

'Ach, the truth be known, Ah dinnae like the darkies maself! Look at this.'

A picture of a gollywog dropped into Jools' mind's eye.

'HEE HEE HEE!' Whiskers laughed.

'How long before you get aw the gear packed away?' Jools asked. 'Will that be me gettin ma heid back then?'

'It'll take us a wee while but Ah don't know when they'll leave you alone. That'll probably be the first of August when they go on holiday.'

Jools felt disappointed.

'Dinnae worry, son. The first's no that far off now. The day will come when you're no a gomer. Ye'll be awright, son,' Whiskers said. 'Ah was hearin ye goat caught oot oan the paedophile monitor? Dinnae worry aboot that, son. Every year it's the same. Some gomer gets caught oot oan the paed tapes. Yer no as bad as some ay them, mind you. Ye should see what some ay them have got in their heids!' he laughed. 'Jools, every gomer in history's been caught oot oan the paed tapes.'

'Aye? The bastards had me nearly believin Ah was a beast,' Jools said.

'Ah heard it was some wee tease had goat ye intae trouble?' Whiskers laughed. 'What did ye dae? Was it stoat the baw?'

'A schoolie nightmare,' Jools said, smiling.

'HEE HEE HEE!' Whiskers laughed. 'Ach, it's no nothin we've no aw done, son,' Whiskers said cheerily. 'Anyway, we better be gettin back tae work or the gaffer'll be moanin'. Ah'll see ye later!' Whiskers left him.

Jools felt a bit better. Whiskers was a funny old coot.

⊙

Jools lay on his bed in the dark. He heard the tea trolley rattling up the hall so he got up and went to the smoking room. The room was full and there were no seats. The students and actors sat around the TV smoking and chatting. Jools poured some tea and lit a cigarette. The Professor suddenly broke into song

'OH FLOWER OF SCOTLAND!' he sang.

'WHEN WILL WE SEE YER LIKES AGAIN?!!!' Everybody in the room joined in.

Jools stubbed out his cigarette in disgust. 'Because ma dad's English!' he thought to himself. 'Well fuck the lot ay them! They call me fuckin racist?!'

He stomped off to his bed.

⊙

Jools lay in bed with his bedside lamp on. His curtain was pulled back and he could see up the ward. A young man with short dark hair came in and went to the bed opposite.

'Alright, mate?' the guy said. 'I'm Jools. If you want anyone with half a brain to talk to, just give me a shout.'

'Ma name's Jools tae,' he said.

The guy turned off his light and went back out.

'Half a brain?' Jools thought. 'Was he a student too? Was he talking about my brain?' he wondered.

A nurse brought round his medication and Jools took it and put his light out. He lay in the dark gazing out the window at the stars.

The high-pitched whine of the signal peaked and faded. Jools fell asleep soon after.

⊙

'Jools, Jools, it's rag week, Jools,' the woman's voice said. 'It's me. I'm in the cupboard in the hall talking into a brainwave monitor. Some of the students are leaving today. The fourth year have finished their exams and they'll be going home now. They've had to stay here all term in the Royal Ed. That's them that do the operations on you from the lab upstairs. They'll all be leaving in the next few days.'

'Thank fuck for that,' Jools said, yawning. He sat up and rubbed his eyes.

A nurse pulled back the curtain at the foot of the bed.

'Medication,' she said cheerily.

Jools swallowed the tablets then lay back down.

⊙

Jools got out of bed, went to the bathroom then went up the hall for a cup of tea. He made a cup and walked back to the smoking room trying not to spill it. He opened the smoking room door, being careful with the cup. Someone had a visitor and the visitor's child ran around the smoking room floor. Jools stopped dead, about turned and left the room with his heart pounding.

⊙

Jools lay on his bed contemplating escape.

'Jools, it's me,' the woman's voice said. 'I'm in the cupboard talking into a brainwave monitor. Stop thinking about escape. You can't escape. "IT" is still in your head and they'll have to de-programme it before you leave. You can't run around with that in your head, now can you? It'll take over eventually.'

Jools noticed the words being typed out across his left eye in transparent letters like on a computer screen.

'That's the Royal Ed computer. It's down in the basement. It records everything about your day so the psychologists can see where to go next,' she said.

'When did they put me on that?' Jools asked.

'Last night while you were sleeping. It's better for you really. We don't have to man you twenty-four hours a day. It records everything. We just come in and read the printout.'

'What aboot ma privacy? This thing's watchin everything Ah dae. Ah'll no get nae peace.'

'Don't worry. If you say or do anything too embarrassing all I have to do is say "NOT".'

The screen on his eye cleared.

'When I say "NOT", it's a signal for it to clear the screen,' the woman said.

Two bells rang in the hall and Jools went to lunch.

⊙

'Assume the position! It's time to do the One!' the voice said. 'One full day without a thoughtwave!'

Jools took up position cross-legged on the bed. He cleared his mind and began to concentrate on staying blank. He stared and stared.

⊙

'Jools, this is Bridget, she's a psychologist. She's here to take you out,' the nurse said. The woman smiled.

'I've got the car downstairs. I was going to take you home for a visit. Would you like that?' the woman asked.

'Aye, sound,' Jools said.

They walked up the corridor and down the stairs. She led Jools out to the car park and they got in the car. A large sandy-coloured Labrador sat panting between the two front seats.

Jools patted the dog as the woman drove through town. He started to feel nervous as they drove across Lothian Road and onto Princes Street. He thought everyone was looking at him in the car. 'There goes the gomer for the Royal Ed!' he imagined them laughing. The woman drove across the Dean Bridge and Jools felt the Royal Ed's signal begin to weaken and drift. The signal crackled and hissed, then picked up again.

'DON'T TOUCH THE DOG!' the voice screamed. 'That's my dog! That's my mother you're with! Don't dare touch the dog! Not ever!'

Jools sighed.

'I'm following in the car behind you so no funny stuff! I'm here to patch up the signal to the Royal Ed. Don't dare touch the dog!' the voice screamed.

The woman drove down Pennywell Road and Jools felt like he'd been away for years. Everything seemed different somehow. They drove along his street and the woman was just parking when Jools discovered he had no keys for the house.

'Ma sister's goat the keys,' he told her. 'Tae look after the cat.'

'Well, never mind,' she said. 'Seeing as we're down this way, why don't we pop into the Royal Victoria for a look around. They want you to attend as an out-patient when you get out.'

'Aye, fair enough,' Jools said.

The woman started the engine and they drove off.

They drove into the Royal Vic car park and Jools got out of the car and lit a cigarette. The woman took her time getting out and they walked slowly to the hospital building and into reception.

'Hold on here a minute,' the psychologist said. 'I'll just see if I can find someone.'

She disappeared through a set of doors. Jools went back outside to finish his cigarette.

He didn't fancy attending this place on a regular basis. It wasn't his scene and he wasn't interested.

The psychologist came back a few minutes later talking to a girl with long red hair and glasses. Jools eyed the young woman up. She was ugly by his standards, he thought, but he'd shag a hole in the barber's floor just now. He was that horny.

The psychologist said her goodbyes and came out. They walked across the car park and were getting back in the car when the voice screamed, 'HOW DARE YOU! THAT'S MY MOTHER! YOU LOOKED AT HER FANNY! JUST NOW, I SAW YOU!'

'Did Ah fuck! Ah was just gettin in the car!' Jools answered mentally.

'Don't dare look at my mother like that! And don't touch the dog!'
They drove back to the Royal Ed in silence.

⊙

Two bells rang in the hall. 'That's dinner, everyone!' the nurse called.

Jools went up the corridor to the kitchen. He took a tray and squeezed in at a table away from Eddie and Danny Love. He ate his food and looked around the room. A tall goofy-looking guy with a curly afro hairdo came into the kitchen wearing a long grey coat down to his ankles and a long stripey scarf.

Jools started to laugh.

'He's just dressed up for rag week, Jools,' the voice laughed.

Jools started to giggle hysterically. He spat a mouthful of custard over the table. His sides started to ache with laughter. The other people at the table chewed on placidly. No one even looked up. Jools nearly fell off his chair, giggling. He tried hard but could not hold it in. The whole kitchen filled with the sound of him laughing.

⊙

Jools was sitting on the bed in his cubicle thinking about escape when he felt a loud click in his face.

'That's the students in the smoking room, Jools,' the voice said. 'They're listening in again.'

Jools heard someone snigger.

'ROAST, BOY, ROAST!' the voice bawled loudly, right up to the microphone. 'YA WEE JEWWWWW! YA WEE JEWWWWWW! ROAST, BOY, ROAST!'

'Aaargh! Fuck off!' Jools growled, clasping his head. The voice was so loud it sent a pain through his head, making him feel sick.

'YA WEE JEWWWW! YOU'RE GONNIE ROAST! RECEIVE UNTO THEE THIS ROASTING FOR WE ARE THEY THAT DO ROAST!' the voice bawled.

Jools couldn't stand the pain and slid onto the floor, covering his ears.

'RECEIVE THIS ROASTING! FOR THOU ART A JEW! AND A POOF! ROAST, BOY, ROAST!'

Jools started to writhe around the floor in agony and his heart began to pound under the strain. The surface of his brain felt like it was burning.

'FOR THOU ART A POOF AND A JEW, AND THOU MUST BE ROASTED! FOR THUS ARE WE! THOSE THAT DO ROAST THY GOMER!' the voice screamed.

Jools started to breathe deeply. He tried hard to stay calm but this was getting too much to bear. The pain flashed through the centre of his skull with every syllable making him want to vomit.

'ROAST!'

⊙

'Jools, it's me,' the woman's voice said. 'I'm in the cupboard talking into a brainwave monitor. You better stay out of the smoking room till later tonight. That was Big Davy Love that just roasted you. He's finished his exams and he's leaving soon so they all want a shot of roasting the gomer before they go.'

Jools's head still spun and throbbed.

'Thank fuck they're aw leavin,' he said. 'Ah'm fuckin sick ay that family.'

'The Love people. They're all in psychology. It's the family business,' the woman said.

'The Love people? Ah've never heard anything sae fuckin cheesy in ma life. Pretentious cunts. Their squeaky-clean image makes me cringe. They're like the fuckin Partridge Family.'

'Maybe, but they're damn good at what they do,' the woman said.

'They're cruel bastards!' Jools snapped. 'They've nae idea how tae treat another human being!'

'Jools, they're all from affluent backgrounds. They're millionaires. They're not used to someone of your social background.'

'So that gies them the right tae treat me like a dog? Fuckin shut up this, stay out ay there, dae this, dinnae dae that! They're daein ma fuckin nut in!'

'Don't you see? The Love people are here to change your attitudes, Jools. They want to make you more like them. They're trying to mould a new you,' the woman said.

'Fuck that! Ah'll never be like them. Never!'

Jools heard the tea trolley rattling up the hall so he got up and went to the smoking room. He poured himself a cup of tea and lit a cigarette. The room was full and everyone sat around the TV. Jools sat in the corner well away from the main group. He smoked his cigarette and was about to light another when the news started on TV.

'Stay off the news!' the voice said.

He took his tea and went out into the hall. He saw the nurse opening the medicine trolley so he nipped in and got his medication first. He went back to his cubicle and lay on the bed.

⊙

Jools lay in the dark. He thought about escaping when suddenly he started to feel a tingle spread up his body.

'Hold still, Jools!' the male voice said. 'Don't move your head. I'm at the Western General and I'm looking into your brain on the computer. You see, I'm looking for some cells that the doctors planted. I have to burn them out with a laser. Don't worry, it doesn't hurt.'

Jools stayed as still as he could and tried not to blink.

'The cells are just artificial thoughtwaves. Probably the paedophile ones. There's one, now hold still.'

Jools felt a mild burning inside his skull behind his eye socket.

'There, that's one of them burned out!' the voice said. 'They're a bit like land mines. They explode if they're not handled with care. That's why I'm practising. I'll have to do this for real some day. Soon it'll all be done this way. Virtual operations. They'll do away with the need to open you up.'

Jools felt another mild burn.

'Got it! That was one awkward little bugger. There don't seem to be any more... no, I think that's the lot. That's me finished for the night. Now Jools, I want you to take it easy for a week or so. I've just burned out a tiny part of your brain. It was only a couple of cells. The burns should heal but if you strain yourself too much they could bleed so take things easy, will you?'

'Aye, awright,' Jools said.

The presence left him. A stick figure of a girl dropped into his mind's eye then vanished.

'This is the Western General Hospital in Edinburgh signing off!' the voice said. 'Goodbye from all the team and stay away fae wee lassies!'

The signal hit its peak then died down to silence. Jools fell asleep thinking of escape.

'Medication, Jools,' Jane, the blonde nurse said, handing him the plastic beakers.

Jools knocked them back and she left him. The sun shone through the window and he looked out across the Pentland Hills. He missed the great outdoors. He'd been stuck away in here all summer and had missed all the good weather. He'd been wrestling with the idea of escape for a few days now and he knew it was only a matter of time. He dressed and went to the smoking room. It was empty so he had a cigarette in peace. His stomach hurt on both sides and he felt drained.

'That's your adrenal glands, Jools. They're swollen again,' the woman said.

'You've been on too long. It's sensitised you. It's me. I'm in the cupboard talking into a brainwave monitor. That was Emma and Davy Love that gave you those operations, Jools. They're all leaving in the next few days,' she said.

A cleaning woman came into the room and asked Jools to leave while she swept and mopped the floor. He left and went to the kitchen.

'Stay off the ward! Ward five are after you!' the voice said, as he poured some tea. Jools took his tea back to his bed. He sat on the bed wondering if he should escape today.

⊙

'Ah'm just goin oot for a walk,' Jools said to the guard at the top of the stairs.

'OK, Jools,' the guard called back.

Jools went down the stairs and through the building. He left by a side door and walked across the lawn lighting a cigarette. The sunshine was warm and he took his denim jacket off and tied it around his waist. He sat down at a picnic bench and smoked his cigarette.

'Ye're a dirty wee poof!' a bird whistled loudly in a tree. 'Ah'm gonnie get you raped!'

He contemplated escape. He had to get away from here. These people were screwy.

⊙

'You'll get frozen out!' a voice said to him. 'No sixteen grand if you don't finish the course.'

Jools was past caring about the money. He just wanted to go home.

'JOOLSY-BOY!' a goofy-sounding voice said.

'Longcoat!' He recognised the voice of the guy with the curly afro. 'How ye daein?'

'Joowls… how come awl your family awl tawlk like that, Joowls?' he said loonily.

'Shut up, ya big bam!' Jools laughed. 'They do not!'

'Not at awl, Joowls! Not at awl!' Longcoat laughed. 'One is a paedophile…'

Jools laughed. 'You're mental man, so ye are.'

'Longcoat's the captain of the Royal Ed fraternity, Jools,' a woman's voice cut in. 'He just wanted a quick word with this year's gomer. You're like their mascot. They think it's funny having a racist paedophile for a mascot. They're all pretty wacky,' she laughed. 'You were our cow. We milked ye for all ye were worth!'

'FIDDLING WITH WOTNOTS!!!' Longcoat called out. 'Stop sssniffing people's underthings!'

Jools started to giggle.

'FIDDLING WITH WOTNOTS?! One… had a wank!'

The word WOTNOTS appeared across his mind's eye in red balloon letters then popped out of existence like soapy bubbles.

Two bells rang out in the hall.

'Lunchtime, everybody!' a nurse called.

⊙

'Assume the position!' the voice said.

Jools sat cross-legged on the bed. He focused on the tack head, blanked out his mind and began to stare.

Two bells rang in the corridor. Jools got up stiffly and went to dinner.

⊙

Jools was sitting on the bed when he heard a woman's footsteps approaching. A nurse popped her head round the curtain.

'That's your sister here to see you, Jools,' she said.

He went out in the hall.

'The nurses said I can take you home for a visit, Jools,' Sarah said. 'D'you want to go see the cat?'

'Aye, sound,' Jools said. They walked along the hall and down the stairs to the car.

'We're right behind you, Jools! Keep your mind blank and don't look out the windows!' the voice said. 'You're on your own this time, it's not stifled so you better keep the thoughts well and truly hidden.'

Jools stared at the dashboard, keeping the One all the way home.

Sarah parked the car and Jools walked up the path to his front door. It all looked strange to him, as if it had been a lifetime ago since he'd been here last. Sarah opened the door and they went in. The smell of fresh paint hit Jools as they stepped into the hall.

'James has done some decorating for you,' Sarah said.

He opened the living room, went to his favourite chair and slumped down. It was good to be home.

'Who's that, puss?' Sarah said, as the cat came in yowling. It sniffed at Jools then jumped up on his knee, purring loudly.

Jools hugged the cat. 'Ah missed ma wee buddy,' he smiled.

He got up and made a cup of tea and had a cigarette. They sat for an hour then she took him back to the hospital.

⊙

Jools had a bath then went to the smoking room.

'Jools, Jools, can Ah get a cigarette off ye?' Archie asked.

'Ah've only got a couple,' Jools said.

'They don't want you in here, Jools,' the voice said. 'The Love people have picked Archie. It's because he joins in and you don't. They don't want you around.'

Jools finished his cigarette and went to bed. He decided he'd escape in the morning.

A nurse brought Jools his medication and he fell asleep planning his escape.

⊙

The curtain pulled back at the foot of the bed and Jools sat up, rubbing his eyes. The nurse gave him his tablets and he swallowed them with the glass of juice. He started to shiver. It was really cold in here. He wrapped the duvet around himself and tried to warm up. A strong cold draught blew through the dorm. Jools stood up and closed the vent window but it made no difference. He noticed someone had left a fan on in another cubicle so he got up and switched it off. He lay in bed listening to the air conditioning buzzing. He heard someone shouting in the smoking room and the door banged shut. A woman screamed in the hall.

'That must be one of the actors hamming it up,' he thought.

The woman screamed again. Jools didn't find her performance too convincing. He thought she was a shit actress. 'Shurrup, ya silly fuckin cow!' he called out.

He lay in bed shivering and finally got up and pulled on his fleece jacket before getting back under the duvet again.

'Is this what they meant by frozen out?' he wondered.

Jools lay shivering in bed. Suddenly a carriage clock appeared in the centre of his head again. He could see it when he shut his eyes and he could feel the wheels and cogs ticking round.

'Get that fuckin oot!' he bawled at top of his lungs.

The clock continued to tick.

'Get it oot ma fuckin heid now!'

Still the clock ticked.

Jools gritted his teeth and booted the wardrobe door.

'Ya fuckin nippy bastards! Get that fuckin thing oot ay me now!'

'Wee man, settle doon!' A close presence filled his head. 'They're just drug testin oan ye! Stop takin bennies every two minutes and settle doon!'

'Fuck you! Ah canny handle this fuckin thing, now get it oot!' he raged.

The clock kept ticking.

Jools got dressed and went down the hall.

'Ah'm just goin for a wee walk,' he said to the tall thin guard with glasses.

'Right-oh, Jools,' the guard said, ticking him off on his register.

He took the stairs two at a time and nearly stumbled half way down. The clock still ticked away in his head making him disorientated and unbalanced.

Jools broke into a jog as he made his way across the lawn. He headed across the grass and into the trees, stopping only when he reached a ten-foot wall. He took a run at it and pulled himself up on top. Train tracks ran along on the other side. He dropped down and made his way across the tracks and up the embankment on the other side. His eyes darted around nervously to make sure he wasn't being followed.

'Ah'm never comin back tae that fuckin place ever again!' he shouted as he scrambled up the embankment and into a quiet side-street. Jools made his way warily along a quiet suburban avenue and came out at a main road.

'Jools! Stay where you are! We know you're escaping! We're on to you. The van is out looking for you,' the voice said.

Jools blanked his mind and ran across the road. A car approached and he ducked down a dirt track leading off the main road. He walked for a while and reached a sign saying Napier University. He looked across to an elaborate old building set in beautiful grounds and wondered if the signal was coming from there.

'Fuck you!' he thought. 'You'll never fuckin catch me now! Now get that fuckin clock oot ma heid or Ah'll track ye doon and fuckin kill ye!'

'I'll chop ye up with a machete!' the voice threatened.

'Aye?! Ye want tae fuckin play wi' knives, dae ye?' Jools bawled. 'Fuckin come doon tae ma hoose then! Ah've got a samurai sword! Ah'll cut yer fuckin heid right off! Now get it oot!'

'Awright, awright!' the voice backed down. 'Ah'll get rid of the clock.'

The clock vanished instantly.

'Now gie me ma fuckin heid back and fuck off! Nae voices, nowt!'

'It'll take me a couple of days. I have to get back into the uni building to switch off the digitiser. It's set up on a desk in the lab. It's only about the size of a wrist watch,' the voice told him.

'Ye've got two fuckin days or Ah start takin cunts oot!' Jools growled firmly.
He decided which way north was and headed homewards towards the Forth.

⊙

Jools reached the top of Pennywell Road. He looked down at his beloved housing scheme and started down through the High School grounds.

'YOU'RE IN A SCHOOL!' the voice screamed.

Jools felt the electric charge building in his body. His legs were almost paralysed and he struggled to remain standing.

'STAY AWAY FROM CHILDREN! STOP! SSSTOP!' the voice bawled.

Jools tried hard to keep moving and had to drag his legs step by step. He felt his bowels loosen and rumble.

'GIVE HIM THE MAX!' the voice screamed.

The electric charge hit Jools in the chest and knocked the wind out of him. The current tingled in his body making him shake violently. Three claws tore away from his brainstem and ripped down along his spinal column. Jools's eyes started to roll and flutter and he thought he might lose consciousness. He fought hard to stay with it and dragged himself onwards, towards the school gates.

'It's not working!' the voice said. 'He's out of range. He's only getting half power!'

⊙

Jools reached home and remembered he'd no keys. He wandered along to the phone box and called his sister.

'I'll be right there,' she said, and Jools went back to wait on the doorstep.

⊙

Sarah pulled up in the car and walked up the path.

'How are you home?' she asked.

'Ah couldnae handle it any longer, so Ah left,' Jools said.

They went in and sat down.

'Ah'm never fuckin goin back tae that place again,' Jools told her.

'I'll have to speak to the doctor, Jools,' Sarah said. 'You can't just walk out like that. You'll be missed. I better call them before they send the police out for you.'

'Fuck them. Fuck the polis! They've got nothin on me. Nowt! Ah'm stayin here, whatever they say.'

'I better get back to work. I'll go up to the hospital later and collect your things. I'll see what they say about you staying home,' Sarah said.

She left the flat and Jools sat in silence in his favourite chair. It was great to be home.

⊙

'Jools, Jools, we'll let you stay home on one condition,' the voice said. 'You must continue the One while we de-programme "IT". I'll expect you to carry on with the One every day as normal. You must stay blank while we work on you. If you don't we can take you back to the Royal Ed.'

'Fuck you! Ah'm never goin back! They're nowt but a bunch ay fuckin screwballs! They nearly fuckin killed me!' Jools bawled. 'Ah'll dae yer fuckin One. If you want me tae stare at the walls, Ah'll stare at walls. Just dinnae make me go back there.'

⊙

The front door tapped. Jools went up to the peephole and spied through. It was Sarah.

'I've brought your stuff back from the hospital, Jools,' she said. 'And I've done a little shopping for you till you can get to the shops. The electricity had run out so I got a couple of power cards. Now the doctors have said they'll let you stay home as long as you take the tablets. You're not to miss any doses. Not even one. You've got to attend the day hospital at the Royal Victoria too. If you don't take the tablets they said they'll take you back in,' she said, handing him two large pink tablets.

'They said to only give you two at a time. I'll have to drop them off every day.'

'Aye, awright,' Jools agreed. 'Ya fuckin beauty! Hame at last!' he rejoiced.

The cat jumped up on his knee, purring loudly.

Jools wondered if they'd let him watch TV again. He was in his own house and to his reckoning, what he said went. He switched the set on and turned up the volume. The picture looked strange to him. Clearer and more life-like than he'd remembered.

'Stay off the TV!' the voice said.

'Naw, fuck off,' Jools said. 'It's ma hoose, Ah'll dae what Ah want.'

'TURN OFF THE TV! It interferes with the signal!'

Jools ignored it and kept watching.

'If you don't turn that TV now, I'm warning you, you'll be sorry!' the voice said.

'Naw, bolt! It's ma telly!'

Jools noticed a high-pitched whine coming from the set.

'TURN IT OFF OR WE'LL BLOW IT UP!' the voice screamed.

The TV whined louder and the picture had a band of interference across the screen.

Jools leaned away from the set and flicked it off at arms length.

'Fuckin oot ay order,' he huffed.

'Jools, just because you're home, don't expect an easy time of it. You're not finished with us yet. We're still waiting on a student finishing his thesis. They still have exams to take. Don't expect all your own way.'

'But how long for?' Jools asked.

'Till the first of August.'

'That's a couple ay weeks away. Ah told that cunt earlier. He's got two days tae gie me ma heid back!' he bawled. 'Now yer sayin a few weeks?'

'Twenty-four hours without a thoughtwave!' The presence left him before he could answer.

⊙

Jools got a plate and put a frozen beef curry on it. He got a fork and was about to pierce the bag when a voice stopped him.

'Don't pierce the bag!' the voice ordered.

'Ah've got tae. It'll explode if a dinnae.'

'No it won't. Do not pierce the bag! The microwaves can leak, spoiling the food.'

'Well, Ah've never heard ay that,' Jools said.

'Do as you are told! Do not question my authority! And stay away from the microwave. It can heat up the coils in your head. They conduct microwaves.'

Jools sighed. 'Awright then, smart-arse. You know best.' He put the frozen curry in the microwave and stepped back.

'Leave the room! It is dangerous for you to be around a microwave. The coils!' the voice said.

Jools went and sat on the stairs to wait.

BANG!

He went to the kitchen and turned the microwave off. His dinner had exploded.

⊙

A voice sniggered in Jools's head. The snigger turned into a giggle.

'What're ye laughin at?' Jools asked.

The voice continued to giggle. 'She was a wee cow!' he laughed. 'That wee bird ye had the ham shank over, she was a wee cocktease! Fuckin wee cow!' the voice giggled.

Jools found it funny too and started to snigger. He started to giggle partly through tiredness, partly because he knew he was on dangerous ground. He felt rebellious.

'Don't dare laugh!' another voice screamed. 'You should be ashamed of yourself! That is a young girl you're talking about!'

Jools giggled hysterically. 'Ah'm no sayin a word!' he laughed. 'It wasnae me!'

'No, but you're laughing!'

'FUCKIN WEE COCKTEASE!' the other voice laughed. 'WEEEEE COWWWWWW!!!'

Jools collapsed in fits of laughter.

The presences faded out.

⊙

'Jools, I need you to assume your position for a while. I'm here to de-programme "IT" for the Royal Ed,' the voice said. The words printed out backwards across his left eye like on a computer screen.

Jools sighed. 'Ah thought Ah'd finished wi' this when Ah left the hospital.'

'It'll take a while,' the voice told him. 'It's just a programme to me. It's all just noughts and ones.'

'Like binary code?' Jools thought.

'Exactly. It's a digital signal. Wow! That thing's evil. It just screamed there and swore at me. It must know it's nearly the end. It's been a really successful programme this year. I can't wait to see the look on the students' faces when they find out you're not really a racist paed. That'll teach them not to make assumptions,' the voice laughed.

Jools sat cross-legged on his futon matress on the living room floor. He stared at a knot in the wooden dado rail on the wall, blanked his mind and stared and stared.

⊙

It had got dark outside and Jools lay in bed on the living room floor. He got up yawning and took his medication. He lit a cigarette and lay in bed smoking and reflecting on his day.

'You know, I like to reflect on my day too, Jools,' a deep male voice said. 'I sit here at night, on my own in front of my laptop and I sort out all the problems and hurdles we run up against during our day.'

'Who are you?' Jools asked.

'I'm the philanthropist. I'm here from the university to study. I'm here to find out why a whole area such as this went so bad over the years. I'm here to live amongst the people, to live what they live for a time so I can really get inside the people. Their collective mind. I want to understand what makes these people tick, discover their essence, as it were. How is it that people can go through so much and still have spirit at the end of it? What makes people from the scheme such a hardy breed? They seem to keep on smiling no matter what you do to them. They have a sense of pride about themselves, of dignity. They're a proud people… I don't know. Sometimes I sit here at night in the wee small hours and I feel like *Midnight Caller* on TV, reaching out across the night. I have to wonder about myself, what I've done to you, and I question myself. What am I doing? Why did I pick on some single guy living on his own and put him through all this? You see, sometimes we have to look inside ourselves to find the answer. To know another man we must look inside ourselves first. You made it pretty easy on me, Jools. Until I found out about your antics with the schoolie. You know, that really annoyed me. It wasn't the fact that you did what you did so much as it made me look inside myself. I had to question my own morals. You made me look at things I didn't really want to see in myself. In the beginning you were starting to get too nosey. You noticed the changes that were going on around you. Most people just walked by, Jools. But you, you started to get in the way. You knew too much. That's when I had to have you removed. I've been having you chased around for months, Jools. You've been on the fear since Christmas at least.'

'What do you mean? Jools asked.

'Do you remember before you took that overdose?' the philanthropist asked. 'Don't you remember all the fear you went through? You thought everyone was talking about you, didn't you? Remember how the feeling of fear was getting so bad that you started staying in? You wouldn't answer the door or the phone. Remember, Jools?'

Jools remembered. He'd known back then there was someone out to get him. The doctor had referred him to a psychiatrist at the Royal Victoria and he'd put him on an anti-depressant and Largactil for anxiety.

'And do you remember why you took the overdose that night, Jools?'

'Someone was trying to set me up for a rape. Ah never done it. Ah've never done anything like that in ma life!' Jools recalled. 'Ah was terrified. Every move

Ah tried tae make, they were one step ahead ay me. Ah knew Ah was dealin wi' a pro. Ah even took ma phone apart cause Ah thought they were bugging the line. Ah could feel the strength ay what Ah was up against. They left me nae choice. There was no way out. Ah had nae alibi. Ah had tae die. It was that or Ah went tae jail for something Ah never done. Ah remember sittin in ma bed thinkin "This is it, Ah have tae dae it." Ah took a whole month's script. Eighty-odd tablets.'

'That was us, Jools. We had you on the fear.'

'Ah thought it was just paranoia!'

'We had to scare you good and proper but you were too strong in the end. We didn't want to kill you. We just wanted you out of the way. You were starting to get too nosey. And then that night on Queensferry Road. We all tried to stop you, Jools. We tried to stop you blabbing. Bigmouth! That was us in the cars. Remember how you blabbed it all out that night? You can't stop progress, Jools. But you should have just saved yourself all this pain and gone when you started to get scared. You had to fight the fear, though. That's when we had you run into the Royal Ed,' the philanthropist said.

'So that was you? You made me think Ah was gettin done for rape?'

'That was us. We put all that fear in you. We started rumours around the area. That you had been talking about people behind their backs. We had them scowl at you in the street. We told everybody to start ignoring you. We had you running around like a headless chicken. You had to go, Jools. We've had you on the fear since Christmas.'

'Could ye no have just told me tae get oot ay Muirhoose? Ye didnae have to scare me that bad Ah nearly killed maself.'

'That's the beauty of it, Jools. No one in particular ever said anything to you, did they?' the philanthropist asked. 'There's no one to tell on. No proof. Try telling your story to the police. It'll be straight back to the Royal Ed for you. By that time we'll be long gone.'

'Ah just... sensed that's what they were daein tae me. Ah knew someone was out tae get me. Ah could feel it. The feelin was so strong,' Jools said.

'Well now you know. I had you run out. Like I said, we didn't want you dead. That was your own doing.'

'Why pick me, though?' Jools asked

'Again I have to look inside myself. I wrestled with it. I really should have some sort of conscience about what I've done to you but... To tell the truth, I think it was because you live on your own. The council have drafted us into Muirhouse to mix with the locals, Jools. They want us to help change the attitudes of the people living in the scheme. They've just rebuilt the place. People like you have to change or move on. There's simply no place for people with your attitude. We've got European backing on this. It's Europe that funds us.'

'Maybe Ah dinnae need re-educatin'!' Jools bawled defiantly.

'Just a thought. Whether you like it or not, Jools, that's how it is. You can't stop progress. You know all this could have been done in the comfort of your own home. You didn't have to go through all that. All you had to do was get with the programme. Not resist it. Others would have seen you and followed.'

'And what make ye sae sure Ah would have helped ye?' Jools asked. 'Ah'm no sure Ah'd be up for you cunts tryin tae brainwash us intae bein placid and responsible citizens. We've goat a mind ay oor ain doon here. It's our identity. Ye canny force us intae thinkin different.'

'That remains to be seen. Just you keep your head down while we're here,' the philanthropist said. 'Stay in the house as much as possible. Until the first of August.'

The presence disappeared.

Jools fell asleep wondering what to do.

⊙

Jools awoke and it took him a few seconds to remember where he was. He got up and took his medication and made some tea. The sun shone in through the kitchen window. It felt great to wake up in his own bed.

Jools left the flat and walked along to the shopping centre. He felt strange being out and wondered how many people would recognise him. He went into the post office and stood in the queue. Someone bumped him and he turned his head to see a short fat woman with black hair standing behind him. She wore a Star of David around her podgy neck.

'She must be a Jew,' Jools thought. 'Probably here to follow me.'

He cashed his benefit book: nearly four hundred pounds, as he'd been unable to cash it for weeks and it had mounted up.

He left the post office and walked round to the supermarket. The same old faces stood drinking by the wall as he turned the corner by the old fruit shop. He ducked into the supermarket and picked up a basket.

'Get out of here!' the voice said.

'Ah'm goin hame after Ah dae some shoppin,' Jools answered.

'Hurry up! You shouldn't be out!'

Jools started to feel a bit nervous being out in the crowds. Everything seemed odd to him as they'd changed the layout of the shop since he'd been here last. He hurried his shopping and went to the checkout.

Suddenly panic ripped through him. His heart pounded as he saw the toddler standing at the checkout with his mum.

'STAY AWAY! CHILDREN!' the voice screamed.

Jools went to another checkout. He was terrified of the tot and was shaking. He gave him a wide berth.

He scurried home and locked the door behind him, panting for breath.

'SHUT UP!' a distinctive male voice said. 'YE'RE A POOF, YE'RE A JEW, SHUT YER MOOTH!'

'Who's that?' Jools asked.

'Jools, just shut up! Simply shut up! SHUT THE FFFFUCK UP, JOOLS! SHUT YER MOOTH!' the voice bawled.

'Ah'm no sayin a word,' Jools said.

'SHUT UP!'

'You shut up! Fuckin weirdo!' Jools said, a bit annoyed.

'YE'RE A POOF, YE'RE A JEW! SHUT YER MOOTH!'

'AH'M NO A FUCKIN POOF! AH'M NO FUCKIN JEWISH! NOW FUCK OFF!' Jools bawled back.

'SHUT UP!'

'Will ye fuck off! Look, who are you?' Jools asked.

'Ah'm Drylaw guy!'

'Drylaw guy? What, are you a student, likes?'

'Ah'm a psych major and Ah stay in Drylaw. You're a poof and a Jew and you live downtown. In the ghettos! Shut the fffffuck up!'

'Well fuck off back tae Drylaw then, ya mongo bastard!!' Jools spat.

'Jew.'

The presence left him alone.

⊙

'It's time. Take up your position. It's time to do the One!' the voice said. 'Twenty-four hours, Jools.'

Jools sat cross-legged on the futon matress on the living room floor. He blanked his mind and began to stare.

⊙

The front door tapped. Jools went to the door and peeped through the spyhole. It was his auntie. He let her in and they went through to the living room.

'How have you been getting on?' she asked. 'Are you feeling any better now you're home?'

'Ah'm awright,' Jools said.

'I've just dropped in on the way home from work. I'm here to give you your tablets for tonight and tomorrow morning.' She handed him two pink tablets in a blister pack. 'I'm not stopping tonight. I have to get home for my dinner. Now is there anything you need? Have you managed to get the shopping in?'

'Ah dinnae need nowt,' Jools mumbled. 'Ah got ma shoppin in this mornin'.'

'OK, then. I'll get away home.'

She left and Jools made his dinner.

⊙

'I need you to take up your position again, Jools,' a male voice said. 'I'm here to de-programme "IT" for the Royal Ed.'

Jools sighed loudly. 'Ah've been starin at the fuckin wall aw day, man!' he moaned. 'How much longer?'

'The de-programming's nearly complete, Jools. "IT" is nearly dead. It keeps screaming at me and swearing. You should hear it. It's really evil. I've just got to make sure it's totally cleared from your head. You couldn't walk around with that thing in your head. It would take over eventually. Now if you could take up your position, it would be helpful. Don't think!'

Jools crossed his legs and got comfortable on the bed as twilight crept in. He cleared his mind and began to stare.

⊙

Jools had a bath. He lay in the hot steaming water and let himself drift. It had been so long since he'd had a really hot bath. He inspected the spot on his manhood. It had nearly healed. He got out of the bath and dried himself then went downstairs and took his medication. He'd allowed himself to unwind and climbed into bed wearily.

'You know I sometimes should let myself relax a bit more, Jools,' the philanthropist said. 'I sit here at night, hunched over my laptop. I get really lost in my work and before I know it, it's five, six in the morning.'

Jools said nothing. He lay listening, relaxed.

'You know, every day you were in that hospital I had to drive up there. I sat outside in my car and tuned into you on my laptop. I had to check on your progress every day. To see if the Royal Ed were making a man of you. It made me ask a lot of questions of myself. Why was I doing this to you? What did I hope to learn? Did you really deserve the treatment they were giving you? I had to look deep inside myself to find out why I didn't feel sorry for you. I didn't have any conscience about what I'd done. I'd taken a thirty-year-old man, single, living on his own, and done this terrible thing to him. And if that wasn't enough, I had him incarcerated in a mental hospital. You nearly died on several occasions because of me, Jools. And you know what? I'm not in the least bit grateful to you. I think you got what you deserved. What you did with that wee lassie that night. It made me question myself, my own morals. A schoolie ham shank, I didn't like what I saw when I looked inside myself, Jools. I found parts of myself that shocked me. But you made me question myself. You made me open those doors. I suppose I lost another piece of my innocence. How naive we are, Jools. But we lose it along with our purity as we experience life… Huh… just a thought.'

'But it was nowt,' Jools said. 'Just a thoughtwave. Does that make me a beast cause she's a couple ay months under age? Naw! That would just be stoat the baw! A laughable offence! No beastin'! Ah bet even you've had a wank over a schoolie before,' he laughed.

'Don't you ever! Not ever!' the philanthropist growled. 'Jools, can you still not see what you did was morally wrong?'

'Whatever a man fantasis…'

'EXACTLY! What a MAN fantasises about! You are a man, Jools. But then I looked around the scheme. I saw the lassie in question. She's not a bairn, put it that way. She's a young woman. She's at that awkward stage between childhood and full womanhood. She's no longer a child but in the eyes of the law… But then laws, who takes much notice of the law? I obviously don't or I wouldn't have had you done up like I have. And what you did wasn't against the law. You're not a paedophile. You never touched anyone. It was simply a disposable, throwaway image in your head. You de-humanised the experience. It must take a cold person to think of another human being in such an exploitative way. Huh… just a thought. Maybe that's why I can be so cruel to you. Anyway, it wasn't my idea to have you stare at walls all day. That was down to my Buddhist friends. Do you remember the Buddhists on the TV that morning, talking to you?'

'Aye, Ah remember,' Jools said.

'Well you were right. They were from Portobello,' the philanthropist said. 'They're good friends of mine, actually. Anyway, when you said he was talking shite that morning he was pretty annoyed with you. He took offence. So I thought I'd let him take care of you his way. It's was his idea to make you shut up. Mentally and physically. He suggested you do the One. Twenty-four hours without a thoughtwave. You've still not managed it, Jools. This will go on and on until you do it, so you better get your finger out'

'And what if Ah dinnae? What if Ah get a squad and we find youse cunts and we run the fuckin lot ay ye oot ay Muirhoose? What will ye dae then?' Jools asked.

'The truth is Jools, you couldn't have me seen to. I control Muirhouse just now. I've got too many people on the payroll. All the hard men are taking my money. I've got them eating out of my hand.'

'Aye, well, ye better hope your money lasts, then,' Jools said. 'Cause they'll keep takin yer money but in the end when it dries up, Ah'll be there tellin them what you're really up tae.'

'Jools, I'll be long gone by then. I'm only studying you while I write my book, then I'll move on somewhere else. There'll be no proof I was ever here. Besides, who'd believe you? There's something to think about. There's nothing you can do… Just a thought.'

The presence left him and he dropped off soon after.

⊙

Jools woke up and rubbed his eyes. He got out of bed and made some tea. His right earlobe throbbed and he discovered he'd grown a large boil on the back of his ear. He studied it in the mirror. His earlobe was red and inflamed.

'It's a stress blister, Jools. Don't squeeze it,' the woman's voice said.

JAB! A needle stuck him in the back.

'Aaargh! Fuck off!' he bawled.

'Jools, it was one of the students. Most of them are on holiday after their exams. They're all out in their cars, gomer-bashing. They drive past and zap you from their cars. They've all got portable thoughtwave generators in their cars,' the woman explained.

JAB! another needle stuck him in the side.

'WILL YE FUCK OFF!' he bawled, running to the window for a glimpse of a passing car.

'They're all out to get you, Jools,' the woman laughed. 'You're the one that got away! There must be at least a couple of them in the area. This'll probably go on all weekend,' she giggled.

'The first cunt Ah catch is gettin a brick through their fuckin windscreen!'

The woman laughed. 'They're crazy, Jools. Just let them have their fun. They'll soon leave you alone. You don't want Bigmooth getting a hold of you.

He's a big fat guy from Kirkcaldy. With a mouth on him. He'll look through your manual and slag you for every private, intimate thought you've ever had. He'll blab the lot out over the radio so all the students can hear. He's the fraternity captain for Fife.'

'Well ay better stay the fuck away fae Muirhoose!' Jools growled. 'He can keep his big fat fuckin mooth in Fife!'

JAB! A needle stuck him in the neck.

'Shut yer mooth!' Drylaw guy said. 'Ye're a poof', ye're a Jew, shut yer mooth!'

'Aw fuck, no you again,' Jools huffed. 'What are ye wantin now?'

'Who's this, Jools? "Jools, Jools, can Ah get a cigarette off ye?"' he said in Archie's voice.

'It sounded just like him,' Jools said. 'How is he?'

'He's daein fine. I'm daein fine WE'RE ALL DAEIN FINE! Just shut up! Shut yer mooth SHUT THE FFFFFUCK UP! YE'RE A POOF, YE'RE A JEW…'

'AYE, AWRIGHT, AH'M A POOF AN A JEW! Whatever you say. Dinnae start aw yer shite again.' Jools really wasn't in the mood.

'Breaker one-nine!' Drylaw guy said. 'Anybody want tae copy the Drylaw guy? C'mon.'

'Is that ye oan the CB?' Jools asked.

'Aye. But so are you. Ah'm thinkin ay puttin you oot on the internet, Jools. Just think, access to a human brain! I'll clean up! Make a fortune! As long as you shut up! Ah'll tell you a secret. Ah've got you out on the CB. Ah've got an elastic band over the mic and Ah've got the mic right up to the speaker. You're going out live on channel nineteen!'

'You better fuckin no have!' Jools raged. 'That's ma private thoughts!'

'BREAKER ONE-NINE!' Drylaw guy said. 'Jools, just shut up!'

'Ah'm fuckin warnin you, ya cunt! Stop fuckin me aboot or Ah'll come up that fuckin road and kill ye!'

'Shut the fuck up! Ah'm easy!'

Drylaw guy left him.

⊙

'It's time to do the One, Jools,' the voice said. 'Take up the position!'

'Aw naw. No again!' Jools sighed.

'Oh yes! Assume the position!'

Jools sat cross-legged on the futon and blanked his mind. He stared and stared.

⊙

The front door tapped. It was Sarah.

'I've just brought your tablets, Jools,' she said.

She handed him another two pink tablets.

'Are you feeling any better? You look more relaxed since you've been home.'

'Ah'm fine,' he said.

'Well, I better be off. I've not been home from work yet.'

She left him and went home. Jools made his dinner and fed the cat.

⊙

Jools heard the ice cream van outside and had a craving for sweets. He needed cigarettes so he pulled on his trainers and left the flat.

'What are you doing out?' the voice asked suspiciously.

'Nowt, just goin tae the van,' Jools said, as he jogged across the road. A short queue had formed and Jools joined the line.

'"There's that guy! The one the uni's got done up like a giant bug!", they'll all be saying,' the voice said. 'They're all just trying to talk beside you because they know we can hear them. You're famous, Jools! You're the One!'

A fat man on a bicycle growled something to someone in the line.

'It's a pal of the wee lassie's family, Jools,' the voice told him. 'They're not happy with the students for using her name. He's going off his head. It's us he's angry with—us, not you.'

'Maybe, but if he doesnae get ays fuckin fat face oot ay ma ear right now Ah'll take ays fuckin eyes oot!' Jools was beginning to get annoyed. He glared at the fat man. The fat guy took the hint and cycled away gingerly.

Jools bought some sweets and cigarettes and turned towards the flat. As he crossed the road his eyes suddenly moved involuntarily. They felt like they were being dragged across a computer screen by a mouse. His gaze stopped on a neighbour's teenage daughter standing at her gate.

'Fuck off!' Jools bawled, trying to move his eyes.

'I was just checking!' the voice said. 'Just looking for a reaction. I wanted to see if you'd ever thought about her…'

'DINNAE BE FUCKIN WIDE!' Jools bawled. 'Ah used tae fuckin babysit for them! That's how fuckin trusted Ah am! Ah'm no a pervert, now fuck off, ya sick bastard!' He was raging. He went into the flat and slammed the door behind him.

'Jools, I'm just the computer operator. I'm just checking. It's my job. I'm just testing for adherance.'

'Well ye can fuck off and test some other bastard! They're ma neighbours yer talkin aboot! Maybe Ah should tell them what you're sayin aboot them! See if Ah did? You lot would get yer fuckin throats cut, Ah swear it! Usin fuckin bairns against me! Well ye'll no find nowt like that in ma fuckin heid!'

'I'm just a computer monitor at Nicolson Square, Jools,' the voice told him. 'I've got a sheet with certain subjects on it and I have to cover them for the uni. It's not up to me.'

'Well who is it up to then?' Jools asked.

'The Dean at the uni.'

'Well maybe Ah should go see the Dean. Tell him what kind ay filth you bastards have been puttin me through. The Royal Ed as well. What would he think of his students' obsession wi' paedophiles? You call this shit their course work? Aw they're interested in is dirt. Filth!'

'The Dean is a very busy man. Anyway, he's on holiday. The uni's empty for the summer,' the voice said.

'The uni's empty, is it? Well what aboot the digitiser? Who's lookin after that? Ah told that fuckin prick the other day he had two days tae switch me off! Now ye'll get nae more co-operation fae me if ye dinnae stop fuckin me aboot!'

'Relax, Jools,' the voice told him. 'The technichians will dismantle your virtual dummy soon. The digitiser's set up on a bench in the lab. They're all set up side by side. All the gomers. They'll get switched off sometime after the first of August. We're just waiting on a student finishing his thesis.'

'Fuck yer thesis!'

The presence left him.

⊙

'Awright! It's Jools isnt it?' a male voice asked.

'Who's that?' he asked.

'I'm a psych major. I live along the street from you. Remember when you were walking with the wind? You stopped right outside my house? We were behind the curtain watching you. We were pissing ourselves laughing, your face looked that serious. I'm studying for my psych major.'

'Aye? How long's that took ye?' Jools asked.

'Four years. I'm glad it's over. Not many from the schemes end up in jobs like that, eh?'

'Are ye originally fae Muirhoose, likes?'

'I've been here all my days. Look, don't worry. You'll get a laugh soon. The monitors will be changing over. You'll get the one fae Muirhouse Drive. He's a sound guy. You'll get a laugh with him.'

JAB! A needle stuck him in the neck.

'Aaargh! Ah wish they cunts would just fuck off!' Jools bawled.

'It's someone driving past, Jools. They've got a portable thoughtwave generator. They're zapping you from a car. Don't worry. They won't stop. They're only brave enough to drive through the scheme. They all just want to zap the gomer. The one that got away.'

'How does aw this gear work?' Jools wondered.

'It's all tuned into your brain frequency. I just switch my radio on and I can hear you think. I don't usually get the chance to talk to you. Normally I just listen in and write about you. That's what I did for my thesis. I've been studying the effects of fear.'

JAB! Another needle stuck him in the stomach.

⊙

Jools ran a bath. The steam filled the room as he got undressed and slipped into the hot water. He lay back and began to relax.

'Jools? Is that you?' a familiar female voice said.

He sat up, wide-eyed.

'Natty? Is that you, Natty?' he gasped.

'It's me, Jools! How ye daein?' his ex-girlfriend asked.

'Natty! How did you get on here? How can you talk to me?'

'Ma uncle works for the government,' she laughed. 'Ah just asked him to get me on.'

'This is pretty wild, eh?' he said.

'Ah ken. It's mental, eh?'

'Ah've been thinkin a lot aboot you, Natty,' Jools said. 'Ah've really missed ye. Ah wish we were still together.'

'Ah've missed you tae, Jools. Ah really have,' she said. 'Ah've thought about you a lot.'

'Ah wish Ah was there so Ah could gie ye a cuddle. Ah wish you were here wi' me.'

'Ah'll see you when this is all over,' Natty said. 'Ah canny wait.'

'Natty, did ye hear what's goin on? They said Ah'm gonnie meet Anastacia and Stephen Seagal! They're payin me a wad tae dae the med research. We could go away wi' the money, start afresh. Natty, would you marry me when this is all over?' he blurted out.

'Aye! Ah canny wait. As long as ye dinnae run away wi' Anastacia though,' she half joked.

'Ach, she wouldnae want the likes ay me. Ah'm no in her league, so Ah guess you're lumbered wi' me. Ah canny wait tae meet her, though. You've made me the happiest guy in the world, Natty!' he beamed.

'You've made me happy tae.' He could hear she was smiling. 'Ah've got tae go in a minute, babes. They've said Ah've got tae finish up.'

'It's been magic tae hear fae ye,' Jools said. 'Ah canny wait till it's aw over. They said the first ay August.'

'Ah'll see ye soon, doll.' She blew him a kiss.

Jools sat smiling. He was on top of the world.

☉

Jools lay in bed. It was too warm to sleep and he'd smoked nearly all his cigarettes. He got up and decided to walk to the 24-hour garage. He dressed and slipped out of the flat. The wind blew strong and seemed to dance around him as if it was excited by his return. A strong gust caught his back and he headed through the deserted streets of Pilton. He got to the garage and bought some cigarettes and a few sweets. The wind howled around him, urging him on.

'No tonight,' he said. 'Ah'm no walkin tonight.'

A strong gust whipped up around him as if in a tantrum.

'No!' he said firmly.

He started to head for home. The wind blew in his face all the way back.

☉

Jools awoke to the sound of the bin lorry outside in the car park. He got up and put the kettle on and made some tea. His ear throbbed and he felt a large boil forming on the back of it. He inspected it in the mirror. It throbbed and had a yellow head. He took his medication then opened his blinds and windows to air the room. The sun shone and it was warm even in the shade. Jools sat on his bed and smoked a cigarette. Suddenly his mind's eye was taken over by a still picture of a courtroom complete with judge. The picture started to move as if in slow motion.

'How does the jury find the accused? Guilty or not guilty?' a voice called out in the court.

'NOT GUILTY!' a reply came.

The court room faded to black.

'This is the Royal Edinburgh hospital signing off. Don't ever speak to us again!' another voice said.

'That's them saying you got a not guilty by jury about the paedophile case, Jools. The Royal Ed says never to speak to them again,' the woman's voice told him.

Something popped in the back of Jools's neck and suddenly his head felt less crowded. Empty.

'That's them unhooking you from the Royal Ed computer,' the woman said.

'Thank fuck for that,' Jools said, laughing. 'See! Ah told ye Ah wasnae a beast! If Ah was a beast ma own people would have taken care of me. We aw hate beasts where Ah come fae. Fuck you, and fuck the Royal Ed!'

'They'll leave you alone now,' the woman laughed. 'That's it all over, finally. Billy Love won't be too happy about it when he finds out his spoiled brat was wrong! The Love people lost this one for sure.'

'The Love people? Fuckin bunch ay cheesy bastards! The fuckin Partridge Family! They can aw suck ma fuckin dick!' Jools rejoiced.

The presence left, another presence joined him.

'Jools, we're aw glad that ye got oot ay the Royal Ed!' the woman said.

'Who are you?' he asked.

'It's me! Ah'm fae the Royal Victoria. You've been signed up to us for the rest of your time. Dinnae worry, we're aw a better laugh than they dirty bastards at the Royal Ed. You should never have went up there, Jools. It's a Tory ward. They treated you brutal. See, we at the Royal Vic dinnae like the Royal Ed. There's a sort ay rivalry between us. We're aw fae Drylaw and Leith and places like that but the Royal Ed students are aw fae snobby areas. You'll get a better laugh wi' us. It was when you crossed the Dean Bridge that night when you were walking with the wind. You crossed over into their territory. You should have always been for the Royal Vic and this would all have been done from your own home. Aw the time you were lying up there in the Royal Ed, you should have been down here talking to us. You should have been having the time of your life! Still, Ah suppose we can steal your sponsorship money back again. You're either sick in the Vic, or sick in the Ed! It's as eeeeasy as that! That's how you ken if we're from the Vic, we say eeeeasy as that! The Royal Ed say, there ye are!'

'Ah was meant tae go tae the Royal Vic day hospital, they told me,' Jools said.

'That doesnae matter, as long as we've got ye on the inner game. They've had ye on the fear too long. Ye wouldnae have been on that long if ye'd stayed wi' the Vic.'

'They nearly fuckin killed ays,' Jools said. 'The Royal Ed were dirty bastards tae me.'

'Well, we'll be takin ye off the fear. Eeeeasy as that!'

⊙

'It's time! Assume the…'

'Ah know the drill,' Jools sighed. He sat cross-legged and blanked his mind.

⊙

The front door tapped, much to Jools's annoyance. It was his aunt. He let her in and she dropped off his medication for the night and the following morning. She left and he made his dinner.

⊙

Jools sat in his bed on the living room floor.

JAB! A needle stuck him in the eye socket.

'Aaargh! Ya dirty fuckin bastards!' he bawled.

He ran to the window to see a small red car passing.

'Ah'll remember that bastard!' he growled. 'If Ah see that cunt in the street he's gettin his windscreen smashed in,' he growled.

He sat back in his bed and lit a cigarette.

'Jools, that's was one of the students that just zapped you. Did you see the car that time?' the voice asked. 'There's a few students down in your area tonight. They're all gomer-bashing. They all want the one that got away.'

'They better fuck off or Ah swear it, Ah'll block the fuckin road off and start takin heids!'

'There's been a few of them hovering around your house all day,' the voice said. 'They're not scared to come near your house.'

'MIAOW!' a male voice mimicked outside the window, a reference to him shagging cats.

Jools ran to the window and opened the blinds. He caught sight of a dark-haired guy of around twenty dressed in baggy clothing. The guy was walking away from the car park.

'That's them taking the piss, Jools. He's saying you shag cats!' the voice laughed.

'Fuck off, ya immature wee bastard. Ah'll rip yer fuckin face open if Ah catch ye roond here again,' Jools growled, but the guy was too far away to hear.

'YE'RE A DIRTY WEE POOF!' a bird laughed from the roof of a nearby building.

⊙

'Jools, we're taking you off the fear!' the man's voice said. 'The Royal Ed had you on the fear too long. It's making you ill.'

'Thank fuck somebody's noticed,' Jools said. 'Ah was beginnin tae think youse wanted me tae die.'

'You're off the fear anyway. Now you'll be on the sexual.'

Jools laughed.

'Don't laugh,' the voice said. 'It's a laugh at first. The gomers all think that but by the time they're finished with you, you'll be crying for them to stop.'

'Aye? Whatever.'

'It's a virtual company, Jools. They've got the franchise off the university to put the gomers through a virtual sex programme. It's just to see if it works. It may be viable for public use.'

'Cool,' Jools laughed. 'What are they gonnie dae?'

'You'll see,' the presence laughed.

⊙

Jools had a hot bath and took his medication. He sat in bed and listened to the night.

'Get a tissue, Jools,' a woman's voice said to him.

'Who are you?' he asked.

'I'm a trainee sex counsellor. I want to have a little talk with you. I'm studying you and taking some measurements. Relax, it's nothing to worry about. Just think of me as a doctor. Now go and get some tissues, just in case.

Jools was puzzled but did as he was told.

'Now get undressed and get into bed,' she instructed him.

Jools lay in bed in the dark feeling sheepish.

'Now, you may have noticed you've had no sexual outlet whatsoever while you've been in the Royal Ed. Well, that was for us. We kept you strictly off the sexual in thought, word and deed for a few months. It was to build up hormone levels in your body. You see, this is what I'm interested in.'

'What? Like testosterone or something?' Jools asked.

'Yes, exactly' she continued. 'We study the effects of the hormone. It's taken a few months to prepare you and build you up for this.'

Jools suddenly felt the muscles in his back contract and spasm, arching his spine and driving his groin into the bed.

'WOW! That isnae me!' Jools shouted. 'But Ah canny stop it!'

He started to get sexually aroused. He tried hard to straighten himself and think of something non-sexual.

Again his back spasmed, driving his groin into the bed. He started to feel embarrassed.

'Ah swear tae God, that isnae me that's doin that! Ah canny stop it!' Jools tried to say.

'Relax, don't fight it!' the woman said smoothly. 'Just think of me like a doctor. Enjoy yourself. Let go!'

Jools turned over on his back. The muscles of his dick stared to contract, then relax, at first slowly, then building up speed. Jools gasped.

'What are you daein?'

It felt like someone was giving him a hand job.

'Relax, Jools,' the woman said calmly. 'I know what I'm doing.'

His prick tensed then relaxed, tensed then relaxed.

'I'm using the simulator on the computer,' the woman said. 'It's supposed to feel just like the real thing.'

'It does!' Jools was embarrassed but beginning to relax.

'All I'm doing is pressing the W key on the computer. Now tell me when you're almost there and I'll stop,' she said.

'Ye better stop right there!' Jools said. 'Ah've no had so much as a sexual thought for months. Ah could shag the buttonhole in a fur coat!'

W... W... W... W she continued.

'Wow! Stop!' Jools bawled.

'OK,' she said. 'One, two, three...'

'What are you daein now?' Jools asked.

'I'm timing your erections. I want to find the time between erection and flaccidity. I'm trying to work out an average,' she told him. 'It's what I'll have to do for a living one day. This is to get me used to doing it gradually. I'll have to do this face-to-face for real when I become a sex counsellor.'

W... W... W... W... W... W she continued.

'Right! Stop again!' Jools shouted. 'Ah'm sorry Ah'm no lastin very long. Ah've no been near a woman for a while. Ah'm sort ay on a bit ay a hair trigger. Ye better stop now,' he grinned.

'One, two, three, four...' she counted. 'Keep that tissue ready.'

W... W... W... W... W... W... W... W...

'Stop! Ye best stop for now,' he said.

'Don't let yourself go, Jools. Hold back. I'm just supposed to take you to the edge and no further,' she said. 'One, two, three...'

W... W... W... W... W... W... W... W... W... W...

⊙

Jools opened his eyes and yawned. The sun shone outside and the room was stifling. He opened the blinds and opened the windows wide to air the room. He made some tea and had a cigarette.

'Hello, Jools,' a distinctive voice said. The voice reminded him of Captain Mainwaring from *Dad's Army*.

'I'm a locum and I'm just here to check on your general health. It's to make sure you're fit to continue.'

'Ah'm no fit tae continue doc!' Jools said. 'Honestly, Ah'm done in. Ah canny take any more ay this. It's killin me!'

'I'm sorry. You see, there's not a lot I can do. I'm only a trainee doctor. I don't have the authority to sign you off,' the locum said. 'I'm just here to patch you up and make sure you don't drop. It says here that they had you on a paedophile monitor. I see… not guilty, blah, blah, blah. Been on the fear… I'm sorry, I'm just looking through your manual. It says you've been on the fear since Christmas. That's quite a while. How are you feeling, generally?'

'Ah'm on ma last legs, doc,' Jools said. 'If they dinnae leave me alone soon Ah'm gonnie die. Ah'm no kiddin doc, ye've got tae help me!'

'It says you're off the fear, on the sexual. I see,' the locum chuckled. 'And how are we getting along there?' he asked.

'It was dead embarassin'! She did me wi' her computer. Ah had tae sit there and let her get on wi' it.'

'Yes,' the locum chuckled. 'Quite. Aren't you lucky? She doesn't do that to just anyone, you know. Well, all I can really say is keep your chin up and try and take it easy. First of… I'm just reading in your manual… they said the first of August. Well, it's only a few days away now. You keep your chin up.'

'Can ye no just put me tae sleep or something? Knock me out till the first?' Jools asked.

'I'm sorry. I wish I could. But you have to be awake. Anyway, they'll take it a bit easier on you now you're with the Vic.'

'Thanks anyway, doc.' Jools's heart sank. He'd just have to stick it out a few more days.

⊙

JAB! Jools flinched as a needle stuck him in the side.

'Fuckin dirty bastards!' he bawled, as he ran to the window. The same red hatchback drove up the street.

'When Ah get that cunt he's fuckin dead!' he growled.

'Relax, Jools. It's just gomer-bashing. I'm the computer monitor at Nicolson Square. I'm just here to fill in before your next appointment. It's a trainee doctor this time, Jools. A woman.'

'Probably another nippy cow,' Jools griped. 'Ah wish they'd leave me alone.'

'Don't worry so much. It's a laugh being on the sexual. It's better than the stuff the Royal Ed had you doing,' the monitor said. 'Most of this lot are from Leith and Drylaw, Telford and places like that. They're a good crowd. You'll have a laugh. I honestly think them up at the Royal Ed are obsessed with paedophiles. They've probably got something to hide. Anyway, none of the Royal Vic team think you're a paedophile.'

'Who keeps fuckin zappin me then?' Jools asked.

'That's the Royal Ed students. Danny Love and Eddie and that. And you better watch out what you think about until after seven at night. We have your head monitored by trusted members of the public until seven at night. They're there to make sure you all behave. If you think dirty or anything they'll zap you.'

'Members ay the public are allowed tae listen tae ma private thoughts?'

'They're there to monitor the students too, Jools,' the monitor said. 'It's to make sure they're not mucking about while they should be studying. The watershed's seven o clock.'

⊙

'Hello, Jools!' a young woman's posh voice said. 'This is my professional voice I'm using. I'm training to be a doctor and I thought I'd try out my professional voice. It gives me an air of authority, don't you think? I'm Miss Well-heeled!'

'You sound toffee-nosed,' Jools laughed. 'Yer patter's shite!'

'Don't muck about,' she said snootily.

'Ah'm no muckin aboot. Ah'm sittin here listenin tae you.'

'I see you did the sex counselling last night,' she said. 'I'll bet that was fun. Did you come? Mmmm… relish!'

'NAW! Ah didnae, ya dirty moo!' Jools choked. 'It wasnae aboot that. She was just timing how long my erections lasted. It's for her sex therapy or something.'

'Sex therapy? That's what she told you,' she laughed. 'Miss Well-heeled!'

'What? Are you sayin she wasnae a trainee doctor, likes?' Jools got suspicious.

'Sex counsellors get turned on too, Jools,' she laughed. 'She probably had a couple of the lassies round for a laugh.'

'Well Ah never done nothin!' Jools said. 'It was aw her that done it. Ah just lay there.'

'She's a lucky lass. That's why I booked you. You're the gomer that's game for anything. Don't muck about!'

'Stop tellin me no tae muck aboot!' Jools snapped. 'Ah'm no fuckin muckin aboot!'

JAB! A needle stuck him in the groin.

'Aaargh! Fuckin stop hurtin me tae, ya cruel cunt!' he bawled.

'That must be one of the Royal Ed students. They still think you should be their gomer. They think you're a racist paedophile, it says so in your manual. We don't think that. It was only a fantasy.'

'Well the Royal Ed canny touch me now so they can suck ma fuckin dick!' Jools said. 'Ah got a "not guilty"! If Ah ever see any ay them again, even in the toon, they're gettin fuckin leathered.'

JAB! A needle stuck him in the armpit.

⊙

'It's time!' the voice said. 'Why don't you try and do the One today?'

Jools sat cross-legged in his position on the bed. He zeroed in on the wall and emptied his mind. He began to stare and stare.

⊙

The front door tapped.

'For fuck's sake! Can they no just leave me alone till the first of August?' he growled. He tried to blank it out.

The door continued to pound. He went to the peephole. It was his aunt.

'Were you sleeping?' she asked.

'Naw, it's awright.' He waved her in.

'How are you managing?' she asked. 'I just popped in with your tablets.'

She gave him two pink tablets in a blister pack.

'Do you want to come up to our house on Sunday for your dinner?' she asked. 'I'll pick you up if you want.'

'It's the Royal Ed, Jools!' the voice said. 'Say no! The Royal Ed are still trying to get you to do their sponsored walk for Safegates.'

'Naw,' he shook his head. 'Ah'm no up for it.'

'OK. I just thought I'd ask. I thought you might want to get out of the house for a while.'

'Ah'm fine,' he mumbled.

'Get rid of her, Jools! The Royal Ed are using her to get to you!' the voice told him.

'Well, I can't stay long. I've got to go home for my dinner. I just dropped in to drop the pills off,' she said, heading for the door. 'I'll see you in a couple of days. Now you look after yourself.'

She left him and he fed the cat and made his dinner.

⊙

'Get a tissue!' the woman's voice commanded.

Jools sighed and started to laugh. He knew what was coming. He went upstairs and got a wad of toilet paper.

'Now take your clothes off and get into bed,' she ordered.

He did as he was told.

W… W… W… W… 'I'm just tapping the W key on the computer,' she said, as his dick contracted and relaxed with each tap.

W… W… W… He became fully aroused and his breath started to deepen. He gasped and his nostrils flared as a wave of testosterone and adrenalin surged through his bloodstream and he grabbed at the bed, almost tearing the mattress.

'You're on the superslide!' the woman said. 'It amplifies whatever you're feeling.'

W… W… W… W… W… W… W… she continued.

'You better stop!' Jools said.

She stopped. 'One, two, three, four…' She counted the seconds.

W… W… W… W… W… W… W… W…

Jools felt his arm twitch, then suddenly start to move down his belly towards his groin. His arm worked independently of himself as his hand slipped down his stomach and touched his balls. He fought hard to stop but could not budge.

'Come 'ere you!' the woman said, as his hand gripped his shaft and started to skim it back and forth.

'THAT'S NO ME! AH'M NO DAEIN THAT!' Jools wriggled and fought but there was nothing he could do.

'Hold back!' she called. 'Stop there! Don't come!' W… W… W… W… W…

Faster and faster he jerked until his body twitched and shook as he reached the point of no return.

⊙

Jools went to the bathroom and had a wash. He came back downstairs and got into bed and lit a cigarette.

'How was it for you, darling?' the woman laughed.

Jools sniggered. 'You're a dirty mare! That was oot ay order!' he laughed, red-faced.

'I just put the virtual glove on and gave you it,' she laughed. 'You had no say in the matter! I could get my books for that. I'm not meant to take you over the edge. I may be a sex counsellor but we get horny too,' she laughed. 'I just felt sorry for you. You're not a paedophile. You're a lot younger than me. Does that make me one too? I did it to get at the Royal Ed. That'll show them. Let them argue with me. Besides, I think you're a sexy wee bugger. There's something about your mind,' she sniggered. 'I fancy your mind!'

⊙

Jools sat in the bath. The boil on the back of his ear was massive and he gave it a squeeze.

'Dinnae do that! Eeeeugh! You're a minger!' a woman's voice said.

The boil burst, spraying green pus and blood all over his face flannel.

'YUK! I heard that pop!' the woman said, disgusted.

'It had tae be done,' Jools said. 'Ah canny walk aboot wi' that on ma lug.'

'It's a stress blister, you shouldn't pop it. No wonder no one fancies gomers. No one ever fancies a gomer!'

'Ah dunno, that bird, the sex counsellor seems tae think Ah'm awright.'

'She can't be shy, that's all I can say,' the woman laughed.

'She says she fancies ma mind.'

Jools washed the wound, got out of the bath and dried himself. He pulled on his shorts and a tee shirt and went downstairs.

JAB! a needle jagged him in the ribs. He didn't flinch.

'Ah wish they'd fuck off,' he sighed. 'They're juvenile. Is that aw they've got tae dae in their sad wee lives? Ah'm gettin used tae the pain now. It doesnae bother me much.'

'I just can't believe you did that earlier,' the woman laughed. 'She got you a beauty with the virtual glove. Edinburgh University won't be too happy about that.'

'What's it tae dae wi' the uni?' Jools asked.

'They've got you wired up to the mainframe. It's a giant computer they're setting up. It records all the thoughtwaves, all the memories that you've ever had and puts them in its memory. It's got a few people's thoughts on it already. They're trying to build a superbrain computer. More powerful even than a human mind. It's recorded your whole personality. Just think, part of you will live forever.'

'Weird,' Jools said.

'I can't believe you had a wank on the mainframe,' the woman laughed. 'Do you realise that'll be recorded for ever?'

'Ah didnae!' Jools spluttered. 'It was her!'

'This is the Royal Vic signing off!' the woman laughed. 'Eeeeasy as that! Yer either sick in the Vic, or sick in the Ed! Either way, you're sick in the 'ead!'

Jools lit a cigarette and made a cup of tea.

⊙

'I'm up at Nicolson Square,' a male voice said. 'I'm your monitor for tonight. Are you the one that had a wank on the mainframe?' he asked, laughing.

'It wasnae me!' Jools said.

'I know. The bird got you with the virtual glove,' he sniggered. 'Was she good?'

Jools just laughed. He went red in the face.

'I wouldn't worry about it. All the gomers are on the sexual now. You're not that bad. You should see some of them. We just did this bird, a gomer bird. We had her goin fuckin mental, man!' he laughed. 'She was gagging for it! Ye should have seen the nick ay her!'

Jools smiled at the thought of some poor cow in the same predicament as he'd been in. It made him laugh.

'We should get you two together one night, see if we can get some virtual shagging going on. I think the bird would be right up for it!' the monitor laughed.

'What, you can give us a virtual ride?'

'Aye, man. It's easy. We just connect you up to each other. Ye should have seen her, man! She was goin ballistic! Horny, did you say?' the monitor giggled.

Jools felt something pop in the back of his neck.

'That's the uni,' the monitor said. 'They've just unplugged you from the mainframe. It must have been that virtual ham shank!'

Jools's head felt empty. Clearer. All the background noise had left him feeling at peace. The black fog lifted from his mind's eye. He could think in pictures again.

⊙

'Jools, Jools, shut up, Jools,' a male voice said. 'Ah'm the fixer-upper. Ah'm just here to patch you up to the students.'

'Are you the one that's rentin ma heid oot?' Jools snapped.

"Ah'm just the fixer-upper. Anyway it says in your manual you had a wank on the mainframe. They switched you off... off the Royal Ed... Ah'm just readin in your manual. Two wanks and a schoolie nightmare it says.'

'Aw, dinnae start aw that paedophile shite again!' Jools said.

'Ah wasnae gonnie. Ah dinnae think you're a paed. So what: a schoolie ham shank. That's nowt. We've aw done it. It's just this wank on the mainframe Ah'm worried aboot. Ah find... Ah dunno, something aboot it pisses me off, dae ye know what Ah mean?'

'It wasnae me!' Jools sighed. 'She did it! Ah tried tae struggle!'

'Aye well... there you go, then,' the fixer-upper said.

'And Ah'm no a fuckin racist either!' Jools added. 'Before ye start! Ah've not even once said the n-word. Ah've no even thought it!'

'What n-word? Nigger? We couldnae gie a fuck if you're racist or no, Jools. It doesn't bother us one way or the other. Ah'm just here tae patch you up. You're back on the sexual tonight.'

⊙

It had got dark outside and Jools sat in the dark, smoking.

JAB! A needle stuck him in the back. He didn't flinch.

'Fuck off! Stop hurtin me!' he bawled.

'Ah dinnae ken what's in the machine!' the fixer-upper said.

'Was that you that just jabbed me?' Jools asked.

'Jools, Ah'm sittin in front of a big desk. Like a sound desk in a recording studio. It's got loads ay buttons and knobs on it. Ah just flick a switch at the time it says on the sheet. Ah dunno what's in them. It might send out a thoughtwave or a picture or whatever. It's for the Royal Ed.'

'Ah thought Ah was finished wi' them!' Jools said.

'Look, Jools, Ah'm just the fixer-upper. Ah just patch you up to the students and every now and then press a button. That's what Ah dae.'

'Fuckin invasion ay the bodysnatchers mair like!' Jools argued.

'Shut up, Jools!' the fixer-upper said. 'Literally shut the fuck up!'

JAB! a needle stuck him in the groin.

⊙

Jools lay in bed.

W... W... W... His dick started to spasm. It contracted then relaxed, contracted then relaxed.

Jools became aroused.

'That's it, just relax,' a woman said in a smooth voice. 'I'm just tapping W on the computer.'

W... W... W... W...

Jools just lay back and closed his eyes. He knew there was no point in struggling.

W... W... W... W... W... W... W...

⊙

Jools woke up and made some tea. He took his medication then had a wash.

'The first of August tomorrow!' he thought to himself. 'Thank fuck! Finally, nae nippy bastards annoyin me.'

'Hi, Jools,' a male voice said. Jools recognised the distinctive voice of the trainee doctor. 'It's me, the locum. I'm just here to see how you're doing after last night,' he chuckled. 'Feeling OK, are we?'

'Ah'm awright,' Jools said.

'It's a lovely day outside. I think I might go out for a while and enjoy the sunshine. She's still in bed.'

'Who's that? Your woman?' Jools asked.

'Oh God, no,' the locum said. 'She's just my flatmate. That was her that did you last night. She's still in bed. A very sensual woman, you know.'

'What's that you're saying?' the velvet-voiced woman butted in.

'I was just saying,' the locum explained, 'that you're a very sensual lady.'

'I suppose so,' she laughed. 'And how did you enjoy yourself last night, Jools?' the woman asked flirtily.

'Aye, well,' Jools laughed. 'Ah didnae have much say in the matter. Ah just let ye get on wi' it.'

Jools heard a door close in the background.

'That's him away out with the dog,' she said. 'I'm just wallking about in my nightie talking through a radio mic. I'm going to miss my wee gomer when I leave. I think I might go back into the bedroom,' she tittered. 'The computer's in there. I've got it set up at the foot of my bed so I can keep an eye on you.'

W... W... W... W... W... W...

⊙

'EEEEASY AS THAT!' a woman's voice said. 'It's me fae the Vic.'

'Awright, pal,' Jools said.

'That's us all off tomorrow,' she said. 'We're all away on holiday. That bird earlier wasnae shy, eh?' she laughed.

'Naw,' Jools sniggered. 'She'll no leave me alone.'

'Yer sick in the Vic, or sick in the Ed. It's as eeeeasy as that!'

'What can Ah dae for you?' he asked.

'Aw, nothing. I just felt like talking to somebody. All the guys are disgusted at you having a wank. It's alright by the girls, though!' she laughed. 'One for the ladies!'

'Honestly, it wasnae me. She done it tae me. Ah had nae say in the matter.'

'That's what I said. The guys all said they feel sick but a few of the girls were getting a bit hot under the collar.'

'What, they saw it?'

'Yeah! We replay all your thoughtwaves on the big screen in the Vic. The whole class watches it. You couldn't see much. It was dark. But a few of the women...'

'Glad tae see Ah've got some fans,' Jools laughed.

'Will ye have one for me?' she asked.

'Whoa there!' Jools said. 'Ah dinnae dae this tae order! What dae ye think Ah am?'

'Just testing for adherence! Eeeeasy as that!'

⊙

'It's time, Jools!' the voice said. 'Why not see if you can really go for it today. Do the One!'

Jools sat cross-legged on the bed. He emptied his mind and began to stare and stare.

⊙

The front door tapped.

'For fuck's sake!' Jools growled. 'Can they no just fuckin leave me alone?' he snapped.

He went to the peephole. It was his sister Sarah.

'Hiya,' she said. 'How are you?'

'Ah'm awright,' Jools mumbled. They went into the living room.

'I just dropped in with your medication. How did you get on at the hospital?' she asked.

'Eh?'

'Don't tell me you didn't go, Jools. They're going to take you back into hospital if you don't keep up the appointments.'

'Ah'm no sittin wi' spastics!' he said. 'Ah'm awright. There's nowt wrong wi' me!'

'Get rid of her, Jools!' the voice said.

'Jools, you've got to trust your family. Tell us what's wrong with you!' Sarah pleaded.

'Ah'm fuckin fine! There's nowt wrong wi' me. Ah just dinnae want tae go oot! Ah wish every cunt would leave me alone!'

'Well, tell the doctors how you feel. That's what they're there for. I better run before the traffic builds up on Queensferry Road.' She left him his two tablets in a blister pack.

He fed the cat and made his dinner.

⊙

Jools lay on his bed smoking a cigarette when suddenly something started to press underneath his right eyeball.

'What the fuck…' Jools said, as an invisible wire pushed its way under his eye and into his skull.

'Fuck off!' he bawled, as the wire began to push into his brain and start to coil around its contours. 'Get that fuckin thing oot ay me!' he bawled.

'Relax, Jools,' the voice said. 'We're just taking a brain cast.'

'Fuckin quit it! Ah'm no kiddin! It hurts!'

The wire continued to wrap around his brain.

'We're just taking a cast of your brain, Jools. We've got the left side already, now we need the right. It just shows up as a model on the computer. It's for virtual surgery. That's how we practice. If you don't calm down, I'll leave you with a spike in your eye.'

'FUCKIN GIT IT OOT! NOW!' Jools howled.

The wire started to recoil slowly from his skull. It took a few minutes to unwind.

'That's it, you can have a spike for that,' the voice laughed.

Jools felt a sharp point go through his eyeball and penetrate his skull like a spike. It went all the way through till it hit the back of his skull.

'FUCKIN GIE IT A REST, YA SICK FUCKS!!!' Jools screamed.

'It's a radio signal, Jools. It's supposed to feel like a spike going through your eye and into your brain. It's a good punishment.'

The spike slowly crept back until it left his eye socket. Relief.

⊙

Jools sat and looked through an Argos catalogue. He looked at camping equipment and priced their best two-man tent.

'Fuck it!' he thought. 'Ah'll get a tent and piss off up the hills for a while. That should take me out of range of their signal.'

⊙

W... W... W... W... He became aroused.

'It's me, Jools,' the sex counsellor said. 'I'm just sitting at the computer tapping the W key.'

W... W... W... W...

'You better go and get a tissue,' she said. 'Just in case.'

Jools started to laugh but did as he was told.

'Now get undressed and get into bed,' she said sexily.

Jools took off his clothes and got under the duvet.

W... W... W... W... W... W... W...

He lay back, smirking. This was crazy but there wasn't a lot he could do so he made the best of it.

'I've been thinking about you all day,' she purred. 'I couldn't wait for tonight. I've been looking through all your sexual memories and thoughtwaves and I'm really into your mind. You certainly know how to please a woman,' she laughed. 'I see you've been told that more than once.'

W... W... W... W... W... W... W...

'Well, Ah aim to please,' Jools sniggered.

W... W... W... W... W... W... 'You know you're a sexy wee bugger, don't you?' she whispered. Jools could hear her breath, slow and deep. 'I've been thinking about you all day.'

W... W... W... W... W... W... W... W... W... W... W... 'You've made me feel horny all afternoon.'

W... W... W... W... His hand started to slip down his belly. He tried to stop it but his arm moved independently of his thought.

W... W... W... W... W... W... W... W... W...

His hand grabbed hold of his shaft and started to skim it back and forth slowly.

W... W... W... W... W...

'Jools, you make me want to touch myself,' she whispered, her breathing quickening.

W... W... W... W... His hand started to move faster back and forth.

W... W... W... W... W...

'Jools, I've got a short skirt on and my hand's stroking my thigh.' W... W... W... 'I'm moving my hand slowly up my thigh, lifting my skirt,' she panted.

W… W… W… W… W…

'My hand's at the top of my stockings. It's moving up slowly to the top of my knickers. Jools I'm putting my hand down my knickers,' she gasped.

W… W… W… W… W… 'Don't come, Jools. Make it last,' she said. 'I just want to take you to the edge.'

W… W… W… W…

His hand skimmed faster.

W… W… W…

'Jools, I'm putting my hand down my knickers and I'm touching myself!' she panted. 'Slow down, make it last,' she whispered.

W… W… W… W… W… W…

Jools was going at it furiously. 'Stop!' he called out.

'Jools, stop! Don't go too far!' she panted.

'OOOOOH YA FUCKER!!!…' Too late.

⊙

Jools went to the bathroom and had a wash. He came back down and sat in bed lighting a cigarette. He lay back grinning to himself.

'You!' the sex counsellor said. 'You'll get me shot! I could get kicked out for doing things like that,' she laughed.

'What was that aw aboot?' Jools laughed.

'It was your fault! You've made me feel horny all day. I had to sit all afternoon and watch all your sexual thoughtwaves. It's been on the cards all day, I can tell you. You were meant to stop before you went too far,' she laughed.

'It wasnae me!' Jools laughed. 'That was your fault. Ah've been off the sexual for months!'

'Well, I suppose. It was what you got up to with your exes that caught my imagination. Natty especially. She was nice, you should have stuck with her. I really fancy your mind! I decided earlier you were getting jumped on. I feel like we've just had sex and we're lying in bed cuddling and having a cigarette. It's nice.'

Jools smiled. He pictured her in his mind. Long dark hair in a loose perm, cuddly figure, big breasts.

'That's nothing like me,' she said. 'I'm not chubby. I'm wee and slim with bobbed hair.'

'What's your name?' Jools laughed. 'After aw that.'

'Lorna.'

'Why don't you come along here?' he asked.

'I can't. I'm not allowed. We can never, ever meet. I'm here to teach you how to get your act together. Make you into the kind of man every woman wants. I'll be showing you that when I get back from holiday. You've got to not be tacky, Jools. I want you to think of a guy you've seen. Could be anywhere. Just a guy you've seen and thought, "I'd like to be like him",' she said.

A man in a flash sports car Jools had seen while out walking with the wind sprang to mind.

'He'll do,' Lorna said. 'See what I mean? That guy was clean-cut. Well groomed. He was flash, but not tacky. He gave out an air of quiet confidence. There was nothing cheap-looking about the guy. That's what I want you to start being like. Take particular interest in your grooming and hygiene. I want you to dress a bit more your age. You can't walk around in denims all the time. And your habits will have to change. No coming home from the pub drunk and pissing in the sink! That's got to stop.'

Jools thought it sounded interesting. 'But it's lack ay money that stops me being like that guy,' he said.

'It's not just that, Jools. He thinks different, acts different. I'm going to teach you how to have more sex appeal. Besides, you'll get paid for this, they said. I'll write in your manual that I think you deserve twenty grand for what you've done. I think you really deserve it.'

'Thanks, doll,' Jools smiled.

'I'm going to turn you into a new man. I'll talk to you soon.' She blew him a kiss.

Her presence left him. He took his medication and went to bed.

He lay in bed thinking. The first of August tomorrow. Then they said all of this would go away. He would be able to think again, picture things in his mind. His head would be his own again.

'Jools, shut up!' the fixer-upper said. 'Ah just dropped in before Ah go tae my bed. Ah'm just finishin ma thesis for the uni. Ah have tae ask ye, Jools, what have you got tae say after all this? When it's all said and done, what are your thoughts on how we've tried to change your thinking? If you could sum it up, what would you say aboot it all?'

'Fuck off,' Jools said bluntly.

'Fuck off? That's all you have tae say? It must have failed then. Ah just wondered. That would make a great endin for ma thesis. All he had tae say in the end was fuck off. It's like you're still defiant at the end. You're stickin two fingers up at the students. Ah like that. We taught you nowt but tae bite back. Resent. That's how ma thesis will end. Shut up, Jools for fuck's sake! Just literally shut the fuck up!'

'Ah'm no sayin fuck all,' Jools said calmly. 'Thank fuck you cunts are away tomorrow.'

The fixer-upper laughed.

'What are ye laughin at?' Jools said, sitting up. 'They said the first of August they'd go away and leave me alone. They've been sayin that for months.'

'Shut up, Jools! Just fuckin shut up! Ah dunno. Ah'm just here tae patch ye up tae the students. Ah'm just the fixer-upper. And what's this? Ye had another wank? Ah dinnae like the thought ay that, Jools.'

'It wasnae fuckin me!' Jools bawled.

'She got ye wi' the virtual glove Ah heard.'

'Aye, well. Dinnae fuckin blame me, awright! What are ye, jealous or something? The bird fancies the gomer and no you!'

'Shut up!' the fixer-upper said.

JAB! Jools didn't even flinch as a needle stuck him in the stomach.

'Is that yer best?' he asked calmly. 'Why don't ye face me like a man? Come along tae ma door and we'll sort it oot like men in the yard.'

'Shut up, Jools! Just SHUT THE FUCK UP! If ye dinnae shut up, we'll have tae hurt ye.'

'What's up? Are ye chicken shit? Ya fuckin wee prick!' Jools growled. 'You better be gone by mornin', Ah'm warnin ye!'

Jools rolled over and fell into a deep sleep.

⊙

Jools opened his eyes and looked around. The first of August was finally here.

He heard a snigger.

'Aw for fuck's sake!' he shouted. 'You bastards are still here. Just fuck off! Leave me alone!'

'Dinnae be like that, Jools. There's a couple of students not finished their thesis yet. It'll take the technicians a couple of days to get round to dismantling your digitiser and virtual doll,' the woman's voice told him. 'The students are on holiday as of today. You best not kick off or they'll leave you till last.'

'AH'M FUCKIN TELLIN YE!' Jools bawled. 'IF YOU'RE NO AWAY IN TWO DAYS, AH'M GOIN TAE THE POLIS! AH'LL GO UP TAE THAT FUCKIN UNI AND START TAKIN HEIDS!!!'

'Jools, calm down,' the woman said. 'They'll be taking your dummy apart soon. Look, you're already off the mainframe. It'll just be a short while now.'

'Fuckin bastards,' he growled. He got up and banged around as he made some tea. He took his medication and had a cigarette. It looked grey and overcast outside and there weren't many people around. Jools had a wash and got dressed. He decided to risk going for a walk and put his washing on before he left the flat. He headed for the beach. He crossed the dual carriageway and wandered down the dirt track in Salvesen. He caught sight of a red hatchback car passing on the road at the foot of the track and wondered if it was the same one that had been zapping him as it passed his house. He crossed the road at the bottom and walked down the steep wooden steps to the beach. The tide was in and he strolled along the grass next to the trees.

'What are you doing out?!' a loud male voice asked.

'Ah'm just goin for a walk,' Jools said. 'Ah've been stuck indoors for weeks.'

'GET HOME, RIGHT THIS MINUTE!!!' the voice screamed.

'Ah'm just goin for…'

'GET HOME—MOVE!'

Suddenly Jools felt a punch land on the side of his jaw. He could smell blood at the back of his nostrils and began to panic.

'Awright, awright!' he said, a bit shaken. 'Ah'm goin, for fuck's sake!' He started to head back home.

⊙

Jools opened the front door and was greeted by the sight of water seeping along the hall carpet. He followed the pool to the kitchen. The hose of his washing machine had been balanced on the edge of the sink and had fallen, draining the water all over the floor.

'HA HA HA!!' the voice laughed. 'That was us! The guys in the lab moved it with the ion generator! They totally flooded your hoose!'

'Fuckin dirty bastards!' Jools growled, switching the machine off. 'Ye've fucked ma carpets!'

He grabbed a mop and bucket and started to clean up.

⊙

Jools was in the middle of working out with his weights when the front door tapped. He went to the peephole in the door. It was Dr La Plante.

'Hello, Jools,' he said. 'How are you?'

Jools took him into the living room and they sat down.

'I came to see how you were getting on,' La Plante said in a posh accent. 'You've not been turning up for your appointments at the hospital.'

'Ah'm awright,' Jools said, trying hard to act normal. 'Ah've just been workin oot.'

'Have you been taking the medication?' the doctor asked. 'You've not missed any doses, have you?'

'Naw, Aah've been takin it. Twice a day, as directed. Ah'm awright.'

'Well we'll have to make a new appointment with the hospital for you. And you must keep up the appointments.'

'Honestly,' Jools said. 'Ah'm fine. Ah'm just no the kind ay guy tae sit wi' them in the hospital.'

'We need to check on you regularly, Jools,' the doctor said. 'We must see you on a regular basis to make sure you're OK.'

He filled in an appointment card.

'Now see to it that you attend this appointment,' La Plante said, heading for the door. 'I'll see you soon.'

He left and Jools closed the door behind him. 'Fuck off!' he said, tearing up the card. 'Ye'll no see me sittin wi' spastics! The Royal Ed can suck ma fuckin dick!'

'You better watch, Jools,' a woman's voice said. 'He doesn't like losing his gomer. He'll try and take you back into hospital.'

A picture of La Plante dropped into Jools's mind's eye. His face was set into a smirk. Jools imagined himself headbutting La Plante's face. He pulled back his head as La Plante's front teeth fell out one by one, cartoon style.

'There's what Ah think ay yer Royal Ed!' Jools laughed. 'They canny fuckin touch me!'

⊙

Jools sat cross-legged on the futon matress. He blanked out his mind and focused on a knot in the wooden dado rail. He began to concentrate and stare.

⊙

The front door tapped.

'Fuckin leave me alone!' He gritted his teeth.

The door banged again and he decided not to answer.

'Jools, it's me!' his aunt called through the letterbox. 'Are you OK?'

Jools blanked his mind and continued to stare. She gave up after five minutes and he heard her put his medication through the letterbox. He got up and unplugged the phone.

'There, nae distractions,' he said to himself. He fed the cat and made his dinner.

⊙

Jools lay in a hot bath.

'Jools,' the woman's voice said. 'I'm speaking to you in my professional voice. I don't really talk like this. It's me!, Miss Well-heeled!'

Jools pictured her with shoulder-length blonde hair.

'I just booked you out cause I had nothing better to do, really!' she laughed.

'Where are you fae?' Jools asked.

'I live at Granton. Crewe Road South,' she said, giggling. 'You're the gomer that had a wank for med research, aren't you?'

'It wasnae me, it was that sex counsellor, Lorna. She made me dae it. Ah had nae say in the matter.'

'Well, would you have one for me? I'd like you to have two for me,' she giggled. 'It's a sort of competition between me and her.'

'Naw!' Jools said, annoyed. 'What dae ye think Ah am?' he huffed. 'Ah dinnae dae it tae order! Beat it, ya skank!'

'Just testing for adherence!' she giggled. 'I think you should leave Natty. She's no good for you. Remember how she treated you?'

'If Ah wanted your opinion Ah'd fuckin ask for it, ya cheeky cow!' Jools bawled.

The girl giggled and her presence left him.

⊙

It had got dark outside and Jools lay on his bed smoking a cigarette.

'Hey!' a male voice called out. 'Hey, GOMER!... GOMER!!!'

'Who's that?' Jools asked.

'It's me! Ah'm pished! Ah just come back fae the pub and Ah was like... Right! Where's gomer? Ah'm on the same course as her earlier,' the student said.

Jools pictured him as having long curly hair and a black leather biker jacket. 'A sweaty', he'd call him.

'It's that bitch!' the student slurred. 'Ah... Ah fuckin love her!'

'Who? Well-heeled? Is that her?' Jools asked.

'That's her! Ah'm in her classes. Ah fuckin love her... but she's a bitch! She says we can just be pals,' he hiccuped. 'But Ah fuckin love the bitch! So Ah went oot and got pished! Hic! Fuckin bitch! And Ah find... what's this? She tries tae get gomer tae have a wank for her! HOW'S THAT FUCKIN MEANT TAE MAKE ME FEEL?!' he slurred. 'Eh? She's nowt but a bitch!... but Ah fuckin love her! SPEAK TAE ME GOMER! SPEAK TAE ME!!! What dae ye think a should dae!!?'

'Mate, Ah didnae ken that was yer woman but Ah told her tae nash anyway,' Jools said. He wanted to help the guy but didn't know what to say. 'Listen, you're pished tonight but it'll all seem differe…'

'Shut up, gomer! Ah fuckin LOVE the bitch! FUCKIN COW! Ah didnae ken what tae dae so Ah says, Where's gomer? Ah'll take it oot oan gomer!'

'Mate, Ah'm tryin tae help ye,' Jools said. 'Forget her, man! If she's no interested, go find somebody else who is. She sounded full ay herself. Ah telt her tae nash anyway.'

The student muttered something but it was incoherent. He started to snore.

'Jools, Jools…' a female voice whispered. 'I'm sorry about that. He's fallen asleep. He still had his radio mic on.'

'Dae ye ken the bird he's talkin aboot?' Jools asked.

'I know her. She's in our classes. She's totally not interested in him but he'll not leave her alone. It's a shame for him. He's not got a chance. He'll probably be too embarrassed to talk to you in the morning. That's probably the last you'll hear of him.'

'He sounds young,' Jools thought.

'He is. He's only twenty-four,' she said.

'She's a dirty wee moo. Ah was talkin tae her earlier.'

'Some of the students are… more mature than others, Jools. You should know that, you've been to college.'

Jools lit a cigarette. The presence left him.

⊙

W… W… W… 'Get a tissue, Jools,' Lorna said.

He did as she said and got undressed and into bed.

W… W… W… W… W… W… W… W…

'I've been thinking about you all day, babes,' she panted. 'I've been watching more of your sexual experiences and I've been thinking about you.'

W… W… W… W… W… His dick contracted and relaxed, contracted and relaxed.

His hand started to move slowly to his groin and he just let it.

W… W… W…

'I… want… that… inside… me!' she purred; his dick twitched with each syllable. W… W… W… W…

Jools lay thinking of her. There was something about her voice that really attracted him.

W… W… W… W… W… W… W… his hand started to jerk off slowly, his arm totally independent of his mind.

W… W… W… 'When I think about you, I want to touch myself,' Lorna purred. 'I've got a short skirt on, Jools, and I'm sliding my hand up my thighs and I'm touching myself,' she said, sighing. 'Don't go too far, Jools. Hold back, make it last as long as you can.'

W… W… W… W… W… W…

His hand action started to quicken.

'Slow down, Jools,' she said. 'I've got to the top of my thighs and I've got my thumbs in the top of my knickers and I'm sliding them down, Jools. I'm taking off my knickers…' W… W… W… 'And I'm touching myself, Jools. I'm watching you on my monitor and I'm touching myself!' she panted.

W… W… W… W… W… 'Stop, Jools,' she said, as his hand got even faster. 'Don't go too far, hold back, babes!'

W… W… W… W… W… W… W… W… She speeded up.

'Jools, I-want-that-in-side-me!' She tapped out the syllables W… W… W… W… W… W… W…

'Stop!… STOP!… WWWWWHOA YAAA FFFFUCKER!!!'

⊙

Jools lay in bed smoking a cigarette.

'You!' Lorna said, laughing. 'I really fancy your mind!'

'Yer no too bad yerself,' Jools laughed.

'I feel like we've just had sex and we're lying having a cuddle after it. I want that!' His dick twitched with each syllable. 'I-want-it!' she purred.

'Ah telt ye! Why don't ye come along here then?' Jools suggested.

'I can't. We can never, ever meet. It's not allowed. Anyway, I'm off on holiday tomorrow.'

'Where are you goin'?' he asked.

'I'm away to Cyprus. I'm away to get shagged,' she said, matter of factly.

Jools felt jealous. Besides, he'd miss her company. She was one of the few he liked.

'Don't be like that, Jools. It's going to be hard enough to leave you as it is. I've got really attatched to you, you know. Don't, cause I've got to be brutal to you before I leave.'

'Ah'm no bothered. Ah still like ye,' Jools said, smiling.

Suddenly he felt the skin of her naked body press against his. The feeling lasted for a split second, then disappeared. It felt just like she'd hugged him.

'WOW!' he said, amazed. 'How did you dae that?'

'It was just a virtual cuddle,' she said. 'I hugged the virtual doll. Aw, I dunno what I'm going to do without my wee gomer,' she said. 'I'm going to really miss you. So what do you plan to do when it's over?' she asked.

'Ah dunno,' Jools said. 'Ah'd like tae write a book some day. Ah always wanted tae write.'

'Well, remember and give me a mention!' she laughed.

'Ah will!' Jools said. 'Seriously.'

'Just remember, Lorna wasn't all bad,' she laughed. 'My wee gomer.'

Jools heard another person in the background. Lorna started to laugh. Another female voice joined in. They both laughed at him for a few minutes and Jools started to feel sheepish.

Their presences eventually left him alone.

⊙

Jools looked at the clock. It was 10pm. He decided now was the time. He emptied his head of all thoughts and began to concentrate. He was determined. The only thoughts he'd let in would be to check himself. He began to stare. He would try and do the One. Twenty-four hours without a thoughtwave.

⊙

Jools awoke next morning with a note in front of his eyes reminding him he was doing the One. He got up and had a cup of tea, being careful to check himself every few minutes to make sure he wasn't daydreaming. He had a wash in cold water to wake himself up then dressed and started busying himself with house work. He checked himself as he worked and soon it had passed lunchtime. He made himself some toast and cheese and continued to blank out his mind.

After lunch he sat cross-legged on his bed and stared for a time.

⊙

The front door tapped. Jools ignored it and kept staring. The sound of his tablets dropping through the letterbox, then footsteps, then silence.

⊙

His stomach started to rumble. He got up and checked himself as he microwaved his meal. He sat down to eat, still blanking himself.

It started to grow dark. He sat concentrating on the knot in the wooden rail. He checked he wasn't picturing anything, he wasn't saying anything to himself, his mind was clear. He shot a sideways glance at the clock on top of the TV. It was almost ten.

'THERE!' he said out loud. 'That must be twenty-four hours at least! Ah've done yer fuckin One!'

His head was swimming, he felt totally drained and his back ached.

There was complete silence for a few minutes. Jools wondered where they had gone. Had they left him alone, finally?

Suddenly he heard a loud bang and a series of crackles as fireworks exploded across his mind's eye.

'CONGRATULATIONS!!! You've done it!' a woman's voice cut in. 'You've done the One! That's it finished! You'll never have to do this again!'

The fireworks continued as Jools lit a cigarette and stood up to stretch his back.

'Jools, you really did it! Well done!' the woman said excitedly. 'Buzz wants to talk to you. She wants to try out a new hypnotherapy technique. It's all done with a two-tone claxon. It's cutting-edge stuff. She discovered a new method herself.'

'Aye, awright,' Jools smiled. He was just happy it was all over.

A siren began to wail in the background. It built up into one continuous tone, then changed pitch to a lower tone. Jools counted. It took eight seconds then changed pitch.

'Just relax, Jools,' the woman's voice said.

He sat up on the chair and got comfortable.

'I see from your thoughtwaves that you know about self-hypnosis. You've actually been hypnotised,' the woman said.

'Aye, that's right. Ma doctor used tae use it. And Ah've read up on it. Ah practised it pretty regular.'

'Well you should have no problems with this, then,' she said, in a smooth, calm voice. 'Just let your body go, and relax. Let your breathing be deep and even as you continue to relax your body, going deeper and deeper.'

Jools started to go into 'state'. His muscles started to relax and he found his breathing synchronising with the two-tone claxon in the background. Eight seconds in, eight seconds out.

'Now just drop all the tension in your jaw, make sure your teeth are not clenched together and allow yourself to relax. Think about the muscles in your scalp... and let go. Just relax, letting this feeling spread down across your forehead... and relaxing all the small muscles around your eyes, letting your eyelids feel heavy, relaxing all your face muscles as you relax deeper and deeper. Now relax your neck, letting your head feel heavy and relaxed and down into the muscles of your shoulders. All the way down your arms to the tips of your fingers. Just really… really… relax. Now allow your torso to relax, letting go completely now as you go deeper and deeper into relaxation. And now just let this feeling of relaxation spread down through your legs, relaxing all the muscles in your legs… all the way to the tips of your toes. Now you are relaxing the whole of your body, I'll let Buzz take over. Just listen and relax…' The woman's presence faded.

A new presence filled his mind as the two-tone claxon sounded in the background.

'*Now ye come and done the One,*' a female voice rapped slowly.

'*That was you, now dae the Two,*
Now talk tae Buzz coz Ah'm wi' uzzzzz…'

The z's made him feel he'd fall asleep.

'*Ah got the name fae sniffin the glue.*
Concentrate, yer doin great,
There's nae point gettin in a state,
Dae the Two, it's up tae you,
Ah'm just here tae be yer mate.
It's up tae me, we'll dae the Three,
It's the way tae be free,
It wasnae you, it was me,
Dae this right and you'll see,
It's gettin sore so try the Four,
It's guaranteed tae open doors,
It isnae you, it was Buzz,
Ye're no a Jew, that was uzzzzzzz.
Relax your mind and come with me,
Ah'll teach ye things you canny see,
Hold ma hand and we'll dae the Three,
Have a sketch, look you'll see,
Ye did the One, nice one son,
Ah hope ye've had a bit ay fun,
And Ah hope ye want tae listen tae Buzz,
Ah only want what's best for uzzzzzzzz.
Dinnae worry,
We're in nae hurry,

But you've got tae listen,
Tae Dr Curry,
Ye've had it rough,
And it's been dead tough,
But we aw ken,
That you're no a poof,
It wasnae you, it was uzzzzzz,
So dinnae make too much fuss.
Now you're here, try the Five,
It's good for you, it'll keep you alive,
Now we see that you're really nae beast!
Yer innocent, no guilty at least.
We had to take you through the fear
For reasons that will be made clear.
That wasnae me, it wasnae Buzzzzzzz,
It wasnae you but it was uzzzzzzz.

The YLT wasnae me,
It wasnae Buzz, but it was uzzzzzzz.
Ye wonder why Ah rap in rhyme?
Ah just dae, aw the time,
We had tae put ye through the fear,
Tae try and get you off the gear.
Ye're no a baddie, ye should be glad,
Ay aw the fuss they've made ay uzzzzzzz.
You werenae silly when they played wi' yer willy,
It wasnae you, it was uzzzzzzzz.
Now listen tae me and dae the Three,
It'll give ye loads of energy,
Listen tae what Ah have tae say,
This is new hypnotherapy.
Ye're no gettin stabbed, Ah bet you're glad,
See that guy? He was mad.
This is where you're meant tae be,
Doin the One, Two or Three.
It wasnae me, it was uzzzzzz
And dinnae blame,
Yer Canadian cuz,
Coz that was uzzzzz, so come wi' Buzzzzzzzzz.

Now open the door and dae the Four,
You shouldnae be scared anymore.
Buzz will help you to dae the five,
You need tae get right oot ay this dive.
Now It's time for Buzz tae leave,
Ah hope in future you'll no be naïve.
Ah hope ye'll start tae pick and choose,
Just what you do and don't believe.
This is uzzzzz signing off,
Ah hope Ah didnae piss ye off.
Buzz was happy tae give ye a shout,
And, by the way, when they knocked you out,
It wasnae you, but it was uzzzzzz,
The decision wasnae down tae Buzzzzzz.
Ah hope this lesson you will keep,
And dinnae worry, ye're no a creep.
'So when ye dae the One, Two or Three,
Ah hope you will remember me,
Name ay Buzzzzzz, Buzz was uzzzzzzz,
And stay away fae the fuzzzzzzz.
Relax now, let yourself be loose,
Drop the tension, there's nae excuse.
Dae the Five, bring it alive,
And Buzz for you will always strive.
Tae help ye oot when you're in need,
Remember the lessons, take heed,
This is Buzz signing off.
Goodbye fae uzzzzz, cheerio fae Buzzzzzzz.'
The presence faded to silence.

'That was Buzz,' the woman's voice said. 'She used to be a glue-sniffer. That's where she started to talk in rhyme. She got on the Love programme and sorted herself out. She's at uni now doing her psych major. Buzz loves everybody.'

Jools felt totally at ease. He lit a cigarette and enjoyed the peace of the night.

⊙

'Jools, keep yer mooth shut tonight,' the fixer-upper said. 'Ah see ye finally done the One. Ye really, really done it! What are ye gonnie dae now yer bird's away on holiday?'

'Who, Lorna?' Jools asked. 'She was just a pal.'

He lit a cigarette and stretched out on the couch. It was dark and a yellow street lamp reflected through his blinds.

'Jools!' a familiar voice barked in the background.

'BULLDOG!' Jools recognised the voice.

'Hiya, son!' he said. 'How ye doin'?'

'Bulldog, it's good tae hear fae ye!' Jools smiled.

'Bulldog's no in the SAS, Jools,' the fixer-upper laughed. 'He's just a writer. We're all just writers. They're a group ay writers fae East Lothian. They sort ay write it as they go along. They took you intae their story. It's like a living book, Jools. You were "IT". The racist paed. Part man, part cyborg when you were hooked up to the paed monitor. But you never find out if he was really a paed. It sort of leaves you hanging on. A racist paedophile called "IT". Part man, part cyborg, it walks with the wind. That was Bulldog's part. They've all had a shot at writing what you do next.'

'When dae Ah get ma heid back?' Jools asked.

'They'll move on to the next person soon, Jools. Then they'll pick up the story where you left off.'

'And what if Ah wanted tae write aboot what's happenin tae me?' Jools thought.

'Ye can never write about this, Jools. It's no your work. It's theirs. They created "IT",' the fixer-upper told him.

⊙

Jools lay on the couch smoking a cigarette.

'*WE ARE PSI PEOPLE,*' a loud whisper said. '*WE ARE FROM EDINBURGH UNIVERSITY DEPARTMENT OF PARAPSYCHOLOGY AND WE ARE INVESTIGATING PSYCHIC PHENOMENA. HAS ONE HAD ANY PSYCHIC EXPERIENCES?*' the whisper asked.

'Aye, sort ay,' Jools said. 'The psychics Ah went tae see asked me if *Roger Rabbit* meant anything tae me. Fuckin does now! That's when aw this started.'

'*THAT IS INTERESTING. WE SHALL INVESTIGATE. HAVE YOU SUFFERED ANY PSYCHIC DISTURBANCE?*'

'Ah remember when Ah was wee, Ah used tae get this nightmare over and over again. Ah'm in a church. It's dark and Ah'm walkin down the aisle. Ah look around and there are benches along each side of the aisle. Ah reach the bottom and there's a raised step at the end. A man in an orange robe sits on his knees with his bald head down looking at the floor. Suddenly his head starts to rise and he starts to laugh. It's a horrible laugh and Ah wake up scared. Ah had that dream five or six times when Ah was a bairn. It always looked like a Buddhist monk or something but Ah was too young to know what one was.'

'*THIS IS OF INTEREST TO PSI PEOPLE. WE WILL GET BACK TO YOU ON THIS,*' the whisper said.

'Was that you lot that crept intae me that night? The shadow, Ah mean?' Jools asked.

'*NO. THAT WAS THE GHOST PEOPLE. GHOST PEOPLE WORK FOR THE UNIVERSITY. THEY GO OUT IN CARS AT NIGHT IN SEARCH OF HEADS TO TAKE FOR RESEARCH PURPOSES. ALL HAPPENINGS WERE MODERN TECHNOLOGY. NO PSI INCIDENTS WERE REPORTED. GHOST PEOPLE ARE SNEAKY.*'

'And what aboot all the animals? Ah saw loads ay animals,' Jools said. 'Ah heard the birds talkin'.'

'*THAT WAS THE ANIMAL PEOPLE. THEY ALSO HAVE THOUGHTWAVE GENERATORS. THEY CONTROL THE ANIMALS. NO PSI INCIDENTS REPORTED. PSI PEOPLE THINK YOU HAVE A NATURAL TENDENCY TOWARDS BUDDHISM.*'

'Well they said it was the Buddhists at Portobello that come up wi' the idea that Ah dae the One,' Jools thought.

'*PSI PEOPLE WILL BE IN CONTACT!*' The whispering presence left him.

He felt totally drained. It had been a long, tiring day. He took his medication and went to bed.

⊙

'Jools, shut up, dinnae say nowt,' the woman's voice said as he opened his eyes.

'AW FOR FUCK'S SAKE!' he shouted, as he sat up. 'CAN YE NO JUST FUCK OFF?! Ah thought you were meant tae be leavin me!'

'Jools, calm down.' The woman started to laugh. 'It's just me. I'm in the lab mucking about with the apparatus. They're going to dismantle your virtual doll.'

'Ye said that the other day,' Jools moaned. 'Ah canny handle any more ay this. When do Ah get tae meet Anastacia?'

The woman started to laugh loudly.

'What are ye laughin at? And when dae Ah get ma cash?' he asked.

The woman laughed even louder.

'Are you sayin Ah'm no gettin tae meet her?' he asked suspiciously.

The woman started to giggle.

'Shut up, Jools!' the fixer-upper cut in. 'Just literally shut the fuck up!'

'Naw, Ah'll fuckin no!' he growled. 'Ah want tae ken what that silly cow's laughin at! Am Ah still gettin tae meet Anastacia?!' he repeated.

The woman giggled in the background.

'Jools, dinnae start takin bennies now!' the fixer-upper said. 'Ah'm in the lab wi' her and we're just messin aroond cause we're gonnie dismantle yer virtual doll.'

'Am Ah gettin tae meet her or what?' Jools bawled.

'Jools, Ah dunno,' the fixer-upper said. 'Ah just work here. This is what Ah dae. Now shut up, yer nippin ma heid.'

Jools was crushed. His heart sank like a lead balloon. 'Ah better be gettin ma fuckin money!' he growled.

The woman sniggered and started laughing again.

'You're no giein me ma money, are ye?' Jools said. 'Ah'm no gettin tae meet anybody, am Ah? This has aw been a lie, eh? This is never gonnie stop, is it?' He began to panic at the thought. 'Fuck's sake, they're tryin tae kill me! Ye are, eh?'

'Jools, shut up!' the man said. The woman giggled loudly.

'Whadda matta Jools, hmmm?' the fixer-upper said in the voice of Grover from *Sesame Street*. 'No paed!'

The woman started to giggle hysterically.

'You do want me deid, eh?' Jools said, shaking. 'Maybe Ah should just gie in, give ye what ye want. Maybe Ah should just make it easy on maself. Maybe Ah should just put maself oot ma misery. Ah'm gonnie end up toppin maself.'

'Kill yourself if ye want, Jools,' the fixer-upper laughed. 'We've no got a death on film yet. It would be interestin tae see what ye go through fae the inside. We could record it on the computer. Aye, fuck it, Jools, why no? Just dae it! Kill yourself!'

Jools couldn't believe what he was hearing. He started to get annoyed.

'Fuck you, ya fuckin dick! You'd like me tae dae that, wouldn't ye?'

'Aye,' the fixer-upper laughed. 'Gomer cops ays whack.'

'And what if Ah didnae kill ma self?' Jools said. 'What if Ah got the polis? What if Ah told everycunt what you people are daein tae me?'

'Shut up, Jools.' The fixer-upper sounded serious.

'Naw, what if Ah did? You keep tellin me tae shut up and keep ma mooth shut aboot what yer daein tae me. What will ye dae if Ah do stick ye in? Maybe Ah should grass! Maybe you cunts will get caught! Is that why Ah've no tae tell? You'll get the jail for a long time for this! And Ah swear it, Ah'll be waitin on ye wi' a big fuck-off rusty blade when ye get oot! YOU'RE FUCKIN DEAD, BY THE WAY!!!'

'SHUT UP, JOOLS!' the fixer-upper warned him. 'Ah'm no kiddin!'

'That's what Ah'll dae, Ah'll grass ye up tae half ay fuckin Muirhoose! We'll see if Ah'll top maself! Ah'm gonnie stick youse in right now,' he said, picking up the phone.

'Jools, Ah'm warnin ye! Ye better no!' the fixer-upper growled.

Jools dialled his sister's work number. His hands were shaking.

'Jools, Ah'm fuckin serious! SHUT UP!' the fixer-upper said.

'Hello, Sarah speaking,' his sister answered.

'Sarah, it's me, Jools. Can ye come doon here? Ah need tae speak tae ye,' Jools blurted out. His heart raced.

'I'm at work, Jools,' Sarah said.

'Sarah, it's important!' Jools gibbered. 'There's somebody tryin tae kill me!'

'Jools, what are you talkin about?' Sarah said. 'Are you feeling ill again? You should speak to the doctor. I thought you were feeling better.'

'Sarah, Ah'll tell ye what's been fuckin goin on!' Jools growled. 'There's these bastards have taken over ma heid! They've done ays up wi' a computer and they keep shoutin at me through a radio mic. They'll no shut up! They said they're students fae the university. They were tryin tae get me tae kill maself!' he blurted out. Jools felt foolish somehow. When he summed it up in words it sounded so crazy, unbelievable.

'Ye canny tell anybody or they said they'll take me back and Ah'll have tae dae it again! They said they'll dae the same tae youse if Ah grass,' he babbled.

'Jools, hold on. I'm coming down,' Sarah said.

'THERE! AH FUCKIN TOLD YE AH'D GRASS YE!' he laughed defiantly as he put the phone down.

'Gie him the polio!' the voice ordered.

Jools tried to stand. His left leg gave way under him and he found himself on the floor. His leg cramped and it was dead from hip to toe. He dragged himself across the carpet by the fingers.

'SHUT UP… SHUT UP… SHUT UP,' a voice repeated over and over.

⊙

Sarah arrived at the flat. Jools was still limping badly. Sarah looked nervous somehow.

'They just gave me a deid leg!' Jools gibbered. 'They were giein me operations and stickin me wi' needles and they tried tae say Ah was a paedophile and Ah was gettin stabbed and…'

'Jools, calm down,' Sarah said.

The front door tapped. Sarah let his aunt in. She looked nervous too.

'They said Ah was a paedophile and they were tryin tae get ays stabbed and they said Ah should kill maself so they can get it on film…'

'SHUT UP… SHUT UP… SHUT UP…' His eye blinked.

'Ah better shut up. Ah've said too much already,' he raved. 'They said if Ah told, you'd be next. They're tellin me tae shut up through my eye.'

SHUT UP… SHUT UP… SHUT UP…' His eye blinked rapidly.

His aunt looked at his sister, bewildered.

'They think Ah'm mad,' he thought to himself. He could see it written on their faces.

The front door tapped again.

'Ah bet that's the psychies!' Jools said suspiciously. 'Well they're no gettin in!' He was determined. 'Ye can tell them they're no gettin in! Ah dinnae want them in ma hoose!'

The door rapped again. 'Jools, could you open the door for us?' La Plante called through the letterbox.

'I'll go and tell them,' his aunt said. She went to answer the door. Jools got up and went to the living room door. La Plante, two women and two policemen stood in his hall. La Plante and the two women came into the living room.

'What are they there for?' Jools asked, his eyes narrowed.

The two middle-aged cops looked at the ground awkwardly.

'AH DINNAE NEED ANY HELP FAE THE MENTAL HEALTH SERVICES!' Jools bawled 'Now leave ma hoose! Get oot!'

'Jools, we're just going to pop you along to ward six,' La Plante said calmly.

'NAW! Ah've no done nowt!' Jools said. 'Now get oot! GET OOT MA HOOSE!'

La Plante looked at him vacantly. They were going to take him back. He'd talked and now they would take him back. There was no way he could take that again. It would kill him. He went upstairs to the bedroom. The two policemen looked away as he passed them in the hall. Sarah followed him into the room.

'I just want you to be back to your old self,' she said. 'We just want the old you back.'

Jools was far from happy with her. He'd trusted her and she'd told La Plante everything. 'Ah'm in trouble now!' he said. 'You dinnae ken what you've done!'

His sister left him alone packing his clothes.

'Fuck this,' Jools said to himself.

He pulled back the curtain and opened the bedroom window. He climbed onto the window sill and dangled a leg out.

'DINNAE DAE IT, JOOLS!' a female voice screamed in his head.

He was in bare feet and his landing would be on stone chips. He lowered himself part of the way and let go.

Jools hit the chipstones below with a loud crunch. He immediately went down into a roll and rolled back up to his feet. He vaulted the garden fence in one movement and ran off into the scheme.

Jools ran around the corner of the high-rise flats and over the top of the field. He climbed up on a wooden fence and jumped in behind the bushes. He sat motionless and watched for a time, staying blank.

'You better no tell them where Ah am!' he said to the woman.

'I'll not,' she laughed. 'Do you remember me?' she asked. 'I'm the one you thought was a gypsy, remember?'

Jools recognised her voice.

'Well just shut up the now,' he whispered.

The two policemen walked across the top of the field towards his position. He froze stiff and tried not to breath too loudly.

'Did you see a guy in a white shirt around here?' one of the policemen asked a young boy on a bike.

'Aye, mister!' the wee boy said. 'Ah think ay went over there!' he pointed away by the high flats.

'Easy, wee man!' Jools grinned as the policemen walked away.

Jools sat for a few minutes then slipped out from his hiding place. He started to hobble slowly back to his block. He'd cut his foot and it bled on the pavement leaving beetroot-coloured stains on the tarmac. He took off his shirt so they wouldn't recognise him and started back across the car park at the back of his flat. He crept up to the window and peeked over the fence. La Plante and the two women were still in the house. Jools started to run.

'Jools, what is it? What's the matter?' Jean, a neighbour, called to him.

'The bizzies are efter me, Jean!' he said.

'What for?' she asked. 'What have ye done?'

'Ah've no done nowt!' he answered, out of breath.

'Come in here,' she said. 'I'll make you a cup of tea and you can tell me what's happening,' she said.

Jools went into the house.

Jean made Jools a cup of tea and cleaned up his foot, putting a plaster on the cut. 'I'll just go out and see if the polis are away,' she said.

'Be careful, Jean,' Jools said. He followed her as far as the front door but was too late to run as the two policemen came in the gate, spotting him instantly. Jools hung his head low.

'Come on now, Jools,' the policeman said. 'We've got to take you back.'

They walked along the path to his flat. Jean put her arms around him and gave him a hug.

'Dinnae worry, Jools. The hospital will make you better,' she said. 'Do it for your mum. Just a wee while, eh?' She gave him a kiss on the cheek and a hug.

Jools went into the flat and got his clothes in a bag. He had a wash and got changed. The policemen led him out to the car in silence.

⊙

The car pulled up outside the Royal Edinburgh Hospital and they got out.

'Ah'm scared,' he said to the policeman.

'There's nothing to be scared of, Jools,' the policeman said. 'Come on, you'll be alright. I promise.'

Jools followed them up to the ward.

The two policemen went into the office and Jools went into the smoking room and sat down to wait. A nurse came through.

'If you follow me I'll show you to your bed,' the nurse said. Jools's heart sank as she showed him back to the same cubicle he was in before. He sat with a lump in his throat and tried not to cry.

⊙

Jools went for a cigarette. Emma was in the room and shuffled over to him.

'Awright, doll?' she said, revealing a toothless mouth. 'Is that you back in?'

The first thing that hit him was that she looked drugged up.

'Aye, the polis brought me in.'

Emma didn't look like a student now he was back. None of them did. The Professor smiled over. Eddie came into the room, still wearing his Hearts top. Jools watched him. He was a patient. The guy wasn't all there. He couldn't be a student either. Above all, there was no sign of Danny Love. Jools assumed he'd left the hospital. This was weird.

They were all patients. Nuts, the lot of them. How could this be? He felt confused and went to lie on his bed.

Two bells rang in the hall.

'That's dinner time, everyone!' a nurse called out.

Jools went for his meal.

⊙

Jools had a quick cigarette before everyone came back from dinner then went to his room. He couldn't stay here, he knew that. He'd have to escape. He lay back on his bed.

W… W… W… his dick started to twitch.

'Aw naw. Fuck off, dinnae start that again!' he said.

'Fair enough,' a woman's voice said. 'If you don't enjoy it, I'll not bother!' she huffed.

Her presence left him.

Jools got up and went to sit in the quiet room.

He went in and pulled up a seat.

'There, you can watch telly now! And read!' the woman said.

Jools flicked the TV on and settled down to watch.

⊙

It had started to get dark outside and Jools heard the tea trolley rattle down the hall. He went to the smoking room, poured a cup of tea and sat down, lighting a cigarette.

'Hiya!' the slim guy with the dark crew-cut said. 'You were in before, weren't you?'

'Aye, Ah'm Jools,' he said.

'My name's Jools too,' he said, holding out a hand.

They shook hands. The guy pulled out his cigarette papers and started to build a joint on the table. Jools watched for the guards nervously.

'Don't worry,' he said, 'they won't come in. Just keep it hidden.' He lit the joint and passed it.

Jools hesitated for a second. 'Fuck it!' he thought, what were they going to do, throw him out? He took the joint, inhaling deeply.

'I'll bring my sounds through in a minute,' the other Jools said. 'I've got all my tapes with me.' He went to the dorm to get them. Jools went for his med. They had changed it to a single white tablet. He knocked it back with a glass of juice and went back to the smoking room. The other Jools came back a few minutes later with a pile of tapes.

'Here,' he said. 'Have a look through them, see what you like.'

Jools sorted through the pile. He selected The Red Hot Chili Peppers *Californication* album and put it on. The other Jools made another joint.

⊙

'AND A GREAT BIG THANK YOU TO LOTHIAN HEALTH BOARD!!! Goodbye and thank God!' a loud voice said. Jools pictured him as a posh-speaking black man.

'Dr David Love,
The Love people, med research, the paedophile monitor!
'Twas I
Bulldog, Mackenzie, the IRA,
'Twas I, 'twas I, 'twas I.
Buzz, us,
'Twas not I, 'twas us!
Lorna, Lorna 'twas us,
Miss Well-heeled, 'twas us,
'Twas us, 'twas us, 'twas us.
Upstairs, 'twas I,
YLT, 'twas I,
Not eye, I,
'Twas I, 'twas I, 'twas I.
Anastacia,
The wind,
Drylaw guy,
'Twas I, Oh why?
'Twas I, 'twas I, 'twas I.
The animal people,
The birds TEE HEE!
That was us,
Ghost people,
'Twas not us, 'twas I.
The Royal Vic, Psi people
Us!
Sick in the Ed,
Longcoat, Western General, Whiskers,
Iga man,
All I.
'Twas I, 'twas I, 'twas I.
Not eye, I!
Bigmooth, us.
Shut up, us,
Students, us.

Rob, Rob, 'twas I.
Prestonpans, us,
Magpies,
Jane,
All us.
Jimmy Saville! 'Twas not us
'Twas not I,
'Twas real!
The max, 'twas I.
'Twas I, 'twas I, 'twas I.
'Twas I…
'Twas I…
'Twas I…'
The voice faded to silence.

Jools sat for a while with his new friend listening to music and smoking joints. He went to bed stoned and fell into a deep, restful sleep.

$\odot$

'Medication, Jools,' The nurse woke him from a deep sleep.

It took him a few seconds to realise where he was then it dawned on him and a sinking feeling filled his belly.

He took the small white tablet and the nurse left him. He went up the hall to the kitchen and made some tea, then took it to the smoking room. A high-pitched whine started up in his head. It sounded as if the signal was trying to get through but it wasn't strong enough. It occurred to him that all was silent. The voices were gone, for the time being at least. Jools's head felt light and empty as if a great weight had been taken from his shoulders. His head was like an empty eggshell, void of contents, and everything was crystal clear.

He started to analyse what had happened to him but found himself backing off at the thought of it all returning. He sat quietly drinking his tea and smoking.

$\odot$

'Jools, Dr La Plante would like to see you,' the Canadian nurse said.

He followed her up the hall and waited while she went in. Jools looked at the stairs. Suddenly it dawned on him. How could there be a lab upstairs? He was on the top floor of the block. The stairs didn't go any further up. He checked the lift. Sure enough, he was at the top alright. He felt confused.

'The doctor will see you now.' The nurse showed him in.

'Take a seat, Jools,' La Plante said. 'Now how are you feeling today? I'd like to speak to you about what you told me yesterday about hearing voices and students taking over your head with a computer.'

'Ah never told you nothin'!' Jools said, embarrassed.

'So that was just a load of rubbish, was it?' La Plante tried to lead him.

'Aye.'

'And what are the voices saying to you?' La Plante asked.

Jools blanked out his mind and began to stare at the wall. He was saying nothing.

⊙

Jools stood in the corridor looking at the notice board. He saw that they had an art class on this morning and thought it might just be his way out. He went to the office and signed his name for it.

⊙

'Jools, I'm here to escort you down to the art room,' the big, quietly-spoken male nurse said. Jools followed him along the hall to the back stairs. The nurse unlocked the door and they descended the three flights down to the basement. He walked along a corridor at the bottom and they went into the art room.

'This is Jools,' the nurse said to the woman taking the class. She was middle-aged with blonde hair and spoke with a west-coast accent.

'Can you give me a buzz when you're finished?' the nurse asked. 'Jools is on escort so I'll have to come back down and collect him when you're finished.'

'OK, will do,' the woman said.

The guard left them and Jools sat down at a paint-stained table. Two women gossiped at the other end of the table and the teacher disappeared into the cupboard to get materials.

Jools seized his chance. He skipped out the door and up a flight of stairs. He went through a set of double doors and along a long corridor. Another set of doors and he was in the main hospital. He kept his head down and marched straight out the front entrance.

Jools headed into Morningside. He reached the main road and hailed a taxi. 'Muirhoose Shoppin Centre please, mate!' he said to the driver.

Jools got out of the taxi outside the pub. He instinctively knew to give his local a wide berth. You didnae fuck aboot in there these days. Big Jim didnae stand for it and would boot your arse personally. That would be you barred for life. He walked to the flat double quick and locked the door behind him.

Home! 'Thank fuck!' He knew they'd be coming for him eventually. He made some tea and sat down to think about what to do next. The cat was pleased to see him and jumped up on his knee, purring loudly.

⊙

Jools left the flat and went into the scheme. He went to the shops and got some cigarettes and papers. Then he visited his friend Sean.

'Awright, Jay,' Sean said. 'C'mon in. Long time no see!'

He led Jools into the kitchen.

'What can Ah do for ye?' he asked.

'Have ye got any hash?' Jools asked. 'Ah'm fuckin gaggin for a smoke.'

'Aye, how much are ye after?' Sean asked.

'Just a quarter,' Jools said. 'Thank fuck you're in. Ah've got tae go away later on and Ah needed a bit hash tae travel wi.'

Sean cut a deal from the bar and put it on the set of digital scales.

'There ye go, ma man,' he smiled.

'Cheers, buddy.' Jools laid the money on the table.

He left the flat and went home for a good smoke.

⊙

Jools left the flat with a rucksack full of clothes. He jumped in a taxi and they headed for Waverley train station.

Jools stopped the driver in the heavy traffic in Stockbridge.

'Ah'll just get oot here,' he said, and paid the driver.

He got out and went into the Raeburn Hotel in the main street. He'd been there many times with Natty and they had a great jukebox.

His first pint of lager went down smooth as silk. He'd worked up some thirst in there and he downed another couple of pints in record time.

He sat in the same seats he and Natty had sat in the last time they were out. He missed her. Those had been better times.

⊙

Jools left the hotel drunk. He got in another taxi and went to the station. He looked up at the notice boards.

'Livingston,' he thought. His cousin stayed in Livingston. He'd be safe there. He boarded the train on platform thirteen.

The train took around twenty minutes to reach Livingston. Jools needed another drink. He hoped his cousin was in a drinking mood. He walked from

Livingston station and headed to a chip shop. He bought a pie and wolfed it down. He noticed a taxi rank outside a supermarket and hailed a cab.

'Eagle Brae please, mate,' he said to the driver.

⊙

'That's us, mate,' the driver said, stopping in a quiet street. Jools looked out the window. This wasn't his cousin's street.

'This is the wrong street, mate,' Jools said. 'Are you sure this is Eagle Brae?' he asked.

'This is definitely it,' the driver said.

'Naw mate, it's the wrong street.'

'Are you sure you've got the right address?' the driver asked.

'Ah dinnae know the address but Ah know his hoose by sight,' Jools said. 'This is definitely the wrong street.'

'Have you not got a phone number? You could call him,' the driver suggested.

'Naw,' Jools said. 'Shit! How much to take me back through to Edinburgh?' he asked.

'Hmmm… about eighteen, twenty pounds,' the driver said.

'Let's go.'

⊙

Jools got back to the flat and locked the door. His mouth felt tacky and his head was starting to swim.

'Fuck it!' he thought. 'Ah'll just get pished.'

He went along to the shopping centre and bought a bottle of vodka and some beer.

He came back home and rolled a few joints while he got wrecked. The night turned into a blur.

⊙

Jools awoke to the sound of his front door banging loudly. He jumped up with a start.

'Hide the ashtrays!' he thought, as he kicked the roach-filled ashtrays under the chair.

'JOOLS, IT'S THE POLICE! COULD YOU OPEN THE DOOR?!' the voice called through the letterbox.

'Fuck!' he started to panic.

He crept up to the door and peeped through the spyhole. He saw the two young cops leaving the gate.

Jools ran upstairs to look out the window.

'Jools, Jools!' the policeman called at the back of the house.

'They're no goin away,' Jools thought. 'What if they come in?'

He pulled the cupboard door open and crouched down inside. He hid his hash on the skirting board and covered it with a box.

Suddenly Jools heard the loud rattle of a drill on the front door. They were drilling the lock open.

He began to panic as he left the bedroom cupboard in search of a better hiding place. He ran to the bathroom cupboard and pulled the door shut just as his front door gave in.

CRASH!

Jools tried hard not to breathe too loudly as the two policemen searched the rooms, calling his name.

'There's no sign up here!' one of them called down the stairs to his colleague.

'Bastard!' the other cursed.

Jools stood motionless, listening.

Suddenly the cupboard door sprang open.

'JESUS!' the young cop said, jumping back. 'You're not going to do anything daft are you?' he asked, visibly shaken.

'Naw, Ah'm awright,' Jools sighed. The policeman led him away. Jools was allowed to have a wash and get dressed.

'We're going to have to restrain you,' the policeman said. 'Hold your hands out.'

He put a set of handcuffs on him.

'Is this how they treat sick people?' Jools asked himself. He was shaking. He hadn't done anything.

The policemen led him out to the car.

⊙

The police car stopped at Drylaw police station and Jools was led through to the cells where they removed the handcuffs. He sat in the dully lit empty cell and waited.

⊙

'These officers are from St Leonards police station, Jools,' the young cop said. 'They're here to take you back to the hospital.'

The two cops led him out of the cells to the back door where a car was waiting. 'Kin Ah smoke?' Jools asked.

'Wait till we get there,' the driver answered.

'We're supposed to be out looking for a ten-year-old girl that's missing, not running round after the likes of you,' the big fat cop ticked him off like a schoolboy.

'Shut yer fuckin hole ya fat, bigmooth fuck!' Jools thought to himself. He looked like some big rugby-playing poof.

'THIS IS HOW THEY TREAT YOU WHEN YOU'RE SICK!!!' he wanted to scream. He had nothing but contempt for these two.

The car stopped in the car park of the Royal Ed and the cops led him up to the ward. The two cops disappeared into the office and Jools went to the smoking room. Emma sat talking to a beautiful blonde girl and Jools wondered if she was a new member of staff. Eddie and Archie sat together. Emma shuffled her way over.

'Awright, doll?' She smiled a gummy smile.

'Who's yer pal?' Jools asked.

'That's Kelly,' Emma said. 'She's a patient. She was a trainee nurse. Tried tae top herself wi' aw the pressure,' Emma said.

Jools found he couldn't stop looking at her. He was dumbstruck by how beautiful she was. The nurse came through to Jools.

'Are you OK, Jools?' she asked.

'Ah'm fine.'

'You can't just leave the ward like that, you know. We have to know where you are at all times,' she said. 'That'll be you on double guard,' she smiled.

Two bells rang in the hall.

'That's lunchtime, everyone!' the nurse called out.

'Hello routine,' Jools thought, as he went for lunch.

⊙

Billy Love was on lunch duty. Jools later discovered his name was Ron and he was a really sound guy. All the staff were great. Ron was just a nurse. It left Jools confused but relieved.

⊙

A week later all was still quiet. Jools had been on double watch all week. Every time he went to the shop or for a walk round the grounds, they'd assign him two nurses to follow him. He stood waiting outside La Plante's office. His aunt and his sister had been in a meeting with La Plante for nearly an hour and Jools was bored waiting. It pissed him off, the thought that they were in there, discussing him.

The door opened finally and Jools stepped in.

'Sit down, Jools,' La Plante said.

'You know everyone here. Dr Bishop your GP, Bill Rae, Jan Raymond, your psychologist, your co-worker and Dr Curry. I've been discussing where we should go from here with your treatment. I've decided to put you back on a section for six months…'

'NAW MAN! Ye're wrappin me up in cotton wool! Ah'll go radged in here for that long!' Jools bawled. 'Ah'm awright!'

'Now it doesn't mean you'll necessarily be in hospital for the whole six months, as we do want to get you home as soon as we possibly can. How are the tablets working?' he asked. 'The Amisulpride is a fairly new drug. Are you still hearing the voices?'

Jools shrugged his shoulders. 'Ah'm no hearin voices!' he covered up. 'There's nowt wrong wi' me! Ah just want tae go hame.'

'Well, I'm giving you the diagnosis of schizophrenia. That's my diagnosis,' La Plante said. 'You'll be on the tablets for at least two years.'

'NAW!' Jools stood up. 'NO DANGER!' He wouldn't believe it. There was no way. He knew they'd think he was mad.

'Now, Jools,' his GP said. 'The man's giving you his professional opinion.'

'When can Ah get oot?' Jools asked. 'When can Ah get passes off the ward? Ah'll no run away again, honest!' he pleaded.

'Well, I've been thinking we'll allow you out on half-hour passes as long as you can assure me you'll come back. You have to build up trust, then we'll increase the passes. Is there anything you want to ask me?'

Jools shook his head.

'Well, I'd like to thank everyone for coming,' La Plante said. They all left the room. Jools went back to his room and sat on the bed.

'Schizophrenia? Surely no,' he thought to himself. But he had been hearing voices. It was just that he'd hadn't thought of it like that. Maybe it was. He decided it was too much to think about. He was scared in case it all came back. He needed a drink. He went to the smoking room where he found the other Jools.

'Are you coming for a pint?' Jools asked. 'Ah'm payin'.'

They went round to Bennett's in Morningside and threw down a few pints and a couple of shorts.

Jools sat in the smoking room. He was still half drunk from earlier and had just finished his dinner.

'Awright, Jay?' Kev said, smiling. He'd come up to visit with Sarah. 'Ah've got something for ye,' he whispered.

'Do you want to go out for a while, Jools?' Sarah asked. 'I've spoken to the nurses and they said we could take you out for an hour.'

'Aye, cool!' Jools said, pulling on his jacket. 'Let go back roond tae Bennetts.'

They took a slow walk round to Morningside and Sarah went to the bar and got the drinks in. Pink Floyd played on the jukebox.

Kev handed Jools an ounce of skunk in the pub toilets.

'There's a bit green tae see ye through,' he said, smiling.

Jools rolled a fat joint for the road home and they took their drinks out to the beer garden. The warm evening sun sank into the Morningside skyline.